Praise for Tyler R. Tichelaar's Children of Arthur Series

"*Arthur's Legacy* is a fresh new take on the ancient and wondrous myth of Arthur. Works of this kind are hugely important because they keep the legends alive and bring them into the 21st century. Strongly recommended for all who love the old and the new in mythic fiction."

— John Matthews, author of
King Arthur: Dark Age Warrior and Mythic Hero

"What if the story of King Arthur was not quite what you thought? And what if its repercussions echoed down the centuries and across the seas? Casting a fresh, inventive and sometimes controversial eye over the rich tradition of Arthurian legend, especially its Welsh roots, in *Arthur's Legacy* Tyler Tichelaar has crafted an intriguing blend of action-packed time-slip fantasy adventure, moving love story, multi-layered mystery, and unusual spiritual exploration."

— Sophie Masson, editor of *The Road to Camelot*

"What if you discovered the famous legends you'd heard and believed all your life didn't happen the way they'd always been told? In *Melusine's Gift*, readers will join Adam and Anne Delaney as they hear the truth right from the mouths of the characters who lived the tales. Readers unfamiliar with Melusine's place in history will be drawn into her world, while the captivating web of multi-layered stories within stories combine and complement to obliterate the preconceived notions of those who consider themselves experts on her legend. I loved *Melusine's Gift* even more than *Arthur's Legacy* and can't wait for the twists and turns of *Ogier's Prayer*."

— Jenifer Brady, author of the *Abby's Camp Days series*

"*Arthur's Legacy* will electrify true fans of the Arthurian legend. Tichelaar's research and his weaving of the Arthurian mythos into a cohesive story for the contemporary reader is second to none. *Arthur's Legacy* will surely take its rightful place among the canon of great Arthurian literature."

— Steven Maines, author of *The Merlin Factor series*

"If you love the mystical magic of Camelot but thrive on the excitement and tribulations of *Game of Thrones*, this book is for you. Tichelaar encompasses the familiarity of contemporary times and skillfully interweaves history and mysticism into the Arthurian legend that has withstood the test of time, and brings the characters all to life."

— Rowena Portch, award-winning author of *The Spirian Saga*

"Tichelaar's ingenious use of throwaway snippets and very obscure sources combines with a powerful imagination to make the old, old story fresh.... The finale brings the two strands of the novel [*Arthur's Legacy*] together, at the same time synthesising its pagan and Christian elements into a Blakeian, poetic pantheism."

— Marcus Pitcaithly, author of *The Realm of Albion*

"Once again Tyler Tichelaar weaves a riveting story that mixes Arthurian lore with fact and fiction. *Melusine's Gift* is skillfully written and is reminiscent of those ancient tales from the *Arabian Nights* where one story flows into the next one and that into the next and so on. In this case, the stories reveal how the descendants of King Arthur are connected through the isle Avalon."

— Cheryl Carpinello, author of *Guinevere: On the Eve of Legend*

"A masterful blend of history, myth-tery and imagination, *Ogier's Prayer*'s inspirational re-visioning of the past, and vivid, suspenseful storytelling will leave you craving the next installment of this thought-provoking, delightfully plot-twisting series!"
— Roslyn McGrath, author of *The Third Mary: 55 Messages for Empowering Truth, Peace & Grace from the Mother of Mary Magdalene*

"Tichelaar deftly weaves together history, myth, and legend into a tale that takes the reader on an epic journey through time, connecting characters and events you'd never expect. In so doing, he creates a present and future where the supernatural is surprisingly real and the age-old battle between good and evil teeters on its ultimate conclusion. A unique series sure to entertain fans of Arthurian legend, literature, and ancient lore."
— Nicole Evelina, author of the *Guinevere's Tale Trilogy*

"So much is asked of saviors that we can forget the beating heart behind the legends. Tyler Tichelaar understands the contradiction between our expectation of heroes and their lonely destiny. In exploring the Arthurian legend, he shows himself once more the master of the complexities of the human heart."
— Diana M. Deluca, Ph.D., author of *A Dream of Shadows: A Novel of Reincarnation*

ARTHUR'S BOSOM

ARTHUR'S BOSOM

THE CHILDREN OF ARTHUR: BOOK FIVE

BY

TYLER R. TICHELAAR

Arthur's Bosom: The Children of Arthur, Book Five

Copyright © 2017 by Tyler R. Tichelaar

Marquette Fiction
1202 Pine Street
Marquette, MI 49855
www.MarquetteFiction.com
www.ChildrenofArthur.com

ISBN-13: 978-0-9962400-4-8
Library of Congress Control Number: 2017905734

This is a work of fiction. All of the characters, names, incidents, organizations, and dialogue in this novel are either the products of the author's imagination or are used fictitiously.

Printed in the United States of America
Publication managed by Superior Book Productions
www.SuperiorBookProductions.com

"Oh, no, he's surely not in hell. He's in Arthur's bosom, if any man ever went to Arthur's bosom."
— William Shakespeare, *Henry V*

CONTENTS

PROLOGUE

THE NOT-TOO-DISTANT FUTURE

CAPTAIN VANDERDECKER LOOKED up into the night sky and reflected upon what a lonely life it was to wander the earth alone on the *Flying Dutchman*; he knew those few to whom he had shown himself believed him cursed, but it was not so; rather, he roamed the seas in his phantom ship to put a little fear into them, a fear that might cause them to repent and turn to good. He had committed no great crime, no great sin, but rather he posed as a terrible sinner for the sake of his fellow men, for they were mostly a weak and cowardly race, and so while fear caused them to do evil, at other times, fear could steer them back onto the right path, and so he had taken the path of fear so they might find their salvation.

Years before, he had agreed to this role, in time playing upon the tales told of how he had been led to this cursed life filled with isolation and misery so that those to whom he spoke would tremble before him and then repent and change their ways before it was too late. Captain Vanderdecker enjoyed his fear-inspiring performances immensely, and once he had released his captive victims from his presence, he spent a great deal of time chuckling to himself, and often, he would use his powerful spyglass to watch them later in life and be pleased by the change he had caused in them.

Yes, at times it had been a lonely life, but Captain Vanderdecker knew his mission was nearing completion, for since Lilith had passed from this world, fear had been slowly losing its grip over much of mankind. Soon it would seem as if all his time spent in this wandering state had never happened at all. And in the meantime, he occasionally met with those who shared his mission—Morgan le Fay and Merlin and several others, all believed to be only characters from legend, but who, in truth, served the Goddess-God by serving mankind to bring about good for all.

Most days, however, Captain Vanderdecker's only companions were the stars in the night sky. They were his true friends, for they guided him upon the sea, and they were loyal and ever-vigilant, never swaying in their trustworthiness. Oh, he knew man's faulty wisdom believed the stars merely to be great flaming balls of fire like the sun, but he also knew that the stars had loving energetic souls that contributed to the music of the spheres, playing a beautiful visual and auditory symphony for him every night as a reminder that he was alone only temporarily and would one day be reunited with the great Source of All Wellbeing that guided the Universe.

And so tonight, like most nights, Captain Vanderdecker lay upon the deck of the *Flying Dutchman*, looking up at the stars, listening to them, sometimes wishing upon them, his wishes actually being prayers for the happiness of the human race, of which he had once been a member before he had tasted of living water and taken up his mission.

The stars entertained him, often singing to him songs of kings and queens, heroes and villains, mermaids and magical beasts, and of a world far better than that he knew currently existed because it was based in the beauty of the imagination and the love that someday the human heart would know when it was free from the fear and strife that mankind caused. Only then would mankind have learned enough to evolve into the next stage of its existence.

Suddenly, in the midst of this beautiful symphony, like a jarring wrong note, from high up in the sky, Captain Vanderdecker heard the whooshing of what first appeared to be a falling star, creating a dissonance as it whirled through the heavens. Standing up to get a better look, he saw it blazon with a fiery light through the night sky. Unsure of what he was seeing, he ran down into his cabin to find his spyglass.

Once back on deck, Captain Vanderdecker put the spyglass to his eye, and looking up, he saw a comet with a flaming tail soaring through the heavens. Then, almost in disbelief, he said aloud, "Despite waiting all these centuries, it seems to have come so suddenly."

Prester John never gave thought to the passing of time. In his sacred kingdom, time mattered little, for he knew that everything happened in the time best suited for it, and so there could be no rushing, no hurrying of it, and certainly never any indication that it was too late—that not enough time remained to achieve whatever wanted achieving, for time was infinite, and hence, no need for worry of any sort existed.

Those who came to Prester John's land to seek wisdom usually came believing time was their greatest enemy, for they had spent all their lives living by its dictates, and they had come to know it as a cruel taskmaster, even if only an illusory one, for humans were ever prone to creating unneeded worry and anxiety for themselves, especially in recent centuries as they invented clocks and timers with alarms and all manner of technological, digital, and electronic taskmasters to capture every second and turn it into profit, affixing a monetary value to it until they came to fear it in their mad rush to produce, produce, produce before it was too late—but too late for what?

When Prester John did think of such matters, he only chuckled, for he knew it was never too late. Still, he felt sorrow for the scurrying madness of the human race, so he rejoiced whenever someone came to his land; once arrived, his visitors would require several days before they were able to relax, to let time's worry leave them, and once they did relax, they felt the freedom from time's restraints to be a great relief and then even a joy.

On this particular day as he walked about his kingdom, Prester John was musing over time's fallacy and reminding himself of the words he had once heard the Savior speak, "Look at the lilies of the field, they neither toil nor do they spin." Was not all mankind's toiling and spinning an effort to fight time, to prepare to have enough before it was too late? The Savior had told them to look at the birds and the beasts of the field and see how at peace they were with the earth, never worrying about the hour or day, but simply walking, running, eating when they felt the need, and not an hour or a minute before or after they so desired.

Prester John gazed out across the fields where he was walking, enjoying the solitariness of the moment, for at times he needed to distance himself from those he nourished when they came to his land, for he could still sense their internal anxiety and questioning as if they were bees buzzing beside his ear, and if he did not distance himself from it until it lessened, it could badly upset his spirit. He much preferred the calming presence of animals over humans, although it was the humans whom he was called to serve.

But now, as he sought out the peace of the beasts of the field, he was surprised to find the landscape before him very empty. Where was the lioness and her cubs that he had visited with for so many days past? And why were there no birds soaring through the air? And looking down to see whether the ants were at least about his feet—he often looked down to be sure not to harm anything—he saw the earth appeared to be bare of moving life. But then, unexpectedly, a field mouse scurried between his feet, and then another, and then two or three, and soon he found himself standing amid a stream of mice, many tumbling over his feet in their panic, but what had so frightened them?

Then like a bolt of lightning, the words that the Savior had once said about him to his friend Peter sprung to Prester John's mind: "If I want him to remain alive until I return, what is that to you?"

Every day since she had become Lady of Avalon some fifteen centuries before, Morgana had looked into the Holy Pool after eating one of the Nuts of Knowledge from the Ancient Hazel that gave the gift of the sight. Some days she saw nothing of concern. Some days she saw the sorrows of mankind. Some days she saw acts of kindness. And now and then, she saw something that required her to take action. It had been several years now since she had been called upon to interfere in the ways of men. The final chapter before the epilogue of mankind's history had been enacted when Lilith had departed the earth, and now there was only waiting to be done; Morgana knew not how many years she needed to wait, but she had learned patience after all this time.

And so Morgana had expected this day to be the same as any other—doubtless there was some minor squabble in the Middle East, but those squabbles were nothing like they had been years ago; not a bomb had gone off in years; there might be a fire in Montana or an earthquake in Japan, but those were not caused by humans, so they were of less concern to her; what did concern her had lessened in recent years, though she still found interest looking into the Holy Pool and viewing the increased acts of charity and kindness she saw being done since Lilith's departure, and Morgana felt finally that the fruits of all of her and Merlin and their many compatriots' works were ripening.

But when Morgana looked into the Holy Pool today, for the first time in many years, she found herself surprised. What she saw was something she had never seen before, and yet something she had always imagined someday seeing since first she had become Lady of Avalon. She watched, eyes wide, her senses more alert than ever before in her life, her whole being caught up in the drama about to be played out, and when she came out of the trance, she knew what she must do.

Through the air, on invisible and inaudible waves, save to the intended receiver, she sent the following message:

"Merlin, the time has come."

PART I
LANCELOT

CHAPTER 1

"SOMETIMES," SAID LANCE Delaney, looking out at the vast sea surrounding his sailboat so that the coast of Cornwall was barely visible in the far distance, "it feels as if time is unchanging, and all the past never happened for us, and even the future will never be; instead, there is only this moment, and us here together in this boat, and the lapping of the waves against it."

Tristan, who was lying on the deck, looked up at his twin older brother for a moment before laughing and saying, "What makes you wax all philosophical?"

Lance, still staring out over the water, replied, "Doesn't it just seem strange sometimes to think of all we've been through—all those years living in Dracula's Castle with Grandfather, and the whole showdown with Lilith, and then Uncle Devin leaving with her for another world—all of it so seemingly impossible that people would think us crazy if we told them? And then, after all that, we simply returned to England with Mom and Dad and took up our lives as if none of it had ever happened."

"Only," said Tristan, agreeing with his brother, "we never knew our parents until we were eighteen, so it's not as if it never happened. We've had to spend all this time getting to know them."

"That's true," said Lance, "but just think—it's been nearly a decade now, and we've gone to college and found jobs and had girlfriends and everything else, and it's almost as if life has always been like this."

"No," said Tristan. "I think life is always changing too much for it to seem as if anything is always. Nothing ever stays the same for even a moment, and I imagine it will all change again soon, and then this moment in this boat will seem like a dream of the past as well."

"But what could make it change like that? Why should we think it will ever be different?" asked Lance, turning the rudder so the boat would move into the wind.

"Nothing stays the same, Lance. Have you been paying attention to the news? Remember when we first returned, the wars in Iraq and Afghanistan were going on, and even after that, there were issues with Russia and North Korea and Syria and ISIS, but as the years have gone by, there's been less war and less famine, and just last week, the United Nations announced that for the first time in memory, there is not a war or skirmish being fought anywhere on the planet."

"Yes, but that doesn't mean it will last," said Lance.

"But other things have changed. Birthrates have severely declined in recent years; the human world population is dropping; people are dying at normal rates, but less people are being born, and—"

"That's a good thing," said Lance. "It means we don't need to fear overpopulating the earth."

"Perhaps it is a good thing," said Tristan, "but I somehow feel as if it's something more, as if some great shift is about to happen for the human race."

"Like what?" asked Lance.

"Well, don't you think it must connect to something, something like the fact that Lilith is no longer part of the earth, so maybe her negative influence is gone and people are consequently becoming better."

"Maybe—that would make sense regarding war, but not a reduced birthrate. More likely pollution or something else is making people unable to have children."

"No, that's too negative," said Tristan. "It's more like—well, maybe souls are no longer interested in having the human experience."

Lance just smirked and returned to looking over the water.

Tristan could see his brother was not yet open to such a discussion, so he let the subject drop.

After a minute, Lance said, "It's a beautiful day; let's not worry about the future of the human race today."

"All right," said Tristan, "but I want to tell you something else, something about my future...because a big shift is going to happen, for me, at least."

Lance's eyes grew wide and he let out a laugh, but a happy one this time, and then he said, "You're going to do it! You're going to ask Elaine to marry you."

Tristan let out a laugh of relief because his brother had guessed and sounded so happy about it. He had worried that the conversation could have gone either way.

"Yes, tonight, after dinner," he confessed.

"Then we should get back to shore so you can be ready," said Lance.

"Oh, she won't be here until five o'clock at least," said Tristan. "It's a long drive for her down from London and she wasn't leaving until noon."

With his foot, Lance nudged his brother's leg, and said, "Congratulations. Just think—we'll have a doctor in the family now."

"Yes," said Tristan. "And we're hoping once we're married to start our own foundation to advance irrigation in Africa. Of course, we'll have a home there so we can run it properly, and so Elaine can open a clinic to care for children—especially all the orphans whose parents died from AIDS as well as the malnourished ones. Although the scientists insist their new discoveries will have the disease wiped out within the year, there are still plenty of children who need love and care after the devastation the disease has wrought in Africa."

"I admire your dedication to good causes," said Lance, who sometimes felt as if he should be more involved in such charities, but he had enough to do overseeing Delaney Castle's estate and farms and the family's other business interests since his father was always busy with politics. Not only was Adam Delaney a member of the House of Lords, but there was also talk he might be chosen for a cabinet position in His Majesty's Government sometime soon. After a moment, Lance added, "I hope all that work doesn't get in the way of you having a family, despite the alleged reduced birthrates."

"No, we hope to have children," said Tristan.

"And when you do, you can't stay away from home as much as you do now. Mom and Dad will want to be seeing their grandchildren, and I'll be wanting to see my nieces or nephews, of course."

"Of course," said Tristan, adding in a little jibe, "but, you know, some of us do need to work for a living; we can't all become the next Earl of Delaney."

"As if you don't have your own fortune," scoffed Lance, who felt little guilt over being the older brother who would someday inherit the title—hopefully, though, not for a long time to come.

"If you were concerned about working for money, you wouldn't be working for a nonprofit now or be thinking of starting your own foundation."

"I just have to do something useful," Tristan replied. "Not that I don't want to be with the family, but I think it best to use my good fortune to help others, just as you do because I know maintaining the estate provides jobs for so many people. It's not a competition between us in any way—we each work our work, and we're always together in spirit if not in body."

"Still," said Lance, "I'm always sad whenever you go back up to London. I sometimes wish for simpler times like those we knew in our childhood."

"I don't know that I'd describe those as simpler times," said Tristan. "We didn't know our parents back then, and while growing up in Dracula's Castle and having all that time to learn and be together was wonderful in many ways, you know as well as I do the sadness we always felt over our separation from Mom and Dad."

"Yes," Lance agreed. "I guess it is easy to romanticize the past. All we can do is enjoy the moment." He took a deep breath of the fresh sea air and tried to tell himself to be at peace and content for now, but he felt burning in him a great desire for something to change, though he feared that desire too, especially when it could be of gigantic proportions as Tristan had just suggested—a change that could alter the destiny of the human race. Lance did not know what kind of change he longed for, though certainly nothing that dramatic. Perhaps just finally to meet the girl of his dreams—he thought he had until Tristan had found the same one and she seemed to prefer him—or was it to do work that felt even more significant than helping his father maintain the family's ancient estate? But sometimes, Lance just longed for the chance to run away from all he knew to have some great adventure and discover new aspects of himself. "Sometimes," he heard himself saying before he had even fully thought out the words, "I feel as if I belong less to the present than to the past—the really distant past—long before our own lifetimes."

"I don't understand," said Tristan, sitting up to put on his shirt because the spray from the sea was starting to chill him.

"I mean far back," said Lance, "as if I would better belong in the age of King Arthur—the age of knights and their ladies, of castles and magic. After all, since we're descended from King Arthur, it's only natural that I should feel a connection to him and his time."

"The sixth century?" said Tristan, wrinkling his brow. "No thank you. I don't imagine it was that pleasant. There were plagues and no technology of any kind—no indoor plumbing, no electricity, no more advanced form of transportation than riding a horse."

"Sounds a lot like parts of Africa today," Lance teased.

"You haven't been there, so how would you know?" Tristan replied. "And besides, with help from caring people, we can change Africa; back in the Middle Ages, there wasn't much they could do about their lack of electricity."

"I know," said Lance, "but somehow it just seems like it would have been more romantic to live back then, even if it's not realistic to think that way."

Tristan yawned, obviously not interested in his brother's head-in-the-clouds ideas. He'd had enough Arthurian connections in his life; not that he did not admire the ideals of Camelot—the justice and fairness that King Arthur had stood for. He just wanted to bring those ideals to people in the present rather than dreaming about them in the past.

"The wind is picking up," he said, "and I do want to get cleaned up so I look my best when I propose to Elaine tonight, so let's head back to shore."

The twin brothers had been staying with their parents at the family's summer cottage near Tintagel for the week. It was only a mile or so from the ruins of the castle where King Arthur had supposedly been born, which was what had enticed Adam and Anne Delaney to buy the cottage. They were proud of their Arthurian descent, despite all the grief it had brought them over the years. They took every opportunity to remind themselves of it by visiting places associated with King Arthur and even buying the land some of those historic sites were on.

"All right," said Lance. "I am getting kind of hungry."

He turned the sailboat back toward the shore, a couple of miles in the distance. But he had barely adjusted the sail when he found himself fighting to keep the boat headed in the right direction as the wind and the waves suddenly picked up.

"Wow, it feels like a storm is coming in," said Tristan. "Maybe I should turn on the radio for the weather report."

Just as Tristan spoke, the sky began to darken overhead. The radio, which had been sitting on the deck, actually slid toward him as he reached for it. Tristan grabbed it to hold it steady as they rode out the sudden waves; then he turned it on and tuned to the weather.

"...cover. The damage could be astronomical. I repeat, go to the lowest level of your homes and between walls where you will be safe.... The comet will pass earth within minutes.... This event is completely a surprise. No one knew it was coming until minutes ago because it is traveling at unheard of speeds. It will be accompanied by several large meteors and other debris. Prepare yourself for a tremendous impact. I repeat, take shelter immediately."

The commentator's panic-stricken voice quickly faded as the wind struck up and the waves began to roar, making the radio inaudible. In a few more seconds, the signal was lost.

"Take down the sail!" screamed Lance as he held the rudder with all his might.

"Did he really say a comet was going to hit?" Tristan yelled back over the fierce wind's roar. Lance could not hear him, and Tristan did not wait for an answer. He quickly struggled to lower the sail, which was swiftly pulling them farther from the coast of Cornwall.

Before Tristan could get the sail even halfway down, a great gust of wind ripped it in half, then quickly tore its pieces from the mast.

Tristan fell to the deck, afraid he would be blown overboard. Lance was struggling to get the motor started so they could head for shore, but the motor would only putter as waves whipped into the boat.

Then the sky went completely black. For a moment, the brothers could not see one another. Then just as quickly, the air filled with a deafening, exploding sound. Its decibel level was louder than the roar of a thousand cannons firing simultaneously. Lance and Tristan covered their ears as they saw a burst of light in the distance coming at them at breakneck speed.

The fiery comet roared through the sky, sending particles of meteors, rocks, and all manner of debris plunging into the sea, causing it to roil about, lifting the sailboat up on waves and dropping it down again. The debris that hit the water was flaming until the sea appeared to be on fire, and only by chance was the sailboat not instantly obliterated as the waves sent the vessel surging back toward the Cornish coast.

"What the hell!" yelled Lance, trying to maneuver the boat through a sea of fire. "How come the scientists didn't know and warn us about this earlier?"

But when Lance looked around to Tristan for his response, he found his brother lying face down on the deck, and beside him was a rock the size of a baseball dented into the ship's deck.

"Bloody hell!" yelled Lance, losing all thought for his own safety and jumping over to his brother to see whether he was okay. At that moment, a giant wave swept up onto the ship, knocking Lance down and sending him floundering on top of his brother. Lance struggled to get his bearing, reaching for the edge of the sailboat, or a rope, or anything; at the same time, he desperately clutched at his brother, refusing to let Tristan be washed away as another enormous wave came up beneath the boat, sending it tilting into the water. Lance grabbed the boat's railing, wrapping his arm around his brother's neck, just as the boat righted itself again. As Lance uttered a sigh of relief, a stream of small rocks—more debris from the comet—came flying through the air. Before he could shield himself, Lance was struck by one on the side of the head, causing him also to lose consciousness.

CHAPTER 2

S EVERAL HOURS LATER, the battered sailboat was drifting just feet away from the shore on a now relatively placid sea. The boat's deck and hull were charred and filled with dents, but miraculously, the vessel had remained seaworthy.

When Lance opened his eyes, he had a terrible pain in his neck, but after rubbing it for a moment and finding he could move his head—a good sign he had not broken anything—he managed to pull himself up into a sitting position and look about him. He saw his brother lying on the deck, his legs twisted oddly, his body face downward. Crawling to him, Lance shook his brother first, then getting no response, managed with difficulty to turn him over, still without any sign of consciousness from Tristan. Next, he gently slapped his brother's face, then listened to his chest for a heartbeat, tried to feel for his pulse, and being unsuccessful in these efforts, nearly panicked.

"Tristan! Tristan! Wake up!" Lance screamed, fiercely shaking his brother, wondering in despair what to do—wondering what he would tell his parents—wondering where or how he would even find his parents. Looking out at the sea, he then saw the land was only a dozen or so yards away, but this was not the harbor they had sailed out of a few short hours ago. No sign existed of a village, a road, a house, or any inhabitants. Just rugged shoreline and trees.

"Tristan, wake up!" Lance shouted, pushing his brother harder than before. "Where are we? I need your help?"

Doubtless, Lance told himself, he was only a few miles down the coast from Tintagel's harbor, but nothing looked familiar to him, and he felt total panic at the thought of being alone if his brother were....

"Damn it, Tristan! Don't do this to me!" Lance hollered, nearly in tears now. "Don't scare me like this. I'll get you to a doctor, but just give me a sign that you're still alive." He leaned over the side of the boat and cupped some water to throw into his brother's face, but even that emitted no response.

"I have to get you to shore," Lance then said, realizing that was his only hope for help. He went to the rear of the boat, only to discover the motor was gone—it must have been ripped away by falling rock and sunk into the sea. The sail was also gone—only a few pieces of string remained, and the mast was charred as if burnt by debris from the comet. If Lance had found time to think about it, he would have been amazed that the boat was even still afloat.

"Tristan, I'm going to pull the boat in. You stay here," Lance said before realizing what a stupid sentence it was—where could his brother go? Then he jumped overboard.

The water was surprisingly warm—like swimming in the tropics—like the Caribbean Sea he had swum in last winter when he had vacationed there with his parents. But this was the Atlantic Ocean off the coast of England—the water should be much colder. No time to think on that now. Lance grabbed hold of the bow and tried to pull the sailboat toward shore. He found he had little strength to do so, but after a few minutes, his feet touched the bottom of the sea floor, and then he was able to make his way inland until, after a quarter of an hour, he had the boat beached.

Lance then struggled to climb back into the boat, thinking if his brother hadn't been dead before, he must be dead now.

Tristan had not moved. Lance nudged him, called his name, poked and prodded him, but he received no response. He noticed there was no blood anywhere. He knew his brother had been hit in the head, but there were no cuts or scratches, and it was too early apparently for a bump to have swollen up. He ripped off Tristan's shirt to look for wounds, but there were none. He pressed his ear to Tristan's chest, but he could not hear anything, nor see his chest rise.

"What am I supposed to do?" he cried, overcome by the situation. "What can I do?"

And then he remembered his smartphone. He dug in his pocket, only to discover he had not brought it with him—he was notorious for accidentally-on-purpose forgetting to carry his phone—he hated technology. Then he dug in Tristan's pockets—Tristan was always texting Elaine—but he found no smartphone there either. It must have fallen out during the storm.

"There probably wouldn't be any reception anyway," Lance muttered.

Should he try to get his brother out of the boat and onto land? Even if he could lay him on the beach, what more could he do? He could not carry him far; nor did he know where to carry him.

Would anyone be able to help him? Lance suspected the comet's debris had done damage on land as well. Just looking at the trees, he could see they were now largely bare, their leaves ripped off by the wind created by the comet, and they looked scorched, as if they'd endured a forest fire. They were completely lacking in greenery. The sky itself was full of the smell of smoke, and the water was full of debris, as if ash had snowed all over it. In his desperation to get the boat to land, Lance had not noticed how very strange everything looked, but now he could see how the land had been devastated.

"Nevertheless, there have to be all kinds of emergency workers around putting out fires or helping the wounded. Someone will help me," he told himself.

Then he turned back to his brother.

"Tristan, stay here. I'm sorry, but I'm going to have to leave you to go fetch help. There's got to be a road just inside those woods, not very far away. I'll be back in just a few minutes. I promise. It won't be long at all before I'm back. Hang on. I know you're going to be all right. I just know you will."

Lance was so caught up in his tears that as he climbed out of the boat, he didn't at first hear the strange yapping sound of dogs, and then when he did hear it, it instantly stopped. He climbed out of the boat, and surveying the area, he saw he was on the edge of a cove. He started to walk along the shore, hoping he could come around the cove's bend to find a sign of civilization, but he was not at all prepared for the sight he did see.

CHAPTER 3

LANCE HAD NEVER seen anything like it. There before him, approaching the shore, was a creature far stranger than any he ever could have imagined. It was a great gray beast—he could not even be sure what it was, for its gray color appeared to be a covering of ash—either debris from the comet or the falling charred remains of tree branches that had burned in the forest.

The creature made its way to the sea and entered it, attempting to bathe in it. Then, after a few minutes, it made its way back to shore, completely unaware of Lance's presence, or not concerned about being watched. It tried to shake the water and the mud formed by the ash from its skin, but the mud had formed into clumps and only a few caked pieces fell off, revealing beneath it skin like that of a leopard. What could this creature possibly be? It was fascinating and horrifying at the same time, and only curiosity kept Lance from running away as he watched it bend now and drink from the sea, the taste of salt water not seeming to bother it.

As he watched, Lance kept trying to figure out just what this great creature could be. It did not seem to be any single kind of animal but an amalgamation of several. It was incredibly tall—it was hard to say how tall from a distance, but perhaps as much as twenty feet. It had a long, narrow, scaled head and a neck like that of a snake, but skin, from what small bit Lance could see, spotted like a leopard; it was much larger than a leopard in size, even larger than a tiger, and it had the haunches of a lion, including its bushy tail, but its legs narrowed down into the pointy hooves of a deer. Could it really be half-mammal and half-reptile? And yet that's what it appeared to be. Was it some sort of giant lizard—perhaps a cousin to the dragon? How was this possible? Perhaps it was a dragon but it had become deformed somehow by radiation from the comet? He wished it was not so covered in ash and mud so he could get a better look at it.

Lance dared not move from fear the animal might attack him, but he knew he must act quickly if he were going to get help for his brother. The creature continued to slurp water from the sea, drinking long and contentedly. And when its mesmerizing snakelike eyes turned and caught sight of Lance, it did not act surprised, but watched him keenly, making Lance feel like a mouse captured in its gaze, and yet, somehow, Lance could sense that the creature wished him no harm.

In another second, Lance's quiet communion with this frightening creature was broken by the sound of an animal running through the forest toward them. Instantly, the strange beast raised its head, and as it did, the sound of a great many hounds barking filled the air. Then the creature turned and fled, its tail flapping behind it, its large body making the ground pound as it awkwardly half-leapt and half-ran into the forest. A second or two later, as Lance continued to look after the beast, just a hundred or so yards farther down the shore, a horse and its rider appeared. The rider was dressed in full armor like the knights of old. The horse was splotched with gray, as if ash from the comet covered it, but the knight's armor seemed to have caused most of the ash to slide off him.

The moment the knight came onto the beach, he saw Lance and turned his horse in his direction so rapidly that Lance jumped up onto a tuft of grass on the forest's edge to avoid being run over.

"Did you see it?" the knight demanded, coming to a standstill before Lance, his black shield just inches from Lance's face.

"The beast—the—I don't know what—"

"Yes, the Beast!" exclaimed the knight. "And did you see the infernal dragon it mates with that caused all this destruction?"

"It didn't look like a dragon. It was—"

"It lit up the sky with fire like a dragon does," insisted the knight.

"No—it—oh, you mean the comet," said Lance.

"I should have known the Beast would bring a dragon to Britain," continued the knight. "Whenever the Beast is seen, it brings grievous misfortune, and now a dragon has charred the forests and caused all the land to be filled with ash for miles around. I must quickly kill the Beast before it works more such witchcraft. Which way did it go?"

"You mean the thing with the snake head and the lion legs and—"

"Yes, yes!" exclaimed the knight. "You saw it. The Beast Glatisant! Which way did it go?"

"Into the woods," said Lance, "that way, but before you go, my brother—"

But already the knight was gone into the forest in fast pursuit of the creature.

"Wait!" shouted Lance. "I need help! It's an emergency! My brother...."

But the knight did not turn around. In another minute, he

had disappeared into the forest, lost amid the ash-covered broken branches and the still smoldering scorched trees. The tree branches, despite the damage to them and most of their leaves being gone, were so entangled that they quickly hid the knight from view.

Lance did not know what to do. He was desperate to help Tristan. Before he could think clearly, he ran into the forest after the knight, hoping he would come across a road or trail of some sort that would lead him to civilization if not to the knight himself, whose help he still hoped to get. He was too desperate even to question why the man was dressed like a knight or what that beast could have been, or why the man thought a comet was a dragon. Lance only knew he had seen how swiftly the strange beast had moved; the knight was unlikely to catch the creature and would eventually grow tired of his pursuit; then, hopefully, Lance would catch up with him, though that could be many miles away, but if he were lucky, he would find someone else before then who could help his brother, even though everything now looked like a godforsaken wasteland.

As Lance penetrated the forest, everything was covered with ash—in some places it was just a dusting on the ground and tree branches, but in other places, the ash was an inch or two deep. Lance was grateful for the ash because it made it easy for him to follow the beast and the horse's footprints. The beast's feet were actually smaller than the horse's, despite its abnormally large size, but its frightening appearance more than compensated for its small feet.

The tracks were so easy to follow that Lance ran through the forest in pursuit, now and then tripping in a hole, but he was a good runner, having had plenty of athletic training and played college football. He ran for a good half-hour, all the while desperately searching for any sign of a building, a passing car, or a nearby road, but all he saw was a thick and devastated forest that seemingly stretched on and on for miles with no sign of human habitation or any other life, for even the birds and small animals had fled the comet's devastation.

Finally, Lance decided to turn around and go back, thinking there had to be a fishing village somewhere along the seashore where someone could help him. He cursed every minute of lost time he had spent in this maddening forest, knowing each second might mean life or death for his brother, although Lance suspected Tristan was already dead and he would have to come to grips with reality. Perhaps he was so in denial of this horrifying experience that he was hallucinating about the knight and the strange beast—and maybe even about this devastated land. No, the devastation at least had to be real for he had seen the damage of the comet firsthand, and it was the cause of his brother's incoherent state.

Just as Lance started back toward the shore, a shout and a great tumbling noise behind him made him spin around again, hoping the noise was caused by humans. Could it be from the knight—had he found and slain the strange creature? Or was the beast devouring him? Whatever it was, the source of that noise might be his only hope, so Lance turned and raced through the forest in the sound's direction. Within a minute, he came across the knight's horse lying on the ground; the knight was struggling to right himself from where he had landed in a barren, though ash-covered bush.

"Are you all right?" Lance shouted, running to the knight and trying to help him stand.

"The foul beast!" exclaimed the knight. "He is cunning, he is. He ran about in circles here to confuse my horse, who ended up turning so sharply that he tumbled over. Help me get him to his feet."

Lance did not know how to help the horse, but the knight said, "Take his halter and try to raise him up, and I'll give him a push from the side."

At their prodding, the horse tried to stand, but after several failed attempts—it tumbling down whenever it put weight on its left front hoof—it was apparent the animal could not raise himself.

"His leg is broken," said the knight. "Damn it! Third horse I've lost because of that foul beast. Step back, good sir."

"What are you going to do?" Lance asked, knowing that lame horses were usually shot, but he was more than surprised when the knight whipped out his sword from its scabbard and gave the horse a murderous slice to its neck.

"It's a great shame, but yet the merciful thing to do," said the knight, bending over to wipe the blood off his sword in the ash-covered grass and among the dead leaves on the forest floor.

"Please," said Lance, "I'm sorry about your horse, but my brother is badly hurt. Can you help me?"

"Aiding those in need is what I am sworn to do," said the knight, looking up at Lance and for the first time raising his visor so that Lance could see him smiling. He was also able to see that the knight had very dark skin, more like someone from the Middle East than from England—although there were so many immigrants in Britain these days that the man's complexion should not surprise him. Perhaps the man was a Pakistani earning extra money by dressing up in a knight costume. "To help and protect others is the first rule of knighthood," the knight added.

Lance was too frantic to pay attention to this speech and hurriedly blurted out, "My brother's lying in the boat back by the shore. I think he might be dead, but I'm hoping he's only unconscious. He was struck by some of the debris from the comet."

"Take me to him," said the knight.

As they rushed through the forest, or rather as Lance rushed ahead, then kept stopping to wait for the knight to catch up with him, since he was much slower in his armor, Lance asked, "Do you have a cell phone? I couldn't get reception with mine? Is there any hospital nearby? I can't even find a road. Do you think we can move him between us to where the ambulance might be able to pick him up?"

"What language do you speak, boy? Is it that of the Franks whose words you are sprinkling in. What is *am-bu-lance*?"

"Ambulance!" Lance shouted, as if the knight were deaf.

"No, I have no magical amulets," said the knight, "but I have a vial of healing medicine my father gave me in case the Beast should ever wound me. It is the very medicine that is keeping my uncle, King Pellinore, alive. My mother traveled to Avalon to receive it from the hands of Lady Morgana herself, so perhaps it will also be helpful in curing what ails your brother."

"Morgana? Avalon?" said Lance in astonishment. "I suppose next you'll tell me you're a Knight of the Round Table?"

"Yes, I do have that privilege," replied the knight. "My uncle is one as well, and it was he who knighted me. You see, since I am not a Christian, my uncle was the only knight willing to do it, but King Arthur has welcomed me to his table nevertheless because of my great prowess."

Lance could not believe these words. He was caught halfway between thinking the man was crazy and that he was himself caught in some strange time-travel experience.

"King Arthur!" he exclaimed. "Are you joking?"

"Anyone who jokes about my liege lord, King Arthur of Camelot, will feel the point of my sword," the knight replied.

"I'm sorry," said Lance. "It's just that…." Lance paused, trying to fathom the situation. Could he truly be in King Arthur's time? "Then how are you not a Christian?" he asked, though it seemed like the least remarkable part of the knight's story. "Isn't everyone in King Arthur's Britain a Christian?"

"Is it not obvious? Is it possible you do not recognize me?" asked the knight in astonishment. "I am the only pagan knight in Christendom, I believe, and I am quite famous, although, unfortunately, mainly for how I have been maligned by my enemy, Sir Tristram."

"I'm sorry," Lance replied, trying to find words to respond to this bizarre statement and deciding it best to humor the knight. "I've been away from Britain for a long time."

"That explains it then," said the knight. "I am the greatly renowned Sir Palomides."

"It's a pleasure to meet you, Sir Palomides," Lance replied.

"The pleasure is all mine," replied the knight. "But what be your name?"

Lance had no more time for pleasantries; fear over his brother was quickly outweighing his curiosity. "I'm Lance," he said quickly, and then "Let's hurry!" and he broke into a run again, shouting over his shoulder, "We need to make sure my brother is okay."

And then Lance sprinted off through the wood back to the shore. As he ran, he thought, *Can this man really be speaking the truth? Avalon? The Round Table? But he is dressed like a knight….* None of that mattered now. He just had to see to Tristan. Still, the curiosity was there. What if he were back in Arthurian Britain? What if the comet had somehow caused him and Tristan to go through some sort of time warp into the past? If that were the case, then even if Tristan were okay, how would they ever get back to the twenty-first century and their parents? But then, if Lady Morgana were involved, anything could be possible. He would just have to figure it out later. Tristan had to come first.

Running was not easy. The ash covered the ground, hiding tree roots and fallen, charred branches, so that a couple of times, Lance tripped and nearly fell. But he followed the footsteps he had earlier made through the ash, and soon, he burst through the woods and back to the shore.

Since he had followed his own footprints, Lance was certain he had returned to the very spot on the beach that he had left, but when he arrived, there was no boat in sight. Now panicking, he quickly ran down the shore, slipping and sliding on the ash where the waves had swept up onto the beach, transforming it all into a gray, muddy mess. He ran for a good half-mile at an exhausting pace without seeing any sign of the boat, and he only stopped when he heard Palomides shouting, "Where is this boat? Where are you going?"

Lance turned around to see Palomides standing on the beach.

"I don't know where it went!" he hollered back while trying to catch his breath. "I'm sure it was here!"

Palomides did not seem to hear him, so Lance began running back toward the knight, who had now turned and started to walk in the opposite direction. Lance hoped Palomides was searching for the boat, but he was too out of breath to holler more.

Palomides walked around the edge of the cove and several hundred feet past where Lance had first seen the strange beast emerge, but he apparently did not sight the boat. Likely finding it cumbersome to walk through the wet ash in his armor, the knight also turned back.

In another few minutes, he met Lance where Lance was certain the boat and his now missing brother had been.

"Where is it? Where's the boat?" Lance moaned, so frustrated he wanted to cry and collapse on the beach, but the thought of becoming covered in the muddy ash made him resist.

"The tide took it back out to sea," said Palomides. "It is the only explanation unless your brother did so himself."

"No," said Lance. "My brother was unconscious, and he wouldn't have left without searching for me. He would have been smart enough to see my footprints in the ash leading from the boat."

Palomides wandered about the site, looking for marks on the beach where the boat's prow had been on the shore, but the tide had come in and the water level was higher now. No sign that the boat had ever been there could be found.

"There is only one set of footprints here—yours," he told Lance. "Your brother must have been washed out to sea in the boat while still unconscious."

"But! But—no, it can't be!" Lance exclaimed. "The boat couldn't have gone that far already. It's not even been an hour since we left the shore. How is it possible?"

"It is the only explanation," said the knight, placing his hand on Lance's shoulder in sympathy.

"But what am I to do?" Lance cried.

The knight looked up at the sky. The sun was setting. Lance looked out at the sea in despair. After a moment, Sir Palomides said, "It will be dark soon. There is nothing we can do. It will be dangerous to venture into the forest in the dark, and the beach breaks off into rocky cliffs a couple of miles from here, so it would be impossible to traverse them in the dark. It is best we rest here tonight and search for your brother tomorrow. Why don't you stay here and rest while I go back to fetch us meat from the horse to eat."

At first, Lance could not reply. He walked up to the forest's edge and sat down on a fallen tree, heedless of getting ash on his shorts.

"Do you hear me?" asked the knight. "Stay here. I will be back shortly."

"All right," said Lance, knowing it would take the knight an hour to walk back to his horse and return—probably longer since he was going to butcher the horse—not that Lance was hungry or had any appetite for horse flesh. But he did not know what else to do. Palomides was right. There was no point in his running about the beach searching in the dark. Better that he calm down, eat something, and get some rest so he could think straight. He was still in shock over everything that had happened, and watching the sun set as he waited for Palomides to return helped him regain a little clarity. He tried to tell himself to remain calm. If Tristan were still in the boat, he wasn't likely to drown at least. Not that it necessarily mattered—Lance hated to admit it, but he believed his brother probably was dead since he had not responded when Lance had tried to awaken him. And if Tristan were dead and the boat did sink, what did it matter if Tristan's body be buried at sea? Lance would have no means to bring the body home to be properly entombed in the family mausoleum—not if he truly were in another time period.

Gradually, Lance accepted that the only answer to all his questions—impossible as it seemed—was that the comet's impact had somehow transported him back to Arthurian Britain. Still, the comet had happened in the twenty-first century. Lance had never heard of such a comet hitting Arthurian Britain, yet here was ash all over the land, and despite Palomides saying it was the result of a dragon,

Lance could not quite believe in dragons, even if he were starting to believe in time travel. Nor could a single dragon have wreaked this much havoc on the land; it could only have been a comet that did this kind of extensive damage. Lance wondered just how extensive the comet's damage was—was it just here, a few miles along the shore and slightly inland that had become such a wasteland, or was it all of Britain—even all of the earth?

From the corner of his eye, Lance could see wisps of smoke rising from some of the burnt trees. He felt glad he had arrived after the forest fire that must have raged but burnt itself out before his arrival, for there were trees and ash that appeared to be still smoldering in places. When his stomach growled, Lance remembered Palomides would be bringing them horseflesh to eat—the thought of eating horse meat was not appetizing to Lance, but eating it raw would be even worse, so he got up from the tree and went over to some of the still smoking wood on the edge of the forest. He managed to grab a few less charred pieces so he didn't burn himself and to carry them to a small area on the beach covered with ash where he thought it would be safe to build a fire. He knew little about cooking outdoors or how to start a fire, but he suspected Palomides might know of such things, and perhaps the smoking wood would be easy to ignite.

Lance had assembled quite a pile of firewood by the time Sir Palomides returned, bearing several large chunks of bloody raw meat wrapped up in what had been his horse's saddle. The sign of the meat was revolting to Lance, but he knew he had to keep up his strength. For a moment, he thought of how he and his brother had been planning to have supper with their parents—and with Elaine—Tristan had been planning to propose to her this very night; it was hard to believe how quickly those plans had changed.

"We will feast tonight," said Palomides, setting the saddle and meat on the beach. "I am glad to see you have collected firewood for us."

"I hope you know how to build a fire," Lance replied. "The wood is still hot, smoking even, from the com...dragon, but I was afraid if I tried to rub it together, it would just start to crumble into ash."

"'Tis not difficult," said Palomides, kneeling down among the wood. The knight took off his metallic gloves and his helmet, and although it was growing dark, Lance could not help again noticing the man's dark skin. He certainly was not English, but what then was the likelihood that he would be in medieval Britain? As Lance pondered all this, he watched Palomides pull out some sort of stone—perhaps flint—from a pouch in his saddle, and although it was too dark now for Lance to see clearly what the knight was doing, in another minute, he saw sparks and then a small flame, and soon, there was a roaring fire.

"I don't know how to cook meat over an open flame," Lance admitted. "I'm sorry."

"I would think a peasant like you would know such things," Palomides replied.

For a moment, Lance was taken aback. Then he realized his T-shirt and shorts must look like peasant garb to a medieval warrior.

"I am not a peasant," Lance replied. "In fact, I'm the son of an earl."

"It must be the dragon's flame then that scorched off half your clothes," Palomides said, looking at Lance's bare legs. But then his eyes fell upon Lance's Reeboks.

"What strange footwear you have," he remarked. "Are you not from Britain? You dress like someone from...I know not where."

"It is a long story," said Lance, "and I am from Britain, but I have been away for quite some time in strange lands."

"I see," said Palomides. Lance knew Palomides would never understand if he tried to explain he was from a different time, and to say he had been in strange lands was not quite lying—he had grown up in Romania and spent his college years in the United States—both of which would have been strange lands to a medieval knight from Britain.

"Fortunately for you," Palomides continued, "when knights go out on quest, they must learn to take care of themselves. I will cook the meat. You look weary from worrying over your brother. Why don't you lie down and sleep for a bit, and I will wake you when the meal is ready."

Lance did feel exhausted, and although he normally would want to do his fair share, he felt it best to let the knight be in charge for now.

"Thank you," said Lance. Then, not knowing what else to do, he walked some feet from the fire. Finding a patch of ground with only a light covering of ash upon it, he lay down to rest. For a moment, he feared that since he had been hit by debris from the comet like his brother, he might also have a concussion, so if he fell asleep, perhaps he would not wake, but the other possibility was that he was simply dreaming and would soon wake to find himself back in the boat with his brother as if none of these strange events had ever occurred.

In another minute, Lance was asleep.

CHAPTER 4

LANCE WOKE TO Palomides gently shaking him awake to tell him the meat was ready. He then stood up, and shivering, walked over to the fire. The ash in the air had created a sort of cloud that blocked out even the moonlight and made the night colder than usual. Lance also worried about breathing in all the ash and dust particles floating in the air, and several times he felt the need to cough. He only hoped that all of this land was not destroyed or covered with ash.

Now so hungry that he was grateful for the roasted horse flesh, Lance ate with relish, using only his bare hands and his teeth to rip loose the pieces of meat. He even told Palomides, "The meat is good. Thank you for preparing it."

"Tomorrow," Palomides replied, "we will make our way to a village that lies about ten miles up the coastline. Hopefully, it withstood the dragon's attack. If so, I will purchase another horse there and we will make inquiries about your brother. We will find you some decent garments as well, for you are not fit to be seen by maidens in your half-naked state."

Lance did not argue or try to explain that his clothing was perfectly acceptable where he came from. Instead, he said, "That sounds good. Hopefully, someone there has seen Tristan."

"Tristan?" said Palomides, sounding surprised.

"Yes, my brother," Lance replied.

"It is a strange name," said Palomides. "Say it again."

"Tristan," Lance replied.

"I am sorry," said Palomides. "For a moment, I thought you said Tristram. You are not Sir Tristram's brother, are you?"

"No," Lance replied, realizing Palomides meant the great knight of King Arthur's Round Table, the same knight for whom his brother had been named since the knight's name was also often spelled as Tristan in the legends.

"It is good," said Palomides, "for while it is my duty as a knight to help all, he is the one exception. Tristram and I are sworn enemies."

"Oh," said Lance. "I see."

"And remind me what your own name is—you said it so quickly, and it is unfamiliar to me," Palomides said.

"I'm sorry. It's Lance."

"It is a strange name."

"I am named for Sir Lancelot," Lance replied.

"Sir Lancelot? I never heard of him," said Palomides.

"Never heard of him!" exclaimed Lance. "Sir Lancelot du Lac, son of King Ban of Benwick, raised by the Lady of the Lake? King Arthur's greatest knight and—" Here he stopped, for he was about to say "the lover of Queen Guinevere," but he realized such a statement might get him in trouble if their love affair was not yet known. If this were Arthurian Britain, at what point in its story was he entering it? Were Lancelot and Guinevere already lovers? Did everyone in

Camelot already know it? And what about the fact that his parents had told him that in reality it was Bedwyr who had been Guinevere's lover? But that explained it—now Lance remembered that Sir Lancelot had been completely fictional—made up by a French romance writer, Chretien de Troyes. No wonder Palomides had not heard of Lancelot—he was not historical. But given that argument, Lance was surprised to find that Palomides was not himself fictional. If he remembered correctly, Palomides had been a Saracen; did that mean his dinner companion was a Muslim? Lance was no expert on history, but he was pretty sure the Prophet Mohammed did not found Islam until about a century after King Arthur had lived. But here was a living, breathing Sir Palomides before him—doubtless the source for the legendary figure. It was mind-boggling.

Palomides had been silently chewing his horse meat while Lance launched into his explanation of Sir Lancelot, so it was a minute after Lance ended his harangue before the knight spoke.

"I apologize," Sir Palomides said, "but I fear, Sir Lancelot, that your fame has not yet reached this part of Britain."

"It's okay," said Lance.

"*O-kay*?" repeated Palomides. "What does that mean?"

"I mean it is all right that you have never heard of Sir Lancelot."

"As I said, it is a failing on my part and not due to any lack of fame on yours, I am sure, Sir Lancelot."

Lance was tired and did not want to try to explain further. Palomides apparently thought he was *the* Sir Lancelot. Maybe he would try to explain it to the knight later, but first Lance wanted to understand Palomides himself.

"It is no matter," Lance replied. "But I would like to hear your own tale and how you came to follow the strange beast."

"It would be with great pleasure that I would tell you my tale, Sir Lancelot, but first, please clear up my confusion. Earlier you said you were an earl's son, but now you say your father is King Ban of Benwick. How is this possible? And where, pray tell, is Benwick?"

"It's a small kingdom in Brittany," said Lance, deciding he might as well play the Sir Lancelot part for what it was worth—after all, if this was Arthurian Britain, no one here would believe he came from the twenty-first century. "It is not surprising you have not heard of it, for my father's kingdom was taken from him long ago and he is now dead. I only reveal to those I trust my true lineage. In any case, I have been far away and have just now come to Britain with my brother."

Then the thought of Tristan caused Lance to become teary-eyed. He stifled a sob but could not help adding, "I wish my brother were here." Tristan would have known better how to answer Palomides' questions, having been a far better scholar of the Arthurian legend than himself.

"Your sadness is understandable," said Sir Palomides. "If your brother is to be found, I promise we will do so. But you are not then an earl's son?"

"You must have misheard me," said Lance, digging himself deeper into his lie. "I said 'grandson.' My mother was the daughter of an earl. That's what I meant." And then he changed the subject to avoid further questioning. "Sir Palomides, I do not mean to be rude, but you are dark of skin, so I do not believe you are a native of this land. Would you tell me how you came to be in Britain?"

"I am, in fact, a native of this land," Palomides replied, "but my father was not."

"Please tell me," Lance continued, "your family history and how you come to quest after that strange beast, for that creature is like nothing I have ever seen before, and I would like to know its story as well as your own."

"Very well," said Palomides. "It is a long tale, but I will try to tell it quickly so we may get a good sleep before the dawn."

SIR PALOMIDES' TALE

To explain my dark complexion and my being here in Britain, it is best I begin by telling the tale of my father, who was King Escabor of Babylon. When he was in his twenty-second year, his father died and he became king. But my father was of an inquisitive mind and soon tired of the petty squabbles and the feigned importance of his court; nor did he like being subject to the King of the Persians, and so after a year, he'd had enough of ruling and decided instead to indulge his curiosity about the world beyond Babylon. Leaving his vizier in charge, whom I understand was later made king in his place, he decided to travel to Rome. He had just heard of the conquest of the eternal city by the barbarians from the North, so he desired to see for himself its new ruler, the Ostrogoth king, Odoacer, who had put an end to centuries of Roman oppression, at least for the subjects of the Western empire.

Once my father reached Rome, after many adventures that I will not trouble your ears with, he did meet Odoacer, whom he found to be just as barbarous as he expected, but he admired him, nonetheless, for bringing down the last of the Western Empire. I have heard it rumored that my father actually saved Odoacer's life, but if this is true, my father never spoke of it, and the bards always will make up details to flower their stories.

While my father was in Rome, he heard tidings of a young man, Arthur, hardly more than a boy, who had been proclaimed rightful King of Britain, after pulling a magical sword from a stone—something he later found out the bards had also made up—but the tale made him curious yet again, and so he decided to visit Britain to see this newly crowned King Arthur for himself. It was rumored that Arthur was wise beyond his years and espousing a code of knighthood, in which only those who show themselves noble in heart and deed are worthy to become knights. My father was intrigued by these beliefs, and although he suspected he would be disappointed by Arthur, he figured he would at least be a better conversationalist than Odoacer.

It was upon my father's arrival in Britain that the Beast Glatisant entered our family history, and here is how it happened. My father always would journey alone, despite his rank and regardless of any dangers, for he hated all forms of royal prerogative and preferred to travel incognito as an adventurer. Upon arriving in Britain, he bought a horse and rode on for Camelot and King Arthur's court. On the second day of this journey, he was riding through the forest and coming down a steep hill when he heard the horrible barking noise that you no doubt heard coming from the Beast. It is said that early in its life, the Beast swallowed whole some thirty hounds that now live inside his stomach and are slowly eating away his intestines, although considering that the Beast is far older than I am, I think this unlikely for he would have been dead by now if thirty dogs continually tore at his stomach. In truth, I do not know the cause of that hideous noise that comes from his stomach, but I digress.

My father, upon hearing this noise, could only think it was a hunting party, perhaps out pursuing a boar. But as he approached closer, the noise increased to an unbelievable level. Then he turned a bend in the road and found a horse lying on the ground and the Beast Glatisant leaning over it; the Beast's horrible serpent head was pulled back like those of the cobras my father had seen as a boy when he had made a visit to India, so he knew the Beast was about to strike. But then he looked closer at the Beast's prey and realized it was not the horse, but a man fallen beside it whom the creature planned to devour.

Quickly, my father, with no thought to his own safety, spurred his horse onward, and pulling out his sword, he smote the Beast aside the head with a blow—a blow that would have severed the head of a human and at least have done fatal damage to any other creature. For a second, the Beast only looked stunned, but when my father struck it again, drawing blood this time, the Beast turned and quickly retreated into the forest, its bellyful of hounds crying as if it had been killed. For some time after that, it was widely believed the Beast had died somewhere in the forest, for it was not seen again for many months, but alas, it finally raised its ugly head again, bringing disaster to the countryside wherever it roamed.

Of course, my father's first thoughts now were not for the Beast but for the fallen knight whose leg was trapped beneath his horse. It was apparent to my father, once he dismounted his own steed, that the fallen knight's horse had died, landing upon and trapping him. The horse itself had been the victim of a sudden deadly kick from the Beast.

My father, who had the strength of three men, quickly lifted the horse high enough with one hand to pull the knight out from under it with his other. He then tended to the knight's wounds, first wrapping him in his cloak and building a fire to keep him warm.

He then gave him medicine that he always carried with him, ancient medicine based on an old Persian recipe, which Christendom had yet to discover; it provided the wounded knight enough relief from his pain that he was finally able to speak.

"What kind of devil are you?" the knight then demanded of my father. "A kind one I see, but nevertheless, you are swarthy like a devil."

"I am a Persian," my father replied. "My name is Escabor, and I am the King of Babylon."

"Babylon?" said the knight. "I've heard tell of that place—is there not a lot of whoring there? Always thought it sounded like somewhere I might like to visit."

"I do not know this word, 'whoring,'" my father replied, for his knowledge of the British tongue was still somewhat limited.

"No matter," said the knight. "What are you doing in Britain?"

After my father explained his desire to visit Camelot, the knight replied, "I can bring you to see Arthur. He and I are good friends, although he has some very strange ideas about how men are supposed to treat women, as if women don't like rutting as much as men, and what's the difference if I have a few bastards in the village? Anyway, as soon as my leg is better, we can go to Camelot, but first you better take me to my castle so I can rest up a few days."

My father agreed to this request, but it was almost nightfall, so they decided it best that they sleep out in the open for that night. Nevertheless, my father wished to know who his prospective host would be, so he said, "Sir, I know not your name. Pray tell me whom I have the honor of addressing, and also what that foul creature was that I saw attacking you. Are there more such creatures about?"

"Pellinore's the name," said the knight. "I guess if we're going to my castle, you'll find out soon enough that I am the King of Listenoise, though it is no great title. Just a little puddle-sized kingdom since my father was a second son, brother to King Bron of Carbonek. Not much glory in ruling such a little place, but there are better things for a man to do, such as going on a quest."

"I am pleased, nevertheless, to meet you, your majesty," my father replied.

"Don't mention it, your majesty," laughed King Pellinore.

"But tell me now, what is that strange beast I saw? It had a serpent's head but legs like a deer and a lion's tail. Truly, it is like nothing I have ever seen before. Is it common in England?"

"No," said Pellinore. "It is a one of a kind, and we can be thankful for that, for it is a foul and horrible creature, and as for what it is, the explanation of that will take some telling."

"I have all night," my father replied, and so King Pellinore told him his tale.

KING PELLINORE'S TALE

Although my kingdom is small because my father was a second son and my grandfather chose to divide the land between his two sons, giving my father the much smaller portion, I come from a family of great significance in Britain. In truth, we are descended from Joseph of Arimathea who founded the line of Avalon long ago, and as a result, my family are distant cousins to King Arthur and his sister, Lady Morgana of Avalon, for their mother Igraine was also of the line of Avalon.

Perhaps you have heard of the Grail family. It is of this family I speak, of which I am a member. My father's older brother, King Bron, was known as the Grail King, but he had no son, and I being the sole son of his only brother, was in turn heir to that title. I am certain you have heard of the Holy Grail, the cup from which Christ drank at the Last Supper and in which Joseph of Arimathea is said to have collected Christ's blood when he was dying on the Cross. It is said that my family's ancestor, Joseph of Arimathea, brought this cup with him to Britain, and consequently, it was passed down in our family.

The strange thing is that my uncle Bron was named for Bran Galed, another ancestor, a pagan who followed the old gods of Britain long before Christianity came to this land. Bran Galed had a marvelous, and some say magical, drinking horn that in those days was considered one of the Thirteen Treasures of Britain. Well, my uncle Bron decided, for whatever reason—perhaps because he treasured the horn but, being a Christian, did not want to keep a pagan relic in the house—that the horn must in truth be the Holy Grail, and that it had been actually passed down in the family not from Bran Galed's side but from Joseph of Arimathea's. And so my uncle had the twisted end of the horn planted in a gold base so that it became a great unwieldy looking drinking cup; it was obviously no grail or even cup of ancient extraction from Jerusalem—obvious to anyone who wasn't half-witted. However, at my father's bidding, I kept silent about this false relic while my father was alive, and my sister Dindrane, who also knew the truth, was never as hotheaded as I, so she also said nothing.

Then one day, not long after my father's death, Dindrane and I went to visit Uncle Bron and his daughter, Elaine. Now, you must understand that since Elaine had been a babe, it had been agreed by my father and uncle that she and I would one day wed to reunite their kingdoms. But now I was a man and king of my own country while Elaine was yet a young girl. I was full of lust and did not want to wait for her to grow up; in truth, I was very impatient to marry and had my eye on several fine wenches in the nearby village, prizing far more highly their ample breasts and sweet kisses than any dowry or title a wife might bring me.

When I told my uncle, who had heard of my roving eye, that I did not wish to wait to marry, he began to lecture me, saying, "You must remain pure and chaste as suiting the future Grail King until the time Elaine is old enough to be your bride. Our Savior would so wish it, and the Grail will not serve a sinner."

I will not repeat how I replied—it was not at all polite, but it is sufficient to say that an argument followed, climaxing in my disparaging the Grail, declaring my disbelief in it, and mocking my uncle for how he reverenced it.

Dindrane begged me to cease my torrent of words, and little Elaine broke into tears, but Uncle Bron and I did not hold back in our exchange of insults, my uncle maintaining a self-righteous tone as he belittled me.

"May you live to regret your words," he said when we parted that day. "For it is by drinking from the Grail that we maintain our health. Its Holy Blood grants us long lives and keeps our kingdoms free from invasion by Romans and Saxons. Pray that God does not punish us and our lands because of your blasphemy."

I had no fear of his gloomy warnings. It was true many of my family members had lived to ripe old ages, but my father had died by falling off his horse at age forty, and the Romans and Saxons had never invaded our land because it was in the West of Britain and we had a well-trained army—none of this had anything to do with some false Holy Grail. So I thought little of my uncle's taunts, and I didn't bother to respond even when he added, "I will not marry my daughter to a blasphemer, and whomsoever I choose for Elaine's husband will inherit my lands, so be assured that you will receive nothing."

I paid little attention to all this, believing his deluded mind was so far gone that he wouldn't be long for this world, and no little maiden was going to stop me from getting his crown. Perhaps I would still marry Elaine, but in the meantime, I would have all the women I wanted.

As Dindrane and I returned home, she begged me to go seek Uncle Bron's forgiveness, but I repeatedly refused. I had made it clear that I was a man now; I was not going to live by anyone else's rules, least of all the moral code of a religious fanatic.

A few days later, my uncle summoned me to his castle. At first, I was foolish enough to think he wanted to reconcile with me, but when I arrived, I was greeted with news that the Holy Grail had been stolen. Worse, my uncle had the effrontery to accuse me of the crime. I, in turn, accused him of intentionally hiding it so he could blame me. I was honestly glad to hear it was gone. That cup had started all the foolishness, and with it gone, I thought perhaps my uncle would regain his senses.

In time, Uncle Bron's anger did indeed cool, and instead of calling me a thief, he came to believe that an angel from heaven had carried away the cup since I was clearly not worthy to inherit it. He went on to insist that the Holy Grail would not be returned until I had shown repentance. When I asked how I was to do that—just out of curiosity; I had no intention of repenting for anything—he said, "You must go on a sacred quest to bring about good in this world, or you must go on a pilgrimage to the holy land. Either way is acceptable to show your great sorrow over your heinous blasphemy and revolting acts of fornication."

I could not help laughing at these words. If God didn't want us to fornicate, why then had He made us so lusty? And furthermore, I told my uncle I had not blasphemed because it was obvious to any reasonable person that the horn of Bran Galed was not the Holy Grail, and furthermore, since I knew the Christ had been a real person and some sort of relative of ours since we were descended from his uncle, Joseph of Arimathea, I could believe in him without needing to worship some old cup.

"God will punish you for your repeated blasphemy," my uncle repeated.

"Maybe so," I replied, "but the punishment can't possibly be so bad as listening to what comes out of your mouth from your addled brain."

As you can imagine, I did not see my uncle again for some time. Besides, I had my own kingdom to rule. I kept myself busy governing my people, reconciling their disputes, giving to the poor, and bedding the kitchen wenches to ensure we maintained a stable population. After all, does not a king have a right to the women of his land? Is he not to be father of his people? Of course, my sister wished me to marry, and to find her a husband as well, but I thought there was time enough for all that. I was having far too much fun, and taking on a bickering wife would only add to my cares, so I was in no rush for one.

And then one summer afternoon, I was out riding in the forest. I was sorely troubled that day because Farmer Giles had come to me that morning with a complaint. Somehow, his entire harvest had disappeared overnight. When I went to investigate, we could find no evidence of what had caused it. It had poured rain early that morning, which erased any sign of footprints that might have given us a clue. I wanted to believe it was some simple theft by his neighbors, but I knew full well no one could have harvested all his crop that quickly. Such a puzzle caused my brain to hurt so much that I sought relief in riding that afternoon, and also in thinking lusty thoughts about the miller's wife—don't get me wrong; I am no adulterer; I might take a woman against her will, but certainly not another man's wife. Still, I see no harm in fantasizing about doing so.

I was enjoying a lovely daydream about fair buxom Martha when I heard a horrendous, deafening noise that sounded like dozens of barking hounds. Immediately, I rode toward it to investigate. The noise only grew louder as I approached it. I assumed the clamor must come from some sort of hunting party. No hunters were allowed on my land without my permission, but nevertheless, I thought I might join them in their sport and, if they were agreeable men, invite them home for dinner to distract me from my worries over Farmer Giles' missing crop.

Then, as I came around a hill in the forest, thinking the hunting party must be just around the bend based on the volume of noise, I suddenly found myself within a mere ten feet of the most hideous creature I had ever seen. It was a veritable amalgamation of beasts, a disgusting mockery of God's creation, a true monster in size and shape. Its great serpent neck stretched up to chew apples from a tree some twenty-feet high. Its body was spotted like that of the leopard I had seen in one of my uncle's old Roman manuscripts. Its tail was like a lion's. Its legs were like those of a deer, but it stood far taller, so tall I could have almost ridden my horse beneath it. I did not know whether it was a dragon or a griffin or some other fabled beast of which I had never heard. And then when it saw me, a great roaring, barking sound came up from its belly and out of its mouth that was nearly deafening.

For a moment, I stared at the Beast while frozen in place until my horse overcame its own temporary paralysis and whinnied in fear. The Beast, hearing this noise, turned to stretch its great ugly face just a few feet from my own so that I thought it would eat me then and there, but my horse had more forethought than I; quickly it turned and bolted back toward the castle, such that I nearly slid off of it and had to scramble to keep my hold, only once daring to look back with relief to see that the creature was not pursuing us.

I was in such a panic that when I reached home, it was all I could do to pass the halter to my stable boy and make my way into the dining hall. Struggling to catch my breath, I practically collapsed into my sister's arms.

"What is it? What has happened?" Dindrane demanded when she saw my pale face.

I could not even begin to describe what I had seen, but somehow I managed through a string of many questions and answers to tell her of the terrible beast I had encountered.

Finally, Dindrane asked, "What does it mean?"

"I do not know," I said. "I do not know what it is, but it must surely mean us ill. It will rend the land naked of vegetation with its appetite, for the tree it was eating from was half-bare, and I do not now doubt it is what ate Farmer Giles' crop."

"We must go to Uncle Bron," Dindrane replied. "Perhaps his bestiary book will tell us what it is and how it may be destroyed."

The last thing I wanted was to go to my uncle with my troubles, but I had to think of my people's welfare, for who knew what dangers the Beast might represent? It might very well seek to devour our live-stock and our very selves after it had eaten all our crops.

Within the hour, Dindrane and I rode to the Grail Castle and I told Uncle Bron my tale. When I had finished, he looked puzzled and replied, "I must pray upon this. Come back tomorrow and I will let you know whether it has pleased God to reveal to me what this creature may be."

I rolled my eyes at this response—knowing very well my uncle had no direct communication with God—but my sister said, "Thank you, Uncle. We will pray as well and return to you in the morning."

I did not sleep well that night, for the monster's face kept reap-pearing in my dreams, but I also felt somehow that the Beast was deeply connected to me, and this feeling both troubled and excited my thoughts.

In the morning, Dindrane and I returned to my uncle's castle, all the way fearing we would encounter the Beast along the road, but we arrived unimpeded, and my uncle welcomed us, eager to tell us the revelation that he claimed God Himself had sent to him.

"I have long been praying, dear nephew," he told me, "that our Savior might send you a sign to make you repent for your sins of for-nication and blasphemy. This night an Angel of the Lord, the same one who has hid away the Holy Grail, revealed to me the truth be-hind this beast that you saw."

I moved to the edge of my chair, interested in what he might say, no matter how skeptical I was about information gathered from an angel rather than from a reliable source like a bestiary.

"You see," my uncle continued, "the Lord does not wish any of His children to be lost and suffer damnation, and least of all does He wish such a fate for one of His own Holy Bloodline. Therefore,

He has set forth a quest for you to pursue, a quest to slay this beast, a quest that only you or one of our family line can fulfill, and only when that quest is fulfilled will your sins be forgiven so you may be worthy to come into His Holy Kingdom on the Last Day. It is this quest upon which you must embark."

Of course, I assumed this was all nonsense, so I asked him directly, "Uncle, do you know what this creature is? Has anyone ever seen one like it before?"

"I most certainly have never seen it myself," he replied, "for the angel revealed that only those who are out of favor with our Lord due to a lack of faith are able to witness it."

"But what is it?" I demanded.

"It is a creature of sin," Uncle Bron replied. His statement did not surprise me at all, and as soon as he spoke the words, I gave up any hope of learning the truth from him. But because Dindrane clearly wished to hear his explanation, I sat and listened as he recited the following excruciating tale of the Beast's origins.

THE TALE OF CASTUS AND INCESTUA, AS TOLD BY THE ANGEL TO KING BRON

Once upon a time in an island kingdom, there lived a king named Philia, whose beloved wife died in childbirth, giving life to twin children, a son, Castus, and a daughter, Incestua.

The kingdom was a small one, and because it was an island, it was quite isolated from the rest of the world, although there was some trade between it and its neighbors. As a result, the royal children had little interaction with others of their rank, and King Philia, being a vain and proud man, did not wish his children to associate with the offspring of servants and others beneath their station. Furthermore, because the king was always busy with affairs of state, he had little time for his children, so brother and sister grew up alone together and were all the world to one another.

Now Prince Castus was a handsome young lad, athletic and ruddy, and fine to look upon. He was also good-hearted and intelligent; he loved the classroom and to learn from his tutor. Princess Incestua, however, preferred to be outdoors. She was just as intelligent as her brother, but her senses awoke to the world earlier than her brother's, and she longed to explore knowledge through experience rather than books.

And then in their fourteenth year, the royal children's tutor became ill and could no longer perform his duties, so King Philia had a new tutor brought from Alexandria, a tutor who had studied in the Great Library of that city, but more importantly, this tutor was a Christian in the days before Christianity had become the religion of the Roman Empire.

In the course of teaching the children, this tutor explained to the prince and princess the wisdom of the ancient Greeks, as well as that of Mesopotamia and Egypt, and all other knowledge known at the time, but Prince Castus was not content with learning solely facts. He sought after wisdom, so he asked the tutor what he truly believed. Incestua found these conversations tiresome and would wander off from the classroom. Meanwhile, Castus listened to his tutor confess his belief in the Christ, and soon after, Prince Castus came to accept Christ as his own savior and to call himself a Christian.

Girls mature more quickly than boys, and so by this time, Incestua had experienced her sexual awakening. Not having anyone else close to her age to set her eyes upon, and having always felt a

close bond to her brother, she began to desire him. Being still innocent, she slowly realized something was strange about her feelings, so
she asked her father to find her a husband. He, however, believed her
too young to wed, and because Incestua reminded him of his beautiful deceased wife, he was loath to have her leave him at such a young
age. Consequently, Incestua remained daily in Castus' company, and
her desire for him grew until she could contain it no longer.

One day, brother and sister were down by the seashore swimming together when Incestua touched Castus in a sensual manner
that shocked and alarmed him. He instantly pulled away. At first,
he thought her innocent enough in her intentions, but then she confessed her great love and desire for him. He explained to her that he
was her brother, so it was against God's law to do what she proposed,
but she persisted in declaring how much she loved and desired him.
He continued to counter her words with arguments for why one
could not engage in sexual behavior with one's sibling. When she replied that Egyptian royalty had often married their siblings, Castus
reminded her that the Egyptians were pagans while he was a believer
in the true God, and therefore, he would not sin, for he had a desire
to see the afterlife.

"There can be no heaven for me but in your arms," Incestua insisted, and yet Castus spurned her, fleeing from her and being ever
wary after that whenever he was in her presence. Not only had Incestua now lost all hope of winning Castus' love, but she had lost the
friendship of her only companion.

A few nights later, Incestua's maid found her mistress crying into
her pillow. This slave girl had been brought from a foreign land, and
her ancestors worshiped the old gods of Canaan, including Molech.
When she tried to comfort her mistress, Incestua spilled from her

lips her love for her brother and revealed her plan to commit suicide if he would not love her.

The slave girl told Incestua that she knew a way to bring about such love, but it could only be done through the power of her ancestors' god. To make contact with this god was very difficult, but the slave girl would do it in exchange for Incestua giving her her freedom. Incestua was so desperate for Castus' affections that she readily agreed. That same night, Incestua and the slave girl went into the neighboring dark forest, and there they participated in a satanic ritual to summon forth the pagan god Molech, who was, in truth, no god indeed, but simply a demon, one of Satan's minions.

A deal with a demon can never lead to anything but trickery, evil, and tragedy, but Incestua was so desperate for her brother's love that she lost all sense of reason. When Molech appeared, she found herself so dazzled by his power that she truly believed Castus could be made to love her.

"Why have I been summoned from the Halls of Eblis?" Molech demanded, coming forth from the ground in a blaze of smoke and fire. When Incestua hesitated to speak, he placed his nose just an inch from hers, and leering, demanded, "Speak, beautiful lusty maiden. I am yours to command, for already I can sense in your heart the strong desire that has led to your summoning of me."

Incestua was overcome by the demon's glamorous appearance. He was not at all unattractive—a head taller than most men, with a chest like a battleship, and his eyes were like wide, deep rivers, rippling in the moonlight, and yet there was a crooked bend to his nose that revealed he was no source of good. Incestua felt both awe and fear in his presence, as well as a strange tingling of desire she tried desperately to suppress.

"Great One, I am wishing to make a man who scorns me fall in love with me," she finally confessed.

Molech let out a roaring cackle, enough to make the leaves blow from the trees, and Incestua and the slave girl were nearly knocked to the ground by it.

"It is often unrequited love that brings humans to communion with me," Molech then explained. "But tell me, fair princess, who would be foolish enough to run from your lovely charms?"

"My brother. I love...my brother," she confessed, looking down at her feet in shame.

The demon let out another burst of howling laughter before replying, "I can well understand that even your own brother would be tempted by your beauty if it were not for the fact that Prince Castus is actually more beautiful than you—perhaps the only being on earth more beautiful. Thankfully, my tastes do not run toward his gender, but to your own, my dear; if you wish me to help you, I must have something in return."

"Oh, I would do anything to possess my brother's love," Incestua replied, initially misunderstanding Molech's intent. "Castus has been my whole world all my life, and I want nothing more than to spend the rest of my days with him and please him in every way possible."

"I do not doubt it," said Molech, "and you will pay the price for it."

Incestua's heart now trembled, for she feared Molech would trick her, but she saw no other way to obtain Castus' love, so she said boldly, "I will pay the price, whatever it is, even...even if it be murder, so long as it will mean that I win Castus' love."

Then Molech replied, "The condition is that I want you, my dear. As you desire your brother, so I desire you."

Shocked, Incestua replied, "Oh, no, I—I can love none but Castus alone."

"I ask not for love," Molech replied. "I ask for your virginity."

"Oh, no, I—but Castus—then he would know—" Incestua protested.

"Oh, do not think of it like that, my pet," said Molech. "I can teach you the joys of the flesh in ways you have never known before, for am I not a god? And by learning from me, you will learn how to please Castus in ways that will make him never want to part with you. It will be a beneficial experience for all three of us, I assure you."

Incestua was by no means a stupid girl, but even the wisest of us may slip into sin when evil lusts tempt us, and so eventually, her desire for Castus overcoming all else, she consented. It would be indecorous to describe what happened next; it is sufficient to say that Incestua sold her body and soul to Molech, and she came away knowing far more about the evils of hell than any of us can ever imagine.

After their evil act was completed, Molech gave Incestua a love potion to use on Castus. Then she returned home with her slave girl, who had watched her mistress' act of sin with great satisfaction. As they passed through the dark forest, the women paused at a pool, and in the moonlight, Incestua stopped to look at her reflection. In horror, she saw that the bloom had left her cheeks and her eyes looked old and wise, but she did not weep, for she knew she could not change what had happened, and she continued to believe her brother's love could restore her happiness.

Once back at the castle, Incestua kept to her room, having her slave girl tell everyone the next day that she was ill. Then that evening, the slave girl departed, having received her freedom. Incestua waited until night, when she expected everyone was asleep, and then she left her room with the love potion and made her way to Castus' chamber. She sprinkled drops from the potion over her brother's eyes so that the instant he opened them, he would see and fall in love with her.

Poor Incestua foolishly thought she could trust the demon, but it was not to be. After she placed the love potion on Castus' eyes, she slid into his bed and began enjoying the touch of his firm young body beside her. After a couple of minutes, Castus awoke. At first, he was confused, then stunned to see Incestua, and then he became angry. He jumped out of the bed, yelling at her to leave his room.

Incestua, shocked and fearful that the servants would hear him, quickly fled to her own room where she wept for an hour, wondering why the love potion had not worked. In her despair, she feared her brother would disgrace her by telling their father.

Deciding her only option now was suicide, Incestua went out onto the balcony of her room, climbed over the railing, and prepared to fling her body into the ocean.

But Incestua's feet had barely left the balcony's security when she felt herself caught up in Molech's strong arms. With his great dragon-like wings, he carried them safely to the privacy of the castle's roof.

"Why did you save me?" Incestua demanded of Molech. "Castus does not love me. You lied to me about the love potion. You have ruined me."

"Shh, my child," said Molech. "I do not break my bargains. You did not utter the magic words I gave you with the potion."

"You gave me no enchantment to utter," she objected.

"Of course I did, but you mortals are of a frail nature and often fail to understand or follow directions. Unfortunately, the love potion is only able to work once. I cannot give you more, but I will help you in another way."

Incestua feared he would desire another favor for his help, but she could not possibly give her body to him again. The thought was repulsive to her, for though his face remained handsome, now his skin appeared to be scaled like that of a crocodile, and his breath was as foul as a dog's after it has swallowed its own vomit.

"I will not give you any more favors," Incestua said, tears springing to her eyes.

"I did not ask for any, my dear," Molech replied. "I merely wish to help you."

"How can you help me?" Incestua asked. "My brother was horrified. He called me unchaste. He said he was a Christian and would never consent to my unnatural desires."

"If you truly love your brother," Molech replied, "you must be willing to win his love at any cost."

"Oh, I am willing. I desire him above all things."

"Do you desire him or do you love him?" Molech asked.

"Oh, both, both," Incestua insisted. "His body is the most perfect and beautiful in all the world so that I cannot control my longing to possess it. If he would only allow me to love him, I would give him such pleasure that I know he would then love me as well."

"Then you must force him to lie with you," said Molech. "You have no other choice."

Suddenly, Incestua felt her stomach curdling, and in another moment, she was vomiting.

"You truly are lovesick," said Molech, laughing.

"I am ill," she replied.

"No, your symptoms are natural for a mother."

"A mother?" asked Incestua, wiping her mouth with the sleeve of her gown.

"My child," said Molech, "surely you know that when maidens copulate, they risk becoming with child."

"But I.... No!" Incestua cried.

"You are carrying my child," Molech confirmed. "Obviously, I cannot marry a mortal woman, for you are living and I am spirit, but you can find a husband before your child is born."

"How?" Incestua asked.

"Do you not see?" asked Molech, circling her in the blackness of the night, and then leaning forward to whisper into her ear. "You must accuse your brother of rape. You must tell your father you are pregnant with Castus' child. Then your father will force the marriage to take place."

"But marriages between siblings are not permitted in our country," Incestua replied.

"You will have to go away with Castus. You will be exiled. Your father's crown will pass to your cousin while you are both believed dead, but what does it matter so long as you possess your greatest desire?"

"That is true," said Incestua, allowing her desire and the demon's urgings to shatter her logic. "I don't care about our inheritance, just about being with Castus, and Castus is a good man. He is a Christian taught to forgive. In time, he will forgive me for wronging him when he knows how much I love him, and as his sister, he's bound to want to help me in my hour of need."

"Exactly," said Molech. "Come now; back to your bed."

The devil then carried Incestua through the air and back to her balcony, and soon she was in bed, content that the devil's plan would work.

In the morning, Incestua went to have breakfast with her father and brother as she did every day. She was still trying to think how to accuse her brother of rape. Fearful the plan might not go as she hoped, she thought perhaps she would put off saying anything until after breakfast so she would not have to tell her father her lies in Castus' presence. However, when she entered the dining hall, she immediately saw her father and brother's jaws drop and their eyes grow wide with horror.

"Incestua!" her father exclaimed.

"What? What is it?" she asked, fearing her brother had already revealed her indiscretion from the night before.

But her father's words were far more shocking.

"You are with child!"

Looking down, Incestua saw that the child had grown in her womb in just a matter of hours so that she looked almost ready to deliver.

"Who has done this to you?" demanded King Philia.

Desperate, Incestua replied, "Castus did it. He raped me!"

Castus' eyes grew wide. Then his cheeks turned pale, but a moment after, he was on his feet, his face red as he shouted, "I never did such a thing. It's a lie! She tried to seduce me."

But Incestua's accusations were louder, and then she began to demand, "Marry me. Marry me, brother!"

Unfortunately, King Philia believed his daughter's lies, but he would not agree to such an incestuous solution.

"No, my daughter; it cannot be," he replied. "Castus has committed a great crime against you and the gods. You cannot be married to your brother. Your child is one of sin. It must be destroyed when it is born, and your brother must be punished."

"I am innocent!" Castus swore, but Philia only replied, "Because you refuse to confess, you must be put to death."

"I cannot confess to a crime I did not commit," Castus argued, and turning to Incestua, he demanded, "Sister, how can you treat me in this way?"

But Incestua turned her face from him in grief; even her great love for him was not strong enough to overcome her fear of being punished for her sins.

Soon Philia had summoned the guards, who dragged Castus to the place of execution.

"Brother, I love you!" Incestua screamed as the executioner raised his ax to decapitate the prince.

Disgusted by his daughter's outcry, Philia clapped his hand over her mouth. Then he told his son, "You shall die and your body will be flung to the dogs so they may tear it apart for the crime you have committed."

"Father," Castus said, "because I am a Christian, I forgive you, for you have not wronged me in seeking to vindicate your daughter. It is she who wrongs me."

"I knew your conversion to Christianity would only cause trouble in my home," Philia replied. "I will hear no more of this dreaded cult. Now ask for your sister's forgiveness before you die."

Then all Christian feeling left Castus. His face grew black with rage as he turned to Incestua and said, "Sister, I know not why you have accused me, but while my God is a loving one, he is also a God of great anger and of justice. I now call upon God to hear my cries and to curse you and your child for how you have treated me. My blood is on your hands. May your child tear apart your belly in the same way the hounds are about to tear me apart."

"Enough!" shouted King Philia, giving the signal to the executioner.

In another moment, Castus' head was severed, and when it fell to the cold ground, his eyes stared directly at Incestua, continuing to accuse her.

But only for a moment. Then King Philia ordered that his dogs be released to tear apart his son's corpse.

The horror of seeing her beloved killed sent Incestua into premature labor. Falling to the ground, she began screeching and wailing, and no one dared even to approach and comfort her. They could only stare in disbelief as they watched the most terrible creature imaginable rip apart her womb, its claws pulling its body up out of her stomach, its head like a serpent's, and its tail streaking the ground with her blood as it burst forth.

For a moment, the foul beast ran about in confusion, and then setting its eyes upon its grandfather, King Philia, it ran up to him, grabbed his nose between its teeth and tore his face apart. Then it swallowed him down whole like a snake swallows a mouse. Next, it slurped up the hounds that had torn apart Castus as if they were mere drops of water. It is those hounds that, being swallowed whole, continue to live and yap incessantly in the foul beast's belly to this day.

When the beast had finished its hideous meal, it jumped over the castle wall into the sea and swam toward Greece. Since then, this infernal monster has been seen wherever evil acts occur, and it is believed that it entices people to sin and make compacts with Satan. It has come to be known as the Beast Glatisant, or the Barking Beast, because of the great noise coming from its belly, though some call it the Questing Beast because only by questing after righteousness and returning to communion with God can one hope to destroy it and free humanity from the sin it perpetuates.

Therefore, let Incestua's story be a warning unto you that sin brings about death, just as the beast now brings death to any land where sinners refuse to repent.

KING PELLINORE'S TALE RESUMES

"What a truly horrible tale, Uncle!" I remarked when he had finished his story. "But tell me, regardless of Incestua's sin, why would God allow such an evil creature as this Beast Glatisant to inhabit the earth?"

"God has a reason for everything that exists in this world," my uncle replied, "and even that which is evil, like this creature, must ultimately do His will. It was conceived by a servant of evil, but it is really the servant of God, for it destroys that which is evil, as it destroyed its mother for her sin of lust and destroyed its grandfather for putting a good Christian to death. It only appears where great evil occurs so that evil might be destroyed, for it is unwittingly the instrument of God despite its own sinfulness. And I daresay, Pellinore, that its purpose to destroy evil is why it has now made its way to Britain and our mutual kingdoms."

"But I am confused," I said, "for what I saw did not have a lion's claws, but rather hooves like a hind, and the hindquarters rather of a lion."

"The Beast is said to be able to change its appearance to suit whatever are its evil intentions," said my uncle quickly, but in a manner that made me think he was making up explanations as they occurred to him. "It is much like Lucifer himself," he continued, "a deceiver, a creature of illusion."

"Whether it be evil or not—" I tried to protest.

"Do not doubt it is evil," Uncle Bron interrupted me. "Do not doubt Satan's power! To do so is to exhibit a false pride, and it was pride which was Lucifer's own sin, the greatest of all sins."

"I thought blasphemy was the greatest sin," I replied.

"Is not blasphemy a sign of pride, for it denies that we are but worms crawling about in the dirt who would be trampled upon were it not for God's mercy."

"I concede your point, Uncle," I said. "But my point is that whether or not it is evil, it must be destroyed before it eats every plant and living creature in sight, thus leaving our people to starve."

"You are right, nephew, for the creature's very nature is to destroy all that is fruitful. But you will never be able to kill it until first you show repentance for your sins—otherwise, you and your land will be haunted by it until the end of your days."

"I have committed no sin," I repeated, knowing I could not commit blasphemy against a false Holy Grail. As for fornicating, it is such a pleasurable activity that I cannot understand why God would forbid it. I've heard that the Bible speaks against it, but since I cannot read, I do not know whether that is true or just something the priests say to control people; I suspect the latter is more likely.

But my uncle insisted, "Denial of your sin is the fault that dooms you to be the Beast's victim."

"Not if I kill it," I replied.

"Would you seek to do battle with the offspring of a demon without first making your peace with God?" Uncle Bron demanded. "Are you so very foolhardy and stubborn?"

"If this creature truly is evil, then it must be destroyed," I repeated. "I will set out immediately on the quest for it, and I will pursue it to the ends of the earth if need be."

"You foolish boy, do you not understand?" my uncle cried. "You need not pursue it. It is pursuing you! Repent for your sins and then perhaps God will empower you to slay the creature."

But I would not listen to him. "Come, Dindrane," I said, grabbing my sister's hand. And then I strode from Castle Carbonek, swearing I would never set foot in it again until the Beast Glatisant was slain. Then I would lay its hide at my uncle's feet to show my contempt for him and his belief in an imaginary grail.

"Go then," he shouted after me, "for I have wasted more patience on your sinful heart than any other saint would."

Apparently, he now fancied himself St. Bron. I thought of him only as Bron the Deluded.

The next day, I set out with sword and shield, intent to find and slay the Beast. I searched throughout my kingdom, but no matter where I looked, I could not find the creature nor its lair. Signs of vegetation stripped from trees and plants eventually made me realize it had left my kingdom, and I found its footprints in a meadow that seemed to suggest it was heading south. I then rode back home to tell Dindrane I would pursue the Beast across Britain or even the entire earth if need be. After the servants packed my supplies and I took a bag of gold from my treasury for my needs, I set off on my quest.

I traveled many days, now and then finding a sign of the Beast's presence that led me onward in its pursuit. A couple of times, I spoke to peasants who claimed they had seen the creature, and once I spoke to a village priest who had seen it peeping into his chapel window while he was saying Mass. These reports set my mind at ease, especially since the priest seemed humble and virtuous enough, which made my uncle's statement untrue that only a great sinner could see it. I began then to believe it was not some supernatural creature sent to punish me, but a foul creature yet unknown to man, sent for who knew what reason to scourge the land. Still, if it were not a supernatural beast, how could one describe the great barking sound that comes from its belly which even the peasants have testified to hearing?

Yet, despite the eyewitness reports I received, it was a good fortnight before I spotted the hideous creature again. By that time, I had heard that High King Uther had died and the young Arthur had been crowned as his successor. Having been one of Uther's vassals, I then thought to ride to Camelot to pay homage to my new liege lord before continuing my quest.

I was less than a half-day's ride from Camelot when one afternoon I passed through an ominously silent forest. I suspected I must now be close upon the Beast's trail, for why else would every woodland creature be so terrified as not to dare make a sound? I was not surprised then when I saw fresh, overly-sized deer tracks in the ground, but I was surprised that if I was so close, I did not hear its incessant barking. Perhaps in the warm afternoon sun, it had become drowsy and decided to nap. If so, I would easily rid the world of the Beast while it slept.

And then, just a few hundred feet from where I had spotted its tracks, I saw it through the trees. It was drinking at a lake—I have since discovered that when it eats or drinks, the ravenous hounds in its belly seem to be temporarily satisfied and grow silent.

Not wishing to startle it until I was close enough to make an attack, I approached slowly. As I did so, I spotted a knight, lying asleep beneath a tree, just a few feet from where the Beast drank. I was not close enough to see the knight well, so I feared he had been killed by the creature and lay dead, only not devoured because of his armor.

I watched for a moment until I saw the man stir. Then I feared moving in case I should alarm the Beast and cause it to attack the man. Suddenly, the knight jumped to his feet, stunned to see the creature beside him. When he quickly drew his sword, its swift sound caused the Beast to lift its head from the lake and turn to look at him. When it did, the yelping of the dogs began once more to rumble from its belly. The knight stepped back, gripping his sword tightly, prepared to swing at the creature if it should attack. I, fearing one knight would be no match for such a monster, quickly pushed my horse forward to aid him in his battle against this minion of Satan.

My approach, however, caused the creature to bolt backwards, then turn around and run through the wood. I hesitated a moment too long, wondering whether I should speak to the knight, and because of my hesitation, I quickly lost sight of the creature. I pursued it for a mile or so, but then I lost its trail. My horse was now winded from traveling all day, so we returned to the lake where it could drink and rest. There we found the knight saddling his own horse, which must have been tied to a tree just out of sight.

"Sir knight," I said, "I congratulate you upon surviving your confrontation with the foul creature. Unfortunately, it has escaped before I could finish it off."

"What was it?" he asked. "I have never seen anything like it."

"It is the Beast Glatisant," I replied. "It is an infernal creature sent from hell, and it is my destiny to destroy it. It is believed only one of my family may succeed in this quest."

I felt great pride as I spoke, and I admit, I dressed up my words a bit, a trait I fear I inherited from Uncle Bron. You will note I did not say why it had been sent from hell, since if any chance existed that I was responsible for it, I did not want my reputation ruined. That said, I had grown to believe it truly was my sole duty to destroy the creature.

"Please, journey to Camelot with me," replied the knight. "You appear to have traveled far, and there I will give you a meal and a bed, and you can tell me all you know about this strange beast."

"I am headed to Camelot now," I replied, "to see King Arthur and pay him my homage."

"What then might be your name?" he asked.

"I am King Pellinore of Listenoise."

"And I," he replied, "am that Arthur of Britain whom you seek."

That is how I met our great king. I did go to Camelot with Arthur, and I have visited there many a time since, but I have never stayed more than a night because my quest to destroy the Beast always drives me onward. I want only to say that as time has gone by, I have come to regret my rash words to my uncle, for after I told Arthur the tale of the Beast's origins, how it was born of sin and the result of a woman seeking to have unnatural relations with her brother, I learned from Arthur's own lips his great sorrow that made him think perhaps he was responsible for the Beast. You see, he had just sent away, at the command of the Church, his beloved wife Morgana, whom he had fallen in love with before knowing she was his half-sister. He had married her regardless until the Pope had threatened him with excommunication unless he put her away. This unfortunate situation caused him to say to me, "I fear there may be truth in your uncle's belief that this creature has come to our land as the result of a great sin, and I fear that sin is my own. The Church says I committed sin when I slept with my sister, but my heart says the true sin is that I sent her away when we loved one another so deeply."

"I do not think love can ever be part of sin," I told him, "so I would not hold yourself responsible for anything to do with the Beast. The coincidence that you should love your sister before you knew who she was could have happened to anyone in the same situation." After all, I thought, how many maidens had I bedded without even knowing their names? If my father had been as lusty as I was, I might well have ended up sleeping with my own sister, and how could it have been helped? When a man's rod becomes ready to tear his trousers in its desperate need for release, he cannot waste time in small talk about his partner's lineage.

"Still," Arthur replied, "it is strange that this creature was not seen in the land until recently."

"Sire," I replied, "I would not think more upon it if I were you, but if it will give your mind rest, I promise you that I will succeed in my quest to destroy the Beast Glatisant."

And so, ever since, I have continued to pursue the Beast. Many a year has now passed in which I have been unsuccessful, always on its trail but usually a day or two behind it. A few times, I have caught up with it, and one such time, I even managed to slice its leg with my sword, but it escaped from me, nevertheless.

And just now, as you can see, it almost got the best of me. Thankfully, King Escabor, you arrived and helped to frighten it off before it could wound me grievously.

SIR PALOMIDES' TALE RESUMES

My father had never before heard a tale like that of King Pellinore, but he could not doubt it, for he knew many strange things happen in this world that cannot be explained, and while he was not a follower of the Christian God, and therefore, not one to give credence to tales of sin, he could not deny that he had seen the Beast Glatisant with his own eyes.

Only one other thing did my father see in his lifetime, as he has often told me, that was as remarkable as the Beast, and that was my mother. The next morning, Pellinore showed my father the way to his castle in Listenoise, and there they stayed while Pellinore recuperated for a few days. During this visit, my father met my mother, Dindrane, King Pellinore's sister. They quickly fell in love, and not long after, they married and I was born. Of course, Uncle Bron objected to his niece marrying a "dark-skinned pagan," but my mother was wise enough to ignore him.

I grew up at Castle Listenoise with my parents. My father took on the role of steward there so my uncle Pellinore could continue his quest for the Beast. By that point, my father had no desire to return home to Babylon, and my mother refused to leave her brother, even though he was seldom home, so Listenoise became my father's home. My parents and I, during those years, saw little of our cousins—the

"Grail family" as we had come to call them disparagingly—and no one cared a bit when we heard that Elaine was to marry the great Sir Bedwyr, Arthur's mightiest knight, who would then rule Carbonek when Uncle Bron died.

Meanwhile, my father trained me in knightly deeds with some additional tutoring from my uncle whenever he was home for a few days. I grew, thus, to be a knight of not only great talent and skill, but also prodigious strength, if I do say so myself, for today, few knights in Britain or Ireland are my equals. I have been many times to King Arthur's court, and I have won several tournaments, but I will not go into the details of all those events. You asked how I came to follow the Beast, which is itself a recent turn of events, but to explain it is a somewhat complicated tale.

For many years, King Anguish of Ireland had allowed his pirates to pillage Britain's shores, and several times, King Arthur had sent forces against them to drive them from our lands. Finally, Arthur threatened to send an army to invade Ireland if the pillaging did not stop, and because of my great strength in arms, he chose me, along with a few of his other knights, to go as emissaries to King Anguish's court. A great tournament was to be held there, and Arthur hoped that by sending his best knights to Ireland, King Anguish would realize the superiority of British men and think twice about waging war with us. While I tried to conceal my awareness of it, I knew well that my dark skin often in-timidated my opponents, who were used to fighting only the fair men of Britain; therefore, Arthur was using my presence to his advantage.

Upon my arrival at King Anguish's court, much was made of me, and the king instantly treated me with great favor, acknowledging me as a prince in my own right. I became a favorite of many others at the court as well, but I fear it was more because I was a novelty among them than because they earnestly sought my friendship. Several jousting practices and mock-fights were held prior to the tournament, and during these, I showed such incredible prowess that I was easily acknowledged as the upcoming tournament's most likely champion. Of course, I do not wish to sound prideful, but I knew I would excel in the jousting for I was one of the greatest knights in Britain, and a British knight is worth two Irish knights any day. But what I did not expect was to fall in love.

Iseult, daughter to King Anguish, was the most beautiful maiden I had ever seen. Already the bards sang of her as "La Belle Iseult," thinking only the romantic tongue of the Franks suitable to describe her beauty. I felt like a fool speaking my British tongue to her, while her Gaelic tongue was like music to me. Her skin was fair and glowing, her hair golden with just a shimmer of red in it. She was shapelier than any maiden I had ever beheld, and I was instantly overcome with love for her. I am sure every man who saw her secretly pined for her, but not like I did, for most knew they did not deserve her, and thus, they did not aspire to her hand in marriage. Nor were any of the other knights at the tournament the sons of kings, as was I, and neither were any of them as prodigious at arms; therefore, when King Anguish made a declaration three days before the tournament that whoever won it should have his daughter's hand in marriage, I could already taste the glory of holding her in my arms and calling her my wife.

But, alas, it was not to be, and through no weakness of my own. Great treachery and betrayal were enacted against me, nothing less in truth than witchcraft. King Anguish was obviously fond of me and knew of my stamina and knightly prowess—I do not doubt that when he made his proclamation, he knew I might well become his son-in-law, but it seemed that Iseult did not think of our marriage prospects as fondly as did her father or I. I know not what, if anything, I did to displease her, but it soon became apparent to me that she loved another.

That man—that villain—was none other than Sir Tristram, a poor Cornish knight who claimed to be some shirttail relation to Cador, Duke of Cornwall, although I remain doubtful of that claim's truth. This Sir Tristram was so poor that he had journeyed to the tournament in an old fishing boat, for it was all he could afford. Not surprisingly, the boat sank while crossing the Irish Sea, and Tristram, whom I hear is a sorry swimmer, was lucky to be washed up on Ireland's shore. I have since heard all kinds of ridiculous stories about the courage of this knight and how when he arrived in Ireland, he was already wounded after some mighty battle against a powerful knight whom he had bested. The truth is that he cut his toe on a nail from the sinking boat as he was floundering in the raging sea. By the time the waves washed him onto Ireland's shore, where Iseult happened to find him, he had a terrible foot infection that made it almost impossible for him to walk.

Of course, Iseult took pity on him because he was goodly to look at, and I admit he is a very pretty fellow with all a young boy's shapeliness, but he is lacking in the bulk of true manhood. Iseult, being hardly more than a girl herself, found him attractive, I daresay, since she had never yet known the love of a real man.

Now it must be understood that because my father was from a foreign land and my uncle Pellinore was rather blasphemous, or so his own uncle believed him to be, no effort had been made to raise me in the ways of Christianity. Not that I was unfamiliar with the subject, for my mother claimed to be a Christian and she told me her religion's stories, but to me, they were no different from fairy tales. Certainly, I believed that all those old biblical people had once lived, but parting the Red Sea, walking on water, and raising people from the dead was all rather too much of a stretch for my imagination. I did not know how anyone could take it seriously, especially when those few I knew who did seemed rather on the dim-witted side, my great-uncle King Bron being foremost among them. Furthermore, I think my mother was too afraid to oppose her brother and husband to force Christianity upon me, and so I had never been baptized, nor had I good reason to desire baptism—until I met Iseult.

The night before the great tournament, I was seated at supper in a place of honor beside King Anguish. Queen Iseult—my beloved having been named for her mother—was seated on his other side. Toward the end of the meal, Queen Iseult made the pointed remark, "I must retire early this evening, husband. I seek to spend time in chapel so I may pray that he who wins the tournament tomorrow shall be not only the mightiest knight in Christendom, but the good-liest and wisest. For when the time comes for him to succeed you, he must govern Ireland as a good Christian should in the ways that St. Patrick taught us."

King Anguish simply nodded to his wife, not thinking anything of this statement, but I quickly discerned that her remarks were pointed at me. Then I was bold enough to ask, "Good queen, would you oppose your daughter's marriage to a man who was not a Christian, even if he should win the tournament?"

"It is not for me to give my daughter's hand," Queen Iseult replied. "That is my husband's prerogative, but I would not like to see any infidel sitting on Ireland's throne, and the people of this land are so devoted to the Faith that I do not doubt they would rise up against such a lord."

"Then let it be clear," I said, "that should I have the great privilege of winning Princess Iseult's hand, I will be baptized in your faith the very next day."

The king nodded in approval of my words, but the queen only stared coldly at me. I then suspected she was only using her religion as an excuse for me not to marry her daughter.

After a moment, she said, "Sir Palomides, do you think you could abide the cold of our winters here, if you were King of Ireland? Are not your kind used to much warmer climes?"

"I daresay the winters in Listenoise are just as cold or colder," I replied. "I was born there and never knew a climate outside the shores of Britain until I crossed the sea to your own fair kingdom."

She frowned and did not apologize for her mistake or ask for further clarification, and I did not give her any, for I saw now upon what she based her dislike of me.

Queen Iseult departed from the banquet hall soon after, and I, deeply disturbed that I should have such a woman for my mother-in-law within a matter of days—for I had no doubt I would win the tournament and be given Iseult's hand in marriage—decided to go to my bed early so I would be fresh and well-rested before the tournament. I also began to feel uncomfortable sitting in the banquet hall, for as I looked out upon the other knights, I began to wonder how many of them felt as Queen Iseult did—how many played at being my friend but secretly disliked me because of the color of my skin?

Then as I made my way to my chamber, I passed a slightly open door and overheard a snippet of conversation.

"You might still be in the tournament tomorrow," said a female voice I immediately recognized as belonging to my beloved Iseult.

"But I am not recovered of my wound," replied a man, whom I instantly knew must be Tristram, for I had heard of his coming and being wounded, though I had not seen him yet. Now I realized I must be standing outside his sickroom. In truth, not a man at the court could help but envy him for having the princess as his personal nursemaid, even though they all laughed behind his back that he should even aspire to participating in the tournament given his lowly status.

"My mother has prepared this potion for you. It will make you grow strong until you are insurmountable," she replied.

I had not even caught a glimpse of Sir Tristram yet, only heard of his arrival. Now I found the princess' words lamentable. Surely, no such medicine could cure him so quickly. I did not mind her kindness toward him, although I certainly did not want to think she would favor him over me or give him unfair advantage. Still, I was in the prime of my manhood, and no potion could make that much difference for him when the tournament was just half a day away.

Refusing to think more upon it, I went to bed where I lay envisioning myself at the tournament, veritably jousting in my sleep so that I might prepare my body for each and every move I would make. And then I fell asleep to a dream of the princess I would call my wife. To her I would show what insurmountable strength her future husband had so she would forget the sickly boy she had been soft-hearted enough to nurse.

In the morning, I was just as confident as I sized up my competition. The only knights worth anything, in my eyes, were those from King Arthur's court, foremost among them being Sir Sagramore and Sir Kei. I had taught them the power of my blows in past tournaments, so I saw no reason to fear them. Indeed, I expected that winning the tournament would be an easy triumph for me.

But I fear I will bore you with all these details. I have listened to many an old warrior who nearly put me to sleep with his battle stories, so I will hurry along my tale. It is sufficient to say that I was challenged by and defeated six knights, including Sir Kei and Sir Sagramore, who both later admitted they had been fools to challenge and fall before me again. Sir Morholt, King Anguish's own champion and the queen's brother, also rode against me, only to find himself tossed from his horse by the blow of my lance. But he was a hot-tempered man, so rather than yield, he jumped up, pulled out his sword, and demanded I engage him in single combat. He waved his sword about like a madman, intent on murder, and indeed, he would have killed me if I had not quickly lunged at him and drawn blood, thinking that would cause him to back off. But the bloodlust was upon him, so he kept coming at me, calling me "infidel" and "black devil" and other horrendous names. He was obviously set upon killing me, so I had no choice but to smite his hand with my sword, slicing off his fingers in self-defense. It was now impossible for him to hold his sword, and a few days later, he committed suicide since he had no identity save that of a warrior. It grieved me that such was his choice, but he had left me no other option than to wound him. I have since heard exaggerated and untruthful tales of how he died at Tristram's hand, doubtless a lie spread by Tristram himself, who will do anything to increase his own glory—save engage in true and honest battle with his fellow knights.

And now Sir Tristram came onto the field, bearing a blue shield and riding upon a steed that Iseult had given him from her father's own stables. He was also wearing armor she must have obtained for him, though I know not from where, for his own armor had been dented and rusted when she found him shipwrecked upon the beach. At first, I thought him a fool to challenge me to combat, but then I thought of the potion Iseult had given him from the queen, which had apparently done wonders to make him well. Nevertheless, I remained confident in my abilities, little suspecting the full extent of Queen Iseult's witchcraft.

After having fought six men, I admit my strength was beginning to wane, but I was not going to yield to a sandy-haired boy with a reputation for being a sorry and largely untried knight; I would never have lived down the shame if I had refused his challenge. And so my pride and my great love and desire for Iseult spurred me on.

Upon our first charge against each other, I struck Tristram with so powerful a blow that it was all he could do to maintain his seat on his horse. I was certain that with one more such blow, I would win the day, but alas, as we began the second charge, a stone caught in my horse's foot, causing him sudden pain and an inability to swerve fast enough for me to avoid Tristram's blow. Caught unaware by the blow and my horse's awkward maneuvering, I lost my balance and fell to the ground. My squire himself confirmed that my horse and not I had been at fault, but the fickle crowd cheered Tristram upon this unexpected change in my fortunes.

Being the true knight I was, I would not show the fiery temper of a Morholt, though it would have been well within my rights to challenge Tristram to single combat. Instead, before I could even regain my feet, the impetuous boy jumped from his horse, pulled out his sword, and, pressing it against my throat, demanded, "Yield!"

I looked to Iseult, but when I saw the anxiety on her face, I realized it was not born from concern for my wellbeing but fear that she might be forced to wed me. And suddenly, I felt my heart breaking inside me. I loved her, or at least I had convinced myself I did. But all my happiness slipped away at that moment. That she would aid Tristram to avoid being my bride hurt me deeply; still, I would not punish her by forcing her to wed a man she could not love. Even the crown of Ireland was not worth being married to a traitorous woman. I longed to believe there would be some way I could convince her in time to love me, but I knew not what that might be. For a moment, I considered grabbing Tristram's sword and pulling it from his hands, for he was so clumsy with it, and I knew that by doing so, I could still win the day, but it would not change Iseult's feelings for me, so what did it matter?

"Do you yield?" Tristram repeated, his nostrils flaring from exhaustion over the exertion he had put himself to, while my own heartbeat had scarcely quickened.

I realized there was only one way I could still please Iseult, and that was impossible—I could no more become a fair boy like the one before me than a leopard can exchange his spots for stripes. And so, heartbroken, I said, "I yield."

"If you seek to retain your life," said Tristram, to my astonishment, for no knight of honor would seek to embarrass his fallen opponent, "you must then do my bidding."

"What are your demands?" I asked, more amused than concerned.

"This shall be your charge," said Tristram. "First, that upon pain of death, you forsake all claim to the hand of Princess Iseult. Second, that you never set foot near her again, and third, as punishment for your fiendish aspirations, you wear no armor and bear no weapons for the next twelve months and a day. Promise me this now, or I will slay you here on the field."

"You are a cruel young lordling," I replied, "while I am the son of a king. You have no right to make such a request of me. It is not seemly, especially not from one who claims to uphold knightly virtues."

"Nevertheless, I make it," he said. His eyes gleamed with hatred, and he gnashed his teeth as he spoke.

"Very well," I said, disgusted with both him and Iseult. "I will have no more to do with the princess. Nor will I bear arms for this coming year as you so say, Sir Tristram. But when that time is done, I will go on a quest to prove myself a better knight than you."

By now, the crowd was applauding Tristram. To meet their acclaim, he made a foppish bow, which required he pull his sword away from my throat. The moment he did so, I quickly rolled out of his path, regained my feet, and motioned my squire to me. With his help, there on the field I removed and cast my armor from me in great disgust. No one even tried to stop me. Then, having no desire to return into the castle for my few belongings, I stomped off the field and made my way to the sea to take a ship back to Listenoise and my family. My flame of love for Iseult was snuffed out, and yet, already I was regretting that I had yielded to Tristram, for now I would be seen as a coward or at least a lesser knight, and I feared none would ever befriend or value me again.

Upon my return home, my parents sought to console me. My mother tried to tell me that I should never find happiness among Christian knights and their ladies unless I was baptized and acknowledged as one of them, but having willingly offered to be baptized in exchange for Iseult's hand in marriage, only to be rejected, I was not going to convert to anyone's religion to be accepted or loved. My father tried to console me in my promise not to bear arms for a year, saying far more pleasure could be found in books and seeking knowledge of nature. I was not interested in scholarship, but I began to think perhaps I could journey east, to my father's lands, and find acceptance there. My father, however, pointed out to me that my northern blood would make me as much an oddity there as my eastern blood made me an oddity in Christendom. And so I stayed home, miserable and biding my time.

As the year passed, occasionally a traveling bard would stop for shelter and my father would pay him to sing. These visits, despite my father's wish to divert me, became the most trying for me, for often the bard would sing of the brave Sir Tristram and the beautiful Iseult. I admit I listened to these tales with interest, though coupled with disgust, for I could not believe how easily they had been embroidered with lies. While I did not like that it was now broadly known that Sir Tristram of the Blue Shield had defeated Sir Palomides of the Black Shield in Ireland and made him promise not to pursue Iseult, I was glad to hear Sir Tristram, at least in my opinion, come off sounding more like a tyrant than a hero.

So much else was also flimflammery in these songs. The bards claimed that Tristram had engaged Morholt in combat and mortally wounded him on some island between Cornwall and Ireland, the fight being over tribute that King Anguish was imposing upon King Mark of Cornwall. Obviously, this tale was a complete falsehood since Morholt had killed himself soon after as I had heard previously. The bards did not even seem to have a basic understanding of modern-day geography and politics; after all, Mark of Cornwall was only a poor lord and a vassal to Duke Cador. Nevertheless, they embellished him until he was a king and Tristram's uncle—I think they were actually second cousins. But then, if Tristram were to be the hero—and more importantly, the lover of a princess like Iseult—he must be of noble lineage, so the bards invented a noble family tree for him. The story grew even more ridiculous when it claimed that Tristram had been wounded by Morholt's sword, which had poison on its tip, the work of Iseult's mother, but Tristram had also broken his sword and left a piece of it in Morholt's body. Morholt then supposedly returned to Ireland, where he died of his wounds. Meanwhile, Tristram needed to be healed from the poison. According to the bards, Iseult was the greatest healer in the world—granted, she had cared for him, but she was hardly a healer—so he went to her in disguise and she nurtured him back to health, and, of course, fell in love with him. But then her mother realized the broken part of Tristram's sword matched the piece she had taken out of Morholt's skull, so there was no chance of marriage between Tristram and Iseult. Tristram returned home, raving of Iseult's beauty. And when King Mark heard of her fair skin and doe-like eyes, he thought that since his cousin could not have her, he would marry her himself, so he sent Tristram back to Ireland to arrange a marriage for him. Surprisingly, King Anguish and Queen Iseult agreed to this marriage, so Tristram escorted his beloved back to Cornwall to be King Mark's bride. Only, Tristram bedded Iseult along the way. The bards sing some foolishness at this point in the story about a love potion Tristram and Iseult accidentally drank being responsible for their behavior, but I doubt any love potion was needed; Tristram was no gentleman, and from how Iseult treated me, I doubt she was any lady. Nevertheless, the bards say she married Mark while Tristram, heartbroken not to possess her love, went off on quests and did all kinds of remarkable deeds. It was all lies, but it was entertaining, and I would have been pleased if it were true because then the lovers would have been parted and miserable.

My vow not to bear arms for a year was now drawing to a close. It was then that Uncle Pellinore returned home. He was still chasing the Beast Glatisant, which always seemed to be just half a league ahead of him. When Uncle Pellinore understood my misfortunes, he told me, "Nephew, you can never win true knightly honor among men. These tournaments are just games they play at to suit their silly notions of love. Grown men fighting for ladies' favors and giving women all the power—I ask you why? Better to take what women you want—they secretly prefer that anyway. Nor will you find glory in their wars, for nothing good comes of killing one another. Join me instead in my quest to destroy the Beast Glatisant, for it is a foul, evil creature, perhaps not one of sin, but nevertheless one that lays waste to the countryside. There can be no better quest than to destroy it, to rid the land of it, and I would be honored to have your companionship in this noble endeavor."

I was not inclined to agree with Uncle Pellinore about the nobility of his quest. Nor had I ever seen the Beast. In fact, it had been more than twenty years since my father had seen it, so I questioned whether it even still lived. But Uncle Pellinore was an amiable companion and one who accepted me despite my dark complexion. Since I badly needed amusement and distraction from my sorrows, I agreed to sally forth with him, seeking this adventure.

Upon leaving Listenoise, we rode for three days before we found any evidence of the Beast. Then we came to a village where the people complained that their crops had disappeared in the night, a sure sign that the Beast had been there. My uncle, with his keen eyesight, soon picked up the foul creature's tracks. We followed it for a day and night before we drew near enough to hear the barking of its belly.

With his many years of experience behind him, my good uncle had by now realized that a sword did not give him the distance needed to fight the Beast and avoid its ferocious teeth; indeed, it was impossible to cut off its long, snakelike neck since it towered above our heads and its hide was too thick and tough for a sword to do more than scratch. Consequently, Uncle Pellinore carried with him a jousting lance and a spear, but also a bow and a quiver of arrows so he could attack the Beast from a distance; he hoped first to shoot and weaken it, so he could then get close enough to hack at its flesh without it being able to kick him with its powerful legs.

That day when we heard the Beast, we were in a meadow beside a strip of forest. My uncle said it would be better if we waited for the creature to step into the meadow so we would not be hindered by trees in our battle. And so we waited, for we could hear the yapping sound becoming a greater roar, signaling that the Beast was headed in our direction.

Now, I had imagined what the Beast must look like many times based upon my uncle's numerous tales, but when I saw it come charging at us through the forest, I was not at all prepared for the sight. It towered as high as the trees, such that I felt overwhelmed, and seeing only its head at first, I thought it truly a giant serpent, but then I saw its great leopard hide, and its giant galloping legs as it broke out from the forest into the meadow. It was tearing across the meadow, directly toward us, and we were a good thousand feet from the forest's edge, yet it covered the distance so quickly that I am afraid I stood there in awe of it, frozen and scarcely even hearing my uncle's cry as he rode toward it with spear in hand.

Then the barking in the Beast's belly became so loud that I could no longer think clearly. Next thing I knew, the monster was towering over me, so tall I could barely see its head as I tilted my own to look up at it; I was aghast at its great serpent-like neck, its terrible beady eyes, and the strange furry ears sticking out from it. It even had queer fur covering its body, which was unnatural for a serpent skin. I was so overcome with dread and disgust that I failed to see my uncle's assault upon it. Then, before I knew what was happening, I heard my uncle's cry and a deafening tumble as the Beast ran completely over my horse and me. For a second, I found myself beneath the creature, and in another second, it was behind me and running off across the meadow for the shelter of distant trees. I shouted, "Uncle, let us go after it. I think you've wounded it!" But when I turned to look at him, Uncle Pellinore was lying on the ground, his horse lying a few feet from him, and his spear sticking straight up in the air, lodged in his groin.

"Uncle! Uncle!" I shouted, running to his assistance. He was alive, but he looked grim and as if his life-force were quickly leaving him. I knew I could not move him with the spear lodged in his flesh, so, before I could give thought to my actions, I said, "Uncle, be strong," and I grasped the spear's handle and drew it forth as he shrieked in pain. Then I ran to his horse, looking for anything that might bind his wound, for I feared his very intestines would gush forth in a moment. I found the horse's skull had been kicked in by the Beast so that it lay dead, but I was able to access the saddle and my uncle's small bundle that included his knapsack, which I realized I could tear into bandages.

My uncle lost consciousness as I bound him up, and he did not wake when I lifted and carried him to my own horse. I laid him across my steed, tying him to the saddle so he would not tumble off. Then, leading my horse, I walked toward the nearest village a couple of miles off, all the while fearing Uncle Pellinore would bleed to death as I listened to him groaning in a half-conscious state. Nevertheless, I did get him to the inn, and then I fetched the local doctor, who further bled him before he stitched up his wound. I was aghast when I saw how bad the wound in his groin area was; it was so frightful that I would not wish any man who prizes his manhood—perhaps not even Tristram—such a punishment, for it was clear that my uncle would never now have children—at least not legitimate ones. That he had even lived was a miracle.

It was a week before the doctor would let me bring Uncle Pellinore home, and then this once great knight had to be carried on a litter, for he could scarcely walk, much less climb up on a horse. His pain has remained great ever since, and to this day, one can see an unsightly bulge in his pants where he is forced to wear bandages and other bindings to hold his intestines and all of his other inner working in their proper places. His wound refuses to heal and often reopens much to his grief. Indeed, he seldom moves but to walk from his bed to the cot in the sitting room where my mother and father can care for him.

I need not tell you how distraught I was to see such a tragedy happen to my uncle after his many years of being active. Most of all, I hated to think that he had spent most of his life questing after the Beast, only to have failed. However, when I expressed this great sadness I felt to him, he replied, "Palomides, it is not a failure so long as the Beast is destroyed. You must now take up this quest for me, for if what my uncle Bron said is true—and I am growing to believe it now that I have been so badly wounded—then only one of my blood may defeat it. You are my sister's son, the closest I will ever have to a son of my own, and so I ask you to take up the quest to destroy this foul creature. It is the child of the devil, and until it is destroyed, many more may be harmed as I have been."

Uncle Pellinore made me swear then and there that I would not rest until the Beast was destroyed, and so I did swear, and I do not doubt it is a good thing that I did, for in defeating my uncle, the Beast has no doubt grown in power. I make that statement because the morning after I made my vow, the foul creature appeared outside our castle walls. I armed myself and rode after it, but I had not gone more than a league before the great dragon appeared in the sky. That creature is no doubt another of the devil's minions. Because of it, everything for miles in every direction, including my uncle's kingdom and also that of my cousin Elaine, has become a wasteland covered with ash and the stink of death. Therefore, I will avenge my uncle if it is the last thing I do. If the Beast be a demon's child as my great-uncle, King Bron, stated, then I have high hopes that when I have killed the creature, Uncle Pellinore's health will be restored and he will no longer linger like a living corpse.

And now you know why I pursue the Beast Glatisant. With the dragon's assistance, who knows what the Beast may be capable of? I have no choice but to kill it or, if it be God's wish, be killed myself by it, but unlike my uncle, I am still pure, and so I have high hopes of succeeding in my quest.

Lance had listened to Palomides' long tale with great interest, wishing he had paid more attention as a young boy to the stories his grandfather had read him out of Sir Thomas Malory's *Le Morte d'Arthur*, but all those knights and jousting tournaments had been enough to make his head dizzy back then, and while he remembered and had enjoyed the main stories of King Arthur, he could not remember much about Palomides. Now, hearing Palomides' tale, Lance realized that all of those knights whom he had assumed had been embroidered into the stories of King Arthur over the centuries had indeed been real people. But Lance had never understood the attraction of the Holy Grail story; now to learn that Pellinore might be the original of the Fisher King of Arthurian legend, who was said to be wounded and waiting to be healed so his land might be healed, seemed disappointing to him; still it was understandable that Pellinore would have been confused with his uncle, the Grail King, whom King Bron claimed to be. What a muddle it all was.

Lance did not even remember from Malory that Palomides and Tristram had been rivals, but he did remember that Tristram had been the greatest knight after Lancelot. His parents had, for that reason, named him and his brother for those two greatest knights—Tristan's name being an alternative spelling of Tristram. So he suspected that Palomides had exaggerated when describing Tristram's youth and poor knightly deeds, and probably even how Tristram had used magic to defeat him at the tournament. Surely, there had to be more to it than all that, but he did not wish to question Palomides on the matter, for to do so might only anger the knight, and for the moment, at least, Lance knew he had no other friend in this strange land.

But what confused Lance most was why Pellinore and now Palomides insisted on pursuing the Beast Glatisant; therefore, choosing his words carefully, Lance said, "Thank you for telling me your story, Sir Palomides. It is quite a remarkable one, and based on what you have said, I think Sir Tristram a horrible brute and a fool besides, so I hope you do give him his comeuppance next time you see him, but I don't think I fully understand why you feel the need to kill the Beast Glatisant. I do not mean to be rude, but your great-uncle Bron does not sound like the most reliable person, and even your uncle Pellinore seems to doubt the truth of what he said, so what do you hope to achieve if you do kill it?"

"There can be no doubt that the Beast is the cause of great evil," Palomides replied. "Why else would the dragon have appeared at the same time I was pursuing the Beast? Clearly, they are allied in their desire to wreak havoc on this land."

"Couldn't it just be a coincidence that you saw the Beast just before the...dragon came?" Lance figured he might as well call the comet by the name Palomides did; the knight would not know or understand what a comet was, and Lance, being no expert in science, hardly understood himself.

"I do not know what you mean," replied the knight.

"I mean, isn't it a coincidence that I met you at the same time you were pursuing the Beast? But I am clearly not a demon, so why think the Beast is allied with one? I'm just saying the dragon and the Beast are not necessarily connected, and while the dragon has done great ill, the Beast appears to be more scared of you and your uncle than it is violent."

Lance watched Palomides' face to see how the knight would take this reasoning; he was clearly struggling with it, but then a spark of realization lit up his brow.

"Perhaps," said the knight, "you are wrong; perhaps your presence is not a coincidence. Since Satan has reinforced the Beast's power by sending the dragon, perhaps God, in His great mercy, has sent you to aid me in slaying this Beast."

It was all Lance could do not to burst out laughing at this reasoning. He certainly had no intention of going on a quest to slay a beast; he wanted only to find his brother. Again choosing his words carefully, he replied, "I thought you said only your uncle Pellinore or one of his family could slay it?"

"That is true," said Palomides. "At least, that is what my uncle told me that his uncle told him, but still, sometimes I wonder, like you, whether the tale Great-Uncle Bron told him was true. Until he received his grievous wound, as you said, Uncle Pellinore always had his own doubts about Great-Uncle Bron's tale. Regardless, there must be some reason for our meeting like this. Do you have any previous experience with slaying dragons or other monsters?"

"No," said Lance, thinking he didn't want to gain any experience either. "Nor do I understand what will happen if we slay this beast."

"We will end a force of evil," said Palomides. "That is enough; it will be doing God's work, whether that God be the Christian one or not. Will you join me in this quest?"

"I'm sorry," Lance replied, "but I have to focus on finding my brother—and then I need to figure out how we can return to our home."

"To Benwick? To regain your father's kingdom, you mean?" asked Palomides. "If you will aid me in slaying the foul beast—understand I must be the one to give him his death blow, but perhaps you can help me to trap him so I might destroy him—then I will help you in finding your brother and regaining your kingdom."

Lance, thinking upon it, decided he really had no choice since he knew no one else in this land. "How about," he said, "you help me find my brother since I fear he is hurt, but if he is well, then both of us can aid you in destroying the Beast. And once he is destroyed, then you can help us find a way to return to Benwick." Benwick or twenty-first century Britain—what did it matter?—both seemed impossible to reach at the moment.

"So it shall be," said Palomides, reaching over to clasp Lance's arm in agreement. "We shall join together in this double quest, and soon the bards will sing of the noble deeds of Sir Lancelot and Sir Palomides."

"Yes, I'm sure they will," Lance agreed, "but not if we don't first get a good night's sleep."

"Yes, I am sleepy myself," Palomides agreed. "We will go to bed now, and in the morning, we will go to the village to find you a suit of armor and a horse for each of us. Then we can sally forth on our great quest."

Lance's head ached too much to reply. With a full belly, he was ready to fall asleep, and now touching the back of his head, he found a good-sized bump had grown there as a result of the rock from the comet that had hit him. He was too tired to think about anything more than sleep.

"Is it safe for us to sleep out here in the open?" he asked Sir Palomides.

"Perfectly safe. The only wild animals in these parts are boars and the Beast Glatisant. They won't harm us. The Beast is too afraid of me and the boars too afraid of the fire. People are far more treacherous than animals, in truth."

"Are there people around whom we need to worry about?" Lance asked.

"That," said Palomides, "is something you never can tell.

There is an evil sorcerer or a witch behind every bush in Britain if you are to believe the bards."

"Well, I won't worry about it then," said Lance, yawning. The Beast Glatisant aside, which he had seen with his own eyes, Lance suspected Palomides was more caught up in superstition than reality.

It was dark by now, and since it was apparently summer, that meant it was quite late.

Palomides rose and wandered off toward the woods. Lance did not ask where he was going, for in a minute, he could hear the knight's activity. When Palomides returned, Lance went to relieve himself as well, and then returning to the fire, he looked up at the sky but could not see any stars.

"Where are the stars?" he muttered.

"The smoke and ash fill the air," said Palomides. "It has yet to clear."

Lance wondered how many days that would take. Would he die from breathing in the floating dust particles in the air before he ever found Tristan? Was Tristan dead already, so that his quest to find him was pointless? No, he mustn't think that way. He needed to sleep before despair started to eat away at him. Everything would appear better in the morning.

"Good night," Lance said to Palomides as he lay down and rested his head on his arms.

"Good night," Palomides replied.

Lance closed his eyes, hoping he would not wake to find his hair filled with ash and sand, for even the sea did not look clean to bathe in with all the debris floating on it. But perhaps by morning, the tide would have carried all that out. Tomorrow would be a new day. It certainly couldn't be worse than today had been.

CHAPTER 6

WHEN LANCE WOKE, he saw the fire had gone out and Palomides was still sleeping. Dawn was just starting to make its appearance in the sky, and it was already a warm morning, so there was no need to start a new fire. Lance wanted to get up and start searching for Tristan right away, but he felt it would be rude to wake Palomides so early; they would have a long day ahead of them if they were going to walk to a village some ten miles away.

So Lance lay there quietly, again wondering what he was doing in this strange land. When he had gone to sleep the night before, he had half-expected to wake and find he had dreamt everything since the comet had struck—perhaps he had been hit by debris from the comet that had rendered him unconscious so that everything since then had been a dream. But now he had woken and found that he was still in this strange and unlikely place—a sad indication that he was experiencing reality, as unreal as it seemed for him to be in sixth century Britain.

Was this whole experience just some strange twist of Fate—perhaps the result of some time warp or a portal he had gone through?

How else could he explain being transported back fifteen centuries? But he also knew from his family's history that the Arthurian world was a real place, not a fantasy land as so many believed in the twenty-first century—after all, years ago he had met Merlin, who had confirmed that his father was descended from King Arthur and his mother from other related lines. And so there must be some reason why he was back in Arthurian Britain. He had no idea what that reason could be, but he would just have to wait and hope it would be revealed—he knew Merlin liked to play games, but everything usually came out right in the end. Still, he would feel much better about everything if he could only find Tristan alive and well.

Tristan and he had always been close companions, the best of friends; in fact, they had been each other's only playmates through their long childhood hidden away in Dracula's Castle to protect them from Lilith. Their grandfather and great-grandfather had trained them in military tactics and the wielding of weapons to prepare them to do battle with evil—with Lilith—but then the situation with Lilith had been resolved with them hardly being involved. In fact, they had later confessed to each other that it had been rather a letdown for them. For a time, Lance had thought that all that training had been a waste—but now he suspected it might have had some other purpose.

Palomides wanted him to aid in fighting the Questing Beast, but Lance could not see the logic in such a quest. More likely, he had been sent back in time to right some great wrong—could it be that he was to stop the fall of Camelot—to stop Gwenhwyvach and Constantine's quest to destroy it so that Camelot could grow into a great shining empire that spread across the globe, bringing righteousness, love, kindness, mercy, and respect to all mankind? For a moment, Lance's heart glowed within him as he contemplated such a possibility, but he remained skeptical, having seen too many time travel films that depicted the consequences of trying to alter the past. And yet there had to be some reason for all of this to have happened—he wished he knew what that reason could be, but as the sun rose, he also felt that to know would ruin the wonder and magic of the experience. He must be open to whatever future lay in store for him; he felt his heart opening to take up this unidentified quest, but he still hoped to find Tristan. He felt he could face anything if only he knew Tristan were well.

"I see you're awake," said Palomides, rolling onto his side and looking in Lance's direction.

"Yes," said Lance, sitting up. "I have been for a while, but I didn't want to wake you."

Palomides stood up.

"It's almost daylight," said the knight. "I should have been up hours ago. Let's get moving then. It's a long way to the next village. It will take us half the morning to get there, and the sooner we leave, the more likely we are to receive word of your brother or catch up with him if he's also on the move."

"All right," said Lance, getting to his feet and dusting the ash from his clothes.

"Just give me a minute," said Palomides, wandering into the wood because nature called. Lance walked a bit farther down the beach for the same reason, glad to see much of the ash had blown away in the night, although the sea, rather than sparkling in the morning sun, still looked gray and murky from all the ash that had settled upon it.

"This way," said Palomides a minute later, passing Lance, who was finishing his business. Lance quickly ran after him, keeping pace with the knight, wanting to ask him what they should do about breakfast; he was used to having his morning coffee, and he was already feeling the caffeine withdrawal, but mentioning it would do no good; Palomides never would have heard of the beverage, and if there were food to be had, Palomides would have said so. Complaining would be of no help, so Lance resigned himself to the belief that he probably wouldn't eat until after his ten-mile hike to the village across difficult terrain, for the ash and the waves combined to make the beach a gray, muddy mess, and Palomides had said there would be some rocky cliffs ahead to cross over.

After a short while, when they were both a bit more awake, Palomides asked Lance, "What were you and your brother doing in that boat, and how did he get hurt?"

"We were just sailing for the fun of it. He got hurt when debris hit him from the comet."

"The comhit? What's that?"

"The comet—it's like a meteor—you know—it has a tail and it lights up the sky, and when it passed by earth, it dropped rocks and debris."

"You mean the dragon? Did your brother get burnt then?"

"Yes, I mean the dragon," said Lance, having momentarily forgotten Palomides had a different explanation for it and not wanting to argue. "And no, he didn't get burnt; I think something hit him in the head—a rock of some sort. The same thing happened to me. I have a bump on the back of my head from it."

"That is strange," said Palomides. "Dragons do not spit out rocks; perhaps it shed one of its scales, and that is what hit you."

"Perhaps," Lance said. "It was pretty scary, whatever it was."

"It was a terrible sight, that is certain," Palomides agreed. "I have heard tales of ferocious dragons all my life, but this was the first time

I have ever seen one. I did not think a creature more horrible than the Beast Glatisant could possibly exist, but now I know there is no end to the evil in this world. Even though the dragon is a far worse monster, I will be glad to slay the Beast to stop what evil in this world I can."

Looking out at the landscape, Lance could not imagine that even a dragon—at least not an individual one—could create so much destruction. Although much of the ash had blown away in the night, plenty of mud from it still clung to the beach, and in some places, the ash had drifted like snow into mounds against the trees and rocks. The trees were bare of leaves, either from being burnt or blown off by the wind, and many a fallen tree, or one standing but stripped of most of its branches, met their sight. The landscape looked like a nuclear holocaust had devastated it. There were no mushroom clouds thankfully, but there was still the smell of ash and smoke in the air. Lance thought the comet must have somehow opened up a portal to transport him back in time—what other explanation could there be?

Lance wondered what Palomides would say if he tried to explain to the knight what had really happened to him. He doubted the concept of time travel was even conceivable to someone from the Dark Ages. He had always understood that medieval people didn't have a good concept of history, as evidenced by their artwork that depicted Jesus in medieval clothes or their blurring the past with the present in their stories; Lance knew that such a lack of historical thinking was largely why the truth of King Arthur had been lost, but also why the medieval writers had been free to elaborate upon his tales as they pleased, creating the rich body of Arthurian literature that retained little of the truth. No, he could not explain time travel to Palomides. But perhaps he would find someone else to whom he could tell his story in full—someone more scientifically minded like Morgan le Fay or Merlin. After all, Merlin might have known that Tristan and he would travel back in time since he could foresee the future; therefore, the great wizard would recognize him as someone from the future he already knew—or would know—it was quite confusing. But how then to find Merlin? If he did not find Tristan soon, he would have to ask Palomides to take him to Camelot or Avalon to find someone who could help him.

Of course, Lance realized that Merlin probably already knew he was here. That the great wizard had not already come to his aid perhaps pointed to a reason for him being here, but one he was supposed to find out on his own. After all, Lance understood from his parents that Merlin was never one to answer your questions until he was ready. In fact, Lance wouldn't be surprised if Merlin had brought all this about; he might have a plan and be manipulating events, but that gave Lance little comfort. For all Merlin's powers, he had not been able to stop the death of Lance's grandmother, Mary Morgan, at Lilith's hands, so there was no reason to believe he could see to Tristan's safety, or even Lance's own.

As Lance pondered all these possibilities, he looked about him for any signs of Tristan, but as he and Palomides trudged along the gray muddy beach, nothing but ocean waves filled with ash met his sight to his left and just the equally ash-covered forest to his right.

"Where do you think my brother's boat could have drifted?" he finally asked. "Would it have traveled along the coast and washed onto the beach, or could it be stranded in some sort of cove?"

"Either is possible," said Palomides, "or I suppose it could have gone further out to sea. It might have ended up off the coast of Gaul or even blown to Cathay by now."

Lance felt confirmed now in his decision not to explain time travel to Palomides, not if the knight thought his brother could drift to Cathay—which Lance knew was the medieval name for China—in less than twenty-four hours. After all, these people thought the world a lot smaller than it truly was since they had no concept of the Americas' existence.

A few minutes later, Palomides drew Lance's attention to a giant stone blocking their path; it was at least six feet tall, and a dozen feet wide, but also half-buried in the sand. "Here," said the knight, "is where the dragon directly breathed his fire. See how he scorched everything that grew upon this hill so it is only rock now."

"Yes," Lance agreed, although he could clearly see that the rock was not a hill but some sort of meteor that had fallen in the comet's wake. It was even still smoking, so he could understand Palomides' interpretation of it. Fortunately, it had landed on the beach and done little damage, but Lance shuddered to think what modern day Britain must look like if stones this size had also hailed down upon it—London could have been destroyed easily, worse than during the Battle of Britain—and even the Coast of Cornwall would have been demolished, its picturesque fishing villages and tourist resorts reduced to rubble. Lance tried not to envision a rock this size striking his parents' summer cottage.

The giant stone was blocking their path, but Palomides was not dissuaded by a difficult terrain. He simply walked around it, wading through the edge of the sea until he got his footing back on shore.

On the rock's other side, the terrain was more marsh than beach and far more difficult to walk through. After a few minutes, Palomides suggested they move up the beach into the forest where the ground was firmer—Lance agreed since he could still see the ocean from there if the sailboat bearing his brother floated by. He followed the knight toward firmer ground, amazed by how quickly Palomides could sprint across the marsh in such heavy armor. Despite all his training, Lance had never worn armor for more than a few hours at a time, and it had now been several years since he had tried on any. He marveled at the knight's prowess and almost envied him for getting to go on quests, although trudging through a marsh was not exactly adventurous.

Lance was having quite a bit of difficulty walking in his tennis shoes. They were already wet and squishy, and they were clearly not made for crossing swamps. He had to watch his step more carefully than Palomides so he could get a firm footing, and only having his shorts on, he was a bit squeamish about getting himself covered in mud.

But when Palomides shouted, "There's a cottage over there!" Lance lost his concentration and quickly found himself knee-deep in the mud.

"Come; we will go ask the peasants there if they have seen your brother!" said Palomides, picking up his pace and not noticing Lance's situation.

Lance tried to pull his legs out of the mud to follow, but his efforts only made him sink more.

"Wait!" he hollered to Palomides as he struggled to free himself. When the knight did not turn back and Lance felt himself sinking even more, he panicked and shouted, "Help me!"

Palomides now turned and saw Lance's predicament, but by that point, Lance had sunk down to his waist and could feel the mud oozing up his leg and into his shorts. Grimacing as the cold mud infiltrated his clothes, Lance hollered, "I'm sinking!"

Palomides ran back in Lance's direction, but he stopped at the marsh's edge, hesitant to find himself in the same situation. Nor did he have anything for Lance to grab onto, except his sword, which would only serve to cut Lance's hand.

"Hold on!" shouted the knight, running back into the forest to find a sturdy tree branch. But Lance could not hold on. Not only was he sinking rapidly, but he felt as if someone were clutching his leg and deliberately pulling him down.

"Help!" Lance yelled. "Something's grabbing my leg! Help!"

By now, Palomides had grabbed a sturdy, if charred, tree branch and was running back to the marsh. He fell to the ground at the marsh's edge and pushed the stick toward Lance, but Lance's shoulders were now level with the mud and his arms flinging about in a panic. His fingers only brushed the stick before he sunk to the point where he could no longer reach it. Taking a deep breath as his head submerged, Lance disappeared into the mud's blackness.

CHAPTER 7

NEVER IN HIS life had Lance felt so panicked, so suffocated, so hopeless as he did while being pulled downward through the mud like an earthworm.

Never before had he experienced anything like the sensation of mud going up his nose and filling his nostrils, sliding over his eyes and ears, and slithering between his toes and fingers, but far worse was the sensation that he could not breathe from all the mud blocking his cavities; in desperation, he wanted to flail his arms and legs, but the mud was so thick and heavy about him that to move more than an inch or two in any direction was impossible.

And still he felt a hand or perhaps even a mouth gripping his leg, pulling him downward, farther and farther, for what seemed like a suffocating eternity until he was certain he would never breathe again. In another few seconds, all went black in his mind, his last conscious thought being the realization that he would never know what kind of subterranean creature had made him its prey.

Lance woke from unconsciousness by spitting up mud and water, coughing and feeling as if he were still choking until, to relieve his agony, he rolled over and realized he had been lying on his stomach on gritty stone. Pushing himself up on his hands, he found he was on dry land, but as he tried to regain his feet, he hit his head on a rock ceiling. After screaming out in surprise and pain, he opened his eyes to find himself in a tiny little cave, not more than three feet high and just perhaps a foot longer than himself; it was more like a ledge just above the water, and he could feel small waves gently lapping at his toes.

"It must be some sort of underwater cavern," Lance said to test his voice. "I must be in some sort of air bubble." Finding he could barely speak from the mud in his mouth and nose, he quickly snorted and spit out the dirt. Then hesitantly reaching into the water—fearing to know what might lurk in it—he cupped just enough water to wash off his face. He was surprised to find very little mud on the rest of his body—a sign that he must have traveled through a great deal of water after his journey through the mud and before he reached his current resting place.

Somehow the current must have pulled him down and trapped him in this little underwater cave with an air pocket. He wondered how long the air pocket would last. Would the tide rise and drown him? He couldn't stay here long, but he didn't have the strength to move yet.

Lance rolled over onto his back and lay there panting. He was surprised then to see light, or at least the reflection of the water on the cave's roof above him. Light had to be coming from somewhere to cause the reflection—perhaps from under the water—which hope-fully meant some sort of tunnel led out of this underwater cave. Otherwise, if the tide rose, he might drown. He would have to swim to find a way out—he dreaded the thought since he didn't know how far down he was, or what creature, which had pulled him down, might still be lurking in the water, waiting to feed on him. He told himself he would just rest a few more minutes; then he would dive into the water and take his chances, for if he stayed here, he was certain to die.

But before those few minutes were passed, just as he was starting to feel as if he had his breath back, the most unexpected event occurred.

A head rose up from the water—at first, Lance didn't know what it was, for it was a hairy reddish-brown color, but then he realized he was seeing the hair covering its face. In a moment, a human hand reached up out of the water to brush the hair aside. Suddenly, Lance found himself staring at a beautiful young woman with sienna hair, rosy lips, and almost translucent white skin.

"Welcome," she said, and her tone, more than the dim light, made it clear to Lance that she was smiling at him.

"Where am I?" Lance asked.

"Just a resting place," she said, "so you can catch your breath before we continue on our journey."

"Are we near land?" he asked.

"Near for me; not near for you," she replied. She folded her arms upon the rock ledge where Lance lay and placed her chin upon them.

Lance rolled onto his side so he could see her better.

"Do I have far to swim?" he asked. "I'm a strong swimmer."

"I'm sure you are," she said. "You look quite strong, and you're very handsome as well."

"And you're absolutely lovely," he replied, unable to help himself, for he felt mesmerized by her strange pale beauty. "What's your name?"

"Ileana."

"It's nice to meet you, Ileana. I'm Lance."

"Yes, Lancelot," she said, nodding and smiling in a way that suggested she already knew all about him. "Come; we have far to travel."

Before Lance knew what was happening, she had taken his hand, and showing surprising strength, she easily pulled him off the rock and into the water. The move was so unexpected that for a moment Lance floundered about, trying to catch his bearings. Ileana let go of his hand to avoid his frantic movements, but after a moment, he realized he wasn't sinking and let his reason and instincts overcome his panic.

In another second, he felt Ileana's hand again in his, and this time she pulled him underwater. Once they were both submerged several feet, she swam slightly in front of him, placing her free hand over his closed eyes, gently pulling at his eyelids to encourage him to open them. When he did, Lance saw the water was very clear, and as he had suspected, they were in a tunnel with a bright light shining at its end. Allowing Ileana to lead him, Lance held onto her hand so that his head was alongside her waist as they swam parallel and up toward the light.

And then Ileana gently released his hand. Lance felt safe and found he could swim beside her without her aid. But after a minute, she began to outdistance him, and then as she began to pass him, he was stunned to see fins where her feet should have been.

For a moment, his shock was so great that he froze in the water, unable to move forward. Ileana, quickly realizing he was not beside her, turned around and beckoned him to follow, and then he woke from his shock, thinking she was too beautiful to fear; he had heard that mermaids were not always kind to humans, but his curiosity and her beauty overcame any need he felt for self-preservation. Nor did he feel panicked swimming behind her in the water, even after he realized several minutes had passed and he was breathing normally through his nose without feeling any aching of his lungs for air. How could that even be possible? He almost thought he must be dreaming. To be able to swim underwater and not feel the need to breathe was simply amazing, and yet, he was grateful when Ileana began to lead him upward.

After a minute or two, they broke the water's surface. Lance did not even bother to look about him to see whether they were in a lake or ocean. He had only one question for Ileana, and she immediately read it on his face.

"Yes, you might say I am a mermaid," she answered before he even spoke. "Mermaid is not exactly an accurate term, but it is the one you humans use to define my kind."

"I thought mermaids only existed in fairy tales."

Ileana smiled and replied, "I did not realize we were in anything but a fairy tale."

"What? I don't understand," said Lance, searching for truth in her smiling green eyes.

Rather than respond, Ileana dove back underwater, her mermaid tail flipping up into the air. Lance looked about now, hoping she would resurface, for he realized they were in a great lake, the distant shore appearing to be several miles away, and he was uncertain whether he could swim to it.

He felt a similar tugging at his leg to what he had felt when he had sunk into the mud, but this time he realized it was Ileana beckoning him to follow her. In a moment, he was underwater again and Ileana had taken his hand. She was guiding him back down below, he knew not where. He wondered whether he should struggle and break free from her. Could she really mean him harm? Surely, she knew humans could not breathe underwater? And yet she kept pulling him down, and he did not let go of her hand; he felt a great warmth come over him just from being in her presence, and it caused his body to relax as he realized again that he was not struggling to breathe. He thought perhaps he was actually drowning, perhaps still, in reality, sunk in the mud and dreaming this experience, or perhaps Ileana had placed him under some sort of enchantment—after all, he was in Arthurian Britain—so why should an enchantment surprise him?

Still, he felt more and more uncertain as they swam deeper into the lake, the water becoming darker and murkier until he could not see anything. He was just about to close his eyes again when a spark of light appeared in the distance below them, and then it grew into a ball of light that seemed to be coming directly toward them, but its movement was only an illusion, for as it grew larger, it broke into multiple lights. Lance then realized the light was not coming toward them, but they were simply traveling toward it. His eyes next began to make out shapes around the various lights—they looked like buildings, towers, pillars, perhaps a palace—a veritable underwater city with strange architecture like he had never seen—pyramids that ended in domes, tall but graceful, with arched windows or doors all the same size, and fish swimming through them—no, not fish, but mermaids and mermen. Lance would have thought it the sunken lost city of Atlantis had it not inexplicably been here, in the middle of an enormous lake in Britain.

Lance dared not let go of Ileana's hand now. And as they swam past her fellow merfolk, he was surprised that not one of them stopped to stare or wonder what he was doing there. Lance wondered himself why he was there, and also how it was possible that he or any of them could breathe underwater, but he had no time to ask questions; even if he should drown in the process, he wanted to see as much of this spectacular land as possible.

Ileana led him through a great arch that appeared to be the city's main gate, although there were no guards of any sort, and then they swam through a passage between buildings—Lance would have called it a street if he had walked along it, but here it was more like a canal. Occasionally, another mermaid swam past them, and when this happened, Lance noticed she would shake her tail in what he guessed was a form of greeting.

Finally, they came to a great stone building, as large as an English cathedral, its walls white as alabaster but decorated with pink sea-shell accents around its eaves and windows. Light shone from within it. Still holding his hand, Ileana led Lance through a window and toward the light, which danced before them, sparkling in the water, reflecting off interior emerald-colored walls. Lance could not help equating the effect of this sparkling light with an underwater disco ball.

Then they turned the corner of a hallway and came to a dead end. Ileana swam upward, as if they were in an elevator shaft, and Lance looked down to see large stone doors closing behind them. Then he noticed drains opening in the walls as Ileana turned down another hallway. Suddenly, the floor rose beneath them and Lance found his feet touching it until he was beginning to walk rather than swim, and in a few more seconds, they had broken the surface and he found himself standing in chest-high water—and in a large crystal-domed chamber.

After spending a moment taking in the magnificent room, whose walls rose up fifty feet to the dazzling ceiling, Lance felt Ileana pulling him forward, and then he looked before them and saw stairs leading up out of the pool onto a marble floor. About a dozen feet past the stairs were a few more steps leading to a golden throne studded with diamonds. And seated on the throne was a beautiful, mature woman with a gold ringlet around her head and a blue coral gown that complemented her auburn hair.

Ileana swam to the pool's edge. Lance followed her until they came to the steps. He let Ileana go up the steps first, amazed to see that she was now dressed in a green dress that hung to her ankles and revealed that her mermaid tail had been replaced by a pair of legs.

"Welcome," said the woman on the throne, pulling Lance's attention back to her. When she stood and stepped forward, even though her gown covered them, it was apparent that she also had human legs. Lance felt surprised and stunned by all that was happening. For a moment, he didn't know how to respond until the woman laughed and said, "You look as if you have many questions."

"He is bound to," said Ileana, also laughing.

The woman came forward and gestured for Lance to walk up the steps. Once he stood before her, she took his hand and led him across the chamber.

"You are probably hungry," she said. "Some food and drink will reenergize you and help you find your tongue."

"Thank you," was the most Lance could manage after all he had experienced.

"Perhaps you have already figured out that I am she who is known in your world as the Lady of the Lake," continued the woman, beckoning for Ileana to follow them. "I am often confused with the Lady of Avalon, but we are not the same, though certainly one in our intentions. That is enough for you to know until you have some food. I don't imagine the burnt horseflesh you ate last night was very appetizing."

Before Lance could ask how she knew what he'd had for dinner, she said, "Follow me."

Her hand still in his, the Lady of the Lake was a step ahead of Lance when she walked right through the wall in front of her, causing Lance to come to a standstill. She pulled gently on his hand—her own he could still see extending out of the wall, but the rest of her body had disappeared. Ileana came up beside him and said, "You think that's amazing, but you can do the same. Go ahead."

The Lady of the Lake's hand tugged on his own again. Closing his eyes, Lance stepped forward with his right foot, wincing and waiting for the cold solid feel of stone against his nose.

Just as Lance felt surprised not to feel anything, Ileana said, "Now the other foot. Keep going."

Slowly, Lance lifted his left foot and set it beside the right. Again, he did not collide with the wall.

"Open your eyes," said the Lady of the Lake, releasing his hand.

When Lance did so, he found they were in a large banquet hall with tall glass windows along one side, through which the sea was clearly visible. Lance could see all manner of fish swimming about, beautiful silver, blue, gold and sparkling fish like none he had ever seen in England.

"Come; be seated," said the Lady of the Lake, going to sit at the head of a great banquet table filled with all manner of fruits, breads, and cups filled with wine, but no meat, Lance observed. He moved forward to take a seat at the foot of the table, but the Lady of the Lake said, "Come; sit beside me." He did so, and then Ileana sat across from him on the Lady of the Lake's other side.

"My name is Viviane, by the way," said the Lady of the Lake, "and you are Lancelot."

"Yes," he said, "but my friends just call me Lance."

"I hope to be your friend," said Viviane, "but I shall call you Lancelot, for it sounds nobler, and I know you have a noble heart. I can feel it in the warmth of your presence, hear it in the tone of your voice, and read it in your eyes."

The word "warmth" made Lance look down at his clothes, realizing he felt warm.

"What is it?" asked Viviane.

"I'm dry. How could my clothes be dry when I just swam through the lake?" he asked, and then after looking at Ileana, he added, "And she's dry too. And...and how did she suddenly come to be wearing a dress when she was not wearing any clothes in the lake? And what— how did her legs form out of fins?"

"I can understand your astonishment," said Viviane, "but it is not difficult to understand. We have become adept at manifesting our transformations in an instant. Some call it magic or sorcery, but it is simply the focusing of the mind with clear intent upon what we want. It is a simple concept, but it takes a great deal of practice and clearing away of old thought patterns that you humans love to hold onto before it can be possible, but even you could do it if you wished, just as you walked through that wall a moment ago, although I admit Ileana and I had to help you with that since your belief is weaker than ours."

"I do not understand," Lance confessed. "Are you both enchant-resses or—or aliens of some sort?"

Lance knew the words sounded ridiculous as he said them, but he could think of no other terms to use.

Viviane laughed and said, "Our ways may seem alien to you, but we are just as human as yourself. We are just better trained mentally and have had many centuries of experience growing up in a culture that encourages us to celebrate the variety of life and to explore our individual desires and creative sides without unhealthy restrictions. It has been that way ever since Lyonesse's beginnings, and it was that way among our ancestors long before Lyonesse was ever founded."

"I've heard of Lyonesse," said Lance, trying to recall what he had heard of it.

"Yes, you have heard of it, but only through what you have read in storybooks," said Viviane. "You see, I know you have come from another time, Lancelot, a time that only dimly recalls this world you have entered. Plus, so much of what you have read of our time is embroidered with men's imaginations—it is not bad at all because of that, but neither is it the truth about the past. But first, before I say more, tell me—what do you think you know of Lyonesse?"

Lance wanted to ask how she knew he had traveled from anoth-er time. He wanted to know whether she would help him find his brother and return home, but not wishing to be rude, and seeing how Viviane peered at him, waiting for his answer, he simply said, "I've heard that Lyonesse was a part of Britain, and I think it fell into the sea during Arthurian times."

"Lyonesse," Viviane corrected, "became submerged generations before the time of King Arthur, and it didn't fall. We purposely sub-merged ourselves. But all this talking is keeping you from eating.

Please, fill your stomach so that your brain may function better."

Ileana passed a bowl of fruit to Lance, who took from it grapes and a peach, and then he accepted the bread Viviane passed to him.

"While you eat, I will tell you of Lyonesse," said Viviane, "and then we will turn to why you are here, for as you've already guessed, there is a reason for it. You could have known it yesterday if you had not let yourself panic over your brother's situation, but this morning, when you calmly reflected that there must be a reason for everything you are experiencing, you allowed yourself to be open to this experience."

Relieved to know Viviane was aware of his brother, Lance quickly asked, "Is Tristan safe?"

"Your brother's journey is to be different from yours. Do not worry about him. Focus instead on what you need to know now."

Lance was not pleased with this answer. Yes, this adventure was all quite amazing, but he could not enjoy it unless he knew his brother was still alive.

"Does that mean that if your brother is dead, you will not go on living?" Viviane asked, as if reading his mind.

Lance did not know how to reply.

"Your brother's journey is not yours," Viviane repeated. "You must focus on your own path. God will take care of your brother. At this moment, you need only be intent on learning what you yourself need to know."

Hesitating, but realizing he was not going to get the answers he wanted without listening to what Viviane wished to tell him, Lance nodded in understanding and acceptance.

"Now, you asked about Lyonesse," she continued, "so let me explain how it is that we live here as we do."

CHAPTER 8

VIVIANE'S TALE OF LYONESSE

I T IS UNDERSTANDABLE that you are surprised about our land and that you should also think of us as being merfolk. I would not even be surprised if you had thought us some branch of the human evolutionary tree that did not move from sea to land to develop. However, you must understand that beyond the evolution of the physical form, there is also the evolution of the mind.

The people of Lyonesse go back to an older culture, that of Atlantis, which is far more famous, but just as misunderstood. In the time you come from, many still seek Atlantis, trying to know its secrets and what became of it, but its story is not to be discovered, and that is by its own choosing.

In those days, our ancestors in Atlantis traded with the rest of mankind, but in time, man became more interested in greed, power, and building empires than in the virtues of love, peace, and the pursuit of knowledge. We were once the marvel of the known world, at least among those few who ventured to our distant shores, but as man became more advanced in developing ships and raising armies, it became clear to us that the time would come when others would seek to conquer our land and take that which was ours. Not that we were attached to property, for we would have given freely, but we came to understand, through the bartering of the merchants who visited us and the behaviors witnessed by the few of our people who ventured to the other humans' great cities, that the human race was never likely to grow past greed. We were dismayed by this situation, realizing Cain's greedy and rage-filled blood had infiltrated all the human race by that time, and we could not bear the thought that our own descendants should be intermixed with it, or worse, subjected to it.

And so our forefathers saw fit to use their powers to make Atlantis sink into the ocean. Because such a decision was beyond what most humans could understand, and because you are all so filled with fear and angst, what became of our land and people was misunderstood and badly interpreted by your historians, and even what little history was recorded has mostly been lost to time, and as a result, men's imaginations have run wild in filling in false details. And so it is now recorded either that our land sunk into the sea because we had done great evil and God was angry with us, or that we advanced to the point of madness, using our technology to destroy ourselves. Neither story is true. We sunk beneath the water to protect ourselves; not that we could not have defeated the armies of man, for I verily believe we could have, but because to engage in warfare, even in our own defense, was seen as detrimental to our souls and incompatible with our mission to live as advanced beings. In council, we debated whether we should simply end our human existences and send our spirits to another planet to begin anew. But we were too fond of the planet earth and its beautiful oceans; we just did not care to associate any longer with our fellow humans, and so we manifested for ourselves the ability to preserve our city underwater and to breathe beneath the surface.

You may well wonder that we of Atlantis had such great technology, but you see, we had far longer than the rest of the human race to develop it. We are just as human as you are, but perhaps we are more closely akin to the Goddess-God's original conception of humanity. You, of course, know the story of the Great Flood as it is remembered in the Bible—how it is said to have covered all the earth and killed all of mankind save Noah and his family, who survived on the ark, but the truth is that by the time of the Great Flood, Atlantis had already been founded and we had already discovered the skills to survive under the sea, and when we chose to do so, mankind falsely assumed we had been destroyed by the Goddess-God for our wickedness, a belief they cherished when in truth it was they themselves who were wicked; they mocked us for holding onto the wisdom and virtues of the Goddess-God. They also hated us for giving shelter for some time to Lilith, who became the lover of our king, Atlas. Atlas promised her all the love and freedom that Adam had denied her, and in return, she helped make possible our existence under the sea. In fact, my sister Helena and I are her daughters. I remember as a small child watching my mother weep when she heard of the Flood and the destruction of mankind, for despite how Adam and Eve had treated her, she had always hoped someday for a reconciliation.

At the time of the Flood, we did not know about Noah and his ark. After the Deluge had ended, Atlantis again rose from the sea because we thought all humanity must have been destroyed and the earth now belonged solely to ourselves and the beasts. Several years passed before we came into contact with Noah's descendants, as well as the Nephilim and Anakim, who because of their strength and size, had also survived the Flood.

And while Lilith had wept for mankind's destruction, she had also felt relief to know its evil had passed away. But then, to discover some of them had survived, and that their wickedness was spreading again, made her incredibly angry. She felt thwarted, as if even the Goddess-God had turned against her; it was then that she chose to leave Atlantis and begin her reign of terror over mankind, including her many reincarnations in the bodies of numerous powerful, manipulative, and destructive women.

My father was so brokenhearted by her decision, begging her to remain with us, that not long after she left, he died of a broken heart. We feared this would mean early deaths for the rest of us as well, but we were made of the sturdy stock of mankind before the Flood; my sister and I were of Lilith's blood, and she had feasted off the Tree of Life, so we have been able to live almost as if we were immortals ever since.

Once my mother left us, we tried to live peacefully with the humans who came to trade with us, but in time, it became apparent again that we could not live with them, for we soon discovered that our children began to imitate their belligerent ways and marvel at the weapons they brought to our shores. We feared that if one of our people should fall in love and have children with one of Noah's descendants, the evil strain soon would mix with all our descendants until all the good that Atlantis stood for would be lost. Consequently, we decided it best again to sink Atlantis into the sea, where it has remained ever since, a civilization still flourishing, yet isolated and hidden away from mankind and its violence.

A few of us, however, dreamed that there might yet be hope for mankind, for now and then a hero would arise among the people who tried to lead them in the ways of righteousness, and even though we ourselves were descendants of Adam and Eve, we did not live like the majority of wicked mankind. Therefore, a small band of us decided that for the good of humanity, we would exile ourselves from Atlantis and set up a small colony, distant enough from mankind that we could observe it and occasionally try to guide it for its benefit, while still being protected from its evil, and so we chose the land of Lyonesse at the edge of Britain, it being nearly the end of the earth as far as mankind knew in those days.

Not long after we set up our colony, the Nephilim brothers, Albion and Avallach, came to Britain. We befriended them and agreed that together we would do that which was beneficial for mankind. The first men who arrived were also of a decent sort, though there were only a handful of them, but they were followed by Brutus and his war-mongering kind, by which time, the human race had reversed back to being nearly as wicked as before the Flood.

It was not long after Brutus came to Britain, bringing with him the murderous ways of Rome and Troy—at that time perhaps the noblest civilizations among the world, which says very little for mankind—that we found we must make the same choice as had been made in Atlantis—to sink beneath the sea for our own protection. But nevertheless, we have continued with our friends at Avalon to keep a watch over mankind, and on a few occasions, we have tried to interfere with mankind for its own benefit, although it has not always worked out as such.

If I have not yet strained your patience too far, I will tell you of one such interference by my sister Helena, for it is tied to the reason why you have arrived here. But first, I need agreement from you regarding the quest for which you have been chosen. I think you will see that our story is not such a difficult one to understand. It is not one of greed or disaster, but simply one of choosing peace over bloodshed and meditation over babbling. We wish to share wisdom with you if you are open to receive it—wisdom that will allow you to continue the quest you are already on, perhaps without you yet being aware of it, so that you may bring back understanding to the rest of the human race when it will be ready to receive it. Are you prepared to take up this quest?

CHAPTER 9

WHEN VIVIANE HAD finished her tale, she looked questioningly at Lance, awaiting his answer.

Lance did not know what to say. His goal was not to make the world a better place, but simply to find his brother. Yet he believed these women were powerful and could help him so he did not wish to burn his bridges with them by outright rejecting them.

"What does the quest entail?" he finally asked.

"It includes finding yourself, healing the faults of your past, and moving forward to help others," Viviane replied.

"I'm willing to do that," said Lance, "but first, I want to find my brother. Can you not at least tell me that he's well?"

"It is not my place to reveal information to you that is hidden from your own senses. If you are to know your brother's welfare, it will be revealed to you when the time is appropriate."

Lance felt irritated by this answer, although he tried not to show it, for clearly Viviane had far more extrasensory powers than a normal human.

"I understand your irritation," she said, again sensing his emotions, if not actually reading his thoughts. "But let us review your past a bit to see how you have done with your life so far; then perhaps you will better understand everything."

"Review my past?" said Lance. He feared that doing so would take too long when he still wanted to find Tristan, despite her saying Tristan had his own path to follow. "What's there to review? I've barely had a life considering all the years I spent in Castle Dracula supposedly for my own protection."

"There are things in your past you must come to terms with," Viviane replied.

"What things?"

"Things you cannot name because you will not admit them to yourself."

"You speak in riddles," said Lance, beginning to feel angry. He could not say exactly what now irritated him about her when earlier he had felt her to be gentle and kind, but somehow, he suspected she was not the benevolent force she claimed to be. Perhaps he was just paranoid, but he had a feeling that she had her own agenda since she seemed uninterested in helping him find Tristan.

"Do not worry; healing your past will go quickly," Viviane promised. "If you cooperate, it will be similar to receiving an inoculation to prevent disease; the needle is sharp, but the pain need only last briefly, and you will then be immune from much that would otherwise harm you. Now just look and observe."

Suddenly, the wall turned into a movie screen, and in disbelief, Lance watched as he saw himself and his brother, as if in a movie—in a film of his past life—but how could it be possible? Who had filmed it?

With the battlements of Castle Dracula looming above them, Lance and Tristan were busily engaged in the castle courtyard, practicing their sword-fighting. They used wooden swords to prevent hurting one another, but that did not make their fighting any less heated or fun, for they both enjoyed it thoroughly and would have thrust and parried with one another all day if their bodies did not eventually tire from the exercise.

"That's enough for now, boys!" called out their instructor, Quincey Harker, who was also their great-grandfather. Though he was well past his hundredth year, he looked no older than twenty-five, in the prime of health, with a muscled torso to make any professional wrestler jealous, while simultaneously being as lithe and quick as a panther. Since his own disappearance from the everyday world, Quincey had resided at Castle Dracula and studied all manner of arts and skills so that he could achieve the perfect balance of intellectual and physical prowess; forty years of such training with an ever-youthful body had made him a formidable force for any opponent, and the perfect instructor for his great-grandsons, who believed it their destiny someday to defeat the evil sorceress Lilith. They had been stolen away as infants by Merlin and brought to this castle to be protected and raised in the art of defense until the hour when they might engage in the great battle with her. Never was there a day when their imaginations did not focus upon this great future battle nor their bodies participate in preparing for it.

The boys now came to Quincey's side, lowering their weapons and laying them on the grass near where he was seated.

"We are not tired yet, Great-Gramps," said Tristan.

"No, but it is almost time for supper, and you know your grandfather does not like us to be late for our meal," Quincey replied.

"We have a good quarter hour still," said Lance.

"Yes, and you will need most of that time to wash the sweat off of you."

"I only needed one more minute," said Lance, "and I would have knocked Tristan's sword from his hand and had mine at his throat."

"You would not have," said Tristan.

"I would so have."

"Why do you think he would not have, Tristan?" Quincey asked. "You cannot deny his skill surpasses yours when it comes to swordplay."

"So? Mine surpasses his in a lot of other things, like horse-riding and math and science."

"Those skills won't keep you from getting your throat slit," Lance retorted.

Tristan's ire could be seen in his eyes, but Quincey placed a calming hand on his arm and said, "Tristan, why do you think he would not have defeated you in another minute?"

Tristan, looking steadily at his brother, replied, "I don't doubt that he might have knocked my sword from my hand, but he wouldn't have put his sword to my throat. He loves me too much to do me any real harm."

"But I'm not fighting you when we practice; I'm envisioning fighting one of Lilith's evil minions," Lance protested. "Of course I wouldn't hurt you, but we must pretend we are each other's enemy if we are to learn to fight effectively."

"It's not possible," said Tristan. "You love me too well to forget who I am, despite your false bravado that you try to hide behind."

"Is this true, Lance?" Quincey asked.

Lance's heart began to pound and his nostrils flared as he declared, "It is not. I would kill my enemy if it had to be."

"Even if your enemy were your brother?" asked Quincey.

Lance thought it best he not answer, but in the end, he confessed, "Yes."

Tristan paled as he quietly, pleadingly, said, "You would not."

"I would if you sought to spite or betray me," said Lance.

"Why would I do that?"

"To win glory for yourself. Because you know I am the older brother and, therefore, deserving of respect; because you know I will be the one in the forefront, leading people in the quest for justice and right, and I think you are jealous because you know it's true."

"Because you were born just minutes before me?" said Tristan. "I don't care about that."

"You do because those few minutes' difference make me a king while you remain but a prince, and if your jealousy should get the better of you, you would try to take that kingship from me, but I will not have it, Brother; that I promise you. I will not allow it."

"You're crazy," laughed Tristan. "Father's only an earl, and I know someday you'll be the earl, but that's fine with me. I'd rather read a book any day than be an old earl."

"That's good because you never will be, and all your books don't seem to help you to dream big. Why be an earl when you can be a king? Did not Merlin tell our father, as Grandpa himself has told us, that you and I are destined to bring about King Arthur's return?"

"That doesn't mean you will be a king," scoffed Tristan.

"I will be a king someday," said Lance, his eyes flaring, "and don't you try to thwart me, or it will go ill with you."

"Someday," said Quincey, his hand still resting on Tristan's arm to prevent his anger, but his eyes now looking into Lance's, "you may need to lead, but true leaders do not seek power over others; they seek simply to serve. Here in this isolation, you should be protected from the petty jealousies and competitions that happen among children; your grandfather and Merlin and I do not want you to grow up with base motives or focus on competing with one another and overlooking the larger goals of humanity's progress toward peace. It is our duty to stop evil, not add to it. Do not forget that the Christ himself was never called the King of Power, but rather the Prince of Peace."

"Then we are to fight for peace?" Tristan asked.

"No," said Quincey. "You cannot fight and expect peace to come from it, but you can, if necessary, defend yourself."

"I will fight," said Lance, "and I will defeat everyone so all will acknowledge me as their king. Then there will be peace because everyone will fear me."

"If that is to be," said Quincey, "I hope I never live to see the day, and perhaps it would be best if we put away the swords for a while."

"Great-Gramps, don't you want me to be king? Won't you be proud of me then?" asked Lance.

"I'm already proud of you," Quincey replied. "You need do nothing to win my love or approval. But I will not be at all happy to see you become a bully, seeking to make others serve you."

"But a king," Lance objected, "must have power so he can control people and keep them from breaking the law."

"I do not deny that such is true in this fault-filled world, but true power is not taken but given by loyal subjects," Quincey replied. "A true king is not a king by birthright but by winning the love of his people. If his people do not love him, he is no true king but a tyrant."

"Then how do I make people love me so they will obey the law and be at peace?" asked Lance.

"By not seeking their love but their welfare, and by serving them. By setting a good example so they need not focus on obeying a law, but will simply long to do what is right and good."

"But how do I become king so I can set an example for the people?"

"Aren't you listening?" asked Tristan. "You need to be chosen by the people."

"Then I would be a president; it would be a democracy, not a monarchy," Lance objected. "And they could vote me out of office. I wish to be a king in full."

"You're impossible," said Tristan.

"And I suppose you're so much better than me," Lance replied. "See, already you try to thwart me; you think you're some sort of prince of peace yourself, but you're really a viper trying to breed anger in me to make me fall so you can have my throne."

"I don't need to listen to this," said Tristan, his brow furrowing in anger. "I'm going in to wash up for dinner." And even though his great-grandfather's hand was still on his arm, Tristan pulled away and entered the castle.

"I will be king, Tristan!" Lance hollered after him. "Don't think I won't, and when I am, you'll be sorry that you mocked me!"

Lance turned to look at his great-grandfather, only to see the start of a tear in his eye.

"It was just a silly conversation," Lance said when the film had ended. He turned toward Viviane and added, "I didn't really mean to be so arrogant; it amounted to nothing; we both forgot it by the time we had finished eating dinner."

Viviane looked at him, but she did not reply, Lance knew it was because he was lying to himself. He had never truly forgotten it. He had always deeply longed in his heart to be a king.

Then Viviane turned back toward the screen and the film began again.

The scene changed to Delaney Castle. It was a month after Lance and Tristan had been reunited with their parents—a month after the showdown with Lilith at Castle Dracula had resulted in the ancient woman choosing their uncle Devin to be her mate and Merlin sending the two off to inhabit another world and begin a new race. There had been no great Armageddon-style battle as Lance had always expected; instead, only one act in which his father, Adam Delaney, had tried to destroy Lilith, but their uncle Devin had interceded, saving her life, which led to her reconciliation with humanity.

And Lance had merely stood and witnessed it all, an observer rather than a participant. In the days that followed, he had tried to hide his disappointment over the lack of his involvement in Lilith's defeat. He tried to bury such feelings in his joy over being reunited with his parents and returning home to England. But as he became settled in his new life, he soon realized that frustration was eating away at his core.

One day after his family had returned to England, his mother and Tristan had gone up to London to do some shopping. Lance had declined the invitation to join them. So his father had decided it was a good occasion for discussing with him the running of Delaney Castle and his role as heir to the earldom.

Father and son had spent about an hour together in Adam's study as they went over the estate's books. Lance had become increasingly bored with each passing minute until finally he said, "Father, why don't you have an agent to take care of all this for you?"

"I do; that is Mr. Hadley's role," Adam replied, "but it is my property, so I must oversee it as well to make sure everything is above board. I trust Hadley, but if something should happen to him, I need to know what is going on, and so must you. It takes more than one man to run this estate. We have thousands of acres of land and employ dozens of people. It's basically like running a corporation."

"But all this fussing over things like sheep and lumber and all that," Lance objected. "Don't you get bored with it?"

"Sometimes," Adam admitted, "but it is our source of income, and beyond that, we have a responsibility to all the people we employ."

"But...."

"But what?" Adam asked.

"Oh, you wouldn't understand," Lance replied.

"Try me."

"Well, you're American, Father, so maybe you just don't get it. I mean, you weren't born like me to be an earl's son."

Adam's eyes grew wide at this remark.

"I mean," Lance tried to explain, "you weren't raised to be an earl. You didn't even know who your father was until you were... what, twenty-two or something?"

"Yes," Adam agreed. "That's true, but what difference does that make? Before I became an earl, I had gone to business school, so I might have ended up running a corporation regardless."

"But that's my point," said Lance. "You Americans are used to working and living like commoners, and if you wish to rise above that, you have to work all the harder in America. But I always knew I was born to be an earl, ever since I was a little boy, even though I grew up in Dracula's Castle."

"Then in knowing that for so long," Adam replied, "you should feel all the more your responsibility to the estate and all of our tenants and employees."

"Don't get me wrong, Father," said Lance, rising from his chair beside his father's desk to pace about the room. "It's not that I don't appreciate these things, but I grew up believing I was raised for greatness."

"Being an earl isn't glamorous enough, then, for you?" Adam asked.

"No, that's not what I mean," said Lance, pausing to look out the window. "At least, not exactly. I mean, Grandpa and Great-Gramps made me think that I was being raised for some great battle against Lilith, and to help bring about the return of King Arthur, and to be some sort of great leader—a hero among men."

"I see," said Adam, sitting back in his chair and smirking a bit, though he tried to hide it when Lance turned his way.

"I don't know if you do see, Father," said Lance. "You told me how overwhelming it was for you to find out you were an earl's son, but in your heart, didn't you always know it? Didn't you know you were born—destined—for greatness, and don't you ever feel bored just to sit here or wander about the estates all day, just to make sure the sheep aren't on the loose?"

"I've had little time in my life to be bored," said Adam, leaning forward. "I had to deal with my father's death, not long after I found him, and the complications of marrying your mother and gaining the title, and then all the horrible years of worry that you and your brother were lost and in danger, and my mother's horrific death, and of course, my grandparents' deaths. It's really only been this past month, now that your brother and you have been restored to me, that I feel I can begin to relax, and even the happiness of this reunion has been marked by some sadness for me because I really miss my cousin, Devin. I can't imagine that I will never see him again in this lifetime."

"I'm sorry you lost your best friend in that way," said Lance, walking back to sit on the edge of his father's desk, "but I still don't think you're getting what I'm trying to say. Look at this." He picked up a small pewter statue of a knight, a paperweight upon his father's desk. "Don't you ever want to have adventures like this knight—to go on a great quest, to right wrongs, and to be a hero? That is what I feel I was destined for—for some sort of greatness—but instead, when the moment came, the great battle with Lilith, it feels like all I did was just stand by while you tried to defeat her, and then Uncle Devin turned out to be the hero of the moment. It...well, it was quite a letdown, you know?"

"A letdown?" Adam half-laughed. "I guess I felt a little of that too, but it quickly vanished when I realized the joy of it all being over and being reunited with my sons."

Lance sighed and stood up again, walking about in the study. After a moment, he turned to face his father from across the room and said, "I want more, Father. I want greatness. I want more than to be the earl of a big estate that's complicated to manage. I want to be a king. I want to wear a crown. I want to be loved and praised by my people, and to know that I have changed the world."

Adam yawned and wiped his eyes, as if he were exhausted.

Lance continued to stare at him, as if demanding answers, as if demanding that his father give him what he sought.

"Lance," said Adam, standing up and pushing his chair under his desk, "I love you, and I do not mean this unkindly, but I've noticed in the short time since we've been reunited that you have a tendency to be arrogant. And I'm afraid you get that from me, which is why I feel I have the right to warn you: Be careful, or your arrogance will get you into trouble."

For a moment, Lance was surprised, insulted even, as if his father had slapped him across the face.

"No, Father," he had then exploded, "it is not arrogant to want to be more than I am. You are the one who should be careful— careful that you are not settling for being a fat middle-aged man with nothing to live for. You can keep your bloody earldom. I won't settle for it!"

And then Lance had stormed out of the study, out of the house, and walked for hours through the gardens and meadows surrounding Delaney Castle, walked until he exhausted his body, but not the craving deep down in his soul.

"It was all forgotten," Lance said as the scene ended. "I know Father didn't hold it against me; we never even mentioned it again...though, perhaps I should have apologized to him...."

Viviane did not reply but simply stared ahead until the next scene began.

After Lance and Tristan had lived at Delaney Castle for a year, their parents felt it was time for the twins to go away to college. Tristan had welcomed the opportunity to explore and learn more about the world because he realized their education had been very limited by the isolation they had experienced at Castle Dracula. Lance questioned whether all the things he would have to learn in college would really be applicable to his becoming an earl, a member of Parliament, and, hopefully, someday a world leader, but he knew he would go to college and excel, for as the future Earl of Delaney, he was determined to be excellent in all things and impress all those whom he met.

Their mother had wanted to send the boys to Oxford or Cambridge, but Tristan had wanted to go abroad, perhaps to a school in France or Australia. Lance had not wanted to leave England, but after much discussion, the twins, who decided wherever they went, they did not wish to be separated, finally chose to attend an American university. They selected a small private college in the American Midwest where the press was unlikely to hound them and where they would not feel overwhelmed by not knowing everyone but could quickly get to know their fellow students. The school only had just over a thousand students, so it was small enough that the brothers, with their English accents, were readily noticeable by all—and even more so when it became general knowledge that they had titles. But Lance embraced the situation, content to be a big fish in a small pond.

The brothers rented a house just a few blocks from the school, and since most of their friends lived at home with their parents or in small dorm rooms, the Delaney twins' house quickly became a gathering place. Tristan was not overly enthused by the constant comings and goings of their many classmates, but Lance quickly made friends, and it became increasingly apparent to Tristan how important it was for Lance that everyone like him.

One night, after a particularly large and boisterous party, and following the homecoming game—in which Lance, as quarterback of the football team, had scored the winning touchdown and been paraded on his teammates' shoulders around the field—Lance, feeling particularly drunk on his popularity, noticed his brother sitting quietly in a corner, as if observing the rest of the party from a distance.

Finally, about two in the morning when the last of the guests had gone, save for a few who were too drunk to drive home and crashed on the twins' living room floor, Lance went upstairs to knock on his brother's door.

"Tristan, are you asleep?" he asked.

Tristan rolled over in bed to face the open door, clearly still awake.

"What is it?" Tristan asked.

"Brother, I am so sorry," Lance replied, stepping into the room.

"Sorry about what?" Tristan asked, confused, as he turned on the bedside lamp.

"Sorry that I get all the attention from our friends; you know it's only because they're intrigued that I will be an earl when father is gone. These Americans are obsessed with English titles."

"I don't care about that," said Tristan, dismissing it with a wave of his hand, but also a strain in his voice that told Lance otherwise.

"I think you do," Lance replied.

"I don't care about the title," said Tristan, "though I think you put too much focus on it. It's not the title but your confidence, your personal charisma, that makes everyone like you so much."

"I don't understand it," said Lance, "but everyone does seem to be very excited when they see me."

"Because you're the best athlete in school," Tristan confirmed, "but you go out of your way to treat everyone well; the way you speak to people makes them feel special. When they talk, you act as if you're really listening to them and like you really want to understand who they are and what their issues are."

"Father and Grandfather and Great-Gramps taught me that," said Lance. "If I am to be the Earl of Delaney and manage the estate, I must understand the people who work for me and whom I am to lead. And someday I will have a seat in the House of Lords, so I hope to make a difference in the world for the better."

"You will," said Tristan. "You will be a great leader someday. You already are. I'm proud of you and happy for you. More to the point, because being a leader or an earl is not something I want personally, there is no reason to apologize to me about your popularity."

"I know, Tristan," Lance replied, "but I never want you to think you are not the most important friend I have. We have been as close as any two brothers could ever possibly be, and no matter how many friends I may have, that will never change between us."

"I know," Tristan replied. "Good night."

"Good night," said Lance.

But it was not a good night for Lance. He felt irritated with his brother, as if Tristan were only half-truthful with him. After all, if Tristan did not want to be a leader or an earl, were those things of real value? Tristan seemed very content with his life, doing what he found to do without ever seriously striving to be the very best at anything. At times, Lance felt irritated that Tristan did not share his drive always to excel, and yet, sometimes Lance felt that drive was a curse, as if he could never relax because he always had to be doing more, achieving more, becoming more. At such times, he envied how Tristan could appear so content. Tristan did not seek out friends or popularity or good grades or even a place on any sports team. He seemed content in the morning to go out jogging in the nearby woods, to sit and study after dinner, and occasionally, to accept a lunch invitation from a friend. Lance just could not understand what was going on in his brother's head. Most of the time, Tristan would not even go to parties or events on campus—other than the football games that Lance knew his brother only attended to cheer him on. Of course, many of these activities involved a great deal of drinking alcohol, something neither brother had ever had any interest in doing, but that did not mean Tristan had to stay home.

Lance participated in most activities, but at the parties, he only imbibed a minimal amount of alcohol; he feared otherwise he would too easily give in to the many drunk girls who came to the parties for one thing only, and as much as Lance was enjoying his American adventure, he did not feel that getting involved with an American girl would be fitting for his station. In fact, there was only one girl at school for whom Lance showed any interest.

Her name was Elaine, and she arrived at the school during her and the twins' senior year. She was an exchange student from England, and best of all, in Lance's opinion, the only daughter of the Marquess of

Astolat, which made her the only female at school suitable to be his girl-friend, and perhaps even his wife. He had assumed when he graduated and returned to England that he would take his place in English society and meet many eligible young women who might be considered for the role of future Countess Delaney, but Lance quickly decided there was no reason not to pursue Elaine. He met her at a party and asked her on a date, and during the date, he shared all of his goals and dreams with her, hoping to impress her, and believing he had.

Elaine certainly impressed him. She had everything he wanted in a wife—good looks, brains, a pleasing personality—plus she seemed quite exotic. The Marquess had caused quite a stir when he had married her mother, an Ethiopian Jew, which had resulted in Elaine having quite striking dark eyes and olive skin and an all-around sexy way about her. He even liked that she was pre-med and wanted to be a doctor so she could one day set up practice in Ethiopia to help others—a wonderful intention, thought Lance, and he planned to help her set up a foundation after they married—but he had no intention of ever moving to Ethiopia; eventually, he figured she'd get over that silly idealistic notion. They couldn't move there—not when he was studying political science and economics and planned either to open his own business or become a lawyer. He was hoping to be involved in politics; in time, of course, he'd end up having a seat in the House of Lords because he would someday inherit his father's title, but the possibility of becoming prime minister was also attractive to him.

Unfortunately, Elaine turned out to be less impressed with Lance than with his brother. When Lance had introduced her to Tristan, wanting to show her off to his brother, you could feel the electricity between them, as if they were long lost best friends. Elaine quickly made it clear she was more interested in having coffee with Tristan while they discussed art, literature, music, and films than listening to Lance discuss how economic policies could change Britain or create effective social change to erase poverty in Africa.

"You don't have to save the whole world, Lance," she had once said when he had joined her and Tristan for dinner and begun to discuss how to improve President Obama's new Affordable Health Care Act without repealing it.

"I want to make the world a better place," he had replied. "What's wrong with that?"

"There's nothing wrong with it," she had said. "But you can do it by being a good person and setting a good example for others. You can't force people to do the right thing."

He had not liked her tone or a good many other things she had said to him that night, and he had told Tristan so afterwards.

"Elaine has no right to talk to me that way," he had objected. "She acts like she somehow thinks she's better than me because she doesn't have the drive I do. I thought she cared about people in Ethiopia."

"She does," Tristan said, "but she's just not a fan of politics like you are."

"I want to create legislation to help people. To make people understand economics so they can use it to their benefit, and to get people to—"

"That's the problem, Lance," said Tristan. "You want to 'make people understand'—you act like you want to force people to do what is right. You act like your way is the best and only way. You can't control everything, and you can't control other people. Some things just have to be worked out for themselves."

"That's bullshit and you know it!" Lance had then exploded.

"People who wait around for things to happen never see effective change. If anything, stagnation only leads to things getting worse. The world won't become a better place unless we do something to make it so."

At that point, Tristan had just walked off rather than argue with him. Lance didn't see what there was to argue about. He knew he was right. The world would have solved poverty and many other social issues long ago if only people would stand up and do something about them.

CHAPTER 10

WHEN THE FINAL film had ended, Lance was speechless. Viviane and Ileana stood looking at him, but for a moment, he felt too ashamed to speak.

"Am I really so obnoxious?" he asked. "I do sincerely want to do good."

"Do you?" asked Viviane.

"Didn't I say so?"

"Yes, but why? Why do you want to help others?"

Lance wasn't sure how to reply.

"Is it," asked Ileana, "because you want to have power? Perhaps you want power, but you want to disguise it in the form of you doing good; maybe you even want to do good, but only if you are acknowledged as a savior—savior to a whole nation even?"

Lance felt offended. He didn't know what to say. For a moment, he thought he might actually cry.

"Ileana, let him sort it out for himself," said Viviane. "Lance, what have you learned from what you have just viewed of your past?"

"I—I don't know," said Lance. "I—well, I don't care about any of that right now. That's all in the past. All that matters to me in the present is finding my brother. I'm worried about him. I don't have time for these mind games right now."

"Maybe you can best help your brother by helping yourself," said Ileana. "Then you will be more bearable to live with; after all, don't they say that charity begins at home?"

"But I'm not that same person," he argued. "I've changed. Those things all happened years ago."

Ileana pulled her head back, flinching as if he were assaulting her with his raised voice.

"I know you have changed," said Viviane. "But have you changed enough?"

"What do you want from me?" Lance demanded. "I want to go find my brother so I know he's all right. Unless you're going to help me find him and then figure out how we can return to the twenty-first century, I don't want to remain here. I think your kingdom is beautiful, and maybe you have the best intentions toward me, but you're not helping me right now."

"It is not a kingdom," Viviane gently corrected. "We have no king. We have no need for such. Since my father Atlas died, we have governed ourselves through sheer reason and goodwill."

"And," Ileana added, "earlier when we were swimming, you were open and trusting to wherever this adventure would lead you. Why have you changed now?"

Lance held back from answering. How could he explain it to them? How could he admit it to himself—that after viewing the scenes from his past, he no longer trusted himself as being worthy of whatever quest these women wanted him to partake in.

"What do you wish me to do?" he finally asked, fearing if he did not give in to what they wanted, they would never help him or maybe not even allow him to return to looking for Tristan.

"You may have heard," Viviane replied, "of the Thirteen Treasures of Britain that Merlin hid away, including the horn of Bran Galed, which some wrongly believe is the Holy Grail."

"Yes," said Lance. "I know of them from what my father was shown by Merlin of Camelot's past, including the horn, which Palomides told me has been mistaken for the Holy Grail."

"Yes," Viviane continued. "All those treasures have been hidden away, and they are not intended to be found for many centuries to come, but two great treasures remain in Britain. Both have also been hidden away for many years until the time came for them to be known again to the world. One of them was returned to mankind's sight not too many years ago by my own hand; the other remains hidden. Can you guess what these treasures are?"

Lance thought for a moment before answering. "You are the Lady of the Lake, and the only item I recall ever hearing that you gave anyone is the sword Excalibur that you gave to King Arthur, so I'm guessing that's one of the treasures, but I really don't know what the other one could be."

"You are correct in your first guess," said Viviane. "I did give the sword to Arthur, and I gave it with great hesitation, for it is not a treasure that we of Lyonesse or our ancestors of Avalon truly prize since it is a weapon of war, but it is Arthur's right to bear this ancient sword. It is in truth the Sword of Troy, which Aeneas, last of Troy's royal family, took with him when he fled during that great city's fall. He brought the sword with him to what would become Rome, and there it passed into the keeping of his great-grandson, Brutus, that same Brutus who came to this isle, bringing misery and bloodshed in his wake. It was with the sword Excalibur that Brutus slew the giant Albion, for whom this land was once named. After his death, Albion became one of the guiding spirits of Britain, and yet, had he lived, perhaps the Old Ways in Britain would have survived and man might be kinder and gentler than he is now. I myself took the sword from Brutus' hand after the murder was committed. It is one of the few times I have interfered in the ways of men, but I did it to weaken Brutus' power so he might not destroy more of those who seek to benefit mankind. I hid the sword here in Lyonesse, and only one other time before I gave it to Arthur was the sword seen by men, and that time was not by my approval.

"My sister, Helena, whose heart and faith were greater than her reason, decided to leave Lyonesse to wed Constantius Chlorus, whom she foresaw would become Roman Emperor. Today, many mistaken stories are told of her origins—from her being the daughter of a British king to her being a stable-maid born in Bithynia—they are all mistaken because she purposely kept her origins in Lyonesse from the world. She chose to enter the world of wicked men because her heart bled for the Christians being slain by the Romans; we had great hope for the Christians in those days since we had met the Christ personally when he came to Britain in his youth with his uncle, Joseph of Arimathea, whom you know better as Merlin. Unfortunately, most of our hope in the Christians was destroyed as an indirect result of Helena trying to help them. You see, she gave birth to her son Constantine, whom she tried to raise to believe in Christianity, though it was a true struggle, for he was an obstinate boy. When she left Lyonesse, she also took, against my will, the Sword of Troy, Excalibur. When Constantine was grown, she gave it to him on condition that if he should win in battle by virtue of the sword, he would convert to Christianity and make it the empire's official religion. If you know your history, you know it is said that Constantine saw a vision that day that caused him to convert. I don't know how true the vision story is—certainly, the sword was of pagan Troy and not Christianity, for Christ himself had said that those who live by the sword will die by the sword, and therefore, I do not think God interests himself in mankind's warfare madness, but nevertheless, Constantine conquered his enemy and then converted the empire to Christianity. At first, it was just freedom of religion he offered to the Christians, but within a couple of generations, a new emperor passed the Edict of Thessalonica, which basically forced all members of the empire to convert. Of course, Helena thought that the empire becoming Christian would be a great blessing to mankind—and I do not deny it was well-intended—but you cannot make men believe in anything by force, and even when they do believe, you cannot make them behave, and so the Church was flawed the moment it became an agent of control. While it taught Christian values, it also taught intolerance of other beliefs. But I am getting ahead of myself.

"Despite his conversion, Constantine went on to commit some horrible crimes, including the killing of his son and wife, and even claiming his mother urged him on to the latter's murder. Helena was so disgusted and heartbroken by these events that she sought to remedy this situation by leaving the court and going on a pilgrimage to the Holy Land. Her aim was to find the True Cross upon which the Christ had died to save the world—not literally save, but to make mankind aware that life after death existed and so fear should have no place in the world; the Church corrupted that understanding as well. In any case, the True Cross is the other great treasure of which I speak.

"Merlin went to Rome with Helena since, as Joseph of Arimathea, he had himself witnessed the Crucifixion three centuries earlier and knew where the True Cross had been placed afterwards. He tried his best to maintain his anonymity, but rumors still arose that the Wandering Jew had appeared to assist Helena; you probably know from your parents that Merlin has at times appeared in that guise. Of course, as is well known, Helena did find the True Cross; in fact, she found three crosses—the one Christ died upon and the ones the two criminals also died upon, only Helena did not know which cross was which, so she had a woman who was near death brought forth to touch each of the crosses. The first two produced no results, but the third cross restored the woman's health, so Helena knew it was the True Cross.

"Helena had the crossbeam left in Jerusalem, and from it, many pieces have been broken off until they were sent throughout Christendom. Helena, however, knowing how easily her own son had turned to man's wicked ways, knew she must preserve the upright beam, so she brought it back to Britain with her. Before she had left Rome, she also took back Excalibur from her son, which I kept safe until I gave it to Arthur.

"As for the upright beam of the True Cross, Helena decided to hide it in a cave in Britain where it would be kept safe until it would be needed to restore mankind to faith—not any specific faith of any church, but simply faith that the Goddess-God loves us well enough to have sent the Christ to us to remind us of our own power, the power that lies within all of us to do what is right and good and even to move mountains if we have such faith. What could be a greater testament of God's love and mankind's spiritual origins than the True Cross? And when would there be a greater need for it than now when

Britain has been struck by this horrible comet that has caused the weak-minded to fear it is a judgment from the Goddess-God when it is really an opportunity to return to Him-Her?"

"But I don't understand," said Lance, "what this all has to do with me."

"Helena never revealed to me where she hid the True Cross. Nor is it for me to know. It is a task that one whom the Christ came to save must undertake to rekindle mankind's faith. I believe you are the one chosen to take up this quest. The sight of the True Cross will reaffirm mankind's understanding that despite the pain wreaked by the comet, all things work according to God's plan and for the betterment of mankind, and it will remind people that they are spiritual beings and, therefore, eternal and cannot truly suffer anyway—all suffering, after all, is an illusion. Will you do this? Will you, Lancelot, take up this quest?"

Lance felt as if Viviane had just asked him to carry the weight of the world on his shoulders. Should he go out looking for the cross—an old rotting piece of wood—when his brother was lost, perhaps dead, or at least wounded and in need of his help? And who was he to play missionary and convert people? Had he not been raised as the son of an earl, a descendant of King Arthur? Was not Excalibur the treasure he should seek over the True Cross? Let a monk or a priest take up that quest.

"Since childhood," said Viviane, interrupting his thoughts, "you have longed to be a king, but you need to understand that a king can wear one of two crowns; yes, there is the earthly crown of glory worn by a king, but there is also the crown of thorns for those who follow the Christ; it is for you to decide which one you shall wear. And while the crown of thorns implies suffering, do not forget what I just said about suffering."

"I am a descendant of King Arthur," Lance replied, boldly. "Therefore, I believe my destiny is to seek a crown. If I am not to be King of Britain now, for clearly Arthur is, then I suspect it is my duty to learn something in this time that will allow me to return to the twenty-first century to be a king in my own time—King of Britain, perhaps, for who knows what destruction the comet may have caused there? I may be needed to lead my people in my own time and land."

"Is that what you truly think?" Viviane asked, her eyes calm but penetrating his.

"Yes," Lance said, trying to stare back and not show doubt—though ignoring the voice in his head that said otherwise.

Viviane was silent a moment—sad, perhaps—but Lance felt too stubborn to change his answer. Then Viviane smiled and said, "It is time for you to leave us, but we cannot let you return to the surface in those ridiculous twenty-first century garments. We will give you armor appropriate for a noble knight, and you shall leave here Sir Lancelot in very truth, for there is none by that name known in Britain, but there shall be henceforth from this day. Oh, you will have a fabulous history once the bards begin to sing about you, and because of your time spent here, they will make up all kinds of tales about your origins and how I raised you, but let them say whatever they might, Britain can be a dangerous place, so I cannot send you back there unprotected."

As Viviane spoke, Ileana had risen from the table and walked toward a curtain against the wall that Lance had not noticed before. When she drew back the curtain, Lance saw a full suit of armor, complete with sword and shield.

"We shall give you a horse too," said Viviane. "You will find it waiting for you upon the shore."

Lance nodded, accepting this gift of armor, feeling it was his due, and also sensing that the time had now come to begin fulfilling his destiny.

"Ileana will help you dress in your armor and then show you how to depart from Lyonesse," said Viviane. "I bid you good fortune, Sir Lancelot, whatever the quest you choose to pursue."

"Thank you, milady," said Lance, only half-surprised by his use of "milady" for he felt truly like a knight now. Viviane simply nodded and then walked through the wall, disappearing from view.

"Come," said Ileana, beckoning Lance forward, and in another minute, she was helping him on with his armor. He found that it suited him perfectly. He was just about to lift up the sword and practice swinging it when Ileana said, "You may be thirsty later, so have one more glass of wine before you go."

She crossed to the table and returned with a goblet. Lance, who did feel parched, thanked her; then he placed the goblet to his lips, raising it up so that it blocked his vision. And when he lowered the cup, he discovered he was standing on the edge of a lake with a horse beside him, his sword and shield lying upon the ground, and all about him, the grass and trees looked dead, as if autumn had come, whereas before it had been summer.

Perhaps the wind has simply blown away all the ash, was his first thought. *After all, the trees were bare before because of the comet.*

It was a disorienting moment, for he had left Lyonesse so quickly and had not expected so suddenly to find himself back on land. "I shouldn't be surprised by anything anymore," he told himself, and yet he was. He just hoped he had not lost months of time in Lyonesse, for he had heard of people going to fairylands who find that years have passed in the human world while they were gone. "I was gone long enough, even if it was just a few hours," he grumbled. He was grateful to Viviane and Ileana for the horse and armor, and he could not deny that Lyonesse had been a marvelous place to visit, but it had taken him away from searching for his brother, and now he was separated from Palomides as well. Plus, he was inland somewhere—he was beside a lake, not on the beach by the ocean—so who knew how far he was from where he had first lost Tristan?

"No matter," he told himself. "I'll ride on until I find someone who can give me directions." Then collecting his sword and shield, he climbed onto his steed and set off for Camelot or wherever Fate might lead him—he didn't care so long as it led him back to Tristan. He felt an even greater longing to find his brother now, though he tried not to focus on those resurfaced memories of the times when he had been obnoxious toward his brother.

Lance rode forward for a few minutes, but then he unexpectedly found himself sobbing. "It's not seemly for a knight to cry," he told himself, "and it isn't helping anything. All I can do is find Tristan and bring him home safely to Elaine so they can be married. That's the only way I can make it up to both of them."

CHAPTER 11

LANCE WENT FORWARD through the meadow to the wood's edge and then followed along it, not knowing where his destination lay. There was no path, no road, no sign of human habitation anywhere. He did not understand why, of all the places he could have been dropped by Viviane and Ileana, he was placed here in the middle of nowhere. Viviane knew his greatest desire was to find Tristan, but she had been completely unhelpful in that respect. He was grateful for the armor and the horse, however, for he knew he needed weapons to survive in this brutal medieval world if it were anything like the Camelot he had read about in storybooks—and from what he had witnessed so far, although he had not experienced any true violence, it was certainly a chaotic world. But she would have been more helpful if she could have told him where his brother was—she seemed to know everything else, so why had she refused to answer him?

As he rode, Lance couldn't help noticing that the ash, which had previously covered everything, was no longer visible. Where before it had coated the leaves of the trees and covered the earth, now the trees were bare and the ground was full of dead leaves. It had also been warm as summer when he had first arrived in Arthurian Britain, but now there was a slight chill in the air, and what little vegetation he saw was dressed in autumnal colors rather than those of summer. How was it possible that the season could have changed so rapidly? Was it even possible?

"La Belle Dame sans Merci," Lance muttered to himself, recalling the poem by John Keats that he had read in college. The poem's title referred to "The Beautiful Woman Without Mercy," and it told of a fairy woman who trapped men in fairyland as her lovers, taking from them their best years. Then they would wake, as if from a dream, to find themselves old men who had lost a lifetime while the dame had held them in her thrall.

Was it possible that Viviane had held him in her thrall—that three months could have passed like that? But La Belle Dame sans Merci was a fairy who seduced mortal men. Viviane had said the people of Lyonesse were human, and there had been nothing sensual between him and Viviane, or even Ileana, though Lance admitted he had felt some healthy urges while swimming with her.

But there was no time to think of that now. He must find Tristan. If he had really been in Lyonesse for months, Tristan either had to be dead, or he may have recovered from his wound or coma by now—at least Lance hoped so.

Lance rode on for several miles until the sun's position told him he was traveling south, for he watched the sun move from being high in the sky to gradually moving to the west, a sign that it was now early afternoon. Was it best for him to head south? How far south could he travel? Ultimately, he would come to the English Channel if he went in that direction, but that could be a hundred miles or more away, depending on where in Britain he was. Hopefully, he was still in Cornwall, so the sea could not be more than a few hours' ride no matter which way he went. Unfortunately, there were no landmarks anywhere to tell him where he was, at least none he recognized, but then this landscape scarcely resembled that of the twenty-first century Britain he knew; there were no highways, no railways, no buildings to be seen anywhere, and the forests covered so much of the land that he could not see far, unlike what had been his experience while riding the railways around Britain. In the past, he had always wondered what it would be like to live in Arthurian Britain. Now he was learning.

In time, Lance came to a peasant's cottage, but it looked vacated, and so he continued on. He wondered whether he should even stop if he did meet anyone. At least he could ask where he was to get his bearings, but where then would he go? Perhaps he could ask the way to Camelot, where he was most likely to find assistance. Hopefully, King Arthur or Merlin would be more helpful to him than Viviane had been.

But Lance rode on all afternoon without spotting a living soul, and when his stomach began rumbling, he realized he would have to find something to eat and somewhere to sleep. Hopefully, he would soon come across some small village or even a farmer's cottage. He had no money to buy food or accommodations, but he would gladly work for a meal and lodging, although he doubted anyone would accept a knight playing a servant's role in what must be a highly class-conscious society. More likely, people would think him a great lord and offer him food and a bed out of courtesy, if not from fear of his sword.

Lance was quickly realizing that being a knight-errant was not all it was cracked up to be. Where did knights get their food? He could sleep outside, but sleeping in armor would be no fun, and if he took it off, someone might sneak up and steal it, and what if it rained overnight—would his armor rust? But without the armor, he would freeze all night, for if it were autumn, the night might be brutally cold; there might even be frost in the morning. Then again, sleeping in metal would be far from warm. None of the storybooks he'd read had ever said what knights did in these situations.

Just as the sun began to set, Lance arrived at the forest's edge. Before him lay a vast plain that gently inclined upward. In the distance, he thought he could see some sort of building, perhaps a chapel or a small castle—it was a long way off, too far to tell what it really was—it might even be a walled city—but whatever it was, it looked like it could provide him with shelter, and he should be able to reach it before dark descended.

The plain was largely barren, but after riding a quarter of a mile, Lance came to what looked to be the remnants of some sort of highway, perhaps an old Roman road. He followed it forward for about a mile, but he soon realized it was leading him away from the structure, so he turned again toward the building, thinking he could always return to the road in the morning. *What does it matter which way I go?* he thought. *I don't know where I'm going. I have no destination. I only want to find Tristan and return home to my parents, and I don't know how to fulfill either of those goals.*

Soon, Lance was riding up a small hill, getting closer to the structure. The sun was descending rapidly now. In another minute, it was right above the structure, and then Lance suddenly felt overcome with awe, for the sun had dipped down and was now shining through the monument. Lance knew immediately where he was. He was not headed toward a city or a castle. Stonehenge lay before him.

He had been to Stonehenge only once before, just happening to drive past it and stopping to look at it, but the area had been roped off and filled with tourists then. While he understood the monument's popularity and the need to protect it, he had walked away from it disappointed, not even taking a photo.

But now he was so amazed by the sunbeams shooting through it that he could well believe it had been built as some sort of temple of the sun, as many had theorized over the years. In any case, it was magnificent, and it looked more complete than he remembered it being. Of course, he was seeing it fifteen hundred years earlier now.

Awestruck, Lance rode forward toward the giant standing stones, feeling compelled, feeling unable to turn back, as if the stones were calling to him for reasons he did not understand.

When he was yet several dozen feet from it, Lance dismounted and led his horse forward, as if treading upon holy ground. He did not understand why he would feel such reverence for the monument when he had scarcely given a thought to it before, but he realized that never before had he time-traveled to the past or had reason to seek out whatever ancient power and secrets Britain's most famous ancient monument might hold.

Lance stood there, watching the sun descend between two of the giant stones, and then in the dusk, he walked among the stones, just daring to touch them, to see whether they would in some way speak to him or give him a sign. He recalled an old made-for-TV film he had once seen in which Dyan Cannon had visited Stonehenge and fallen through a tunnel into Merlin's cave; there Merlin had shown her the "true history" of Camelot. Of course, Lance already knew the real true story because Merlin had told it to his father, and it didn't match the version Dyan Cannon had seen—plus, the film's Candice Bergen was a far cry from the real Morgan le Fay. Still, the memory of the film caused Lance to walk cautiously, not relishing possibly falling into a hidden cave. He wouldn't complain, though, if Merlin appeared to tell him where his brother was.

Soon enough, it was dark and no sorcerers, fairies, or ancient druids had appeared to enlighten Lance. It was too dark to travel farther, and while the monument could not provide him much in the way of shelter, he resolved to stay where he was for the night.

By now, Lance was hungry after several hours of riding, so he dug into his saddlebag and retrieved some bread and cheese that Ileana or Viviane had been kind enough to give him. He was glad to see his horse eating the grass since there did not appear to be enough food for him as well. But he was even gladder when in the saddlebag he found a matchbook. It took him a moment to realize what it was, for he did not expect to see anything so modern here in the Arthurian world, but he could not resist shouting out a "Thank you!" in case Viviane or Ileana happened to be listening—and he would not have been surprised if they were.

A few small scrub bushes were scattered about the plain from which he could make a fire. Of course, he did not wish to set the grass on fire, so he would need to dig a firepit. He had nothing in the way of a shovel, but he found that his helmet would serve his purpose. He could always rinse it out later, and he didn't plan to wear it again anytime soon since it was too warm. So getting down on his hands and knees, Lance dug a trench around a couple of the scrub bushes, thinking he would simply light them on fire. It took him nearly an hour to finish this task, and it was none too soon, for he doubted the temperature was much above five degrees Celsius by that point now that the sun had gone down and the stars had come out. But he then quickly got a fire going, and after he took the saddle off his horse, he got it to lie down close enough to the fire to be warm without being frightened. Then Lance sat down to eat his bread and cheese and consider what he might do in the morning.

He had no grand ideas. All he could do was continue to journey on, hoping to find a town or village, and then perhaps someone could point him onward toward Camelot, where hopefully, Merlin would be able to help him, or if not, perhaps he could get directions to Avalon to seek help from Morgan le Fay.

His long journey combined with the late meal were now making Lance sleepy. With the fire burning, he told himself he need not fear being attacked by wild animals, but what about people? How was he even to know who was his friend or foe in this strange land? So far, he had only met Palomides, Ileana, Viviane, and the Beast Glatisant; except for the Beast, they had all seemed to want to help him, but in all honesty, none of them really had. And he knew there were plenty of villains lurking about in Arthurian England—black knights, sorcerers, and perhaps the evil Gwenhwyvach herself, who was Lilith's reincarnation in Arthurian times. Would she be likely to realize he was not her enemy? In the future, of course, she was redeemed, but he was back in the past now, so he doubted he could count on her goodwill.

But whatever fears he might have about spending the night outside, his body's fatigue soon got the better of him. He could feel his head nodding forward as he sat staring into the flames. He was just thinking he should take off his armor and lie down when his horse bolted up, whinnying. Instinctively, Lance jumped to his feet, grabbed his sword, and looked about. He saw nothing, but something must have startled the horse.

After a moment, he heard a twig crunch beneath a foot. He turned in its direction, his sword before him, but again he saw nothing. For a moment, he feared perhaps he was hearing things. No, perhaps the place was haunted; the ghost of some sacrificial victim might be here—although he didn't think Stonehenge had ever been an altar, but....

Enough musing.

"Who's there?" he demanded. "There's nothing here for you. Get away!"

"Please," said a male voice. "Can I just warm myself by the fire?"

Lance was startled by the response. The voice sounded familiar, but it was not that of Palomides.

"Who are you?" he asked. "Show your face!"

"I am a stranger in these lands," said the voice. "I'm lost and just looking for shelter from the cold."

And then the man stepped forward. For a moment, Lance stared at him, shocked, and then he dropped his sword and ran forward with more joy than he had ever felt before.

"Tristan!"

In a moment, they were in each other's arms, so excited that they bear-hugged each other to the ground and rolled around on it, laughing and shouting, "Thank God!" and calling out each other's names and asking simultaneously, "Where have you been?" and exclaiming, "I'm so relieved to see you!"

And finally, they sat up, and then Lance got to his feet and helped his brother up, and they sat down beside the fire.

"Have you any food?" asked Tristan.

"Yes, a great deal of it," Lance replied. "I swear, this saddle is like a horn of plenty; it is packed with food." He pulled out bread, cheese, and some apples and handed them to Tristan. He felt so happy that he realized he was ravenous himself and sat down to eat with his brother.

"Where have you been all this time?" Tristan asked as he accepted the food.

"It's a long story, and I have the same question for you," Lance replied. "I feared you were dead; I left the boat only for a moment when it came to shore, but it was washed out to sea with you in it."

"I didn't even know," said Tristan, "that you were alive. I thought maybe the comet had knocked you out of the boat since the people who found me said I was all alone."

"Well, we're both alive now," said Lance, "but I don't know how we will get out of this strange land."

"Actually, I've been rather enjoying my time here," said Tristan, "at least all but the last couple of days. But please, tell me all that has happened to you, and then I will tell you my tale."

Lance readily agreed, and though the night was wearing on, he told it all, and when he had finished, he urged his brother to tell his tale before they should sleep, and Tristan quickly complied.

PART II
TRISTAN

CHAPTER 1

THE LAST TIME I remember seeing you, Lance, was when we were out at sea. As the comet swept overhead, we were trying to take down the boat's sail, and then I remember excruciating pain from being hit on the back of the head by a rock or some other debris from the comet. I must have blacked out a second after that. I have no memory of the events you describe that followed—not of you pulling the sailboat to shore, or my lying in the boat while you sought Palomides' help, or of the boat drifting back out onto the sea. Nor do I know how long I drifted on the water, although I daresay it was a day or more.

My next memory is waking up in a bed beside a window. First, I felt the sun's warmth on my face, and then I opened my eyes and saw I was in some sort of room beside an open window. Through it I could see the sky, but not the land below, so I realized I must be several stories above ground. Before I could look around more, I heard a rustling sound, and turning my head in its direction, I saw a woman in a long pink gown, looking like a princess from a fairy tale, standing over my bed.

"Good sir, you are awake at last," she said.

She was the single most beautiful, most feminine, most delicate, and yet most sad-eyed woman I had ever seen. (I mean no disrespect to Elaine by saying that, but I must admit it is true. Please do not tell her so, if we ever see her again.) In any case, after a moment, this beautiful stranger recovered from her obvious surprise over my being awake. Then she smiled, and I instantly sensed that she was trying to hide the sadness still creeping through her eyes. In that moment, I also recognized her beautiful accent, and although I had yet to marvel at my ability to understand the Breton tongue, I was delighted by the sheer musicality of her words.

"We have waited many days for you to get better," she said. "How do you feel now?"

I did not know how I felt. I tried to sit up, which I managed to do with a little pain, grimacing and feeling weak and dizzy, and then I realized I must have been ill. I tried to find words to say so, but my head felt a bit muddled at first.

"Do not strain yourself," she said, placing her hand on my shoulder. Her touch should have been ecstasy to me, but it hurt so much that I felt like I might faint, which was how I realized I must be wounded in my shoulder.

When she saw me grimace, she asked, "Does it still hurt?"

I nodded my head in confirmation and then finally thought to ask, "Where am I?"

"My father's castle," she replied. "Should I change the dressing on your wound?"

I turned my head toward my shoulder where a moment before her hand had been. I saw that the blanket on me covered my chest, but my shoulder and upper arms were naked, and a bandage was tied around my bicep.

"Your body was full of scratches and bruises as if you had rolled down a cliff," she said, "and there is an enormous bump on the back of your skull. We were afraid you would never wake."

"How long have I been here?" I asked, still wondering where exactly I was.

"Three days," she said.

"But how did I get here?"

"A fisherman found your boat floating out in the bay. He saw you were dressed like a foreigner, so he pulled your boat to the village and then notified some soldiers; he feared you might be an enemy of some sort. My father and I immediately came down to see you, and I insisted we bring you up to the castle so I could look after you."

"But who are you, and who is your father?" I asked.

"I am Isolde. Some call me Isolde of the White Hands," she replied. "I am the daughter of Hoel, Duke of Lesser Britain."

"Duke Hoel," I repeated, trying to place the name, for it sounded familiar. "But Lesser Britain—that's Brittany—that's in France. Did I really drift here from Cornwall?"

"Brittany most certainly is not in France," Isolde replied, her nostrils flaring. "Nor will it ever be if my father and King Arthur have anything to say about it. We will not let that pagan Clovis' monster children take over our land."

"Clovis?" I said, trying to remember my history. "Clovis of the Franks?"

"Yes. I have nothing against his wife, who is a good Christian, but even though he was baptized, it did not keep his sons from warring against one another and causing discord among their own people, as well as their constantly leading raids into Lesser Britain. I will have nothing to do with such sinful warmongers."

As she spoke, my head began to throb and my eyes to blur. I kept blinking, trying to bring the room back into focus—and it was a curious room that I definitely wanted to observe better. Was that really a tapestry with a unicorn on it that I saw hanging on the wall at the foot of my bed? Could I really be in a medieval castle in Brittany?

"Did you say King Arthur?" I asked as the name finally registered in my brain.

"Yes," she replied. "He is my father's cousin."

"And you said your name is Isolde—Isolde of the White Hands?"

"Yes," she said, "but lie down. You are terribly pale. You look as if you are in shock. Should I fetch the surgeon?"

"No. I'm...I'm just surprised," I replied.

"So am I—surprised that you are alive. But you must be hungry. Let me go get you some food. You have not eaten in days."

I realized I was starving. In fact, my stomach decided to growl.

"I will be back in a moment," she said, smiling at my stomach's demands, but I noticed that her eyes did not light up as they should have when her mouth smiled.

Isolde left, and I lay still until she returned, thinking I must be dreaming, but I did not want to wake up until I saw what might happen next. In about ten minutes, she returned with a tray containing some delicious broth with pieces of fish in it, as well as some bread and water.

"I would have brought you wine, but I feared your stomach might not handle it well since you have not eaten in days. Be sure to eat slowly so your stomach can adapt."

I pulled myself up into a sitting position again, ignoring the pain in my back in my eagerness to eat. Isolde set the tray upon a table and then handed me the bowl of broth and a piece of bread. She gave me no silverware, not even a spoon, and she did not seem to know what I meant when I asked for one, so I took the bread and dipped it in the soup, soaking up the juice. When I had finished the bread, I tipped the bowl to my lips and drank down the rest. I felt strange eating in such a vulgar manner with a beautiful young woman watching me, but I was too hungry to be polite, and with no spoon, she gave me no other choice. Within a few minutes, I felt the strength coming back to me.

But no sooner had I eaten than I needed to relieve myself. Embarrassed, I admitted this fact to my hostess.

"There is a chamber pot in the corner there," Isolde replied. "Are you able to steady yourself upon it, or should I call one of the male servants to come and assist you?"

It was such a little pot that I could not imagine it supporting my weight. I would have to squat over it, and I did not know if I had the strength to do so, but neither did I want to ask for assistance, so I told her I would be fine. I was afraid I'd end up splayed on the floor, but I would risk it rather than let anyone see me in so compromising a position.

Isolde assisted me out of the bed, casting her eyes away as I wrapped the sheet around my waist, and then when she saw I could take a few fairly steady steps, she said, "I will wait outside the door. Call me when you are finished or if you need anything."

"I will be fine," I replied, hoping she would not be the one to empty the chamber pot after I had finished; after all, she was a duke's daughter.

Somehow, I managed to balance myself over the tiny pot, and when I had finished, I used the water she had brought me to wash myself. I did not ask for toilet paper. I knew there would be no such thing in the Middle Ages. I could not imagine how these people lived in such a way, but such was the case.

Isolde must have been listening for my movements because I had scarcely sat on the bed, not even put my legs back beneath the sheets, when she returned.

"I will take the tray away," she said. "You should probably rest for a while now."

"I have been doing nothing but resting," I objected. I wanted to get up and walk around the castle, but I knew I was not strong enough.

"Nevertheless," she said, "you must not strain yourself the first day you are awake. Lie down and rest. I will come and check on you later."

I know not whether she did check on me again because I was asleep within seconds of her leaving the room.

The next thing I remember was waking to see the first streaks of dawn in the sky. For a long time I lay there, marveling at the beautiful tapestry of a unicorn hanging before me and wondering why people in the twenty-first century did not still have such tapestries in their homes. And then I sat up to look out the window and watch the sun rise over the most picturesque little village and harbor I had ever seen. I knew then for certain I was in a castle, for I could see its ramparts below me and soldiers marching upon them.

After a little while, Isolde opened the door. The sun was shining right where the door was so that when she entered the room, she was momentarily blinded, which gave me the opportunity to notice how red her eyes were, as if she had been crying. But when she saw I was awake, her face lit up into a smile, and she said, "Good morning."

"Good morning," I replied.

"I have asked my maid to bring up your breakfast, and I'll stay to serve you," she offered.

"That's not necessary," I said. "I feel quite well today. In fact, I'd like to move around some."

"I was hoping you would say that," she replied. "After breakfast, I'll find you some clothes to wear. Perhaps you could go for a walk in the gardens, and then, if you are not too tired, my father, Duke Hoel, would like to meet you."

"I would like that," I said, now accepting that somehow I was not dreaming but truly in medieval Brittany. My adventure was about to begin.

CHAPTER 2

L EAVING MY ROOM that morning was an event in itself. Isolde brought me fresh clothes to wear, which looked far too expensive for anyone but a nobleman. "Thank you. They are very fine," I said with gratitude. "Are they your father's?"

She hesitated, then said, "No." Because of the painful look in her eyes, I thought it best not to inquire further. Perhaps they belonged to someone whom she grieved, maybe a dead brother since she had mentioned no other family member than her father, and that would explain the sadness in her eyes.

She gave me instructions on how to find my way to the banquet chamber where her father would receive me, and then she left me alone to dress myself.

Once I was clothed, I followed her directions, making my way down a large stairway that left me wondering how anyone had ever carried me up it on a litter. When I reached the bottom, a serving maid curtseyed and said she would lead me to the banquet hall. As I followed her, I noticed how stark and cold the walls were. There were tapestries, but they did little to enliven the castle. It was quite primitive, truly, with great cold gray stones everywhere that made me long for the warmth of Delaney Castle, a few centuries old itself, but with modern heating and other conveniences.

The banquet room held several tables, placed together and able to seat fifty or more men. Seated at one end was an older man, perhaps sixty or more years of age as evidenced by his gray hair, but I could see he had the bulk to have once been a warrior.

Although I knew Hoel to be a duke and not a king, in politeness to him as my host, I bowed when he saw me. He acknowledged my act of respect with a nod of his head, and then he gestured for me to approach, saying, "Come; sit and have a glass of wine."

I did as he bid, seating myself at an angle from him, as I said, "It is a pleasure to meet you, Your Grace." I used what I knew was the proper form of address in twenty-first-century England for a duke since I did not know what was proper in sixth-century Brittany.

Duke Hoel gave a wave of his hand to dismiss formalities, and after asking me to be seated and pouring me some wine, he asked me to tell my story.

I was hesitant to share all the details. I feared he would think me crazy if I told him I was from the twenty-first century, and I was still having a hard time believing that I was not dreaming, so I simply told him that my brother and I had been fishing off the coast of Cornwall when we had been caught in a storm, and somehow, I had been hit on the head and blacked out. I concluded by saying that I did not know what had become of my brother, but I understood from Isolde that I had been found in the boat, washed up on the shore of Lesser Britain.

"Yes," Hoel replied. "We suspected you might have been the victim of the dragon's wrath. While our land was not ravaged by his attack, even here in Lesser Britain we saw the great dragon pass through the sky, and in the days since then, I have heard many tales of devastation from emissaries sent by my cousin, King Arthur, to see how we have fared and to report that much of Cornwall and southern Britain was devastated. Thankfully, the dragon has not been seen since, but the damage is clearly extreme."

"Was my brother found?" I asked, realizing that by the dragon he meant the comet, but I did not bother to correct him. I was more concerned to learn about your welfare, Lance.

"We only know," said Hoel slowly to soften the blow to me, "that you were found alone in the boat. I daresay many were lost at sea; I do not know whether we shall ever know what became of your brother. I am truly sorry to say so and wish I could give you more details."

I nodded, struggling to hold back my tears as I tried to accept that I might never see you again, Lance.

"It was a curious boat you were in," said Hoel, after a moment. "Very strangely made. Is it Roman?"

"Yes," I replied, thinking it best not to try to explain it was a modern sailboat. "My father had it made for us."

"Then you traveled far to come all the way from Constantinople," said Hoel, "for I doubt you came from Rome where the Goths now rule."

"Yes, from Constantinople," I agreed, thinking that saying the boat came from what is the most civilized and advanced city on earth in this time would be the best way to explain it.

"Your clothes were quite strange as well, more like undergarments, and yet with strange metallic bits to them."

"You refer to what is called a zipper, I believe," I said, knowing he referred to my shorts I had been wearing, and to sound authentic, I added, "They are newly invented in Constantinople."

"But what were you doing in Cornwall, then? You're not Cornish, are you? I warn you, I think little of Cornishmen, and for good reason."

"No, I am not Cornish," I replied, reluctant to say more.

"That is good. I would not refuse a guest in need of refuge, regardless, but I do not trust Cornishmen."

"May I ask why?" I asked, curious and surprised by his remark.

Hoel hesitated a moment before saying, "I have my reasons. I do not know you well enough yet to share my miseries with you. But tell me, stranger, what is your name?"

"Tristan," I replied.

"Tristan! Why, it is a Cornish-sounding name!"

"It may be," I said, "but my parents simply chose it because they liked the sound of it."

Hoel growled and then took a long drink of wine as if to calm his nerves.

"I don't suppose you can help what your parents named you," he finally said, setting his cup down. "Tell me; how do you feel? You had quite a lump on your head when you arrived, but it looks as if the swelling has gone down now."

"I'm still a bit dizzy," I replied. "At least I felt that way when I was walking down the stairs, but overall, I can feel my strength coming back to me."

"What will you do when you are recovered? Where will you go?"

"I do not know," I admitted. "I would like to try to find my brother to learn for certain whether he is dead or alive."

"I'm sorry to say that he probably is dead if he were not found in the boat. Drowned most likely," said Hoel. "I'm certain the dragon's fury has resulted in many dead, many of them burnt so badly their corpses will never be identified. The messengers from Britain say the land there is now like charcoal for miles and miles, a veritable wasteland."

"Still," I said, "I must look for him. I will go back to Cornwall to make inquiries."

"How will you get there? You have no money, no possessions. All we found in the boat was yourself and your torn clothes. The sea's waves clearly washed away everything else."

"I do not know," I admitted, feeling defeated. I was alone in a strange world without a friend or resources.

"How will you earn your living?" Hoel continued. "Do you have any trade, any skill?"

I took a sip of wine before answering, thinking that to say I was involved in supporting twenty-first century charitable organizations would make me sound like a priest. After a moment, I said, "I have been trained as a knight and soldier." It was true—since Great-Gramps had trained us as such—and while I did not relish warfare, I was not going to become some sort of serf in this medieval world.

"Very well. I have need of good knights," said Hoel. "There are always foul Saxon pirates about and petty lords seeking to invade my land to rob me. If you wish to remain here, perhaps I could give you a commission in my army."

"I would be grateful so to serve you, at least for a short time," I replied, thinking there was no sense in my wandering about the medieval world aimlessly. I thought I could still make inquiries for you, Lance, while serving Hoel, and after I had earned some money, I could then journey back to Cornwall to seek you. Otherwise, I would have no resources to travel at all.

"Good. We will pay you soldier's wages then," said Hoel, "provided you are worthy. I will have you tested by my sword master in a few days after you have regained your strength."

"I much appreciate it," I replied. "I fear you are correct that all my possessions were destroyed by the dragon. I will have no home to return to, no money, no clothes. I will earn even these clothes on my back if I am permitted to continue to wear them, and I thank you for your generosity in the meantime."

"No," he said. "I have sent for clothes from the village for you. I do not want to see you wearing these garments again."

He said it so adamantly that, unable to restrain my curiosity, I asked, "Did they belong to a family member? I noted some sadness in your daughter; I apologize for intruding upon you if you are currently in a time of mourning."

"My daughter's emotions are none of your concern," he replied, taking another long drink of wine as if to stifle his anger. After wiping his mouth, he added, "Isolde is kinder to strangers than most of them deserve. I warn you that if you take any advantage of her kindness, it will go ill with you."

"I understand," I said, sensing it was best to placate him, and I certainly did not wish to hurt the beautiful and kind Isolde in any way.

Hoel took one final swig of his wine, and then slamming his cup down on the table, he got up from his chair. "I have a dukedom to oversee," he said, "so I will leave you now. You are free to walk about the castle and gardens as it pleases you, and once you feel your strength has returned, I will have my sword master test your skills and prowess."

"Thank you, my lord," I replied, standing up and bowing to him.

He again dismissively waved his hand, and with a grunt, he left me alone in the banquet room.

CHAPTER 3

AFTER HOEL LEFT me, I could not bear returning to my room upstairs, so I spent that day wandering about the castle. I introduced myself to the servants, who bowed or curtseyed and asked how they might serve me, but their manner was cold when I tried to be friendly, causing me to think they were uncomfortable associating with their betters. I soon realized they mistook me for some great lord from Constantinople, for Hoel must have said something to one of them about my origins, and word had spread among them so that they thought me something I was not. But I decided I could use that to my advantage; I did not wish to deceive anyone, but I also knew that if I maintained an illusion of being someone important, I would have more mobility in this class-conscious world, and therefore, be better able to search for you, Lance.

As the days passed, my strength returned. I began to ponder how I might eventually escape this medieval world and return to the twenty-first century, but first, I wanted to see what I could of this time in history; after all, I was living in the time of my ancestors, and since Hoel was King Arthur's cousin, I hoped in time he would decide to visit Camelot, and then I could accompany him there. It would not only give me a thrill to see our ancestor, King Arthur, but perhaps then I could speak to Merlin or Morgan le Fay, and one of them could help me locate you and figure out how to return to our own time.

After a few days, I did have my trial with Hoel's sword master, Sir Cowan. He had me engage in mock combat with several of Hoel's other knights, and when it was finished, I had bested three of the four, and the fourth only won because I had grown fatigued, so I received high praise from everyone. I was quickly added to Hoel's army, and in our daily trainings, I was proud to see not only my strength and skill returning to me, but that my muscles grew larger and firmer, and my endurance and stamina greater than they had ever been when we trained as teenagers.

During this time, Hoel grew to like me, and he often insisted I dine with him and Isolde and the one or two other intimates of his household, including Sir Cowan. Hoel said I had the makings of a great champion someday, and even Sir Cowan admitted he had never but once in his life seen a man with such skill at arms as I had.

"And who might that man have been?" I asked.

"We do not speak his name in this household," Hoel snapped before Sir Cowan could answer. I was surprised to see the anger in the duke's eyes, matched only by the pain I saw arising in Isolde's. Quickly changing the subject, Hoel said, "Of course, King Arthur is a great soldier, second only to Sir Bedwyr. Had Arthur arrived in time, he would have saved my niece from being killed by that damned giant."

"Father, please, let's not talk of that," Isolde said. "It's been years now. Let it rest in peace."

Hoel again changed the subject, though it left me wondering whether this niece's death was the cause of the sadness I continually sensed in the household. I wanted to ask whether it truly had been a giant, but I dared not interrupt Hoel, who had begun recalling his own glory days as a soldier.

"In my youth," Hoel said, "I fought beside Arthur's father, Uther Pendragon. Oh, how we used to send the Saxons scurrying back to their ships and frozen lands." And he launched into a long and tedious tale of battle, complete with army maneuvers and graphic descriptions of slaughter. I tried to follow all the disorganized details he spewed forth since Uther Pendragon is our ancestor, but I admit I was deathly bored by Hoel's stories. He seemed content, however, just to have me nod to show I was listening; when I occasionally asked a question, he seemed irritated, as if I were not paying close enough attention, and I admit I often wasn't.

I was wondering instead what could have caused this family so much pain. The loss of a niece was sad, but Isolde had said the niece's death was years ago, while the pain in her eyes seemed far fresher. The garment Isolde had given me that first day could not have belonged to anyone but a male, yet I saw no other man of high enough rank in the castle to dress in such finery. Perhaps the clothes had belonged to the great knight whom Sir Cowan had referred to that Hoel would not speak of. Was this mysterious knight the cause of Isolde's sadness?

One evening, Hoel began telling me about the beauties and wonders of the Forest of Brocéliande, and how Merlin had supposedly been imprisoned in a cave there by the Lady of the Lake. I expressed a desire to see this place since, Lance, we had visited there last year with Mom and Dad when we were traveling in France. You'll remember all we saw then were a few stones, an old broken down dolmen I think it was, so I was curious to see what it had looked like fifteen centuries earlier. Furthermore, I knew Merlin had told our parents he had never been trapped in a crystal cave or any other such place by anyone, so I wondered what, if anything, had inspired such a story. Hoel told me that Brocéliande was the source of many other remarkable tales besides those associated with the cave—fairies had been sighted making their homes in the trees, mysterious women had appeared beside sparkling fountains, and magical beasts roamed about freely. When I expressed a desire to see this legendary forest, Hoel said, "We will go a-Maying there; the fresh air and summer sunshine will do us all good."

At first, Isolde did not seem interested in going, but Sir Cowan also urged that we go on such a pleasure outing; he said his knights would enjoy the excursion and Isolde could bring some of her ladies-in-waiting. When Isolde saw the enthusiasm of the rest of the court, she did not wish to disappoint them and finally agreed that we should go the next day.

It was a warm summer's morning when we left the castle—just a couple of days past midsummer; I found it hard to believe I had already been at Hoel's court for a month by then. Because I hoped this outing would lead to others, including a longer journey to Camelot, I kept mentioning to Hoel and Isolde as we rode how much I enjoyed traveling.

When Hoel asked where else I had traveled, I mentioned only places of antiquity I had seen in my twenty-first century journeys, such as Rome, Constantinople, and the older places in England like Stonehenge, since I obviously could not explain the United States to him, or even the Eiffel Tower. He seemed receptive to hearing my descriptions until I mentioned Ireland, and then it was Isolde who said, "I think we've had enough of chattering today. We are missing the lovely bird songs." I was surprised by this remark since she had always seemed eager to talk to me before. I could only think that the mention of Ireland had somehow upset her.

When we were well into the wood and not far from where Hoel said Merlin's Tomb lay, we stopped to have a picnic lunch, and after we ate, several of the knights and ladies-in-waiting wandered off in small groups to frolic in the forest, collecting flowers to make garlands and simply teasing each other as young men and women will do.

Being eager to see Merlin's Tomb, I asked Duke Hoel whether he would now show me the way.

"I'm afraid I'm too old to walk so far," he replied, "and after eating all that food, I need a nap, but take Isolde. She knows the path."

I was overjoyed by this suggestion. I had not dared to ask her, fearing her father would think me forward, so I was glad to think he trusted me to be alone with her, and I would not betray his trust. Nor would I have done anything to upset her, for I found I was falling in love with her, and I also sensed that she was like a wounded animal who needed delicate care.

Isolde, however, was not keen on the idea and suggested she should remain with her father. Was she uncomfortable being alone in my company? Could she not see by now how I felt about her?

"Nonsense," Hoel told her. "Ranulph here will keep me company." Ranulph was his squire, and I was glad to hear he would stay behind. I felt sorry that the young boy would not get to explore the woods, but I would not forsake my time alone with Isolde for his sake.

"I would be honored, milady," I told Isolde, "if you will show me the way. You cannot know how greatly I desire to see this place."

"It's not really worth seeing," she replied. "It hasn't changed since I was a little girl, and no one called it Merlin's Tomb in those days. Besides, I don't think Merlin would have been foolish enough to get locked up in it."

"No, but legends have to start somehow," Hoel said, lying down. He closed his eyes while he waved his hand to dismiss us. "Go now and let me sleep."

Isolde hesitated another second, then said, "Very well," and sighing as if irritated, she gave me her hand so I could help her to her feet. I was surprised she would even let me touch her, for she had grown more distant since I had recovered from my illness, but I still believed she liked me. And I was beginning to like her a great deal, but I also knew that to love her could only bring me pain if I were still to return to the twenty-first century.

After we had entered the forest together, I asked, "Would you like me to collect flowers for you?" I had seen the other knights doing so for her ladies-in-waiting, so I did not want her to think I was any less gallant.

"Oh, no," she said. "I'm too old for such things."

"Too old?" I replied. "You can't be a day past twenty."

"Most women are mothers by my age," she stated.

"Still," I said, forgetting at what young ages medieval women married, "you are young and beautiful, and you deserve to be clothed in flowers. I do not know how to weave them into garlands, but I will gladly collect them for you."

"No," she said. "Flowers are for the young and innocent—and the joyful."

"You certainly qualify in all those categories," I replied, although I knew I was wrong about the last one.

"You mean to be kind," Isolde said, walking on ahead of me a little, "but you do not know me well enough to make such a statement."

I followed behind her for quite a ways, not knowing how to respond. She walked on for about a hundred yards, not looking back, but looking up at the sky, as if to listen to the birds' songs. I did not want to be obtrusive since she clearly wanted to be alone with her thoughts, but I stayed close enough to protect her if the need arose.

Finally, we came to a clearing with a large boulder in its center.

"Here," she said, turning around to face me, "is one of the marvels of Brocéliande that you came to see."

"This big rock?" I asked, seeing nothing remarkable about it.

"It is a magical stone," she said, and she smirked, as if teasing me, but my heart beat faster to see her spirits lift a little.

"What kind of magic does it have?" I asked, joining in the joke.

"You do not believe me, do you?" she replied.

"You look as if you are jesting," I said.

"It is an old fairy tale," she explained. "It is said that if you throw water on this rock, a great booming sound will be heard and then the sky will open and rain shall fall."

"Have you ever tried it?" I asked.

"No," she said, definitely smiling now.

"Why not? How else will you know whether or not the story is true?"

She laughed and said, "I've always been afraid of getting wet and ruining my gown."

"I am sure you would look beautiful wet," I replied. "Are you game to try now?"

She looked at me, mischievously, and then, shrugging her shoulders, said, "Perhaps, but I haven't any water."

Reaching for the drinking flask on my belt, I said, "I do." I removed the flask and held it out to her, saying, "I dare you."

She looked at the flask and then at me. For just a second, she hesitated, and then laughing, she grabbed the flask and quickly poured water onto the rock.

We waited, but nothing happened.

"I guess that solves that mystery," she said, "and now you are out of water."

"It is worth it," I replied, "because it made you laugh, and it is the first time I have seen you do so since I have come to Lesser Britain."

I had barely finished speaking when a loud clap of thunder filled the air. Isolde jumped with surprise, and then I looked up and saw lightning flash across the sky.

"Quickly," I said. "It's going to pour, and we need to get away from these trees before lightning strikes them."

Grabbing her hand, I looked about, wondering where we should go, and then she pointed across the clearing to a small cave in the side of a hill. We set off running, I trying to go slow enough that she would not trip on her gown, which I admit gave me extra time to relish the touch of her hand in mine.

The rain started before we were halfway to the cave, but it fell lightly until we could take shelter. We had just stepped into the cave when the raindrops began to come down in sheets.

"Are you cold?" I asked, pulling off my cape and putting it around her shoulders before she could answer. I admit my hands lingered on her shoulders a tad longer than necessary.

When I had finished, I returned to standing before her. She giggled, as if enjoying our little adventure, and for just a second, I thought about kissing her, but then I saw she was shivering and her face had turned pale. Was she afraid of me?

"Come farther back," I said, gently taking her hand. "The wind is blowing the rain inside."

But she held back, even when I released her hand and stepped back myself. Did she fear I would take advantage of her? Could she not see how much I loved but also respected her for all her kindness toward me?

"Come; you'll get wet," I repeated.

"No," she said. "You do not understand...."

"What don't I understand?"

But rather than answer me, her eyes grew wide, and then I realized she was looking over my shoulder. Fearing perhaps we had entered a bear's den, I spun around, my hand reaching for my sword, but I was not at all prepared to see the cave's walls glowing white, much less to see them spring to life with images, as if they were multiple movie screens. Of course, Isolde would not know what a movie screen was, so she was far more surprised than I, but I was quite astonished myself.

"What is it?" she gasped, clutching my arm and looking terrified as we saw a knight riding his horse across the screen as if he were headed directly for us. She leapt out of his way, but I grabbed her, saying, "They are just images; they are not real."

And then we watched as Isolde herself appeared on the screen.

"It—it can't be me," she muttered. But it was. The knight had stopped his horse beside her and dismounted, and when he removed his helmet, the Isolde on the screen kissed him, but the Isolde beside me let out a shriek.

"How? How?" she asked. I could not answer now, for I was engrossed in watching the knight passionately sweep her up in his arms. But I did not see more, for then the real Isolde swooned into my own arms, and I grabbed her just fast enough to prevent her from falling to the ground. Then the cave went completely dark. Everything was eerily silent for several seconds as I held her, not knowing what to do. Finally, a thin beam of sunshine shot into the cave from outside. Turning, picking Isolde up to carry her, I saw the rain had stopped. I brought her out of the cave, and seeing no one, I hollered for help.

In another minute, Sir Cowan and a couple of Isolde's ladies-in-waiting came running. Upon seeing Isolde in my arms, the women ran up to us and began fussing while Sir Cowan said, "Stand back. Give her room to breathe." After drawing the women away, he asked me, "What happened?"

"I—I don't rightly know," I said. "We went inside the cave to seek shelter from the storm...and then...and then she fainted."

"Merlin's cave," muttered one of the ladies.

"Witchcraft," said another. "How could you let her go in there?"

"It was pouring rain," I replied.

"Do you need help carrying her?" asked Sir Cowan.

I felt embarrassed and sternly said, "Certainly not. I only hollered because I didn't know my way back."

"It's this way," said one lady, starting off in the direction where we had left Duke Hoel. I quickly followed her, Sir Cowan by my side, acting as if he feared I should drop Isolde, but nothing on earth would have caused me to do so.

In a few more minutes, we found Duke Hoel and his squire waiting for us. Upon seeing the unconscious Isolde in my arms, he quickly jumped to his feet with concern.

"It's all right," I said. "She just fainted." I laid her down on the picnic cloth, and then one of the ladies pressed a flask of water to her lips. After a moment, Isolde opened her eyes, looking dazed and bewildered. When Hoel asked her whether she was all right, she did not reply at first, but she sat up. He had to repeat the question before she answered.

"I had the strangest dream," she said, and then looking at everyone in turn, she finally focused on me and said, "I think Sir Tristan did as well."

"She is confused," I said. "I think the lightning must have frightened her." I did not want to reveal the truth, for I suspected she had recognized the knight whose image we had seen in the cave and that he was the cause of her fainting and the sadness I had sensed in her since we had first met.

"No, I—I—" she stuttered, trying to find the right words. And then she seemed to think better of it and said, "I'll tell you later, Father. I would like to go home now please."

And so we did, although she did not feel strong enough to ride alone on her horse, so Hoel asked me, "Sir Tristan, will you let my daughter ride with you to make certain she reaches home safely?"

I was surprised but honored by the request, sensing that because of his age, Hoel did not feel steady enough on his own horse to hold his daughter as well.

"I would be honored," I replied, and after mounting my horse, I reached down a hand and pulled Isolde up in front of me.

Honored indeed was I to have the most beautiful woman in the world sitting before me, resting her head against my chest, with one of my arms about her waist. For miles, we rode like lovebirds, all the way back to the castle. *If only she truly did love me*, I thought, but I feared she only sought the comfort and not the love of my embrace. I had, at least for now, been defeated by the image she had seen in the cave.

When we reached the castle, Isolde's maids quickly led her up to her own room. I was about to bring my horse to the stable when Hoel stopped me.

"Sir Tristan," he said, "you look as if you need a good warm bath and a fire after being caught in the rain. Take your time, but when you have finished, come to my private chambers. We will dine together there in private, for there is something I wish to discuss with you."

I bowed, accepting his command. Then after returning my horse to the stable, I went up to my room where my squire had already drawn me a bath beside a crackling fire. I took my time about bathing, for I was lost in thought, pondering the strange events in the cave and how they might be related to the mysterious sadness I often saw in Isolde's eyes.

An hour later, I was in Hoel's chamber, where a meal had already been laid out for us. I joined him at a small table, and after the servants poured our wine, he dismissed them, ordering them not to interrupt us.

"Help yourself to the food," he said, "and while you eat, I will tell you what you no doubt have wondered about since you have arrived here—namely, why my daughter appears to be overcome at times by sadness—and I will explain to you the strange occurrence she has just now told me that you both saw today."

"Yes, please do explain," I replied. "She seemed very upset by the vision."

Hoel's eyes teared up at these words, and he took a moment to compose himself before sighing and saying, "Then you will not doubt what I am about to tell you. Please understand how difficult it is for me to speak of these matters, but I fear that not to do so will only cause that pain to grow in my daughter's heart. There is no one else with whom I can share my sorrow, for a ruler does not tell his troubles to his steward or his stableboy, but because you are the son of a great lord of Constantinople and have shown yourself noble in speech and manner, I feel I can trust you with my tale. I find it difficult to trust anyone, understand, for the last man I trusted and gave shelter to under this roof turned out to be the cause of all this trouble that has come upon our household."

Hoel paused and took another sip of his wine, as if choosing his words carefully. Then he launched into the story of the great unhappiness that had marred Isolde's life, as well as his own.

CHAPTER 4

HOEL'S TALE

I HAVE TOLD you that in my youth I fought alongside King Uther Pendragon. And perhaps you are aware of what soldiers were like in those days before King Arthur took the throne and established a code of honor among soldiers and knights. In short, they were lovers, but far from respecters, of women. The behavior of men such as King Pellinore and many another lusty young knight were legendary, and King Uther himself was just as bad as the rest of them, for no doubt you know how our good King Arthur was conceived through deceit when Uther Pendragon disguised himself as Gorlois, Duke of Cornwall, to trick Gorlois' wife Igraine into sleeping with him.

I was one of those who remained aloof from this sort of behavior. In many a village we visited after a battle, I saw for myself the horrible treatment of women being raped and brutalized by men. Knowing how I would feel if my own mother, wife, or daughter were treated in such a way, I vowed always to be gentle and kind to all women. I also vowed that I would only love one woman rather than bring a string of bastards into this world. And not until peace came to Britain and Uther rewarded me for my service with this dukedom did I even think of marriage.

Unfortunately, I was not wise in my choice of a wife. As soon as I began to think of marriage, I let my eye be caught by a young maiden who served in this castle. From the beginning, I was surprised by her forwardness to me, her lord, but she was a beautiful woman, and I was greatly flattered that she was so eager to please me. I soon found myself every night fantasizing about her until I decided there was no reason to put off marriage any longer, for why fantasize about a woman when you can have one in truth? And being Duke of Lesser Britain, I felt I could marry whom I pleased. Of course, vassals are to ask their king's permission to marry, but as a relative to Arthur, who had just come to the throne, I dismissed it as a formality I should not trouble him with. And considering the debacle of his marriage with his half-sister, Morgana, he was in no position to upbraid me for marrying a serving girl. And so I proposed to this maiden whom I thought I should love for the rest of my life, and she, with much gratitude expressed toward me, accepted. Her name was Isolde; our daughter is named for her.

I did not seek to inquire about Isolde's family background. She told me her parents were dead, and since she did not seem to have any relatives, I saw no trouble in that. Only later did she confess to me the truth about her parents' deaths. She had come from a village many leagues hence where her father had died of sickness and her mother, who was a wise woman, knowledgeable in herbs and their healing properties, had been accused of witchcraft and poisoning her own husband. Isolde's mother was taken by the villagers to the village square and burned alive. Isolde had been forced to watch this horrible event, and then she had been imprisoned; only by luck did her jailor one night forget to lock her cell, and so she managed to escape.

Of course, Isolde wept as she revealed all this to me, and I was much grieved to see all her distress. I proposed then that I go and destroy this village and slay its inhabitants, but she would not have it. She told me the villagers were narrow-minded Christians who refused to understand the Old Ways, but to condone murder would make her no better than them; then she promised me that her mother had not killed her father, but had simply been trying to heal him with her herbs.

That my wife might be the daughter of a witch did, I admit, disturb me, but I did my best to dismiss it. For some time after that, Isolde and I were quite happy. She gave me my beautiful daughter, whom I insisted we name for her, and just a year later, she gave birth to our son, Kahedin. I gather you have guessed that I had a son. In truth, he is still alive, though dead to me now, but that is getting ahead of my tale. One day, when Kahedin was but a few months old, he became ill with fever. I wanted to fetch the doctor, but Isolde refused, saying she could heal him. I was aghast when she not only gave him strange smelling potions but spoke words over him in a tongue I did not understand. I began to fear now that my wife herself might be a witch, but that same night, Kahedin's fever broke and he was soon well again, so once more I dismissed such thoughts.

When the Feast of Pentecost came that year, the spring weather was good, so I thought it time I should present my wife, of now two years, to King Arthur. And so we traveled to Camelot and stayed as guests at the court. Another guest at the court during that time was the young King Anguish of Ireland, who had come to participate in the tournament being held as part of the festivities.

For three weeks, we were at Camelot, and in all that time, I suspected nothing. And then the morning we were to begin our journey back to Lesser Britain, I woke to find that Isolde was not beside me. I quickly dressed and then made inquiries of the servants, but no one had seen her. When I went down to join Arthur and Guinevere at breakfast, Isolde was still not to be found. I continued to make inquiries and soon learned that the only other person missing that morning was King Anguish of Ireland. It did not take me long to realize he had run off with my wife. That he was a villain I could believe; what I could not believe was the message Isolde sent me the next day: "Do not come after me. I love Anguish. I will not return to you." It was Isolde's handwriting, her name was signed to the letter, and I was made a cuckold.

You can imagine the shame I felt to have everyone at Camelot know my wife had left me for a man who was scarcely old enough to have a beard. Nor did I have any means of redress, for the King of Ireland was no subject to King Arthur, and therefore, clearly felt no need to uphold the moral code when he was beyond the reach of punishment. Arthur refused to lead an army against Anguish, saying he would not begin another Trojan War over a woman who clearly had not been abducted but had chosen to leave me. Arthur did try to speak words of comfort to me, but I despaired over the situation's hopelessness. I was too proud to chase after Isolde, and realizing she had equally abandoned our children, I focused my energies upon raising and loving them.

After a year's time, I learned that this evil woman—for what else could she be if she would abandon her own children?—had given birth to King Anguish's child. Worse, she had the audacity to name the girl after herself, thus also giving the child the same name as her elder half-sister, save for using the Irish spelling of Iseult, instead of Isolde.

I cannot tell you how difficult it was all those years to answer my children's questions about their mother. I was tempted at first to tell them that their mother was dead, but I knew in time the truth would come out, and so I simply told them that she lived in Ireland, and a little at a time, I gave them additional information, such as that she was a queen there, and she had chosen to be a queen rather than a duchess. When they asked me how she had become a queen, I told them she had married another. My children were loyal to me, and without my having to say anything derogatory about their mother, in time they realized she had betrayed me, and I think they loved me all the more because of it.

Far too quickly, the years passed, and soon my children were nearly grown. I knew it would not be long now before Kahedin would be Duke of Lesser Britain, for I was growing old, my body suffering the aches and pains that result from years of warfare. Not having the stamina any longer to train my son in swordplay as I would have liked, I hired Sir Cowan to be sword master and tutor to him. As for Isolde, I began to ponder who might be her future husband, considering all the eligible young men in Britain—earls, dukes, and barons—as possibilities. I admit, I even thought Prince Mordred might be a potential husband for her, until he decided to marry that Saxon wench; she's nothing to look at from the glance I got of her at their wedding. I scoped out many prospective grooms for Isolde at that wedding, but I would not let my children attend it, for I feared King Anguish and their mother would come, and I did not wish a scene between them and my children. If that woman wished to see her children, which she clearly did not, she could visit us in Lesser Britain. Fortunately, their absence from the wedding saved me a confrontation with her.

Not long after I returned home, I received a message from Lord Mark of Cornwall, asking whether I would take his nephew, Sir Tristram, into my service since he desired to serve under a foreign ruler. Of course, I agreed, for I had heard high praise of Sir Tristram's prowess as displayed at various tournaments, and I had not yet heard any gossip about him. I could not imagine why Lord Mark would wish Sir Tristram to serve at my court since it is hardly as splendid as those of the truly great kings and princes of Christendom. But I cared not what his reasons were because I thought Sir Tristram would be a good companion to Kahedin; perhaps he could even teach my son more about modern warfare and knightly skills since Kahedin had now learned all Sir Cowan could teach him.

About this time, the Earl of Grippe's men began to raid my lands. Kahedin, being a headstrong and brave lad, rode out to punish the earl and his knights. My son was of good prowess and skill, but the earl and his men were treacherous, so they managed to ambush him. Though Kahedin fought valiantly, they outnumbered him, eventually relieved him of his sword, and took him captive. Then for three days, they beat him, starved him, and finally sent him home to me, a bloody misshapen mess.

You can imagine the grief I felt at the sight of my beaten son, but Isolde told me not to fear, for unknown to me, she had been studying some of her mother's old books about herbs and medicine, and through what she had learned, she was able to heal her brother's wounds; only a scar on his cheek remained to show he had ever been ill. I feared her having such a skill, for it was rumored that her sister, Iseult, had also learned to be a healer from her mother. I worried that their common interest might eventually draw these half-sisters together; for all I knew, Iseult might be a shameless woman like her mother, and I did not want her to influence my daughter away from the path of virtue.

I thought it best then that I marry off Isolde quickly before she could cast eyes on any other man. Since Prince Mordred was now taken, I selected a neighboring wealthy baron for my daughter's husband. When I raised the matter of such a marriage to Isolde, she did not object, but simply said she wished to wait until Kahedin was fully recovered from his wounds.

While Kahedin was still healing, Sir Tristram arrived at my court. I did not think very highly of him at first, perhaps because he was young and strong while I was well past my prime and, thus, jealous. I admit he was a veritable Adonis with his golden hair and brawny arms, but perhaps it would be more accurate to compare him to Narcissus; it was immediately apparent that he thought very highly of himself, and women obviously did as well, for I caught several of the serving maids casting glances at him.

And instantly, I feared the worst—that Isolde would fall in love with him. He was beneath her station, but I could have gotten past that. It was how he was so obnoxious, the way he swaggered about as if he feared nothing, that irritated me most; at the same time, I admit I wished perhaps Kahedin could be bolder like Tristram, especially since my son's courage had seemed to desert him after his first failed skirmish. When Tristram learned how Kahedin had been wounded by the Earl of Grippe's men, he declared he would teach them a lesson. I think Tristram would that very moment have mounted a horse, ridden to Grippe Castle, and sliced the earl's head off if we had let him. Kahedin, however, insisted that if there were to be revenge, he would be part of it—well, I hesitate to admit it, but what my son actually said to Tristram was, "I want to be there to see you give him what he deserves." I was alarmed to think my son would merely be an onlooker and not a participant in our revenge, as if he needed this brash young knight to fight his battles. And in the days that followed, I noticed more and more how my son's eyes grew large with worship for Sir Tristram's skill and abilities as the two of them trained in preparation to attack the Earl of Grippe.

A few days later, though I dreaded the contest, Tristram and Kahedin rode out together to the Earl of Grippe's lands, and when four of that ignoble man's minions attacked them, Tristram quickly cut down three of them, while Kahedin managed to wound the fourth, who went back to the earl with terms that demanded the return of all that he had taken from me.

We waited then two days for the earl's emissary to send retribution for raiding my people's crops and stealing their livestock, as well as robbing travelers upon my lands. When no emissary came, Tristram led my army, invading the earl's domains, putting all who opposed him to the sword, burning the earl's people's crops, battering down the gate to Grippe Castle, and returning with jewels and golden goblets wrapped in rich tapestries.

I was astonished, delighted, and embarrassed all at once. I had not sought revenge to such an extent, but Kahedin told me not to be unhappy. "No one will dare attack or raid us now that it is known Sir Tristram is your champion, Father," he said, adding, "and someday mine as well when I am duke."

And so Sir Tristram came to hold a place of respect in our home. Unfortunately, he thought this gave him the right to be disrespectful by looking at my daughter. I would have put a stop to it immediately except that I caught her looking back, and then I began to fear that if I tried to stop it, she would run off with him, just as her mother had run off with King Anguish. I also noticed about this time that Tristram and Kahedin's discussions would often lead to disagreements, and in the heat of the argument, Tristram would raise his voice, yelling at my son, despite Kahedin being his better by birth, until Kahedin would give in to him. There was little I could do. I felt old and helpless, and I grew fearful of what might happen if this bullying continued, especially after I was gone.

Then one day, Kahedin told me he had given Tristram his blessing to take Isolde's hand in marriage. I was furious. I told him he had no right to make such an agreement. I was Isolde's father, so only I could give her hand in marriage, and I was planning to marry her to a neighboring baron. But Kahedin said, "Father, if that is so, Tristram may leave us, and you know I am not strong enough to hold your dukedom on my own."

"Not strong enough!" I exclaimed. "You are skilled in swordplay and combat, and did not you defeat the knight who went running back to the earl as his messenger?"

"I was bold only because Tristram was with me," Kahedin confessed, "and I knew if the other knight got the best of me, Tristram would intercede. Father, I am afraid of battle. I am ashamed of myself, but the truth is that I am a coward. You do not know how easily the Earl of Grippe's men bested me—"

"They ambushed you and they outnumbered you, but you fought bravely and—"

"No, I lied. I grew fearful when I faced just one of the earl's men; I could barely lift my sword to defend myself. I am a coward. I am not fit to tie Tristram's bootstrap. Please, I hate to think what will become of our land once you are gone because I will not be fit to hold it on my own."

"I suppose next," I retorted, "you will hand over your dukedom to Tristram, as well as your sister's hand?"

"No, Father. Tristram does not expect that."

But I had my doubts. It seemed like Tristram found a way to take whatever he wanted.

Immediately, I called Isolde to me and demanded to know whether she truly wished to wed this upstart knight.

"He is the greatest knight in the world, Father," she replied. "I know people say Sir Bedwyr is the greatest knight, but I have never seen him, and Sir Bedwyr is one-handed now, so he cannot possibly be greater than Tristram. Would you not wish me to marry a great knight? And Tristram is of noble blood, related to the Dukes of Cornwall."

I was not convinced by this argument—he was but a nephew to Lord Mark, who was a distant relative—a second cousin at best—to Duke Cador of Cornwall. But I could not deny my daughter's wishes when I saw how badly she longed to marry Tristram, and if Kahedin were as much a coward as he himself confessed, I had to admit it would be for the best. Perhaps Tristram would not make a great duke, but he would keep the lands in my family's possession until Isolde should have a son grown who could rule, especially since Kahedin also seemed to be afraid of women; hopefully, Isolde's son would inherit his father and mother's best qualities.

And so, with great sorrow, I saw my daughter wed Sir Tristram.

Not long after, Tristram began to act as if he ruled my household.

When I reminded him that it was I who was Duke of Lesser Britain, he wisely held his tongue, but I did not like the menacing look in his eyes. Still, I knew all families must go through times of transition when someone new enters the fold, and so I told myself all would be better once my grandchildren were born.

However, as the months went by, I found Tristram's behavior more and more domineering and unbearable. He often spent the evening drinking with the other knights. He ordered about my servants as if they were his own, and he bullied Kahedin into doing whatever he wanted, including spending his money on him when I refused to give Isolde any more for him to use.

Meanwhile, I waited and waited for Isolde to become with child, but it never happened, and when I questioned her about it, she refused to answer. I even questioned her lady-in-waiting, but she only shook her head and told me the sheets were always without stain in the morning.

And then came a letter from Cornwall, from Lord Mark's wife, Iseult. Understand that we were all ignorant until that time as to the reason Tristram had come to my court, thinking it solely that he sought to see the world beyond Cornwall. I had no idea then that he had ever been to Ireland, much less that he had known Iseult before she had gone to Cornwall to marry Lord Mark. I did not even know that Iseult had married Lord Mark. By that time, my children knew they had a half-sister, but they had never expressed interest in seeing her. Now she was married to Tristram's uncle and communicating with us for the first time.

Iseult wrote to congratulate her husband's nephew Tristram on his marriage, and she invited him and his new bride to Cornwall for a visit. She made no mention of her relationship to Tristram's wife—I do not know whether Iseult realized yet that Tristram had married her half-sister, or whether she even knew the truth of her mother's past and that she had siblings. But the invitation made Isolde very happy, for she was eager to meet Tristram's family as well as her own half-sister.

I cautioned Isolde that she might well be disappointed by such a journey. I had not heard pleasant stories about King Anguish's character, and I, of course, had a poor opinion of Iseult's mother; therefore, I feared Iseult would not be a pleasant woman, but I also knew I should not judge her for her parents' sins.

When I told Isolde I feared her expectations for this journey were too high, she confessed, "I will be able to have time alone with my husband during the journey. He will be away from his drinking companions and have nothing more to do on the ship but spend time with me, so I hope finally to conceive his child."

I doubted it would work out how she dreamt, for I knew too well the fickleness of men, but I did not wish to dash her hopes, so I consented to her making the journey.

Alas, none of our hopes were to become reality! The morning Tristram and Isolde were to leave, my daughter woke to find a letter penned by her brother Kahedin, saying:

> Dear Sister,
>
> Tristram bids me write to tell you he cannot insult his true lady, La Belle Iseult of Cornwall and Ireland, by bringing you as his wife to her court. He has long loved her, and he deeply regrets his marriage to you and any pain it causes you for him to leave you in this way.

As for myself, Tristram is the greatest knight in the world and my best friend, and so I have decided that rather than remain here, I must see the world and travel with him. I do not know when or whether either of us will return.

Give my love and apologies to Father.

Kahedin

You can imagine how heartbroken Isolde was by this letter. I can't say I was surprised by Tristram's departure, but that he was Iseult's paramour, or whatever their relationship was, did surprise me. Worse, to think that my own son should be foolish enough to leave with the man who was betraying his sister! And yet I had to admit that I had suspected how jealous Kahedin was when Tristram gave his affections to Isolde rather than him. Like his sister, I am certain Kahedin will also have his heart broken by this ignoble knight.

We did not hear from Tristram or Kahedin again, but about a month later, Isolde received a letter from Iseult.

Dear Sister,

You cannot have Tristram back. He is mine and I have loved him since first I healed him of his wound when he came to Ireland. I have made him heartsick with love for me so that no other woman's affections will ever be a remedy for what only I can provide him. Do not pursue him. Do not seek to have him back. Just as my father proved himself more capable than your father of winning our mother's affections, so I have won Tristram's love from you. I have left Lord Mark. Tristram and I will now be together even if it means spending our lives wandering from one land to another, going wherever fortune brings us. It matters not so long as we can always be together.

Iseult of Ireland & Cornwall

This venomous letter nearly broke Isolde's heart. She was miserable for three days, and I feared she would truly die. Fortunately, Sir Tristan, you then arrived on our shore. I am certain your presence has distracted her enough to keep her alive, but I know she remains miserable.

I cannot bear to see my daughter in so much pain. I have seen in your eyes, Sir Tristan, that you are fond of her. I fear she may never love anyone but Sir Tristram, yet I suspect you are as strong a knight as him, and I am certain you are a far better man. In any case, I have no one else from whom I can ask such a great boon. Will you go to Britain, find Sir Tristram, and persuade him to return? I do not mean for you to persuade him by words. I want you to fight him. Defeat him. Shame him so if he will not return, at least he will no longer dare to call himself a knight, for knights should be loyal and true to their ladies, and that whorish young lady he loves is not his lady in the eyes of God. I know I have no right to ask this deed of you, but there is no one else I can ask. My own son has been fool enough to fall under Tristram's spell. Understand, King Anguish stole my wife and my happiness. I will not permit his daughter to steal my daughter's husband and her happiness. Will you do this for me and for Isolde?

CHAPTER 5

TRISTAN'S TALE CONTINUES

WHEN DUKE HOEL had finished his tale, I was saddened, horrified, and also puzzled as to how to answer him. I was horrified that any man could treat Isolde as Sir Tristram had, but I was also puzzled whether it was my place to take up this quest. I was no marriage counselor. Yes, I could go and plead Isolde's case, but I doubted very much that Sir Tristram would listen to me if he were so enamored of Iseult, who seemed—well, quite frankly—to be a real bitch.

"Let me think it over," I finally said to Hoel, but as soon as I said it, his whole posture drooped in dejection.

"I am sorry I have asked," he sighed. "You do not owe us this favor. Even though we rescued you from possible drowning and took you in and fed and clothed you and welcomed you as if you were a family member rather than a stranger, I cannot expect it from you."

"It is not that I am ungrateful," I said, searching for words. "It's just...."

"It is not your duty. It would be different if you were Isolde's brother, but you see, her brother has proven himself a fool, pining af-

ter Tristram like a lovesick girl and pursuing him around the countryside. I do not understand why God has decided to treat me like
Job and let such ills fall on my head in my old age—to have a milksop
of a son, an injured and heartbroken daughter, a whore of a wife, not
to mention a niece killed by a giant. If I were twenty years younger, I
would go myself and demand justice from Sir Tristram, but instead,
I am a no-account, bone-weary old man. I may be a duke, but I can't
lead an army against him. You are my last hope for resolution of this
matter. If it is not resolved quickly, that daughter of a whore may become pregnant with Tristram's child, and then he will never return
to his rightful wife."

Hoel's anger was getting the better of him now, and I watched as
he turned red until he saw the surprise on my face and tried to calm
himself.

"I see," he repeated, shifting his eyes to the floor, "that I am imposing upon your goodwill and asking you to intercede in a matter
that is truly none of your concern."

Feeling sorry for the old man, and simultaneously angry at myself for letting him manipulate me, I replied, "I can go and plead
your daughter's case...but I cannot force Sir Tristram to return."

"You can if you defeat him in battle," said Hoel, his whole frame
perking up with hope at my words. "You can if you shame him," he
continued, becoming quite animated, flinging about his arms to il-
lustrate his words, "if you place a sword to his throat and make him
swear on his honor—though the blackguard has little of it—to do
your bidding."

I was surprised by these heated words. I again reminded myself
that I was no longer in the twenty-first century, but in a time when
vigilante justice was perfectly acceptable. I admit, I did rather like

the idea of thrashing Sir Tristram, and I did feel sorry for Isolde, but I would have preferred to comfort her in other ways. If I had not been trapped in the wrong century, I might have considered replacing Sir Tristram in her affections, but I knew that to try to do so now would only hurt her more. So, in the end, I agreed to take up this quest because it would allow me to return to Britain and search for you, Lance, and find someone like Merlin who could help me.

So, finally, I replied, "Duke Hoel, I will go to Britain and try to find Sir Tristram, and if I do find him, I will plead your daughter's case to him. But please understand that I am still concerned about what became of my brother. If on this journey, I find my brother before I locate Sir Tristram, I will have to abandon this quest because my first duty is to my brother, and he and I will need to return home to our family. If that happens, or if I cannot find Sir Tristram or persuade him to see reason in this matter, I will send you word so you know the result."

"Oh, I have no fear that you will complete the quest," Hoel replied, his eyes lighting up, "for I have seen how honorable you are in the short time you have been here. Therefore, I agree to all your conditions. I am not overly hopeful you will succeed, but we cannot know what might happen unless you try. In three days' time, you will leave. In the meantime, we will prepare for your trip; I will provide you with money and rations for traveling, and clothe you in the best armor, and I will write you a letter of introduction to King Arthur so he will aid you in locating Sir Tristram. It would be best that you go to Camelot first. Surely, someone there will have heard of Sir Tristram's whereabouts."

Camelot! Finally, I would have a chance to go there. Of course, King Arthur was Hoel's cousin, so doubtless he would help me in making Sir Tristram return to his wife. More importantly, Camelot was the home of Merlin, the only one I thought might have the power to tell me, Lance, where you were, or how to return to the twenty-first century.

But one matter still troubled me.

"Shall we be telling Isolde of my mission?" I asked Hoel. "If not, what shall we tell her is the reason for my departure?"

"We shall tell her," Hoel replied. "It will give her hope."

"But what if I should fail?" I asked. "I do not want to see her more disappointed than she already is."

"If you fail, then she will come to realize what a worthless man is her husband, and hopefully, her grief will turn to anger, which in turn will make her strong again."

"Anger is not strength," I replied.

"It can be," said Hoel. "But, hopefully, she will not have to find her strength through it. I will go tell Isolde of your quest now; she may have a specific message for you to give her husband."

After Hoel left me, I went for a walk in the forest to ponder over this matter and ask myself whether I was doing the right thing. But now that I had agreed to this mission—to bring a wayward, adulterous husband home to his wife—I could not go back on my word.

I found Isolde glowing when I returned to the castle. She must have seen me approaching, for she met me at the outer gate to the gardens. Instantly taking my hand, she said, "Come; you will be my champion in this mission to my husband, and I will send you off in the best armor possible." Then she led me upstairs to her very own chamber. I did not think it seemly for me to enter there, but she insisted, and there she opened a wardrobe, which contained within it the finest suit of armor I had ever seen, complete with a blue shield.

"It is Tristram's armor," she told me. "I bought it for him as a wedding gift. It matches perfectly the armor he always wears; his old armor was quite battered, so I wanted him to have something new. But he left so swiftly that he forgot to take it with him."

Or perhaps, I thought, *he did not want any reminder of the wife he left behind.*

Wearing Tristram's armor did not in any way appeal to me, but I could not refuse Isolde.

However, she had not yet finished making her requests.

"When you reach Britain and before you find my husband," she said, "you must seek out the Lady of the Lake and tell her of your mission. She is a great lover of justice, so she will clearly understand how my husband has wronged me; she can provide you with the means to make him return to me."

"I don't understand," I replied. "What is this 'means' you speak of?"

"A love potion, most likely," Isolde replied. "For it is said that the Lady of the Lake is skilled in spells and potions."

"A love potion? But how will I get Tristram to drink it?" I asked. "And how do you know it will make him love you and not Iseult?"

Suddenly, my mission seemed ridiculous; I was not to go on a knight's quest, but rather to play Cupid to star-crossed lovers.

"The Lady of the Lake will know what to do," Isolde simply replied.

"And where am I to find this Lady of the Lake?" I asked.

"In a lake...it does not matter which one, for she has the ability to appear in many of them, but simply call for her at each lake you pass and she will eventually come to you."

Isolde spoke as if she had complete faith in this plan. I had not known that the Lady of the Lake gave out anything but magical swords, but here I was in the time of King Arthur, and I had already seen water on a rock create a rainstorm, been in an enchanted cave, and heard how Hoel's niece had been killed by a giant, so why should I doubt the Lady of the Lake's abilities?

And so I agreed to find this mysterious water fairy, or whatever she might be, and seek help from her so Isolde could regain her husband. In three days' time, I set off for Britain. After I crossed the channel, I asked for directions and headed toward Camelot. I have traveled now for several days, stopping at every lake I come to, shouting for the Lady of the Lake to show herself, but I have never received any response to my greetings.

Earlier this evening, I crossed a river, and in doing so, I fell from my horse. My saddle came loose and was washed away with what little food and money I had left. Then my horse ran off, and I was left to wander the land on foot with only my sword and my armor. I did not know what I would do, but then I came to this great plain as night fell. I saw Stonehenge on the hill as the sun set—I recognized it instantly and walked toward it. But when I saw your fire, I became fearful, for I did not know what kind of reception I might receive. I had only stepped close enough to see you were alone when you jumped up and demanded to know who I was. I recognized your voice just the second before you called my name, and I cannot tell you how happy and relieved I am to have found you.

PART III
THE QUESTING BEAST

CHAPTER 1

"TRISTAN, WHAT A remarkable story," said Lance when his brother had finished speaking. "The marvels you speak of seem to be nearly as surprising as those I've experienced myself. They confirm for me that I am not crazy or dreaming, for here you are in the flesh, and you have also experienced at least one magical event and been told to seek the Lady of the Lake, whom I have seen, though I am not inclined to seek her out further. This world we are in, then, must truly be real if we have both experienced it, and hopefully, together, we will figure out how to get home to the twenty-first century."

"Yes," said Tristan. "I am relieved to find you also, and I want to figure out how to get home, but I also feel I must finish my quest. Will you help me?"

"What? To find the Lady of the Lake so you can help her convince Tristram to return to Isolde? I don't think we should mess in such affairs. You know from movies we have seen what happens when people time travel and mess with the past. I feel sorry for Isolde, but we must let Tristram meet his fate on his own or it might alter the future and then we won't be able to return to our own time as it was. Furthermore, Viviane does not seem willing to help me."

"How can you be certain of that?" asked Tristan. "Did she not give you a quest also—to find the True Cross? Perhaps finding it will help to bring about what we seek. Yes, I want to get home, but I also think there must be a reason why we have been sent back in time to Arthurian Britain, and now that we have found one another, we should embrace this opportunity. After all, mankind has dreamt of time travel for centuries, yet here we are, the first to have ever succeeded at it. Think of what we can learn here, what knowledge of the past we can bring back to the twenty-first century, to make available to those of our own time so they have a better understanding of history; our findings might even advance science for all we know!"

Lance did not share Tristan's enthusiasm. Yawning, he said, "I am too tired to think of all that now. It must be long past midnight, and we have both traveled a long way, and who knows how much farther we have yet to travel? I think it best that we get some sleep. Then we can make our decisions with clear heads in the morning."

Tristan readily agreed to this. Soon, they had made themselves comfortable on the ground and fallen fast asleep.

Lance slept soundly, yet he woke early, too excited by his reunion with Tristan to let sleep hold him in its clutches for long. The morning sun was just coming over the horizon when he woke, and he again enjoyed watching its beautiful rays shine between Stonehenge's pillars. Then he got up and dug in his saddle for some fruit and bread and also his flask of water so they might have breakfast.

By the time Lance had finished this simple chore, Tristan's eyes had opened.

"Good morning," said Tristan, immediately smiling, and he quickly jumped up to join his brother, equally sharing in Lance's joy at their having been reunited.

They ate and talked again of their adventures, asking each other questions while Lance's horse found breakfast in a patch of grass nearby and from a couple of apples Lance tossed to him.

When they had finished eating, the brothers dressed in their armor. Lance rinsed out the dirt in his helmet from using it to dig the night before, and it quickly dried in the morning sun. Once they were dressed, Tristan asked, "Can we both ride on your horse?"

"I don't see why not," said Lance.

"I'm sorry I lost my horse," said Tristan. "It would have helped us to travel more quickly, and if we end up being challenged by a black knight or some such opponent, I won't be much use."

"I have not been challenged yet," said Lance, "and the only knight I have met is Sir Palomides, but it wouldn't hurt for us to practice our swordplay a little and limber up before we go riding about the countryside in search of another lake."

"You mean you're willing to help me find the Lady of the Lake?" asked Tristan.

"If that's what needs to be done before you will help me find our way back home, then I guess I'll have to," Lance said. "I wouldn't want you breaking a promise. But first, let's practice a little. It's been years since we were trained in dueling and swordplay, and we want to be ready if we do meet a foe."

Tristan smiled broadly. After putting on his helmet for protection, he pulled forth his sword.

Lance gave the horse a pat and told it to "Stay." Then he also donned his helmet and unsheathed his sword.

The brothers were soon moving in a circle, distancing themselves from the horse, before they engaged one another. They did not, however, distance themselves from Stonehenge, but rather, losing all sense of propriety and reverence for the monument in their sudden joy and boyish play, they were soon leaping up on the stones, hiding behind them, and ducking to allow the giant boulders to take blows intended for themselves.

Quite the sword contest ensued, and any Hollywood director would have loved to film it all in one take. Arms swung, swords rang together, and there was also much laughter and many good-natured taunts.

Both brothers were so intensely focused upon their contest that neither saw a mounted knight approaching across the plain. Nor did they hear him until he had dismounted some twenty feet from them. Suddenly, Salisbury Plain rang out with the words:

"Prepare to die, traitor!"

Tristan turned his head to see a knight running toward him with a sword. The momentary distraction kept him from raising his sword quickly enough to block Lance's blow. Before anyone knew what was happening, Lance's sword had struck just beneath Tristan's helmet and deeply wounded him in the neck. Blood squirted forth as Tristan dropped his sword, his hand reaching for his neck, his eyes staring into his brother's before he collapsed on the ground.

The unknown knight now approached. His sword still raised, as if to do battle with Lance.

"You fool!" shouted the knight. "You have stolen from me my righteous vengeance. I should kill you in his place."

"Be silent!" exclaimed Lance, dropping his sword and rushing to Tristan's side. He pulled off his brother's helmet, allowing more blood to pour forth. Then he saw the shock on Tristan's face and watched his eyes roll back into his skull.

"Tristan, I am so sorry," cried Lance.

But Lance's words were interrupted by the assailant knight, who seeing Tristan's face revealed, exclaimed, "No, it is not him. How can this be? He wears Sir Tristram's armor."

At these words, Lance looked up, recognizing Sir Palomides' voice. He instantly removed his own helmet so the knight should know him.

"My friend, I—" stuttered Sir Palomides, removing his own helmet now. "I did not know—"

"It is my brother," said Lance; then he turned back to Tristan. "Don't leave me, Tristan, please. How will I ever explain this to Mother and Father? Please, stay with me."

Tristan was struggling to breathe.

"Go to my saddle and get me some cloth, anything, so I can stop the bleeding," Lance ordered Palomides. Still in shock, the knight did as he was bid.

"It's no use, Lance," said Tristan. "I—I feel the life going out of me."

"Don't talk," said Lance. "You'll only make it worse. I'm so sorry, Tristan. I didn't mean to do it. I didn't—"

"It's not your fault," said Tristan.

By now, Palomides had handed Lance his old T-shirt. Viviane must have placed it in his saddlebag. Lance quickly rolled it into a ball to apply pressure to Tristan's neck.

"Don't worry, Tristan. As soon as we get the bleeding to stop a little, we'll get you to a doctor." He did not know where he would find one, but for the moment, he spoke to comfort his brother.

"It is too late," said Tristan, beginning to tremble.

"No," cried Lance. "No, don't say that. Do not leave me, Tristan."

"Lance," Tristan said, now gasping for air, "finish my quest. Find the Lady of the Lake. Get the potion. Send Tristram back to Isolde."

Palomides let out a swear at these words; Lance wasn't sure what the knight said, but he recognized the tone. Ignoring him, Lance replied, "No, Tristan; you will do those things yourself." But he could see death creeping into his brother's eyes.

"I cannot," said Tristan, "but do not fear, Lance. It will all be well."

"I do fear," cried Lance. "Please, do not leave me. Do not die on me. Do not leave me alone here."

"No, you do not understand," Tristan calmly replied. "I die *for* you."

And then Tristan's eyes glazed over and his shaking ceased.

Lance clasped his brother's hand, but it was already limp.

"I am sorry, friend," said Sir Palomides, who now placed his hand on Lance's shoulder. "Sorry it was your brother. I did not mean to hurt him."

For a moment, Lance felt he should be angry, but Tristan looked so peaceful now. Lance breathed deeply and then closed his brother's eyes. And after a minute, he let go of Tristan's hand and stood up.

Palomides looked cautiously at Lance, as if afraid of his wrath, but Lance said softly, "You did not mean it. You could not know, and you are not...the one who killed him. I understand why you mistook him for Sir Tristram."

"It is not your fault either," said Palomides, but he could see Lance was lost in grief and not listening to him.

"It is my fault," said Lance. "Why did I ever touch a damn sword? I killed him. I may not have meant to. It may have been an accident. But I killed him, regardless."

Palomides again placed his hand on Lance's shoulder. "I did not have the honor of knowing your brother," he said, "but I am sure he would not want you to blame yourself."

Lance looked down at the ground as tears began to spring from his eyes.

After a moment, Palomides said, "I will leave you alone with him for a little while." Then he went and stood by his horse, waiting until Lance was more composed.

Lance sat down again beside his brother's now lifeless form. He was overcome with grief. The tears streamed from his face. Exhausted, he lay down on the ground and held Tristan. Then anger consumed him. He pounded on the earth, he shook his brother's corpse, begging him to come back to life, and finally, he lay on his back, staring up at the sky, his eyes closed, his throat sore from sobbing, until he felt calm enough to think rationally again.

He did not know what to do now. Tristan was gone. What unkind Fate had brought about this strange turn of events? First, Tristan and he had been thrown into this strange world; almost immediately, they had been separated. And then, after what appeared to be some three months, they had been reunited. Lance had never known such joy in his entire life, and yet now they had been separated again after only a few hours together, and this time permanently.

A million confused thoughts passed through Lance's mind, one quickly replacing the other so that none of them were really coherent. He felt exhausted, dazed, grief-stricken, frozen, completely unable to know what he should do next.

Finally, he heard Palomides approach him again. "Let me help you bury him," the knight said.

Bury? At first, the word was incomprehensible to Lance. Bury his brother? So he would never see him again? To leave his body cold and in the ground? How could he do that?

"No, I—I must bring him home to my parents," Lance said, feeling overcome with despair as he realized the impossibility of such a task even as he said it.

"And where is that?" asked Palomides. "To Constantinople? You cannot bring the body that far. It will begin to decay."

"I can't bury him!" cried Lance. "I just can't."

"Some cultures," Palomides replied, "set their loved ones on barges; they send them off to sea. We might do that if you wish, or we could build him a funeral pyre."

"No, I will not have him burnt," Lance insisted. He knew cremation or burial were the two most normal ways to dispose of a body, but somehow, he could not bring himself to do either. How could he leave his brother here? How could he return to his parents without him—if he ever did return?

"Come; you must decide what to do with his corpse," said Palomides. "He will soon start to smell, and that will draw maggots and wild animals who will want to feast on his body."

Lance shivered at the thought. He almost wanted to reprimand Palomides for such a grotesque remark, but he knew the words were true.

Sighing, he finally said, "We will send him off on a barge."

"There is no lake here," Palomides replied.

"We will bring him to one then," said Lance, suddenly beginning to think coherently again. "And he wished me to finish his quest—to find the Lady of the Lake and receive a love potion from her, so I do not doubt she will know we are searching for her."

"A love potion?" asked Palomides.

"Yes," Lance replied, and he briefly explained to Palomides about Tristram and Isolde and Iseult, and why Tristan had been wearing the adulterous knight's armor, which had caused Palomides to mistake him for his enemy.

"I am not surprised by any of this sordid tale," Palomides said when Lance had finished. "Nor do I like the idea of seeking out the Lady of the Lake. I have heard many contradictory tales of her, and I am not certain we can trust her to aid us."

"I have actually met her," Lance replied as he stood up. "It was through her powers that I survived sinking in the mud. I believe she will help us." And yet Lance had his doubts, and for that reason, he held back from telling Palomides all he had experienced in his own visit to the Lady of the Lake, for parts of that visit still disturbed him, and he remained skeptical that Viviane was willing to help anyone. She might only wish to use him for her own purposes. Still, Lance did not know whom else he could turn to if he wished to complete his brother's quest, and he knew he would dearly like to see Ileana again, for her beauty had been unsurpassed in his eyes. Whatever Viviane's motivations, she had made it clear to him that there were reasons for everything, and perhaps he should not doubt that since she could see all things; she might even be watching him now. She would know he was looking for her. "There must be a body of water somewhere nearby," he said to Palomides. "Will you help me find it and bring my brother to it?"

Palomides nodded, adding, "We should be able to carry his body on one of our horses, and while we walk, you can tell me all about your meeting with the Lady of the Lake."

Lance was reluctant to do so, but he was too exhausted to argue.

"All right," he said. He had no one but Palomides now to help him, and while he knew the knight could never fully understand what he had gone through in coming to this strange land, he thought perhaps Palomides would also tell him what he knew of Viviane, and that would enlighten him on what course now to pursue.

CHAPTER 2

WITHIN THE HOUR, Lance and Palomides had hoisted Tristan's body onto Lance's horse and managed to tie it down with some rope Palomides had. Lance hated to see his brother in such an awkward position, so they covered Tristan with Lance's cape. Then, because Lance was too nervous about watching the body to lead the horse, Palomides led it while Lance led Palomides' horse a few steps behind so he could keep an eye on Tristan's remains.

As they walked toward where Palomides believed a lake lay several miles in the distance, beyond the edge of Salisbury Plain and Lance's view, Lance told Palomides about his visit to Viviane's underwater kingdom and how she had given him his horse and armor to continue his journey. He explained in great detail all the wonders of Lyonesse, but he did not mention the scenes from his life that Viviane had caused him to witness, nor how she had known he was from the twenty-first century since Lance knew Palomides would not understand such matters.

"It is hard to believe," Palomides remarked when Lance had finished, "that your meeting with the Lady of the Lake seemed to take but a few hours, and yet you were gone for three months, but I know it was at least that long since I saw you sink into the mud."

"Yes," said Lance, "but tell me what you have been doing all this time. Have you found the Beast Glatisant since I last saw you?"

"I have not seen the Beast," said Palomides, "though it has not been from lack of searching for it. I did find what your brother told you to be very interesting because while I was parted from you, I traveled to Camelot. I learned that Tristram and Iseult had sought refuge there, but Queen Guinevere sent them away, refusing them hospitality because of their adulterous ways."

"So where have they gone then?" asked Lance. "After we find the Lady of the Lake, I will need to find Tristram."

"I heard they had headed to Scotland. King Anguish has reputedly refused them entrance to Ireland, but I think in time they will return there, for King Anguish has no son and will need an heir, or else the other Irish kings will seek to overthrow him."

"I don't know how I will convince Sir Tristram of anything," said Lance, wishing he could relinquish his quest; going to Scotland to find the wayward knight was not something he relished. He only wanted to learn how to get back home to his parents, but he would not forsake his promise now to his brother.

"I doubt Tristram can be convinced of anything; he is much too pig-headed," Palomides agreed. "It would be better if we killed him; it would be righteous punishment for his sins."

Lance was silent. Palomides' hatred of Tristram had led to the killing of his own brother, and while Lance did not blame Palomides, realizing it had been an accident, he could not understand how people in this time could be so ready to murder each other. No doubt, Tristram was a louse, but did he deserve the death penalty for his actions?

"Surely," Palomides continued, "this Lady Isolde of Lesser Britain can do far better for a husband. If she is as beautiful as your brother said, perhaps I could wed her myself."

"Do you really think that after you kill her husband," said Lance, "she will wish to marry you?"

"And why not?" Palomides asked. "I would not be the first man to do such a thing, and I am no Christian who turns the other cheek. Sir Tristram has wronged me, and I would be doing both her and myself a favor to rid her of such a villain. Furthermore, I would be proving myself the stronger man and, therefore, the one better able to be her protector."

Lance was speechless. How could these people think in such a way? Lance did not want to be privy to killing anyone for any reason. Wasn't it horrible enough that he had caused the death of his own brother? He wanted to vomit at the thought of it, and at the sight of his brother's corpse lying on the horse before him; to think that he would never speak with his brother again was overwhelming.

As Lance began to sob, Palomides kept his eyes before him, unwilling to embarrass his new friend by taking note of his unmanly behavior.

After an hour or more of walking, it became clear that Palomides had been mistaken about the location of the nearest lake. Nevertheless, they kept moving forward, Palomides saying they were headed in Camelot's direction anyway, so Lance hoped he might still receive help from Merlin, and there was bound to be a lake eventually.

As they walked, Lance could not believe how sparsely populated Britain was that they should not see a soul all day. Not until late afternoon did they come upon any sign of habitation, and that was only a small cottage, built against a mountain; in fact, it was built over the mouth of a cave, and a hundred feet from its door, a small spring ran through the meadow. Neither Palomides nor Lance had eaten, and they were both thirsty, having nearly emptied their water skins that they carried, so Lance stopped to water the horses at the spring while Palomides went to the cottage to ask for sustenance.

From a distance, Lance could hear Palomides exchanging words with the cottage owner, although he could not make out what was said nor get a good view of the man. But after a couple of minutes, the knight returned with a man of middle-age, slightly graying hair, and substantial build and strength. Despite his powerful physique, the man was no warrior but dressed in a brown robe that made Lance think him a friar or member of some other religious order. The man approached Lance with a glowing smile.

"Welcome!" he said. "I am Brother Baudwin. I am a hermit here, but I welcome passersby, and my friend Palomides tells me you are in need of assistance."

"I am Lancelot," Lance replied, allowing the man to clasp him by the forearm in greeting. "It's a pleasure to meet you. Do you and Palomides already know each other?"

"Indeed, we do," Baudwin replied. "I have met him at tournaments in times past when I was myself a knight."

Lance was not surprised by this remark, though his curiosity could not keep him from asking, "Whatever possessed you to leave off being a knight to become a hermit?"

Baudwin raised his eyebrows. "Do you not think a hermit is as good as a knight?"

"It—it's not that," said Lance, embarrassed and afraid that he had offended the man. "It's just...being a knight is exciting; the quiet life of a hermit must be a big adjustment."

"It is a big blessing," Baudwin replied. "But my personal reasons would only bore you, and you must be famished. Come inside and I will find you something to eat. My supplies are meager, but there is bread and cheese, and I have some berries I will be happy to share with you."

"We should not stop," Lance replied, gesturing toward his brother's corpse. "We seek a lake in which we may send my brother to eternal rest, and we also seek the Lady of the Lake."

"You have my sympathies for your loss," said Baudwin, making the Sign of the Cross with his hand in the direction of where Tristan's corpse remained on the horse. "But it will be nightfall in a couple of hours. You will not reach a lake in time, but in the morning, if you follow this stream, you should reach the lake by noon. Your brother will keep until then. Come; I will help you carry him inside where the cave's chambers are cool, and there he will be well-preserved. If you leave him out here in the sun, his body will quickly begin to rot or wild animals might try to feed upon it during the night."

Lance had to admit it had been a long day of walking, and he also realized he did not yet feel ready to bury Tristan. Another day would make little difference.

"Very well," said Lance. "Palomides and I thank you for your hospitality."

Fortunately, Baudwin's cottage was warm, if not really comfortable. There were only rushes on the floor for a bed, one small cot that Lance could not imagine Brother Baudwin even fit upon, and a couple of hard wooden benches beside a table. The cave opening off the back of the cottage reminded Lance of a walk-in refrigerator; there Baudwin kept a store of fruits and vegetables as well as herbs, for Palomides said he was a great healer, "and once Constable of Britain under King Arthur."

"That was a long time ago," said Baudwin, dismissively. "Come. Let us eat. There will be time for talk later."

In truth, there was plenty of time for talk, for Palomides' tongue loosened at the sight of an old comrade in arms, and for the first time, really, Lance was able to observe the knight in the presence of others. He found that Palomides loved to boast of his skill at arms and he took great pride in telling Baudwin of one tournament after another he had been in, occasionally recalling Baudwin's own skill at arms. "But all that is past now," Baudwin would say, as if embarrassed by his past. "I barely ever think of those days now."

"Tournaments are the past for me as well," Palomides said, "for now my quest is solely to slay the Beast Glatisant, so that in destroying such evil, my uncle may be recovered from his wound and the land healed."

"The land healed?" asked Baudwin, pouring them each a new glass of wine, which he had made himself. "What do you mean?"

"Healed from the destruction that the dragon did this summer," said Palomides, "and also from the way the Beast ravages the land."

"I know of no dragon or destruction," said Baudwin, doubtfully.

"He did not damage this part of Britain, fortunately," Palomides replied, "but my uncle's kingdom of Listenoise and the land for many dozens of miles around it were all badly damaged by the dragon."

"He speaks the truth," Lance chimed in. "The dragon burnt everything—the trees were scorched and all the land filled with ash for miles and miles, although I imagine most of it has blown away now, and I'm sure the plants and trees will begin to grow again this coming spring."

"I have so few guests and receive so little news," Baudwin replied, "that I have not heard of this dragon. It is truly marvelous to think of—that Satan's minions would dare to scorch our Christian land; it doubtless is because of the sins of those who continue to follow the Old Ways in Britain, but this Beast you seek, Sir Palomides, have you ever even seen it? Are you certain of its existence?"

"I saw it wound my uncle, and I saw it again the same day the dragon passed overhead. Sir Lancelot here saw it as well."

"I did," Lance replied. "It was covered with ash from the dragon's destruction, so it tried to bathe in the sea, but the ash was thick and turned to mud upon it, and before it could finish bathing, it ran off because it knew Palomides was in pursuit of it."

"But what exactly is it?" asked Baudwin.

"It is a beast of sin," Palomides replied, "and though I am no Christian, we know it seeks to work evil among mankind, being the child of a demon."

Palomides went on to tell Baudwin all he knew about the Beast Glatisant, including the Tale of Castus and Incestua, which Lance seriously doubted could be true. He did not know what the Beast was, but he knew better than to believe in some medieval allegorical monster, the love child of a demon. Such a tale sounded like something out of a bad Vincent Price film.

Finally, long after dark and after Lance thought Baudwin should have lost his patience with the chattering knight, Palomides ceased his talking and said he was ready for bed.

The cottage was warm, but Baudwin still found a blanket for each of them to cover himself. He wanted one of them to take his cot, but they both refused and lay down on the floor's rushes, quickly falling into a sound sleep.

CHAPTER 3

JUST BEFORE DAWN, Lance woke, still in a drowsy state, to a soft murmuring voice. Opening his eyes, he saw in the dim morning light the figure of Baudwin kneeling before a cross on the wall. Lance did not understand the words, though he suspected they were in Latin. He listened until the hermit had finished his prayer. Then Baudwin quietly rose from his knees, trying to be thoughtful of his sleeping guests, but by then, Lance had sat up, and turning around, the hermit saw him.

"You are awake early," said Baudwin. "It is not quite daylight yet."

"I couldn't sleep," said Lance. "I—I've had a hard time sleeping lately."

"Yes, I imagine so...considering you have lost your brother," said Baudwin, crossing the room and placing his hand on Lance's shoulder.

The gentleness of Baudwin's touch caught Lance unawares. He had known no true tenderness since he had arrived in Arthurian Britain, but now he found that it opened up his tear ducts. He tried to hold back his grief, but Baudwin, apparently seeing the pain in his face, said, "Shh, we do not wish to wake Palomides. His tongue is too loose, and it would be better if you tell me of your sorrow in private. Let's go outside."

Lance wondered at the man's kindness. The hermit had not even asked how his brother had died or tried to intrude upon his grief in any way, but he now expressed willingness to listen. Feeling the need to talk to someone, Lance followed Baudwin outside. They sat on a bench beside the cottage's front door.

"It is a new day," said Baudwin. "See how the Lord blesses us, giving us the perpetual opportunity to start anew and make today better than the one before."

Lance did not know what to say. He did not see how any day could again be good after he had lost Tristan, and all his family actually, and everything he had ever known or had. He had nothing now. He had been so busy trying to figure out how to get back what he had that not until now had he realized how desolate he felt.

"The Lord is our Shepherd," Baudwin continued. "Everything we need He gives to us, whether we realize it or not, whether we accept it or not."

Lance still did not reply. He wanted to ask why the Lord did not give him what he most wanted—to return to the way his life had been.

"Your brother must have been a good man for you to mourn him so greatly," said Baudwin. "If it would be a comfort for you to speak about him, my ears will bear hearing your tale, no matter how heavy it might be. I have known my own share of grief, and I know what it is to wish someone could carry the burden of it with you."

Lance felt the need deeply to confess what troubled him, but to say it—what he continually thought and yet tried to repress—that seemed too much for him. And yet it would be said; it was forcing itself up from his throat, no matter how he tried to repress it, until the words broke forth in sobs.

"I—I killed him. I killed my brother."

"I see," said Baudwin, nodding his head in acknowledgment.

"I did not mean to. It was an accident. Palomides mistook him for someone else—Sir Tristram—and when he came upon us, he shouted, and that made me lose my focus—you see, we were practicing with our swords—and so I accidentally struck him in the neck with my sword, killing him. He lingered for a few minutes, but...."

Here Lance broke into tears and could not speak further.

"Sometimes accidents happen," said Baudwin, "and we are not at fault for them. When they do happen, I imagine they are to teach us something."

Lance, not able to process Baudwin's words in his grief, continued. "He knew I didn't mean it, but it was still my fault. I just acted—I—I don't know why I was ever so stupid even to pick up a sword."

"In this world," Baudwin replied, "sometimes a sword seems like our only protection. We forget that God is our true protection. But in any case, I'm sure your brother knew you would never intentionally harm him."

"Yes, he knew that. He forgave me before he died. He was not angry, but still, I...."

"Do not blame yourself," said Baudwin, placing his hand on Lance's shoulder.

"I know it wasn't really my fault, but how could something this horrible happen to me? How is it possible that I would kill my own brother? You are a holy man. Tell me why God would allow such a thing to happen."

Lance turned to search Baudwin's eyes, but the hermit turned away, pulling back his hand from Lance's shoulder and resting it in his lap. He then struggled in his search for appropriate words.

"I do not know," he finally admitted. "I wish I could tell you there is a reason for everything; I believe there is, actually, but I cannot tell you what the reason is in this situation. The Lord's ways are mysterious. Even if you knew now the reason, you would probably take little comfort in it, for it would not bring back your brother. And your brother is doubtless in another place now since you thought him a good man. Someday, hopefully, you will understand, but for now, just trust that the experience is intended as the best possible thing that could have happened for you—"

"Best possible thing!" exclaimed Lance. "To lose my brother? How can that be?"

"Please," said Baudwin. "Let me finish."

The hermit waited until Lance's ire lessened, and then when Lance breathed deeply and looked ready to listen, he continued.

"I did not say the best possible thing in this world, for you will no doubt grieve your brother for the remainder of your life, though the pain will greatly lessen as time goes on. But do not forget that there is a world beyond this, and that this world itself is just an illusion."

"Yes, I know you will say I will see him again in Heaven, and I hope that is true," said Lance, "but I still don't see how there is anything good about this experience."

"Such tragedies are not necessarily good for the heart and mind of mortal man," Baudwin admitted, "but they are often the best things possible for the evolution of the soul."

"Evolution of the soul?" Lance repeated. "I don't understand."

"I do not fully understand myself," said Baudwin. "I only know that the soul does evolve. I know that it evolves in this lifetime and perhaps across many lifetimes or at least here on earth and then through time in the afterlife."

"Are you talking about reincarnation?" asked Lance, feeling he was beginning to understand. "But I thought Christians didn't believe in reincarnation?"

"I don't know where you got that idea," said Baudwin. "Yes, there are those in the church today, mostly those bishops and clergy of the East and the remainder of the Roman Empire who deny the reincarnation of souls, but I must believe that they are wrong, for did not Christ himself say that John the Baptist was the Prophet Elijah come again?"

"I—I don't know," said Lance. "I don't remember."

"You should pay more attention to the Scriptures," Baudwin said softly. "They can be a great comfort to you and lead to wisdom that goes beyond man's understanding. I know you may not know how to read—most men of your class do not—but you can listen to the priests to learn about holy writ and also gain knowledge of God and His wisdom through prayer."

"I can read," said Lance, realizing this ability made him unusual in Arthurian Britain. "But now I wish I had paid more attention to what I read. There is much I have read that could help me in this world if I could only remember it." Lance knew Baudwin would not understand his words, and despite how wise the holy man seemed, Lance did not think that revealing he had come from another century far into the future would help him any.

"I understand," said Baudwin. "Plus, it is difficult to find copies of the Scriptures, much less carry them with you when you are a knight-errant. I am fortunate to have a copy of the Bible, and it is my greatest treasure. I read it day and night so I might live by its wisdom."

"And you really believe in reincarnation?" asked Lance. "But how—how does that…. Well, I guess it means I might see my brother again, right?"

"I can only tell you that the Scriptures clearly express that men can live many lives, and many a wiser man than myself has been led to believe it. Men who are truly knowledgeable in the faith, such as St. Gregory of Nyssa, have said that it is absolutely necessary for the soul to be healed and purified, and if it does not happen in this life, it will happen in another."

"Whether I go to Heaven, or I reincarnate," Lance replied, "I guess that means I'll see my brother again."

"I believe so," said Baudwin, "and if reincarnation is true, you and your brother have probably enjoyed one another's company in many lives, so I would not be surprised if you made an agreement before this life for exactly what has happened between you to occur. Your brother must have loved you very much, I think, if he was willing to die so that you might learn from it what your soul needs to know."

"I—I—." Something was stirring up in Lance. Something Tristan had said before he died. What was it? "I think…" Lance said, trying to put his thoughts into words, "I think you must be right. I wonder…. No, I do believe Tristan knew that somehow—that there was a reason for his death. It was very strange, and I didn't understand it at the time because I was so full of grief, but his last words—well, I said to him, 'Do not die on me,' and he replied, 'I die *for* you.' I didn't understand it then, but...but how could he know this—that he had a reason for his death? But then, he always was more introspective, more thoughtful, more of a reader and philosopher than I am. I shouldn't be surprised, I guess, if he did understand."

Baudwin patted Lance's leg. "Your brother appears to have been very wise indeed."

"Yes," said Lance, and then he felt the first bit of relief since his brother's death, and that relief soon turned into a hint of happiness.

Baudwin, as if seeing the seed of healing had been planted, now turned to easier topics. "Tell me, what was your brother like?"

"I'm not sure how to answer that," Lance replied. "He was a wonderful brother in many ways, but we had a very odd childhood. I mean, I can't really explain it to you well because...because my brother and I are not from this place, and so you would not understand."

"Where are you from?" asked Baudwin, raising his eyebrows. "You do speak with a different accent. Are you from Gaul?"

"No," said Lance, wanting to explain his situation but afraid that as open-minded as this religious man was, he might accuse Lance of witchcraft if Lance tried to explain to him about time travel. Not knowing how else to answer, Lance just repeated, "No, I am not from Gaul, or from Britain."

"I am from Lesser Britain myself," said Baudwin, "so I have had dealings with Goths and Franks and many others, but I cannot place your accent."

Not seeing any harm in it, Lance replied, "I grew up in Romania."

"I am not familiar with it," Baudwin said. "Is it far away?"

"It is near Constantinople," Lance replied.

"Constantinople?" said Baudwin excitedly. "Have you been there?"

"Yes, many times," Lance replied.

"What is it like? Does it really shine like gold?" The hermit's eyes were ablaze with longing to hear of the fabulous city of legend.

"Yes," said Lance, thinking that for all he knew, the city might have shined in the sixth century, and he did not wish to disappoint this kind man. "It is everything you ever dreamed it was."

"I am mostly content in my simple life," said Baudwin, "but if I were to travel, it would be only to see that great city." For a moment, the hermit appeared caught up in daydreaming, but then he turned again to Lance and asked, "But then how did you come to be in Britain?"

"I cannot tell you that," said Lance. "I guess you might say I am on a personal quest. I—well, I am seeking Merlin because I believe he is the only one who might be able to help me fulfill it."

"I see," said Baudwin, politely not making further inquiries. "Unfortunately, Merlin has not been seen in Britain for more than twenty years. No one knows where he has gone. Some say the Lady of the Lake has locked him up in a cave in Lesser Britain. Others say he has gone to the Isle of Anglesey. I do not know myself where he has gone, and I only met him once or twice when I first was at Arthur's court in my youth; still, I believe he was far too wise to allow a woman to trick him."

"Actually," said Lance, "part of my quest also involves seeking the Lady of the Lake. Do you know where I may find her?"

"What do you seek from her?" asked Baudwin, sounding alarmed. "She cannot heal your brother. Is that why you are carrying him about the countryside rather than giving him a proper Christian burial—in hopes she will use her magic? I would not trust her if I were you. Her ways are those of pagans. I hold no hatred toward any man, but somehow, I do not think she always works for the good."

"I do not know whether or not she does," Lance admitted, "but it is also possible we do not understand her intentions, just as you said we cannot understand God's reasons for everything."

Brother Baudwin seemed taken aback by this argument, so he did not pursue the discussion on this point but simply replied, "Why do you seek her?"

"It is not to raise my brother from the dead," said Lance. "I know that is impossible. It is to fulfill my promise to my brother to complete the quest he was on." And then Lance explained how his brother had sought a love potion from the Lady of the Lake and the reason why.

"It is an ill-conceived quest," said Baudwin when he had heard all, "and Hoel should know better; I am surprised that he or my niece should be so fanciful as to think a love potion can change anything."

"Your niece?" said Lance. "Are you...but you did say you were from Lesser Britain, didn't you?"

"I am Hoel's younger brother," said Baudwin. "When I was young, I married and my wife died in childbirth. I was overcome with grief, so I threw myself into serving Arthur as a way to cope with it. I was a very poor father I'm afraid, so I left my daughter in the care of Hoel. He had recently married himself, and his wife had just given birth to a daughter of her own, my niece Isolde. I thought my little Enid would be better off with them while I went to Camelot. I visited her now and then, but I knew I could not care for her as well, even after Hoel's wife abandoned him. It is my daughter who was killed by the giant. When she was first taken by the creature, Hoel sent word to me, and Arthur and I immediately set forth to rescue her, but...I do not like to speak of it. We were too late. Arthur slew the giant, but that could not bring back my child. It was because of that event that I left the court and chose to become a hermit. I could not bear to be involved in any sort of violence after that. I watched Arthur kill the giant, and I saw the pain it experienced, and while I had thought I would enjoy such revenge, it only left me feeling great sorrow. I wondered what it must be like to be a giant, persecuted by humans continually, not having a mate, for there are so few of their kind left. I—my feelings are not normal, I suspect; any father would hate his daughter's murderer—but I have come to forgive that creature."

Baudwin's words left Lance astounded. How could anyone forgive the murderer of his child, and especially when that murderer wasn't even human? But after a moment, he heard himself say, "If you can forgive a giant for such an evil deed, then I think...I can forgive myself for accidentally killing my brother."

Baudwin smiled and said, "Violence accomplishes nothing. We cannot fight evil with evil, and sometimes the worst evil is punishing ourselves. Only in forgiveness does healing lie."

"Yes," Lance agreed.

"But," Baudwin continued, "to return to your quest, I have learned that it is not our place to force people to do anything, and so I think it an ill-conceived idea to try to trick Sir Tristram into coming back to Isolde. And while I do not understand the Lady of the Lake or her ways, I suspect she will be of the same opinion and refuse to help you in this endeavor."

Lance silently considered what that might mean. Should he abandon his quest to find the Lady of the Lake? All he really wanted to do was find a way to return home, but he still didn't know how to do so.

"That said," added Baudwin after a moment, "I do not wish to tell you what to do, but Palomides told me you seek to let your brother float off to sea in a barge. It is many miles to the nearest lake, and I feel you are ready to be relieved of your burden of grieving for your brother. May I suggest you leave his body here? I can give him a proper Christian burial in the cave behind my house. Then you may always return to visit his remains if you like, and I can assure you that his grave will not be desecrated. In fact, I will daily pray over his soul for you."

Lance was moved by this generous offer. He had not even thought to pray for his brother's soul, even though he now believed that on some higher spiritual level, Tristan had intentionally wanted to die for the good of Lance's own soul.

"I would like that," Lance said. "Thank you."

"Good," said Baudwin. "You must move past your grief now. Your brother's life has ended, but you have much life ahead of you yet, and just as you and your brother may have had a purpose in what happened to you, I suspect Isolde and Tristram must learn from their own situations, so we should not interfere in them."

"I think you're right," Lance agreed, feeling a great burden lifting from his shoulders—two burdens actually—that of burying Tristan and of fulfilling his quest.

"I believe I hear Palomides stirring inside," Baudwin said, standing up. "Let us go in and have some breakfast. Then we will give your brother his proper funeral rites before you continue your journey."

CHAPTER 4

ONCE PALOMIDES WAS awake and they had all eaten a simple breakfast, Brother Baudwin prepared Tristan's body for burial. Lance could not bear to look at his brother's face again, being afraid to see it already pale and beginning to decay. Instead, he waited in the cottage while Palomides assisted the hermit in the cave, preparing a hole in the stone wall so that it became a catacomb. Baudwin used some herbs or medicines for the body's preservation so it would not smell or rot too quickly, and then he and Palomides wrapped Tristan in a sheet. Finally, Lance came into the cave and helped Palomides lift Tristan and slide him into the little rock shelf that would be his final resting place. Baudwin said that later he would place stones over the cavity to hold the body in place. Then he said a prayer in Latin that Lance did not understand, but found comforting nevertheless.

Lance knew he had no choice but to leave his brother behind, and since Baudwin would pray for Tristan's soul, he could not think of a better solution for Tristan's final resting place. He reminded himself he would also have to begin praying for his brother, as well as for himself, and after speaking with Baudwin, he was beginning to understand that the best prayer he could offer would be to accept, if not understand, his presence in this strange land, for it must have some purpose. Perhaps that purpose was only to make him disillusioned with it all, for once he had dreamed of being a king, or at least a great knight, but now he saw how little glory there was in knighthood when violence was everywhere and death could happen so quickly. Even amid mermaids and magical beasts, he felt the Middle Ages was a far scarier time than the twenty-first century.

After Brother Baudwin finished praying, Lance thanked him. Then the hermit gave him and Palomides some bread and cheese for their journey. Once they bid Baudwin goodbye, Palomides and Lance mounted their horses and followed alongside the stream, uncertain where they were now going.

After a little time, Lance said, "Brother Baudwin did not think I should seek the Lady of the Lake or try to force Sir Tristram to return to Isolde."

Palomides shook his head, saying, "Sir Tristram is of bad account, and so is Iseult of Ireland, and so I would say they deserve to be left alone to make one another miserable."

"You are a noble knight," said Lance, who did not agree with all of Palomides' views but still appreciated his friendship. "Perhaps you should travel to Lesser Britain to see whether Isolde will marry you since she must be beautiful to have won Tristram's affections even for a short time."

"To take his cast-offs?" exclaimed Palomides, changing his previous viewpoint and acting as if it would bring shame upon him.

Lance did not reply, afraid he had offended the knight, but after another minute, Palomides remarked, "I shall think on the idea. No doubt, she would appreciate a knight who is true and would console her, and she sounds like a kind woman, which I find often lacking in the women of Britain because of my complexion. Most women, unlike my mother, are not willing to see beyond a man's skin to the nobleness of his heart."

"That is probably sadly true," Lance agreed, "but it is the women's loss in those cases."

"No matter," said Palomides. "For now I am committed to my quest, and you did say you would aid me in it; I will have plenty of time for romance later."

"I did say I would aid you," Lance agreed, "but I do need to find Merlin and speak to him."

"Merlin has not been seen for many years," Palomides reminded him, clearly thinking that finding the Beast Glatisant took priority over finding a wizard.

But Lance was not willing to give way. "I do not think Camelot is far—Tristan had expected to find it in another day, so why not ride to Camelot? We can both make inquiries along the way to learn whether anyone has seen Merlin or the Beast."

"And if we do not find Merlin, you will aid me in my quest?"

"If we do not find Merlin, I wish to find the Lady Morgana of Avalon, for she might also be willing to help me. I have come to Britain for reasons I cannot fully disclose to you, but can only discuss with Merlin or Lady Morgana. Please understand this, for it is of the utmost importance to me. And since you do not know where the Beast is, we are just as likely to stumble upon it while on the way to Camelot or Avalon as looking elsewhere."

"You wish to keep secrets from me, your fellow knight?" Palomides replied.

Lance did not want to anger his only friend, so he chose his words carefully before replying.

"It is...not a secret," Lance replied, "but simply certain...esoteric... information I have learned from living in Romania and Constantinople that I need to share with them. I believe it is something only they will understand."

Palomides' nostrils flared a bit at these words, but he did not reply. They then rode in silence for a good quarter hour or more before the knight finally said, "We will head toward Camelot, though it is farther than your brother believed. After that, I may leave you to continue my quest, for I cannot allow all of Britain to be destroyed by the Beast's voracious appetite. He is raping the land with his hunger, leaving whole forests leafless. Surely, your quest is not so important as mine, but in deference to your brother's recent death, I will accompany you to Camelot."

"I thank you," said Lance, trying to sound as grateful as possible despite how irritated he felt. Hopefully, with Palomides to introduce him at court, King Arthur or someone else of significance would trust him enough to take him to Avalon if Merlin were not there. First, though, he must reach Camelot. He could figure out what to do next once that was accomplished.

They continued on, not saying much, for there was nothing much to say. Lance simply enjoyed observing the trees and vegetation and noticing how sixth century Britain's forests were somewhat different than those he had known in the modern world—many of the trees he was familiar with were missing, and there were also some flowers and plants he had never seen before, although he had traveled all over Britain in the past—or rather, what had been his past, which was in the future. Keeping the difference straight was making his head ache.

In the afternoon, they stopped in a village to find food. For the first time, Lance found himself around a large group of people, and he found it fascinating to watch the children playing in the dirty streets, to see how the people dressed, to listen to their conversations, and to see ducks, pigs, and sheep wandering about or being herded everywhere. All these nameless people were actively going about their own lives, showing no sign of interest in him, and yet he was fascinated by them, especially when he remembered what he had learned in the modern world about DNA and mathematical calculations that said everyone who had lived in this time and had descendants was likely his direct ancestor, from the toothless hag begging for alms to the ruddy young farmer drinking in the tavern—and perhaps even Sir Palomides himself.

Palomides, however, was no fan of villages because everyone in them kept staring at his dark skin. Lance found this somewhat amusing since if these people knew he had traveled here from the future, he would be the far greater novelty. He and Palomides only stayed in the village long enough to buy some food, water their horses, and ask for directions to Camelot. Within half an hour, they were on the road again.

When Lance tried to ask Palomides about the village, the people he had seen, and what their lives must be like, the knight quickly grew irritated and said, "You ask too many questions." Lance reminded him, "I am just curious because I am from a foreign land." But Palomides replied, "They are just peasants; they are not worth taking interest in. You must have peasants and pigs where you come from. They are the same all over the world." These words shut up Lance, who now remembered there were other forms of prejudice besides racism. Palomides was, after all, a prince by birth, so he gave no thought to lumping pigs and peasants together. In the modern world, Lance would have objected to such rhetoric, but being dependent on the knight as his sole friend, he bit his tongue.

When darkness began to fall, they found themselves beside a small lake. Palomides suggested they rest there for the night, but Lance was leery of spending the night beside the water.

"I'd rather we stayed somewhere else," he said. "I'd like to avoid all chance of meeting the Lady of the Lake again. The more I think about it, the less I want further encounters with her, and certainly, I do not want her to sneak up on me in the night."

Palomides, who had become more fatigued and surly as the day progressed, replied, "The horses need water now, and they will again in the morning, and so do we. It must be a strange land you come from if you have not common sense enough to know this." And with that, he dismounted from his horse and began to make camp.

Lance realized Palomides was right, and he was sorry that the knight was annoyed with him. He was certain his friend was irritated that he would not quest for the Beast Glatisant with him, but just as he had accepted that solving Tristram and Isolde's marriage problems was not his duty, so he felt no need to help slaughter some magical creature.

The two companions hardly said another word to each other that evening. They were both tired, and rather than try to find game to eat, they made due with the bread and cheese that Brother Baudwin had given them. Not long after, they lay down on the ground, wrapped in their capes and using their saddles for pillows.

Long after Palomides began snoring, Lance lay looking up at the stars, wondering what was the possibility of another comet appearing in the sky that would carry him back to the twenty-first century. Then he thought how funny it would be if Palomides were to be transported into the future with him. He could just see the great knight's reaction the first time he saw an automobile. *He'd probably chase after it as if it were a new version of the Beast,* thought Lance. And then he was surprised to hear himself laughing when his brother had so recently died, and that reminded him to say his prayers. He did not know what to say, so he simply asked God or whoever was listening to take care of his brother and his parents wherever they were. Scarcely had those thoughts passed through his head before he fell asleep.

CHAPTER 5

LANCE WOKE TO the early morning sun shining directly into his eyes. For a moment, he was blinded, but he could hear a female voice saying, "There's a good boy. I bet you like apples, don't you? Here you go. Oh, look at how big your teeth are. You like that apple, don't you? Yes, I know you do."

At first, Lance thought someone was talking to him. But who would talk to him in such a way, as if he were a puppy dog? But puppies didn't eat apples. Someone must be feeding the horses.

Lifting his hand to block the sun, Lance looked in the voice's direction, but he could see nothing. A good-sized clump of tall trees and bushes were a dozen or so yards away along the lakeshore, and the voice seemed to be coming from behind the clump.

Slowly, Lance stood up, not wanting to surprise whoever was speaking. He hesitated for a moment, wondering whether he should wake Palomides before he ventured forth, but he did not think a woman and a horse could be very frightening. Still, just to be safe, Lance picked up his sword. Then he quietly crept forth so as not to startle the woman or animal.

"What are you doing so far from home?" the woman was saying to the animal.

Lance saw movement between the trees, made by something large, something yellowish and brown, and something very tall. He could not see the woman yet, but he could not imagine what kind of creature was behind the trees—no horse could be that size!

Gripping his sword tightly, Lance picked up his pace. In a few seconds, he had made a large circle around the trees. He saw the woman; her back was to him. And then looming up above her was—

"Why, it's a giraffe!" Lance exclaimed.

The woman turned at hearing his voice, and even the giraffe perked up its ears.

"It's a giraffe!" Lance repeated, laughing now. "What is a giraffe doing in Britain?"

"There you are," said the woman, diverting Lance's attention from the giraffe. He recognized her instantly. She was dressed in the green gown she had worn in Lyonesse.

"Ileana, what are you doing here?" Lance asked. "And what are you doing with a giraffe?"

"Good morning, Sir Lancelot," she replied. "Come and share breakfast with me."

Ileana held out her hand to Lance. It contained an apple, but before Lance could approach to take it, the giraffe bent down its long neck and stole the apple from her hand.

Ileana laughed and turned around to look at the creature, and Lance joined in the laughter.

But the happy moment was only a moment. In the next second, Lance heard Palomides shouting.

"Do not harm her, foul beast!"

Lance turned to see the knight already mounted on his horse and riding at an alarming pace toward Ileana and the giraffe. Palomides obviously thought the giraffe was going to harm Ileana.

Of course, thought Lance. *A serpent's head, spots like a leopard....*

But before Lance could complete this thought, Palomides raised his sword, riding toward the giraffe. Lance froze as he watched the knight's sword slash through the air at the giraffe's head, which was still lowered to eat Ileana's apples. Now realizing the danger that threatened it, the giraffe raised its head and bolted backwards, and....

Ileana's head went flying, severed from her body.

As if watching a slow motion film, Lance saw Ileana's body slowly collapse to the ground.

Palomides, unaware of what had happened, rode forward, still waving his sword as he pursued his beast, which went running in fear across the meadow, its hooves and screams combining to sound like a pack of wild hounds.

Lance could not move for several seconds. Then he found himself running toward Ileana's corpse and her head, which had fallen just feet away. As he approached, he saw her eyelids blink and her mouth open as if to speak, but then her eyes closed...forever.

"Noooo!" screamed Lance. The horror was too much for him. He turned, not knowing what he was doing. He went charging along the lakeshore until he reached the nearby wood. Then he ran through it; he ran and ran and ran, stumbled and fell, pulled himself up from the earth, and continued to run, seeking to erase the memory of what he had just seen. But this last shock was more than he could bear, and his mind became clouded over with madness.

CHAPTER 6

I N THE TIME of King Arthur, in those peaceful years following the Battle of Mount Badon when Arthur defeated and made peace with the Saxons and before the horrible Battle of Camlann that brought about the Fall of Camelot, there lived a wild man in the forests of Britain.

Most people did not know who he was or where he came from, but rumor said he had once been a knight named Sir Lancelot, and once the rumors began, they grew until stories spread that he had been one of the greatest knights of Camelot, that he had defeated all the other knights in many a tournament, that he was the son of a king, that he had been raised by the Lady of the Lake, and even that he had gone mad because Queen Guinevere had refused to return his love.

Whether or not these stories were true, no one questioned them because they became so widespread that everyone heard them from someone he or she knew and trusted. Yet no one trusted the mad Sir Lancelot. Whenever he came out of the forest into a village, people ran from him, and with good cause, for he looked undoubtedly like a wild man. True, the occasional maiden said he might be very handsome if only he would shave and take a bath, and many a man secretly envied his strength when he would lift up a rock or a log to use as a weapon of defense if he thought someone would attack him. But no one ever got close enough to attack him, for as soon as he was seen, people would scatter, and then the wild man would run deeper into the forest.

The mad knight dwelt in the forest, laying hidden beneath the ash trees, unwilling that anyone should see him, perhaps fearing his fellow men more than they feared him. His clothes were old and so torn that he appeared half-naked. He lived off berries, nuts, and roots, and although his demeanor was frightening, he never seemed to harm a living thing. Indeed, not even the forest animals appeared to fear him, for they had better instincts than men and sensed he was of a peaceful nature. The forest did not provide him a great deal of sustenance so he grew thin, but the hard labor of climbing trees to find fruit or digging in the ground for nuts that he stole from the squirrels kept him lithe and strong.

When winter came, the wild man made his home in a cave, creating a bed from dead leaves and any scrap of cloth or paper he might find in the forest that could help to keep him warm. Throughout winter's coldest months, he lived a miserable, mad existence. He would have thought death preferable had his madness allowed him to know what death was, but all his wits, memories, thoughts, and reasoning had left him until only his survival instinct remained, causing him to eat, drink, seek shelter, and hide from humans and any other creatures that might hurt him. Somehow, he knew to pile up food for the winter, keeping it refrigerated in the pile of snow he kept in his cave. He would not harm a creature, but he did dine on the occasional frozen mouse or bird he found lying dead in the snow or on the cold earth. He was not knowledgeable enough to fear that the creature might have died from anything other than the cold.

When spring came, the wild man began to venture out from his cave, for it was a few miles from any source of water, and he could no longer eat the snow, which had melted, so he needed some other way to quench his thirst. And as the plants returned to life, so too, but slowly, did his mind. He had moments when he could almost re-member something. For the first time in months, he would see some-thing and a word, scarcely more than a grunt, would escape his lips. "Bird," he would say or "Tree." And if his stomach growled, "Food" or "Hungry."

After a few ventures from his cave, the wild man one day walked far enough through the forest that he came to a clearing where he saw a village. Occasionally, people had spotted him in the forest and he had run from them, and from those incidents, the stories of Sir Lancelot had spread. He seemed to have some memory of a dark-skinned man even once grabbing hold of him and trying to speak to him, and this man had called him "Lancelot." If the wild man had known of the stories told about him, he probably would have realized this man had been the start of them. But the wild man had not even wondered why he was called such; he had only let the dark-skinned man hold and speak to him for a few seconds, and then he had bro-ken free of him and run to hide in the wood.

But now the wild man did not run, for he was hidden among the bushes on the forest's edge and watching. He saw two little boys walking together, one good-naturedly pushing the other's shoulder, and seeing the two boys triggered something in his mind, something small, but powerful, like a small hole in a dam that grows larger until a torrent of water breaks forth and washes away all trace of its former barrier.

The trigger was a great pang of grief and loneliness. And then a sob worked its way up through his throat, and not even knowing yet what he was saying, he found himself softly crying out, "Tristan! Tristan!"

And then he watched as more people walked about. He saw them smiling, laughing, greeting one another, patting each other on their backs, exchanging items from baskets they carried, and he found himself fascinated by them.

He went back to his cave that evening, but he returned to the forest's edge the next day, and the day after that, to watch these humans interacting with one another.

And then one morning, he came early to the forest's edge near the village before anyone was awake, and he felt brave and curious, for the humans' dwellings were strange and looked far more inviting than his damp cave, and so the wild man ventured forth from the forest's darkness. Coming out into the open, he crossed the field into the village and walked the street between the houses. When he saw a cart of apples in front of a door, he stopped, picked up an apple and began to eat it, for he had no concept of personal property.

"You thief!" someone shouted, and before the wild man knew it, he was struck on the back with a stick. And before he could run, he was struck again. And when he turned to look at his assailant, he felt the stick strike his legs, and then he tumbled to the ground.

Suddenly, a great many people were shouting, running toward him, and surrounding him. Apples and tomatoes were being flung at him, and a small child kicked him. Fortunately, the child was grabbed by his mother and pulled away from "the madman."

The wild man tried to dodge the blows. He managed to get back on his feet, and then he grabbed the stick from the man who had been beating him.

"Run! He'll kill us all!" shrieked a woman, but before she could run, she fainted.

"He was once a great knight. He is trained in killing. Run for your lives!" screamed another woman.

But the men continued to circle the wild man, stepping in closer. When one of them pulled out a knife, the wild man swung his stick, knocking the knife from the man's hand, but then two other men pulled out knives and ran toward him, ready to kill.

"Hold off!" screamed a voice. "In the name of God, do not hurt him!"

The wild man's assailants backed up a few steps and turned to look in the voice's direction.

"It's the hermit of the forest," someone said.

"He's as mad as the madman!" shouted another.

But if the hermit heard his detractors, he paid them no mind. He was only intent on rescuing the man they persecuted.

"Back off, all of you!" the hermit shouted, pushing his way through the crowd with his walking stick. A few among the crowd shouted, "Beware!" or "You don't know what you're doing, old man!" but they all backed up and did not try to stop him. In a minute, a large circle of onlookers had formed, surrounding the hermit and the wild man.

The hermit slowly approached the wild man, who now cowered on the ground. He tried to run away while on all fours, but the crowd surrounded him. After running about in a circle for a few seconds and shouting nonsensical words, he became still, like a captured beast, and waited as the hermit approached him.

"Brother, do not touch him!" shouted a boy from the crowd.

"He is like a rabid dog. He will bite you!" screeched a woman.

"Fie on all of you, to treat a man like an animal!" replied the hermit, turning around to glare at them all with disgust. "Be off, every one of you, or I will have the king's army come to teach you all a lesson, and do not doubt I have the power to do it."

The villagers must have had reason to think the hermit would make good on his threat for they swiftly began to disperse; those few who dallied behind to watch soon found the hermit shaking his staff in their faces; then they too turned and ran several paces to watch from a distance.

Then the hermit turned back to look at the wild man, who still cowered on the ground. Approaching him again, the hermit knelt down before the wild man and placed a gentle hand on his shoulder.

"Are you all right, sir?"

The wild man raised up his head, his eyes peering into those of the hermit. He tried to catch his breath, not knowing what to do.

"Can you stand?" asked the hermit, standing up and giving the wild man his hand to help him to his feet. The wild man struggled, but he stood. Still stooping a bit, he rubbed his shoulder where he had been struck.

The hermit looked him in the eyes, as if to discern whether there were any sign of reasoning in the man.

"Are you hurt? Do you need a doctor?" the hermit asked.

The wild man shook his head.

"Do you know your name?" the hermit asked.

The wild man looked confused, but he did not answer.

"Do you know my name?" asked the hermit.

Again the wild man shook his head.

"I am Baudwin, the hermit of the forest, once Sir Baudwin, Constable to King Arthur. We have met before. You do not remember me?"

The wild man's eyes appeared to be searching, and he looked about him as if for familiar objects to help him remember.

"I was once a great knight. Do you know what a knight is?"

The wild man stared blankly at the hermit.

"You were once a knight also," said the hermit, this time receiving a look of surprise from the wild man, which encouraged him to continue. "You were once a knight named Sir Lancelot, and you were great friends with Sir Palomides, and you came to my cottage. Do you remember coming there? I thought you to be a very good and kind man then. I am very saddened to see you now in such a state."

"Lan-ce-lot," the wild man said slowly, as if considering this matter. "No, Lance...Lance...Lance."

"Lancelot," the hermit said, trying to complete the word for him.

"No," said the wild man. "Not Lan-ce-lot. Lance...just Lance... Lance De-lan-ey."

The hermit did not understand what Lance was trying to tell him, but he felt they had made enough progress in understanding one another for now, so he said, "Come; let me take you home with me. It is not far. We will find you some clean clothes and some food. I know you have experienced a great shock. Last autumn, after you ran into the forest, Sir Palomides tried to find you. When he finally did, he tried to talk to you, but he could not reason with you and you ran away. He came and told me what had happened. Both he and I have been looking for you ever since. But this may all be too much for you to think about now. We will speak of it later when you are ready. Will you come with me, Lancelot?"

The hermit put his hand on Lance's arm to pull him gently forward.

Lance pulled back his arm and said, "Lance!"

"Lance," the hermit repeated. "We will have it your way, but come along. You must be hungry."

Lance looked uncertain, so the hermit slowly started walking through the village street with his staff. He walked about ten feet, then turned around to see whether Lance was following, but the wild man stood silently, questioning what to do.

"Come along," the hermit said. "I will not hurt you. I will give you food and shelter, and I will try to help you however I may."

Lance saw the old man was kind. Something about him seemed familiar. Had he known him before? His mind was a muddle, but somehow he felt he could trust him.

"Come along," the hermit repeated, beckoning with his hand.

Lance took a few cautious steps, and then when the hermit turned around to continue walking, Lance ran up and walked alongside him into the forest as the villagers watched, several of them making the Sign of the Cross and all of them feeling relieved to be free of the wild man.

Brother Baudwin talked softly to Lance as they traveled through the forest. Lance did not listen because the hermit spoke of things such as herbs for healing, his understanding of the human mind, and how evil spirits can possess a man when he has experienced a great shock. None of these things made sense to Lance, although they related directly to what he most wanted at that moment—to remember.

They walked for nearly an hour, Baudwin sometimes slowing down for Lance's sake because his knee had been hurt in the scuffle with the villagers; he limped a bit, and now and then he stumbled over a tree root or a small rock in the path, but in time, they came to Brother Baudwin's small cottage attached to a cave.

When Baudwin opened the door, Lance hesitantly peered inside, but the small dwelling did look familiar to him.

"Welcome to my home," said the hermit, holding the door open and motioning him inside. "Watch your head."

They ducked inside, and then the hermit walked Lance to his own cot in the back of the room and bade him sit down.

"I won't let you sleep on the floor this time," Baudwin said.

Again, Lance looked confused, so Baudwin said, "Of course, you don't remember your last visit here."

"It seems...familiar," Lance replied, almost surprised by his ability to find the right word.

"You stayed here with your friend Palomides...and you came bringing a great burden with you...something that brought you tremendous sorrow. Do you remember what it was?"

"Tristan!" exclaimed Lance. It was as if a light bulb had gone off in his head, and suddenly, he was flooded with warm memories of his brother. "Yes," he said, "you agreed to have him buried here in the cave."

Buried! Lance's expression made Baudwin realize what a shock his words had just imparted.

"I...I...." Lance stumbled. "He's...dead?" He found it hard to believe, but as his memory came back, he knew it to be true.

"I'm sorry. I shouldn't have mentioned it yet," said Baudwin. "Let me get you some wine."

Lance sat staring about him as Baudwin found some wooden drinking vessels and gave him something to drink. The hermit also gave him some fruit and a bit of bread, which Lance ate ravenously.

"I do remember being here," said Lance, once he had eaten, "and I was with another knight. A Middle Eastern man, he was."

"Do you remember his name?" asked Baudwin.

"No, I think you told me in the village, but I don't remember. No, I do remember that he...he was chasing a...a giraffe."

"The Beast Glatisant, you mean," Baudwin corrected.

Lance didn't reply. He was sure it had been a giraffe...and...there was...there was....

And then he remembered how he had seen the giraffe...and Ileana feeding it apples, and how Palomides had attacked...and missed the Beast...and sliced off....

"The lady—Ileana—Palomides, he...!" Lance shrieked, and in his horror, he dropped his cup of wine, spilling it on the floor.

"Yes," said Baudwin. "You do remember."

"She...did she really die?" asked Lance.

Baudwin nodded in confirmation as he bent over to fetch the fallen wine cup. "Palomides did not realize what he had done at first. When he returned to the spot about an hour later, he found her head lying beside the river. Overcome with grief, he realized what must have happened, and so he carried her body to me to bury here in my cave. She rests now beside your brother."

"She...she...do you know who she was?"

"I only know she must have been a beautiful maiden," said Baudwin.

"No, she was more than that," Lance replied, struggling hard to remember. "She was a...oh, you'll think I'm crazy, but...."

"I don't know what 'crazy' means," Baudwin replied.

"Mad. You'll think I'm mad," said Lance.

"Everyone already thinks that," laughed Baudwin, "so fear not. Just tell me what you know of this fair maiden Ileana, as you call her."

"She...she was...well, not quite human. She was from Lyonesse, and she had a mermaid's tail, and—"

Baudwin laughed.

"I knew you'd think I was crazy," said Lance, his shoulders slumping.

"I am sorry. I have heard of Lyonesse, but it is under the sea. It sank centuries ago."

"It did, but intentionally. It...." Lance still had to struggle to remember. "It's the home of...the people of Atlantis founded it...and... Ileana was the...no, not her, but...I can't remember her name...but she's a powerful woman who lives underwater...and—"

"Do you mean the Lady of the Lake?" asked Baudwin.

"Yes, exactly!" said Lance. "She lives in Lyonesse, and that is where Ileana lives."

"Tell me how you know these things," said Baudwin.

Lance tried to think how he could explain to Baudwin everything that had happened to him, but his brain hurt, and after a moment, he shook his head and said, "I'm sorry. May I lie down? I have a terrible headache. I need to rest, and then maybe it will come back clearly for me."

"Of course," said Baudwin, getting up and walking with Lance to the cot since he still did not seem steady on his feet. "Lie down and rest. It is almost evening. Sleep as long as you need to. When you wake, hopefully your mind will be clear, and then you can tell me all."

CHAPTER 7

LANCE SLEPT UNTIL the morning, and when he woke, Brother Baudwin gave him breakfast. And then the moment finally came when Lance felt he could tell his story. He felt desperate to tell it, for the madness had now left his mind, but he feared its return. He knew his words would sound mad to Brother Baudwin, but he also knew the hermit seemed to be the only sensible person he had met since his arrival in this strange land, now nearly a year ago. Palomides was well-meaning, but highly uneducated, as apparent from his views about the Beast Glatisant—but then, the knight never having been to Africa, how was he to know the difference between a beast and a giraffe? And Lance obviously could not speak to Tristan or Ileana, and Viviane had seemed completely unwilling to help him, being too involved in her own concerns. And so Lance found himself trusting Baudwin by elimination, but also because he thought the hermit would at least try to understand.

"I need to get to Camelot," he began, "and I think I need someone like yourself who is known there and will be trusted to help me get the help I need."

"Your words are flowing much better this morning," said Baudwin. "Tell me; what kind of help do you need?"

"I need to get home, and when I tell you where home is, you probably aren't going to believe me, but I need to get there regardless. And I don't think anyone can help me get there except for Merlin or Lady Morgana of Avalon."

"Merlin has not been seen in many years," Baudwin reminded Lance, "and when I left Camelot, no one knew his whereabouts. It is possible that Lady Morgana can help you, but first, please, tell me what it is you need. Where is this home you speak of?"

And then Lance let his tale pour forth from him, not caring whether Baudwin believed him or not; just needing finally to relieve himself of the truth. "I come from the future," he admitted, "from the Britain that will exist fifteen-hundred years from now." As Lance spoke, he watched Brother Baudwin's face change from an expression of surprise to one of disbelief and then to one of confusion as he sought to understand. Lance explained not only where he had come from, but what the twenty-first century was like; he told Baudwin of his parents, and how Tristan and he had come to Britain, and everything that had happened to him here, even the visit to Lyonesse. And finally, he ended his tale by stating, "So, if you believe me, you can understand why I want to return to the twenty-first century."

Baudwin lowered his eyes. The hermit was speechless. Lance waited a couple of minutes for his reaction, but when there was none, he asked, "Do you think I'm crazy?"

Baudwin replied, "I think I need to relieve myself. I'll be back in a moment."

The hermit stood up and went outside. Lance realized nature was also calling him, but he was too nervous to move. He said a silent prayer that the hermit would believe him and help him get to Camelot, for he knew not how else he would get there. He had left his sword, his armor, and his horse behind the day he had run stark raving mad into the forest. He had nothing but the torn clothes on his back—not even those, for Baudwin had told him to undress and put on a robe instead to sleep in; Lance did not know what the hermit had done with the remnants of his clothing.

When Brother Baudwin returned, he sat down again at the table, and after a moment, he said, "It is three days journey to Avalon, and I cannot guarantee that you will reach there, for you must take a boat to the island, and even then, you might not find it, for it is shrouded in mists. I have never been there myself. I only know in which direction it lies. However, I am sure King Arthur must have a way to summon his sister when he needs her aid. Therefore, I think your best chance is to go to Camelot first so someone can show you how to reach Lady Morgana."

"Then you do believe me?" asked Lance.

"I am not sure I believe you," said Baudwin, "but that is neither here nor there; I do believe that our existence is full of mysteries we cannot explain with our limited knowledge, but they are mysteries that could be explained if we only had the ability to understand them. I am willing to give you the benefit of the doubt that your story is one of those mysteries. Had you boasted to me of how you had come from the future, I might not have believed you, but I see the anguish in your eyes, so I will believe you are in earnest. Furthermore, from the descriptions you give of the twenty-first century, I cannot conceive that any man alive today could imagine such things. I would be shocked to see these creatures called airplanes and automobiles that you describe, so I can well imagine you are also shocked to be here. It is no wonder you went mad. Seeing Ileana die before your eyes would have been enough, but to have come from another time, to have lost your brother, to have journeyed to an underwater kingdom—these wonders would deform the strongest of minds, so yes, I am inclined to believe you."

"But will you help me? Will you go with me to Camelot to persuade King Arthur to help me?"

"I will need to think upon that," Baudwin replied. "I have sworn off the world and all its trappings; I have made a vow to God to avoid courts and kings with their pomp and circumstance, their vanity and hypocrisy. Not that Arthur is not a good king, but my soul is more important to me than the comforts and intrigues of his court."

"But surely you would help a fellow man in need?" Lance begged.

"I will not make a rash decision today. You have spent most of the day telling me your tale, and so I think it best we have some supper. Tonight, I will ask God to give me guidance in this matter, and then you will have my answer in the morning."

Lance was not satisfied with this response. He was impatient to begin his journey to Camelot or Avalon or wherever it might be that he needed to go so he could learn how to return to twenty-first century Britain, but he also realized that the only person who could help him at the moment was Brother Baudwin. Repressing his anxiety and frustration, Lance reminded himself that patience was a virtue he needed to work on, and he recalled that a lack of patience was also something for which Merlin had often scolded his father. Therefore, Lance replied, "Fair enough. Thank you," and then to hide his disappointment, he went outside.

He remained outdoors for half an hour; he felt so tense and exhausted that he took a bath in the stream, washing himself for the first time in many months, and when he had finished, he felt rein-vigorated. He breathed in the fresh air, marveling at the beauty that springtime brought to the forest, and he thought that if it were not for wanting to see his parents again, he might resign himself to re-maining in such a beautiful place. In fact, if not for the violence he had witnessed that had resulted in Tristan and Ileana's deaths—albe-it both accidents—he might have thoroughly enjoyed his adventure in the Arthurian world.

When Lance returned inside the cottage, he and Brother Baud-win had a late supper, and then Baudwin knelt down before the cross on the wall. He invited Lance to pray with him, but Lance could barely hold back a yawn, and excusing himself, he sought sleep on the cot instead. Soon Lance was snoring, but Brother Baudwin was too occupied with petitioning for His Savior's assistance to notice.

CHAPTER 8

WHEN LANCE WOKE in the morning, he found the cottage empty. He could hear the birds outside singing, and he suspected that Baudwin had not gone far, perhaps just to collect some herbs or find something for them to eat. Nevertheless, Lance was anxious to know whether Baudwin would take him to Camelot.

Lance got up from the cot, finding his body was less stiff than it had been the night before. Then he took off the robe Baudwin had loaned him to investigate whether he had any wounds; he was filled with bruises from the beating he had received in the village, and he had a couple of scratches, but they were already healing, so it didn't look like he had anything serious to worry about. In another day or two, he would feel like his old self and be ready to travel to Camelot or Avalon or wherever he might get help for his situation.

He was about to put back on the robe when, out of the corner of his eye, he saw something glittering. Turning around, he was astonished to see a full set of armor standing near the mouth of the cave. He slowly walked toward the suit, becoming more astonished when he realized it was the armor the Lady of the Lake had given him, and there, beside it, was also the sword she had given him. Somehow, either Palomides or Baudwin had retrieved his armor and sword and brought them here for safekeeping. It was almost as if they had known he would eventually return. Baudwin must have set the armor out last night while Lance was asleep so that he could have it this morning.

Lance felt eager to begin his journey now that he could be dressed again as befitted his station—but then he realized that was not a humble thought, so he changed it to being grateful that he would now have armor to protect him from the dangers of this violent world. He spent a moment admiring the beautiful armor, gold in color and the finest he had ever seen—far finer than that which Palomides or Tristan had worn. He even thought perhaps he should not hold such a bad opinion of the Lady of the Lake since she had given him something so beautiful and fine to wear. Next to the armor lay a simple shirt and pants like a peasant would wear; without doubt, Baudwin had intended them for him. Lance quickly put on the clothes, and then he reverently began to dress himself in the armor, as if he were performing a sacred ritual.

Lance was only half-dressed, however, when he began to feel thirsty. Looking about the room, he saw a pitcher sitting on a rude table against the wall. He went to it and found it filled with water. After quenching his thirst, he was about to return to putting on the rest of his armor when he noticed for the first time that a small cracked mirror hung above the table.

"I didn't think Baudwin would be so vain," said Lance, smiling, for he could not imagine that the hermit, whose robe was unkempt and whose hair revealed that it had not seen a comb in weeks, ever used a looking glass.

Lance finished putting on the armor, and then he went to see how he looked in the mirror. But first he had to wipe the dust from the glass—apparently, Baudwin wasn't so vain after all.

At first, the mirror only presented Lance with a shadow of himself in the cottage's dim light, but as he looked at his reflection, admiring the armor's fine workmanship, he noticed that the metal began to glow in the mirror. Looking down at the armor itself, however, he did not notice any actual change in its appearance.

"The mirror is playing tricks on me," he thought.

In fact, it seemed as if the mirror were somehow being illuminated from behind. Suddenly, its interior became as bright as if it were outside in the midday sun, and for the first time since he had arrived in this strange land, Lance was able to see himself. He marveled at how healthy and strong he looked, as if he had never been hurt and was the very embodiment of strength and energy. He couldn't say the matted beard he had grown during his months of madness was so nice to look at, but then he noticed a razor beside the pitcher—he was surprised by its appearance, but not going to question it. He picked it up and began the laborious process of shaving until his bare skin appeared again. It took a while, but despite the razor blade's roughness and no shaving cream or hot water, Lance managed to create a fairly close shave. Then he looked at himself some more. His skin had never looked smoother, his eyes bluer, nor his hair blonder. His face had the ruddy glow of health about it, and he honestly could not help admiring how very handsome and attractive he was. For a moment, he wished he could be seen by several attractive women, all of whom would doubtless wish to kiss him. But then he remembered that there had only been one woman whom he had really, truly wanted to be with—Elaine. But she had quickly decided she preferred Tristan to him. Poor Elaine. She would be heartbroken to learn Tristan was dead.

This sad thought overpowered Lance's senses. Feeling stricken with grief, Lance was about to go look for Brother Baudwin when he noticed a movement in the mirror's reflection, a movement he had not made.

Looking again in the mirror, he was astonished to see that his reflection had been replaced by that of a beautiful maiden with long, flowing hair, red lips, and green eyes, and she looked like—Ileana? But Ileana was dead. Could it be—Elaine? But she was in twenty-first century Britain. He was not sure who it was, but he suddenly realized how much Elaine and Ileana resembled one another, despite Elaine's Ethiopian background and Ileana's Atlantean one. And then he was further surprised when the woman's lips moved and he heard her say, "Like you, Lance, I am half-sick of shadows. I am waiting for you."

Lance was so shocked by these words that he did not know what to say or do. How could this be possible? Mirrors only spoke in fairy tales, but then, wasn't he living a sort of fairy tale? He seemed to remember Ileana saying something to that effect.

"Do not fear," the woman in the mirror continued. "Your journey will soon come to an end, and I will be there when it does."

"Who are you?" he asked. "How do you know me?"

She did not answer, only smiled, and then Lance watched the mirror's image begin to fade.

"Ah, you're awake!" said Baudwin, suddenly coming through the cottage door.

Lance turned from the mirror for just a second at the sound of the hermit's voice, and then he turned back to see the image had vanished.

"Don't go," he said to the mirror.

"What's that?" asked Baudwin.

"Where did you go?" asked Lance of Baudwin, trying to cover his confusion. He still felt uncertain how much Baudwin had believed his story last night of being from another time, so he hesitated to mention this newest strange experience.

"I just went for a walk to think further on what you said," Baudwin replied. "I see you found your armor."

"Yes. Thank you for keeping it for me. Did you come to a decision?"

"I'm afraid your horse ran off when you fled into the forest after Ileana's death, and Palomides never found it," Baudwin replied. "But I think you can make it to Camelot wearing your armor. It should only be a three-day walk. I am sorry, but I find in my heart that it will not be well for me to go with you—I might be too tempted to return to the glamorous evils of this world. But I have written you a letter of introduction to give to King Arthur. He will recognize my handwriting and know it is authentic. It explains that I am sending you on a personal mission to see the Lady Morgana of Avalon, and it asks for him to give you assistance. I will point you in the right direction, and then you can ask directions when you reach the next village, just a couple of miles from here. I am sorry I cannot do more for you."

"I understand," said Lance, though he really did not understand why the hermit would not accompany him.

"Let's have some breakfast, and then I will wish you well on your way," said Baudwin, "and I pray God guides you on your journey."

And I pray this will be the last leg of my journey, Lance thought.

PART IV
THE CROSS AND THE CROWN

CHAPTER 1

LANCE SET OFF on foot, heading in the direction Brother Baudwin had told him to travel. He was glad to have his armor back, but he soon found it was a lot harder to walk in it than to wear it while riding a horse. Furthermore, lugging around his sword and shield made his arms quickly grow tired, but having seen so much violence already, accidental or not, he did not wish to risk discarding them. Nevertheless, he was reminded of gun safety arguments he had often heard. So far, he had not seen any good come from carrying swords—yet one never knew when a belligerent knight or monstrous beast might attack.

It was a cool spring morning, but Lance knew that by noon he would be sweating from the heavy armor, especially when the sun reached its highest point. Baudwin had said it would take him three days to reach Camelot by foot, but Lance suspected it might take longer for one like himself not accustomed to bearing such weight; he felt more like he was hiking up a mountain than walking through a meadow.

"I thought I read somewhere that this kind of heavy armor was only worn in the late Middle Ages," he remarked to himself. "I thought they just had light chain mail prior to that, but then, I guess Viviane gave me the best armor possible—cutting-edge armor, you might say. Even so, Palomides and Tristram's armor was no light matter. Still, I can't imagine the history books are inaccurate, so how can such an anachronism be possible?"

Lance passed a couple of peasants walking along the road and then a farmer with a cart, all of whom looked at him strangely. Apparently, it was a rare sight to see a knight without a horse. Lance only nodded at them, feeling no need to converse or ask directions since Baudwin had told him he wouldn't come to a village until afternoon, where he would find another road to take him to Camelot.

When noon came, Lance was so hot that he felt the need to stop and rest. Baudwin had given him a satchel with some fruit, bread, and cheese, so he decided to eat half and save the rest for supper. Baudwin had also been kind enough to give Lance a few coins, so hopefully, he could buy enough food to sustain him the rest of the way to Camelot.

Lance found a shaded tree and sat down to eat, but the armor was so uncomfortable and awkward, and he was sweating so profusely inside it that he decided to remove it while he ate, and maybe even lie down and rest under the tree for a little while. It was far too miserable walking in the hot sun, and he had plenty of hours of daylight left, so he could spare an hour or two of rest before continuing on. By then, the hottest hours of the day would be over.

Lance did not plan to take a nap, but once he had eaten, he found the food and the long walk had made him drowsy, and before he knew it, he had fallen asleep.

What Lance dreamt he couldn't later remember, but he had one of those strange dreams in which a sudden sensation of falling makes you snap awake.

And just as he regained consciousness and before he even opened his eyes, he heard a woman shouting.

"Fool!" she screamed. "Drop him and you'll pay for it with your life!"

As he opened his eyes, Lance tried to move his legs to stand up, but he was shocked to find he couldn't. His legs felt paralyzed. And then he felt something hard, metallic even, beneath him. And he saw a man before him, but with his back to him, and two more men, one on each side of him. Lance could at least move his neck since he turned to look at the men on his sides. He could see he was between them on something—then he realized he was being carried—which accounted for the falling sensation he had experienced. One of the men must have stumbled and nearly dropped him, which is why the woman had yelled, but where was she?

"Now look what you did!" the woman shouted again. "You woke him up, damn you!"

Struggling to move his neck, Lance managed to look a bit around the man in front of him, and then he saw four women riding ahead of him and his bearers. The women appeared to be seated on white mules. They were dressed in rich red gowns, complete with furs, jewels, and elaborate headpieces, making them look like queens, princesses, or at least duchesses.

Again Lance tried to sit up, but his back would not move—and nor would his arms, so he could not lift himself up.

"Where am I?" he asked, glad to hear that at least his voice worked. But no one replied to him; the men looked as if they were purposely trying to ignore him.

"Where am I?" he repeated in a louder voice. "What are you doing? Where are you taking me?"

When again no one answered him, Lance began yelling.

"I demand to know where I'm being taken!"

"Shut up!" a woman screamed, and this time Lance saw one of the women turn her mule around and ride toward him. The men stopped walking as she approached and so did her female companions. The man to Lance's left moved behind him so he could continue to support Lance on what Lance now realized was his own shield. The woman now rode up alongside him.

"So you're awake," she said. "I didn't think you'd wake so quickly, though you are quite strong. I should have given you another dose, but no matter, even if your tongue is wobbling about in your throat, the rest of your body will not be able to move before we reach the castle."

As she spoke, Lance observed her. She was a beautiful woman, just past her prime, but certainly not older than forty. She had no sign of wrinkles and not a touch of gray marked her dark raven hair. Her lips were lush and sensuous, but they curled upward in a stern way, and her eyes were almost icy and fiery at the same time.

"Who are you and where are you taking me?" Lance demanded. "I am a knight. You cannot kidnap me like this."

"Who made you a knight?" the woman laughed. "You are no Knight of the Round Table. You have done no knightly deeds. All you have is a golden suit of armor given you by that treasonous sea witch who helped to set a false king and queen on the throne of Britain."

"Who are you?" Lance asked. "And how do you know these things about me?"

"Your armor gives away who your mistress is," said the woman, "and I know well all the Knights of the Round Table. You, Sir Lancelot, are just a fake, an interloper, a pretender to knighthood."

"How do you even know my name?"

"I know many things—things it is not your right to know."

"Who are you and what do you want with me?" Lance repeated.

"I am Guinevere, High Queen of Britain, and some say I am your lover. Would you like to be my lover?"

As she spoke, she ran her tongue upon her full lips in a teasing way. Lance felt repulsed, despite her beauty.

"Come," she continued. "I understand you think yourself to be of great knightly prowess. You can't blame a lonely woman for wanting to find out the truth for herself, can you?"

Lance could not believe she was so crude. How could Queen Guinevere behave this way? It couldn't be possible, and why would she kidnap him? What did she have to gain in doing so?

"What is not to be gained by seducing a powerful knight and making him into my slave?" she replied, as if reading his mind.

And then something in her eyes, in her mannerisms, and in her claim to be King Arthur's wife caused Lance to have a sudden epiphany. "I know you!" he shouted. "You're not Queen Guinevere. You are Gwenhwyvach, her evil half-sister! You are the False Guinevere."

Gwenhwyvach's eyes grew wide and then filled with rage, but she controlled her reaction, only sneering as she replied.

"And you are a fool. Do you think I want the whole forest to hear you making such ridiculous accusations? For you to say I am someone other than the queen is an act of treason, and I will make sure you are thoroughly punished for it."

"You have always been one to twist others' words and cast your guilt onto them," Lance replied, his whole body aching to jump up and get in her face with his words. Perhaps he had feared her in his childhood, but no longer.

"You are a liar and no doubt a thief as well," Gwenhwyvach continued. "I wouldn't be surprised if you stole that armor from Viviane."

"And you stole your looks from Queen Guinevere," he replied. "No, in truth, you do not even resemble her. In fact, you are not even her half-sister. I know your true identity."

Gwenhwyvach cackled and said, "Pray tell me, who do you think I am? The lily-livered Elaine of the Wastelands, or perhaps La Belle Iseult, or the Saxon Princess Edythe? Come. I can't wait to hear."

But her laughter ceased when Lance replied, "You are the incarnation of Lilith, Adam's first wife, though in this lifetime you go by the name Gwenhwyvach, Queen Guinevere's half-sister. Do not waste your breath trying to deny it."

Gwenhwyvach actually seemed taken aback by this remark. The fire momentarily died in her eyes, and for just a second, her face lost color.

"Why would you even make up such a ridiculous story?" she laughed, looking at her guards and fellow ladies to see whether his words had made any impression upon them.

"I doubt," Lance said when none of them answered, "that your companions know much about Jewish or biblical history, these being the Dark Ages. I doubt they can even read. But you cannot fool me, Lilith. I know you well."

"You know me well," she mocked. "Pray tell how you know me. We have not met before."

"We have, in the future."

"What nonsense is this?" she replied. "Don't tell me you have magic yourself? I did wonder how you so strangely arrived in this land."

Ignoring the confused look on her face, Lance continued, "I know you very well, and I even know how all your acts of evil will end. Oh, do not fear; you will remain powerful for another fifteen centuries, but in the end, you will lose your battle against the children of Adam and Eve at the hand of King Arthur's descendants."

"Lose?" she cackled. "How can I lose? I am far more powerful than you or anyone else—even that fool wizard Merlin."

"Nevertheless, you will lose, for I know the future."

"Know the future!" she scoffed. "I suppose you think you are some sort of prophet."

"No, but I have come from the future and I know your fate."

"No one can know my fate or anyone else's—the future can never be fully known. And even if it could be known, it can always change based upon what we do now. How about I kill you?" she asked, laughing. "Then you won't have any future at all."

Lance refused to be intimidated by her. "Nevertheless," he coolly stated, "I know your reign of evil over mankind will one day end."

"No one can kill me," she taunted him. "You are mere mortals, but I have eaten of the Tree of Life. You think you know things, but you are a fool and should not meddle in things beyond your understanding."

"I am not a fool," Lance replied. "I know what I know, and I promise you that your reign of evil will come to an end, but I also promise it will not be through your destruction but through the power of love."

"The power of love?" she snorted. "What do you as a man know of love? All you men want is one thing—a pretty miss to plow each night. The only thing you desire more is many pretty misses to plow. Do you deny it?"

"There is a man who desires more than that," said Lance. "A man who desires love. His name is Devin Purcell. He is my father's cousin and my mother's half-brother, and someday he will choose you for his mate and take you from this world so you may experience a new Eden."

At these words, Gwenhwyvach's face turned pale again, and for just a second, she looked as if a tear might spring to her eyes. Then, after a moment, she said, "It cannot be. There is no man capable of loving me." And instantly the ire rose up in her again, and she spat out, "There is no man good enough to love me—no man deserving of my love."

"My uncle Devin is," Lance replied calmly. "He will be able to see the beauty in you."

Infuriated, Gwenhwyvach whipped around to call to one of her women.

"Petronilla, come here!" she exclaimed. The woman, who looked like a queen to Lance, rode her mule over to Gwenhwyvach's side. Then the ancient witch demanded of her, "Give me your scarf," and when the woman offered it, Gwenhwyvach nearly ripped it from her hand and began to wrap it around Lance's mouth.

"My queen," Lance begged Petronilla, "I beseech you, as a good and gentle woman, do not let her mistreat me like this."

"Queen?" laughed Gwenhwyvach. "You're calling her a queen? The only true queen in this land is myself. Look at her more closely." Suddenly, Lance saw this richly dressed and beautiful woman transform into a kitchen wench, her skin covered with grease and soot, her skin smelling of onions, her teeth rotted, and her breath foul.

"They are all such," said Gwenhwyvach, gesturing toward the other two women who stood at a distance. "All ugly as sin and more ugly than I can abide, but they are my slaves, and so I disguise them to make them bearable to my sight as well as to aid me in my schemes. You see now there can be no help for you."

As Gwenhwyvach spoke, she gagged Lance's mouth with Petronilla's scarf.

Then Gwenhwyvach ordered the men to continue, and she and Petronilla rode on ahead again. There was nothing Lance could do except pray to God for some means by which he might escape her clutches. Perhaps he had softened her heart by mention of his uncle Devin, but his words would take time to sink into her being. He was sure Merlin, even back in the sixth century, had the power to see into the future, so why would Gwenhwyvach, who was centuries, even millennia, older than the famous wizard, not be able to? Was she in denial, unwilling to see the future, or was the event that would turn the tide of her evil still too far in the future for it to strike her yet? Lance pondered these thoughts as he continued to be carried on his shield by the evil woman's knights—or, for all he knew, perhaps they were farmers also under a spell.

Lance did not know how he was going to escape, but escape he must. He wondered why she wanted him—hadn't Merlin feared when he and Tristan were babies that she would seek to kill them? Was it not possible then that she had been the one to send them back in time through the comet? Perhaps her plan had been to destroy them in the past before they ever had a chance to live in the future. But if she had wanted to do that, she would have had to take them when they were still children, long before she met them in Castle Dracula. Besides, they had turned out to be no true threat to her. Wouldn't it have made more sense for her to bring Uncle Devin back in time to destroy him before he could save her from her own evil? And would she really work in such a way against herself? It was so confusing since Lance knew Gwenhwyvach's future was good—he could not imagine the good woman he knew in the end would seek to hurt him now. His head hurt just trying to wrap his mind around all the possibilities this crazy time-traveling had created.

Lance could not see where he was going, but in time, he realized they were approaching a small mountain. As they began to climb up it, Gwenhwyvach returned to his side and said, "I want to forewarn you that I have insatiable appetites. Tonight I will use you for my pleasure, and if you do not please me, I will kill you. If you do please me, I may kill you anyway, or just let you live until I weary of you. Either way, it would be safe for you to think of me as a black widow."

Lance shivered at the thought. Whether the future had any in-fluence on the past or vice versa, she clearly planned to kill him, and he did not like that possibility at all. He was a man, a knight, heir to an earldom, and one who had once dreamed of being a king. He could not just lie here and do nothing, and yet, how was he to do otherwise?

CHAPTER 2

WHEN THEY REACHED Gwenhwyvach's castle, Lance was carried on his shield up two flights of stairs to a bedchamber. Still paralyzed, he was dumped upon the bed by the knights while Gwenhwyvach watched.

After the knights removed themselves from the room, Gwenhwyvach stood over Lance, again rolling her tongue over her upper lip, before she said, "I will see you tonight, love. You will greatly enjoy your death, I promise."

Did she plan then to kill him in bed? Lance was not going to wait to find out.

As soon as Gwenhwyvach left, turning the key in the lock so he could not escape, Lance's adrenaline began to kick in. He could not yet move his limbs, but he knew from what she said that the potion or drug or whatever she had given him was bound to wear off soon. Hopefully, that would happen before she returned, and he must be prepared to act the second he could move.

Immediately, he began turning his head to scan the room for a means of escape. The walls were solid stone, no doubt a foot or more thick. The only window was a small one, six feet from the floor and covered with bars; even if he could remove the bars, the window was too narrow for his broad shoulders to squeeze through. The door looked to be made of solid oak and was several inches thick, so even if he had his sword, which must have been taken from him while he was still asleep, he could not have broken it down. Gwenhwyvach had also taken his armor. He was simply dressed in the peasant garb Brother Baudwin had given him. Without his armor, his shoulder would be useless in trying to batter down the door by force. Nor was there anything in the room he could use as a battering ram. Other than the bed, the only piece of furniture was a small bedside table that looked as if its legs were about to fall off. Perhaps, though, he could break off one of those legs to use as a club and attack whoever next entered the room. He would attempt it as soon as life returned to his limbs.

Lance had to accept that he could do nothing except wait for the door to open and then either trick or fight whoever entered the room so he could escape. Gwenhwyvach said she would return tonight; he did not expect that to be before dark, which according to the sky, looked to be another hour or two away. He also doubted he could do anything to fight her when she returned—not if she again used her sorcery upon him. But if she should send someone to him with food before then, he might have a chance.

Another hour passed before Lance felt the drug really begin to wear off. Not since Christ had healed the lame did anyone rejoice so much to be able to move his limbs again. First, he felt a tingling in his fingers and toes. Then, after a few minutes, the tingling moved into his hands and finally up his forearms. By the time he was able to make a fist and move his toes, he could feel tingling up his legs and back. The first signs of sunset had appeared in the sky when Lance was finally able to sit up. Then slowly, he lifted his legs, massaging them with his hands as he did so, to swing them over the side of the bed. After a minute of steadying himself, he was able to stand up and carefully walk the few steps to the window the way someone half-hops when his leg has fallen asleep. It took Lance another minute for enough strength to return to his legs so he could stand on his tiptoes to get a good view out the window. The view disappointed him, but it did not surprise him. He was clearly on the third floor of the castle, and the castle was perched on a mountain crag at least five hundred feet up. For a moment, he wondered where in Britain he might be. Had he traveled so far west to be near the mountains of what he knew in the twenty-first century as Wales? If so, it would take him a good week to walk to Camelot from here, if not longer. He wished now that he had studied Britain's topographical geography better.

But first things first; he would never get to Camelot if he didn't discover a way to escape.

Then Lance heard a key turn in the lock. Unwilling to give away his renewed mobility, and having no way of knowing who might open the door, Lance quickly leapt back into bed, surprising himself by how swiftly he moved. His paralysis must have completely dissipated now.

In another second, Petronilla—the fine lady he had thought a queen—entered the room. Only now she was in her natural state as a kitchen wench, and besides being dirty, when she opened her mouth to speak, Lance was repelled by the reek of onions and garlic on her breath.

"I bring you food and drink, good sir," she said, approaching the bed with a tray.

She stopped a moment to push the door shut with her shoulder, but not so quickly that Lance did not get a chance to see that his door was unguarded. Gwenhwyvach must think her spell still effective if she would let a serving girl come alone to bring him food.

"I cannot eat it," Lance replied. "I am still paralyzed."

"You must keep up your strength," said the wench, approaching him and setting the tray on the bedside table. "My queen will want you limber for tonight's exercises."

"I cannot eat," he repeated, trying not to focus on the image Petronilla had just planted in his mind. "Would you feed it to me?"

She looked at him questioningly, then said, "I suppose it would not hurt me to help you."

All she had brought was a bowl of onion soup, some of which she must have eaten herself, considering the stale smell of her breath. He found he was hungry, however, so he let her hold the bowl up to his mouth—when were these people going to invent spoons?—and drank it down. But then before she could pull it away, he quickly grabbed her wrists and said, "You must help me escape."

For a moment, Petronilla looked startled, but she had not screamed when he grabbed her, which impressed him.

"Aye, I will help," she replied. "Why else do you think I have come? Do you truly think that foul witch wants you fed? Or did you think I only came to get some of what she wants from you before she does?"

She smiled, and for a moment, Lance thought she might be flirting with him, but he had no time for that.

"How can I escape?" he demanded.

"You're hurting me," she said, nodding toward her wrists, her hands still clutching the empty bowl.

Lance released her and she set the bowl down. Then sitting down on the side of the bed, she said, "So you can truly move all of your body now?"

"Yes," he said. "I am ready to go the moment the coast is clear."

"Oh, there's no way you can reach the coast to escape," she replied. "You must go through the forest."

"It's just an expression," Lance replied. "I mean, whenever you think I can get away without anyone seeing me escape, I'm ready to leave."

"I see," she said. "Very well. I will help you, but only if you promise to help me as well."

"I will try," he said. "What do you require?"

"There is a man I love," she began. Lance smiled as she said it, but seeing the glimmer in his eye, she quickly corrected him. "A knight I love as a brother. He and another young knight are locked up in the dungeon of a castle a half league from here by a lord who is in conspiracy with Gwenhwyvach against King Arthur. This man is a knight of the Round Table, and so he has been captured to weaken King Arthur's defenses. Will you help them to escape also?"

"I will if it's possible and you tell me how," said Lance, for while he did not wish to be delayed on his trip to Camelot, he saw no way to reach there unless he gained help from this woman, and he also now understood from personal experience that no one deserved to be held unjustly as a prisoner.

"There is to be a great tournament tomorrow afternoon at this lord's castle," said Petronilla. "If I help you to escape, and I restore your armor to you and find you a horse, will you ride in this tournament, seeking to defeat this lord?"

"Yes," said Lance, "but how will my fighting in a tournament help to free these knights?"

"Once you have defeated this wicked lord, you will demand that he grant you a boon on pain of his life. When he agrees, you will demand the release of these knights from prison."

"I see," said Lance, nodding his head in understanding. "I will gladly do so if I am able, but first, tell me how you will get me out of this castle?"

"That is easy enough," she said.

Lance waited for her to explain, but before she said anything more, he began to smell roses, and the smell overcame that of onions. In fact, the scent was so overpowering that he turned toward the window and said, "Do you smell that?"

And she, laughing, replied, "Smell what?"

And when he turned his head back to speak to her, he discovered that not the kitchen wench but Gwenhwyvach was sitting on his bed.

"How—what—?" he began.

"You thought you could escape from me," Gwenhwyvach replied. "You thought you and a stupid kitchen wench could outsmart me—I who have the cunning of centuries within me."

"I—I—there is no excuse for such trickery!" Lance explained. "What right have you to think I would try to do anything but escape when you hold me against my will?"

"Oh, but you see, there is all the reason for trickery now," she replied. "When it is for good, it is completely—"

"What good have you ever done?" Lance interrupted her.

"Let me finish," Gwenhwyvach snapped. "You too easily believe what you see before you, but remember, appearances can be deceiving. I am just joking around with you. I am not Gwenhwyvach; I am still the kitchen wench you saw before you. Gwenhwyvach believes only she can change my appearance to that of a queen as you saw in the meadow this afternoon, but what she does not realize is that when she first made my acquaintance, I had already disguised myself as a kitchen wench to gain entrance to her castle."

"I don't understand," Lance replied. "If you are not Petronilla or Gwenhwyvach, who are you, and why are you taking on this appearance?"

"I, dear Lance Delaney, brave but silly boy, am Lady Morgana of Avalon, more famously known as Morgan le Fay."

Lance was too stunned by this statement to speak, but he felt relief flood through him.

"You—you—oh, thank God, you know my name," he finally said. "You know who I am."

"Yes, of course," said Morgana. "I have been watching you since you arrived on Britain's shore."

"Then you know how I arrived here by mistake," said Lance. "You know that I am not from this time. And you will help me return to the twenty-first century, won't you?"

"There are no mistakes," she replied. "No mistakes at all, but we have no time for explanations now. We must move quickly. So long as I am disguised as Gwenhwyvach, her minions will obey me, but we must leave before she returns, for I fear her powers are greater than mine—as I said when mimicking her—I confess I do so love to do it—she has the cunning of centuries, so we do not want to risk a confrontation with her."

Morgana quickly stood up. Lance crossed the room behind her as she carefully opened the door to peek out. She looked both ways, then motioned for him to follow her.

Soon they were walking down a long dark hallway, lit only by torches, since night had now fallen. Had they waited another minute or two, no doubt Gwenhwyvach would have come upon them, but it wasn't until they reached the stairs that they saw anyone, and then it was just a serving wench who curtsied in fear while Morgana ignored her in keeping with Gwenhwyvach's behavior.

At the bottom of the stairs were two guards, but Morgana swept past them. They simply stood at attention in deference to her, not even daring to question why she was followed by her prisoner. Another flight of stairs brought them to a male servant, who looked askance at Lance's presence, but Morgana said, "Do not worry. He is under my spell." The servant then simply bowed in obedience until they had passed.

Morgana next led Lance down another long corridor to a door. Once Morgana opened it, Lance's sight was greeted by an armory filled with several hanging suits of armor, including his own.

"Be quick now," said Morgana. "I shall help you put it on. Remember, Gwenhwyvach could be upon us at any moment."

Lance had never dressed so quickly in his life. He was about to grab up his sword and shield, but Morgana said, "Give those to me so it does not look suspicious." He did as she bade, and then they returned to the corridor and proceeded down it. Soon enough, they were in the courtyard where two armed guards met them.

"Milady?" said one.

"I am going to kill him," Morgana told the guard. "I wish to do so in the forest so no one else need be bothered by his screams."

"Do you wish me to accompany you for protection, milady?" asked the guard, trying not to show his fear of her—after all, she appeared quite confident in her ability to destroy such a powerful-looking knight.

"No," Morgana replied, completely staying in character. "I wish to have privacy. I plan to have my way with him first, you understand." Then she stepped up to the guard, lifting Lance's sword until its point reached his chin. "Until his own sword is as erect as this one," she laughed, "and then I will force him against his will, and when he still fails to please me, I shall take great pleasure in killing him, and if that still does not satisfy me, I will return to see whether you are capable of satisfying my lust, and if not, perhaps you will die also."

The guard looked as if he were about to cry, but he managed to say, "Very well, milady. My only wish is to serve you."

Morgana cackled, perfectly imitating her enemy, before replying, "Yes, it is good you know your purpose. Now open the gate!"

The other guard quickly ran to do so while Morgana continued to point the sword at the first, gently twisting it into his chin until he began to sweat with fear.

"Come!" Lance shouted, too nervous to delay longer and nearly giving them away by his plea, but Morgana remained calmly in character.

Swinging around and removing the sword, much to the guard's relief, she said to Lance, "You do not give me orders, little man! I will get around to killing you when I so choose." And then marching like an Amazon warrior, she passed out of the open gate. Lance meekly trailed behind her.

"Close the gate!" Morgana shouted once they had passed through it. And then, without looking back, she continued into the forest until the trees and darkness hid her and Lance from sight.

"You were marvelous!" Lance said once they were out of hearing.

Morgana laughed and said, "Here; take these. I hate weapons."

She handed him back his sword and shield; then she admitted, "It was rather fun pretending to be evil. I can see what a thrill it is to hold power over others, but I could also sense how easily it can consume your soul, and that feeling frightened even me."

"Where do we go now?" asked Lance as his eyes tried to adjust to the forest's darkness.

"I don't know how long it will take before Gwenhwyvach realizes we are gone and sends men out searching for us," said Morgana. "I will change back into my normal form so we are less likely to be recognized."

Morgana then transformed from Gwenhwyvach into the Lady of Avalon, a change that was not dramatic—no smoke or lightning, but just a soft transformation of features, which Lance found remarkable even though he had difficulty seeing the full effect in the growing darkness. He could just tell that she was beautiful—and there was a kindness in her face that far surpassed Gwenhwyvach's haughty beauty.

"Now," said Morgana, "I think we should travel at least an hour into the forest to ensure our safety. Then we can find a place in the woods to sleep. At the break of dawn, we will travel to the castle where the tournament will be held tomorrow afternoon."

"Oh," said Lance, trying to keep up with her pace on the treacherous rocky path before them. "I thought maybe you had made up the stuff about the tournament; I thought that was all just part of your character as a serving maid."

"No," said Morgana. "The castle where the tournament will be held is under a spell, and I have been unable to penetrate it. Nor is it my duty to be the hero of this tale. You must rescue the imprisoned knights to prove yourself worthy."

"Worthy of what?" asked Lance.

"You will know in time."

Lance did not reply at first, but then his frustration burst forth. "Everyone acts as if I'm supposed to be learning something here, but I never asked for any of this. You do realize I don't belong in this time. Do you know how I can return back to the twenty-first century and my parents?"

"I know what I need to know," Morgana replied, picking up her pace.

"What does that mean?" asked Lance, nearly having to run to keep up with her, for his armor was heavy and slowed him down. "You do understand I was caught in some accidental time warp because of the comet, don't you?"

"I told you before there are no mistakes," said Morgana, "so there can be no accidents. That said, it is not for me to enlighten you, but for you to enlighten yourself."

"But I don't understand what you're saying?" Lance replied. "Are you saying you will not help me?"

"I am saying it is not my place to help you beyond a certain degree. I rescued you from Gwenhwyvach, and I will do one more thing for you so that you may win the tournament, but you cannot expect more than that from me."

"I don't care about your bloody tournament!" Lance snapped. "I didn't ask to participate in it, so help me in another way. Help me to get home."

"It is true you did not ask to participate in the tournament," said Morgana patiently, "but you agreed to in exchange for my help, so you must keep your promise. But more to the point, is it not when we help others that we most help ourselves?"

Lance felt chastised, but he could not resist muttering, "I am sick of all these riddles."

"I, on the other hand," said Morgana, "enjoy them a great deal, and they are not all riddles, but the ways to wisdom. They exist for your benefit, whether you realize it or not."

"Nothing in life can ever be easy, can it?" Lance asked.

"You are on a quest," said Morgana. "You cannot expect a quest to be easy; otherwise, what you seek would not be worth questing for."

"But I don't even know why I'm on this quest," said Lance, "or what it is."

"Perhaps that is the very reason you are on it," said Morgana, stopping to look him in the eye, although in the darkness, they were little more than shadows to one another. "Perhaps you must figure it all out for yourself. Now, shush. We must not risk Gwenhwyvach's men overhearing us; they may already be in pursuit."

Lance said no more but followed her in silence as she began walking again. He felt bone weary, but he continued to wonder why he had been brought into this strange situation, and why even the most knowledgeable people could not give him the answers he sought.

After an hour, Morgana walked off the path about a hundred feet until they came to a thicket where she said they would sleep. They had to fight their way into the thicket, but the thorn bushes did not seem to bother Morgana, and Lance's armor protected him until they were inside it. "We will sleep here," said Morgana. "I do not think we need fear being disturbed." They found the clearing inside the thicket just wide enough to lie down beside each other for the night.

By this point, Lance was exhausted. He did not relish the idea of sleeping in his armor, but he managed to make a pillow out of some dead leaves, and after carefully positioning himself so he would not roll over and crush the Lady of Avalon beneath his armor, he soon drifted off to sleep.

CHAPTER 3

ONLY A SLIGHT glimmer of morning light graced the sky when Lance opened his eyes. He lay there for a moment, feeling disoriented and almost thinking he was home at Delaney Castle. Not able to recognize his surroundings in the darkness, he slowly remembered being in Baudwin's cottage, but it was another few seconds before he felt the forest floor beneath his fingers and remembered falling asleep in the thicket with Morgana.

When he looked over, however, Morgana was gone.

He jumped up in a panic. Where was she? Should he go looking for her? Had Gwenhwyvach's men captured her? But they couldn't have without waking him—and if they had come, wouldn't they have taken him too?

"Calm down," he told himself. "Maybe she just went to find something to eat, or to relieve herself in privacy—something I also need to do."

He struggled out of the thicket and found a tree to hide behind to relieve himself, all the while looking about for any sign of Morgana. He hoped to spot her, but he did not wish her to see him until he was finished, which took some extra time, considering he was wearing his armor.

Finally, he stepped from behind the tree and continued to look about him. The darkness was lifting, but the forest was so thick that he could not see more than twenty feet before him. Where had she gone? Why would she have left him? He bent down to look about the thicket for footprints or any matted grass to reveal where she had gone, but he was no woodsman or tracker, so he could not find any sign that would give him answers.

"I'll walk in a big circle," he told himself. "That will help me find her." So he walked into the forest about fifty feet and then proceeded east, slowly circling around in a clockwise manner, hoping he truly was going in a circle since he had to make little side trips around all the trees and bushes in his way. The worst thing he could imagine would be to get lost when he already didn't know where he was.

As he searched, he slowly felt himself starting to panic. Was it possible that after all the time he had spent searching in this strange time and place, he had finally found someone who could help him, only to lose her? And now he had no idea where he was, no idea which way was Camelot, or even which way was Gwenhwyvach's castle. How could he possibly know without Morgana's help whether he was heading toward his salvation or future imprisonment?

Lance was nearly about to give into the panic fighting its way up his chest when he heard a horse whinnying. Immediately, he froze. Morgana did not have a horse, but Gwenhwyvach's men probably did. If the horse belonged to anyone else, he would not know whether its owner was friend or foe. Carefully, he looked about for the horse, but it wasn't until he heard it whinny again and Morgana say, "Whoa, boy. It will be all right, I promise," that he turned in the right direction. Then, feeling so joyful he nearly wanted to run, he tramped quickly through the forest for fifty feet until he saw Morgana—and the amazing creature she was with. At the same moment, the creature saw him, and it reared up on its hind legs in surprise, but Morgana quickly placed her hand on its mane to soothe it.

"It's okay," she said to the creature, a creature Lance could not believe was standing before him—it was the most beautiful horse he had ever seen, and from its forehead grew a beautiful, twisted, ivory-looking horn.

"You didn't really believe unicorns existed, did you?" Morgana said, turning toward Lance once the magical creature was again standing still.

Lance shook his head, speechless. He did not think he had ever seen anything so beautiful...except—but he could not think of Elaine now. She loved his brother anyway.

"Come closer," said Morgana. "Gently, so you do not startle him. He does not fear you, but he has only been here a minute, so I haven't had time to explain to him yet that you are my friend."

Lance carefully stepped forward. The unicorn now bowed its head down to the ground as if to greet him. Lance came up to Morgana, stopping just a couple of feet from her, and then he stood staring in awe at the beautiful white creature as it lifted its head again and looked him in the eye. Lance felt as if the unicorn were reading him like a book, seeing all his faults and flaws, and yet sending him love regardless.

Then Lance felt Morgana reach for his hand. She pulled it up and set his palm upon the unicorn's head, beside its horn.

"He likes to be petted," Morgana said.

Lance barely dared to touch such a beautiful part of God's creation, yet he could not resist stroking its mane, and as he did so, a great feeling of peace and contentment came over him.

"Unicorns are simpler than we are," said Morgana. "More pure, and far less full of anxiety than humans. They are wiser, too, because they lack mankind's foolishness."

"Are there many unicorns left?" Lance asked. "They always seem, even in medieval literature, to be special and few."

"Special, yes," said Morgana, "but not few. Men would hunt them for their horns, which have great medicinal properties, so they are forced to disguise themselves to hide from man. They do so here in Arthur's time, and they do so in your own time as well."

"You mean there are unicorns in England in the twenty-first century?" Lance asked, raising his eyebrows.

"Lance," said Morgana, shaking her head at his ignorance, "if you would only pay attention, you would know there are unicorns in the very stables of Delaney Castle, and you have seen them many times. You just never really took the time to look at them. You humans tend to see only what you are looking for; you do not bother to consider what you might see."

The unicorn now stepped forward to rub its nose in Morgana's hair.

"He likes you," laughed Lance. "He wants to be your friend."

"More than that," said Morgana. "We are old friends. We have been for centuries."

"Then you knew he was here in the forest?"

"No, he came to find me," she said. "He sensed that if we are going to the tournament today, you will need a steed, and so he came to fulfill that need. I told you I would arrange one more way to help you."

Lance could not believe what he was hearing. This unicorn was to be his steed! He was to ride it in a tournament!

"But...but I don't think...people will," he said, trying to make his sentence intelligible. "Won't everyone be shocked to see me ride a unicorn?"

"You did not listen to what I just said," Morgana replied. "Did I not say that you humans only see what you are looking for?"

"Yes," said Lance, not understanding.

"At the tournament, people will be looking to see knights on horses, not unicorns."

"Yes, that is my point exactly," Lance replied. "They'll be shocked by it."

"No, because they won't be expecting to see a unicorn, but a horse, so they will only see you upon your steed."

This response left Lance in awe. He did not quite understand whether it was magic or the fault of human imagination that would keep others from seeing the unicorn for what it really was, but he was grateful just for the opportunity to be near it.

"Stand back now," said Morgana, taking Lance's hand and walking backward with him several feet. "Watch," she then said.

Lance's surprise over seeing a unicorn felt like nothing compared to what he now witnessed—unbelievably, he watched as enormous wings sprouted from the unicorn's sides. The magical creature immediately flapped its wings, and then, leaping forward, it effortlessly lifted itself up into the air.

"It's—it's a Pegasus!" Lance exclaimed, watching it fly into the distance so quickly that it was but a speck in the air within ten seconds.

"That's just insulting," said Morgana, laughing, as the unicorn began its flight back toward them. "Pegasus was said to be born of Medusa's blood, and Medusa was one of Lilith's many incarnations—no unicorn could be born of Medusa's blood, though I will say that Gwenhwyvach's current hairstyle is a big improvement on the one she wore as Medusa. But regardless, Pegasus never lived. He was just made up by the storytellers; after all, how can a horse be born of a woman, even if the sea god Poseidon sired him? So no, he is not a Pegasus. He is Papillon, my own steed, and a rare and beautifully gifted creature, the progeny of two very special unicorns."

"He must be the eighth wonder of the world!" Lance declared as Papillon continued to fly in circles above them.

"More a wonder," Morgana replied, "than your friend Palomides' Beast Glatisant at least."

Lance looked at her, wondering whether she was joking. "That beast is a giraffe from Africa," he said. "Surely, you know that."

"Of course I know that. How else do you think it got to Britain? At the rate Pellinore was going, I was afraid every other child in Britain would someday be his bastard, so just about the first thing I did as Lady of Avalon was have that giraffe brought by magic to Britain to give Pellinore a quest and the women of Listenoise some respite. I won't say it was my best act of magic—Merlin was still training me back then, but at least I picked a giraffe—Merlin wanted a more hideous beast like a rhinoceros, but I was afraid a rhinoceros might really hurt Pellinore if it charged him, and I also feared it would be an easier target for him. Giraffes are faster, and I didn't want anyone to get hurt. I regret that Pellinore ended up being wounded, but I thought after a couple of years of chasing the beast, he'd come to his senses and settle down with a wife. I guess I misjudged him. I'm sorry to see him bedridden now, but at least he can no longer go around trying to assert his *droit de seigneur.*"

Lance was only half-listening to Morgana as he continued to stare with wonder at Papillon—he felt he could never tire of watching the wondrous creature. But after a few minutes, Morgana motioned for the flying unicorn to return to earth.

Papillon landed gently, and then he bowed his head again. Lance watched as the unicorn horn disappeared at the same moment Papillon folded his wings. Then the wings also dissolved into the sides of his body. In another second, the unicorn had been transformed into what appeared to be a knight's everyday steed.

"I don't think," said Lance, feeling almost breathless, "that from this day forth, I will ever find anything impossible to believe."

"Wise words indeed," replied Morgana. "Come now. We will both ride him to the tournament. I have some fruit I found in my satchel that we can eat along the way."

Lance hesitated a moment.

"Will he let me ride him?" he asked.

"He is my special steed," Morgana replied, "and therefore, he will not let anyone else ride him without my permission. Only one other, Ogier the Dane, has ever ridden him until now, but yes, he will let you ride him, for it is his pleasure to do as I wish, but count yourself fortunate for the honor."

Papillon now lowered his head, almost as if bowing out of respect to Lance, making it clear Lance was welcome to ride him. Lance then smiled and no longer had any qualm about climbing onto Papillon's back. Once mounted, he reached down and pulled Morgana up so she could sit in front of him.

In another minute, they were returning to the road through the forest and on their way to the tournament.

CHAPTER 4

IT TOOK SOME time for the wonder of riding on a flying unicorn disguised as an ordinary horse, even though they were only trotting down an ordinary dusty road, to wear off for Lance. And then he began to have some serious concerns about how well he would perform in the tournament. It was one thing to agree to participate in a tournament when you were locked in a castle by a witch and had no other way to escape; it was another thing when the tournament would take place in just a few hours, you weren't really a knight, and you hadn't had any sword practice for several years.

Often in the past when Lance had felt self-doubt or had a great task to perform, he had found strength in remembering the great men and women from whom he was descended; their courageous blood ran in his veins, and if he did not always remember the details of their lives, he always felt certain that wherever they were, they were cheering him on. That thought comforted him for a moment, but then he realized that chief among those ancestors was King Arthur; how could King Arthur be cheering him from heaven or Avalon or wherever he was in the twenty-first century when Lance was here in the sixth century and King Arthur was still alive and in Camelot? And that made Lance realize that if he were in the past, the other great ancestors he looked to for support—Melusine, Roland, Ogier the Dane, and many others—were all yet to be born so they would not have the power to support him. And then he remembered that Ogier the Dane, as Morgana had just recently told him, had once ridden the very horse he was riding upon now. That had been a curious thing for Morgana to say when it would not happen for nearly three more centuries.

"Lady Morgana?" Lance began respectfully, for he felt a bit awkward to have her seated in front of him, the scent of her hair wafting up his nostrils, and now he was beginning to realize she was quite attractive besides, yet she had to be something like his thirty-greats-grandmother.

"Yes," she said, patiently waiting for him to finish his question.

"I was wondering," he continued, "how you could remember that Ogier the Dane rode Papillon when that event is three hundred years in the future? Do you know everything about the future including what you'll be doing in it?"

Morgana hesitated for a moment, as if unsure how to explain it to him.

"Please," said Lance. "I want to understand."

Morgana took a deep breath, choosing her words carefully, before replying. "It is not an easy matter to explain, and at this moment, there are reasons why I cannot reveal it all to you, but you will know in a short time now I believe."

"But can't you explain any of it to me?" Lance persisted. "Give me the dumbed-down explanation at least?"

"The reason I can know the future," said Morgana, "and also

what is the past and your own past, which lies in the future, is be-cause there really is no such thing as the past or the future. In fact, there really is no such thing as time. It is far too complicated for me to explain in detail to you, but when you get back to your own world, I recommend you read a book about quantum physics; that may help you to understand it better."

"When I get back to my own time," Lance repeated. "Then you know I will eventually return to my family and the twenty-first cen-tury?"

"I have already said too much," Morgana replied, "and we are approaching the main road to the tournament, so we cannot discuss it further with all these people around us."

Indeed, the trail through the forest they had been following now merged into a wider, main dirt road, and it was filled with small groups of people, all of them headed in the same direction.

"Are they all going to the tournament?" asked Lance in surprise.

"Yes," said Morgana. "Such an event is a great holiday for them."

Lance was amazed; he had never seen so many people since he had arrived in the past. He had been to Renaissance faires in En-gland, but he had found them rather disappointing and trite—a few players in costume mobbed by crowds of people in twenty-first century clothing. But here it was as if everyone were in costume—except these were their real clothes. It was quite an amazing sight, with women and men in every color imaginable, and far more color-ful than the black and other drab colors most modern people wore. These people's clothes were far more decorative, with buckles and bells and ribbons, long poufy dresses and long-sleeved shirts with great drooping sleeves. Women with flowers and all manner of or-naments in their hair walked beside large strong men who were not afraid to sport pink shirts and tan trousers, and monks and friars, still in sober gray and brown robes, wore smiles of great mirth. All had come to enjoy what felt like a festive day in Merry Olde England—or rather Britain. And nothing but festivity and frivolity seemed to matter at this moment.

"But I will return to my own time?" Lance asked for reassurance after a moment of watching the teeming crowd.

"You will return," said Morgana, "but hush now." And she gave a little pat to his leg to comfort him. It was the first sign of affection Lance had known since he had arrived, and he greatly appreciated it. For just a moment, he lay his hand upon her own, only to be surprised to touch great bejeweled rings on her fingers that he had not noticed before. And then looking at her to question why she was wearing them, he was so startled that he nearly fell off Papillon—for Morgana had taken on the guise of Gwenhwyvach again.

When Morgana realized he was staring at her, she explained, "It will better serve our purposes for me to take on this form, as you will soon understand. You are to tell everyone you are my champion when we arrive."

"All right," said Lance, swallowing hard, for now the thought of the tournament was making him nervous again.

Most of the people on the road were peasants and clergy, all walking to the tournament, while the occasional young lord and his lady rode past Lance and Morgana. These young men often would slow their horses to lift their hats and nod to Morgana, who was apparently not recognized as Gwenhwyvach or mistaken as her half-sister Queen Guinevere—after all, there was no television or even photographs in this time, Lance reminded himself, so only a handful of people might truly recognize her.

In half an hour's time, Lance and Morgana arrived at a great open field surrounding a large castle. Morgana told him the castle was called Dolorous Gard because it was believed by the local people to have been under an enchantment since ancient times. Lance, however, could clearly see it was not more than fifty years old. Surely, the uneducated peasants were quick to spread rumors and tales. Morgana went on to say that the castle's owner was known as the Copper Knight, and he would challenge all who approached his castle, defeating them and throwing them into his prison. "His prowess is so great," said Morgana, "that many say it is he and not the castle that is under an enchantment, for no man could have such strength or such a winning streak in combat—not even the great Sir Bedwyr of Camelot. Nor does anyone know the Copper Knight's true identity or how he came to possess the castle, so they fear him all the more."

The field before them was filled with hundreds, if not thousands, of people. Tents and small pavilions were set up all around the field with the tournament green at the far end. Many booths were selling ale and mead, as well as all manner of breads, meats, and cheeses. Primitive games were being played, ranging from some form of horseshoes and beanie bag tosses to tug-of-wars. The entire stream of people present seemed to be eating, playing, and enjoying themselves.

"Do not be misled by all this merriment," Morgana whispered in Lance's ear. "The Copper Knight is happy to show his hospitality to lure more knights to him so he can defeat them and make them his prisoners. He is in league with Gwenhwyvach to weaken Arthur's forces, for nearly every knight in Britain serves the High King, but this man and Gwenhwyvach seek to change that very quickly."

"Do you know the Copper Knight's identity?" Lance asked.

"He is called the Copper Knight because of his armor," Morgana replied, "but Gwenhwyvach acquired that armor for him. She also had this castle built to serve as a prison, so I imagine you can guess his name."

"Is he Constantine of Cornwall," Lance asked, "the one who will eventually conquer Camelot and overthrow Arthur?"

"Yes," said Morgana, "but at least for today, he shall not succeed. Not after you have finished with him. But first, you must rest and recoup your strength. Do you see that red tent over there? My servants have set it up for us."

Lance rode toward the tent, glad to hear he would be allowed to rest for a short time. He was surprised Morgana had servants already here. But he was more surprised when, as Papillon carried them toward the tent, the Copper Knight—his identity obvious from his armor—suddenly appeared and rode up beside them. When the knight blew Morgana a kiss, Lance's skin began to crawl until he realized the man thought Morgana was Gwenhwyvach—his mistress. Lance was relieved when Morgana only nodded to Constantine, who then rode off in the opposite direction.

Once Lance and Morgana arrived at the tent, they dismounted. Morgana bid a squire come feed and water the horse and allow it to rest before the tournament began in a little more than an hour. Then she and Lance went into the tent, which Lance was surprised to find had a beautiful bed inside it with soft cushions and furs upon it. There was even a table and two small chairs at one end, and on the table was a bowl of fruit.

"I don't think I'll ever get used to the beauty of everything medieval," Lance said, admiring the roomy tent and carved wood of the chairs, "or that everything here is so magical."

"It is good when life continues to have surprises," Morgana agreed, "but let me help you off with your armor so you may rest. I fear you did not sleep well last night, and you will need all your strength for the tournament. While you sleep, I will also cast a spell over you so your strength and prowess increase and you are protected from being wounded."

"Is that fair?" asked Lance, who after the spell Gwenhwyvach had placed him under, was uncertain he wanted to experience another.

"No, it is not," said Morgana, "at least, it would not be if your opponent were anyone else, but remember, he is not just an opponent; he is our enemy, and if we are to fight witchcraft, we need magic."

Lance nodded assent, and with Morgana's help, he quickly had his armor off and then lay down on the bed to rest.

"Once I cast the spell, I will leave you to sleep while I try to gather word of the prisoners from the townsfolk," said Morgana. "But do not worry. I will be back in time to help you get ready for the tournament."

Lance was already drifting to sleep, so he did not reply, and he barely heard the first foreign words Morgana muttered over him before he was snoring.

His eyes still closed, Lance stirred in his sleep, feeling something fuzzy and rough rubbing against his cheek, even though he had the sheet covering most of his head. He was still too much asleep, however, to be bothered by it and simply hoped it would go away.

Then he heard a male voice say, "My love, I so desired you when I saw you that I had to come to you immediately. Please tell me you have not spurned me for that lily-faced boy I saw you with."

It took a moment for Lance's fogged brain to register these words, but it took less than a half-second for him to register the kiss placed upon his cheek.

Lance bolted out of bed, reaching for his sword that lay beside him on the floor. He quickly grabbed it and swung around, placing his sword at the throat of his would-be lover. The man was himself so stunned that he had frozen and remained kneeling beside the bed.

"You!" exclaimed Lance, surprised to find Constantine, the Copper Knight, in his tent. "What are you doing here?"

"You...I thought.... What are you doing in milady's chamber?" Constantine demanded, cautiously regaining his feet at the point of Lance's sword.

"You thought me Gwenhwyvach?" demanded Lance.

"Yes, yes," spluttered Constantine. "You do not think I would— but you have not answered me. I am her paramour. Therefore, I demand to know who you are!"

"I," said Lance, "am her champion."

"Her champion?" exclaimed Constantine. "How can that be? She loves me! You are a scoundrel, a woman-stealer!" Enraged, he reached for his sword.

"Relax, my love," said Morgana, appearing at the tent's entrance, still disguised as Gwenhwyvach.

"I demand to know what you are doing with this man!" Constantine raged.

"You know I have many purposes," the False Gwenhwyvach replied. "You have no need to question me."

"Do not lie to me!" shouted Constantine. "Is he your lover? Tell me. Tell me the truth. If he is, I will kill him—I will run my sword through him before your very eyes."

"You well may do so during the tournament," said the False Gwenhwyvach, "but he is not my lover."

"Please do not lie to me," said Constantine, now looking as if he were about to cry. He approached her, knelt before her, took her hand in his own, and placed it against his cheek. "Do not spurn me, Mistress. You know how I love you. You know I would die for you. I am only well when I am in your presence. You are my queen, and I seek only to make you Queen of Britain as is your right, and then I will glory in serving you all my days as your king and your knight true."

As Lance watched Constantine's submissive display, he couldn't decide whether he should laugh or gag.

"Rise; do not make a fool out of yourself," Morgana snapped, playing well her bitchy role as Gwenhwyvach so Constantine would not suspect her. "This knight is Sir Lancelot, and he has come here in the guise of my champion only so that no one will suspect my relationship with you. Furthermore, Sir Lancelot is a knight of great prowess, unlike many of those puny weaklings from Camelot whom you have already defeated. Some say he is the greatest knight in the land now that Sir Bedwyr has lost his hand. Therefore, my love, if you defeat him, you will make all Britain marvel at your strength and skill; people will praise you, and they will seek to follow you; then we will raise an army that you can lead to victory against King Arthur."

"You are so wise, my mistress," said Constantine, looking up at her with tears in his eyes. "You do love me, don't you?"

"I am always seeking to do everything I can to help you," Morgana lied.

"Forgive me, Mistress. I never should have doubted you, but please understand that my devotion sometimes blinds me to logic. I am but a worm seeking to find his home in your love."

The False Gwenhwyvach smiled, and then stroking his face with her fingers, she said, "No, you should never doubt me." Lance watched Constantine shudder with delight at her touch. Then he was aghast to see the False Gwenhwyvach shove her index finger into Constantine's mouth, which he sucked like a babe. Fortunately, only Lance saw the look of disgust on the False Gwenhwyvach's face as she kept up her ruse by placating him.

After a moment, the False Gwenhwyvach snapped, "That is enough!" and yanked her finger from Constantine's mouth, wiping off the spit on it on Constantine's own beard. "The tournament is beginning soon. You must kill Sir Lancelot so you may achieve great fame today. Sir Lancelot is a proud and haughty knight, so he has it coming."

"I shall not be defeated," Lance declared, keeping up his part in the game. "I will prove, milady, that it is I who deserve your affections; that I am the only one capable of leading your army to defeat Arthur. And when I do so, I will gratefully allow you to place Britain's crown upon my head."

At these words, Constantine jumped to his feet. He swung around, pulled out his sword, and pointed it at Lance. "Do not for a moment think you will ever know the pleasures of being with this woman!" he warned, "or that you will ever receive the crown that is rightfully mine!"

"Enough!" shouted the False Gwenhwyvach. "There will be no bloodshed in private; that will not enhance your reputation, Constantine. Go now. Sir Lancelot will soon follow to challenge you in the tournament."

Constantine looked at her, then lowered his sword. His face begged that she kiss him, but she waved him off, refusing to look at him more. After a moment, he departed, but not without first glaring at Lance.

"You're amazing!" Lance told Morgana once their enemy was gone. "Although that part with your finger was more than any actress should have to pull off."

"Shh!" Morgana replied. "He may be listening. Be quick now; we must get you into your armor."

Morgana helped Lance to dress, and he was just about done when the trumpets sounded for the tournament to begin. Lance quickly went outside to mount Papillon and await his turn in the jousting. Morgana, meanwhile, went to the spectator stands where she joined the other noble ladies watching the tournament.

As Lance waited, he saw the Copper Knight ride against several strong and sturdy-looking young knights. Some of them even appeared to be quite skilled in jousting, but each time one of their lances struck the Copper Knight, the blow was scarcely felt, the Copper Knight riding on past his opponent and knocking the man from his horse in the process. Only one knight lasted for a second tourney with the Copper Knight, and soon the Copper Knight had defeated all five of his challengers. It had been decreed before the tournament began that each loser was to be publicly humiliated, so Constantine had chosen to have a barber at the ready to shave off each fallen knight's beard and send him home in shame. Lance was surprised that Constantine did not seek to make the knights his prisoners, but perhaps that would be going too far at a public event.

When the trumpet sounded again, it was Lance's turn. Taking the jousting lance that a squire handed to him, he rode to his station.

Another blast from the trumpet and the joust began. Lance spurred on Papillon, and holding his lance tightly, he rode straight toward his opponent. Constantine was also coming at him full speed with great determination; for a second, Lance winced, thinking how much the blow from Constantine's lance would hurt. But he managed to hold steady, and while not striking a blow to his opponent, he did maneuver his lance to strike Constantine's, knocking it aside so neither rider was struck.

The two knights returned to opposite stations; then they charged each other again, with similar results. A third sally saw Constantine wait until their horses were nearly nose to nose, and then he threw his lance sideways in an attempt to knock Lance from his horse. Scarcely knowing what possessed him, Lance dropped his own lance and grabbed onto Constantine's to block it from hitting him. Lance's grip was so strong that Constantine's horse rode on without its rider; Constantine found himself momentarily suspended in the air by Lance's strength, and then Lance released the lance, sending Constantine tumbling into the dirt.

The crowd roared with laughter. Once Constantine had fallen, Lance slowed Papillon to a walk and moved to the end of the field. Before Lance could turn his horse around, Constantine was on his feet, and grabbing Lance's own lance from the ground, he charged Lance from behind.

The crowd cried a warning, but Lance did not turn around in time, and in the next second, Constantine had struck Lance a blow upon the back that sent him toppling from his horse.

"Boo!" sounded the crowd, but Constantine only lifted the lance again, and this time, he whacked the fallen knight across the chest with it.

One such blow would have killed a man not protected by the enchanted armor of Lyonesse, but Lance simply rolled over and got to his feet. Constantine, amazed that his opponent could still walk, now lifted the lance back over his shoulder as if it were a baseball bat, preparing to whack Lance with it again. But as the lance came forward, Lance grabbed hold of it. The knights were now engaged in a tug-of-war, but it was quickly apparent that the Copper Knight was the weaker man. Making one last valiant effort to shake his opponent, Constantine ground his feet into the earth, and leaning backward to use his full weight, he unexpectedly found himself falling into the dirt when Lance let go of the lance.

"You bastard!" shouted Constantine, but he was not heard over the crowd's roaring laughter. While Constantine struggled to his feet, Lance patiently waited, like the schoolyard bully who knows the little boy he torments is no match for him; only this time, the true bully was getting his comeuppance.

Once on his feet again, Constantine motioned to a squire, who came running to bring him his sword. When Lance saw his enemy armed, he also motioned that a sword be brought to him. A squire ran forward with one for Lance, but before he could reach him, his neck encountered Constantine's sword; the squire dropped headless to the earth, and the sword intended for Lance fell from his hand.

"Foul!" screamed the crowd, but Constantine ignored his detractors. He now stepped forward, flourishing his sword, intent on quickly dispatching his enemy.

Lance had nowhere to run; the spectator stands were at his back. All he could do was hope to dodge Constantine's blows. Relying on the footwork he had learned in fencing and boxing practice, Lance danced about the tournament ground while Constantine, now exhausted and letting his anger interfere with his skill, clumsily swung the sword about until his arm grew tired while Lance's footwork was only getting warmed up. Finally, Constantine swung a bit too hard, and when Lance ducked from the blow, Constantine lost his balance. As the Copper Knight struggled to regain his footing, Lance circled behind him, and then, with the slightest nudge, pushed him to the ground. Constantine's sword fell from his hand, and before the villain even felt the earth collide with his chest, Lance grabbed the sword and pointed it at Constantine's back.

The crowd rose to its feet, cheering and applauding. Lance took a moment to look up into the stands. When several spectators stuck out their fists and then pointed their thumbs downward, he realized that the old Roman customs hadn't yet died in Britain, and for just a second, he marveled again that he should be in Arthurian Britain. Then he turned his attention back to his opponent.

CHAPTER 5

"**I** SHOULD KILL you," said Lance, his sword hovering over Constantine's back. "I know if the situation were reversed, you would show no mercy to me. But I am not like you, and so I shall let you live."

"Do not do me any favors," Constantine spat, struggling to keep his mouth out of the dirt.

Lance pulled back his sword, but he kept it pointed at his fallen opponent. "Get up. No, kneel," he ordered Constantine.

"Kill him!" screamed a bloodthirsty woman in the crowd, thinking Lance intended to behead the Copper Knight, but Lance ignored her.

"How dare you embarrass me before my mistress," said Constantine, nevertheless kneeling as bid, "especially when you also claim to serve her! What do you want with me?"

Lance looked into the stands for Morgana, still in disguise as Gwenhwyvach, and beckoned for her to come to him.

As Morgana rose and made her way from the stands, all the spectators began muttering among themselves, wondering who was this beautiful woman who had two great knights vying for her affections.

From the corner of his eye, Constantine saw her approaching, and when she was only a few feet from him, he cried out, "Why do you betray me, my love? Why do you seek to disgrace me?"

"You have disgraced yourself," the False Gwenhwyvach replied. "Your conduct is unseemly for a knight."

Constantine was astonished by this remark. "When did you come to believe in fair play?" he demanded.

"Silence!" shouted the False Gwenhwyvach. "You have embarrassed enough knights, and no doubt through trickery, so now you must be embarrassed. It is only fair."

"I have no beard to be shaved off," Constantine taunted.

"No," said Lance, pushing the tip of his sword into Constantine's shoulder, "but you have a castle full of prisoners. In exchange for your life, you will free them immediately."

Constantine raised his eyebrows. His nostrils flared. He looked at the woman he thought to be Gwenhwyvach, not believing she would agree to such a condition. When she said nothing to oppose Lance's condition, he said, "I do not take orders from anyone save my mistress."

"It is my wish as well," the False Gwenhwyvach told him, "that you free these prisoners."

"But, Mistress," Constantine argued, "those knights will only go to King Arthur and tell him of us, and then he will come seeking to overthrow us before we are prepared to face him."

"Shut up and do as you're told!" the False Gwenhwyvach snapped, and then lowering her tone so no one in the crowd should overhear her, she added, "Do you plan to ruin us by revealing our plans before all these people? Just play along. It's all part of my plan."

Constantine's eyes now widened in surprise, but the words gave him hope again.

The False Gwenhwyvach now turned to the crowd and proclaimed, "For too long, the Copper Knight has oppressed all those who come to this land, but today, his reign of terror shall end. The gates of Dolorous Gard will be thrown open and its prisoners freed. And I declare that from this day forth, it will be known as Joyous Gard, and this knight, Sir Lancelot, shall be its rightful owner!"

The crowd rose to its feet, cheering. The ladies waved their handkerchiefs. Several beautiful young maidens blew kisses to Lance. And Constantine scowled, but he dared not object, desperately hoping Gwenhwyvach would yet compensate him for such humiliation.

Lance now gave Constantine's shoulder a little jab with his sword, just enough to make a flesh wound, and then he said, "Go now, on to the castle. Let us set about freeing your prisoners."

Constantine turned with a look of disgust on his face.

"No dilly-dallying," said Lance, pushing the sword under Constantine's elbow as if to help him to his feet.

The walk to the castle only took a few minutes, and by the time they had reached its gates, the spectators had left the stands and flooded onto the tournament ground to follow them.

"Open the gates!" the False Gwenhwyvach ordered. When the gate remained solidly shut, Lance gave Constantine another poke with the sword until Constantine nodded permission to the gatekeeper, who stood on the other side.

Once the gate opened, into the castle poured the crowd, led by the False Gwenhwyvach, with Constantine and Lance trailing behind.

"Where is the jailor?" the False Gwenhwyvach demanded.

He stepped forward from a small group of servants who had gathered in the castle courtyard, all astonished to see their master so degraded.

"Jailor," the False Gwenhwyvach told him, "release the prisoners and tell them to come to me."

The jailor did not look to Constantine for permission. He simply exited the courtyard into a tower where a staircase must have led down to the dungeon.

While they waited for the prisoners to arrive, Constantine turned to Gwenhwyvach, nearly in tears now. "Why are you doing this? Please do not desert me. You know I would do anything to please you. Be merciful to me."

"You will understand in time," said the False Gwenhwyvach. "But for now, it is best there be silence between us."

Lance guessed Morgana feared too many words would make Constantine suspect the truth, but Constantine was now too distraught and confused to question the absurdity of her orders. For a moment, Lance even felt a bit of sympathy for the villain.

Within a couple of minutes, a dozen knights trailed out of the tower and into the courtyard; they were a ragamuffin bunch, looking dirty, blinking their eyes at the sunlight that many of them had not seen for weeks. They all clearly needed food, but for the moment, their focus was solely on thanking Lance and the False Gwenhwyvach for their release. Last to exit the tower, much to Lance's surprise, was Sir Palomides. Upon seeing Lance, he ran forward and embraced him, leaving Lance no choice but to lower the sword he had directed at Constantine. By this point, however, the bully knew he was outnumbered, so he dared not try to escape.

"Sir Lancelot, it does my heart good to set eyes upon you," said Palomides. "I did not know whether we should ever meet again. Forsooth, I thought you mad forever."

"I am glad to see you again as well," said Lance, "and I will tell you all the story later."

"I will be glad to hear it," said Palomides, "but let it wait, for there is one more knight still in the prison; he is too sickly to come to us. Will you help me carry him out? I fear he is close to death, and behind bars is no place for him to die."

"What is wrong with him?" asked the False Gwenhwyvach.

"I wish I knew, milady," Palomides replied, bowing his head to her. "I hesitate to say it, but I fear, in truth, his heart is broken."

"His heart is broken?" Lance repeated, wondering at first whether Palomides meant he had a heart condition.

"Aye, of the lovesickness I fear," Palomides replied, "and it is all the more sad, for truly the object of his affection never deserved such devotion."

"He pines for a lady who would not have him?" asked Morgana.

"I wish it were so simple," said Palomides, looking truly woeful. "But please, Sir Lancelot, come help me carry him from the dungeon. I promise he is one you have reason to wish to meet, and then he or I will explain all."

Lance did not want to waste another moment in explanations if the poor knight were truly suffering. After handing his sword to Morgana, who kept it pointed at Constantine, he quickly followed Palomides into the tower and down the steps into the dungeon.

Lance had never been in a dungeon before, and the sight of the place was truly awful, for not only were there jail cells but plenty of strange instruments, which Lance suspected were used for torture.

"This way," said Palomides, directing Lance through several corridors that twisted and turned until they came to a cell so dark and damp that Lance's eyes could barely adjust to it and he found the smell of mold overwhelming. After a moment, Lance made out the figure of an emaciated man, lying on a pile of straw upon the floor. Palomides grasped the man's shoulders and lifted him, while Lance grabbed the man's feet. The man groaned in pain, but Palomides said, "Go! Do not delay!" and so Lance obeyed, walking backward as they carried the ailing knight down the passageway and then up the stairs until they emerged out of the tower.

Once in the courtyard, they found one of the other knights waiting for them. "The great lady—I fear I know not her name," said the knight, "has ordered the servants to feed us in the great hall. I will show you the way."

Lance and Palomides, now assisted by the knight, carried the wounded man into the castle. There they found that Morgana had already had the castle steward and jailor bring down a bed for the heartbroken man to rest upon.

Once the sick man lay on the bed, fast asleep, Morgana approached and told the other knight to go dine with his fellow freed prisoners. She told Lance and Palomides to do the same, but both were too concerned over the invalid before them.

"What is his name?" Lance asked.

"He is Sir Kahedin," Palomides replied, "the brother of Isolde of Lesser Britain."

"Kahedin!" exclaimed Lance, surprised that Isolde's brother should be imprisoned with Palomides. Surely, it was no coincidence that Morgana had led him to this castle. Lance suspected now that he must still be intended to finish his brother's quest, for doubtless,

Kahedin would know how he could find Sir Tristram so he could deliver Isolde's plea to return to her.

However, Kahedin appeared to be unconscious; his forehead looked heated, as if he were suffering from some great fever; he did not speak, nor move, nor open his eyes. He simply moaned in his sleep, unaware that he had even been moved.

"Go and eat," the False Gwenhwyvach again insisted. "In the meantime, I will see whether I can aid him."

Palomides and Lance reluctantly left Kahedin's side, though not going farther than twenty feet. Still, they knew they could do nothing for him. But Lance explained to Palomides that "the great lady" was a renowned healer and could be trusted.

"I am glad to hear it," said Palomides. "For a moment, I thought at first she was Queen Guinevere, but then I realized she could not be."

Lance changed the subject by asking Palomides how he had become the Copper Knight's prisoner. Palomides then launched into a long tale of his many adventures after Lance had fallen into madness. At least twice since their last meeting, he had been hot on the Beast Glatisant's trail, but each time, he had failed to kill the creature, for which Lance was very thankful, although he knew it would be pointless to explain to his friend that the Beast was but a harmless, hungry giraffe. Eventually, Palomides had chased the Beast into the Copper Knight's domains, resulting in his being challenged by the Copper Knight, who defeated him and made him his prisoner.

"It must be witchcraft," Palomides concluded, glancing over at Constantine, who now sat sniveling in a corner of the room, guarded by two of his former prisoners while the others ate. "No other man has ever yet defeated me in fair combat."

Lance was beginning to suspect Palomides was not the great knight he claimed to be, but he simply asked, "How did Sir Kahedin come to be the Copper Knight's prisoner?"

Before Palomides could answer, Morgana called, "Sir Lancelot, Sir Palomides, your friend is awake!"

They rushed to the bed where Kahedin's eyes were indeed open, but the knight stared at them, looking bewildered, as if he were not long for this world.

"He is very ill," whispered Morgana. "I gave him some medicine so he could regain consciousness, but I doubt he will live more than a day or two. I fear it is beyond my powers to save him."

"We cannot let him die," said Palomides. "His sister will be heartbroken, and he has told me so much of her that I...I believe I love her. He promised me that if ever we escaped from this prison, I might go with him to Lesser Britain to see whether she would have me as her husband."

Lance could see how heartbroken Palomides was, though clearly more heartbroken over the loss of his future prospects for a wife than he was for Kahedin. Lance patted Palomides on the shoulder to console him, but he could not resist asking, "But how can you marry Isolde? Is she not still married to Sir Tristram?"

At hearing Tristram's name, Kahedin let out an agonizing wail that caused everyone in the room to cringe.

"What is it?" Morgana asked him. "Where does it hurt?"

"In my heart!" Kahedin cried. "In my heart. Oh, I wish I were dead so that my agony might end!"

"Are you truly in that much pain?" Morgana asked him.

"Yes, and I will never be well again," he wept. "My dearest friend, Sir Tristram, is dead at the treacherous hand of Mark of Cornwall."

"Dead?" exclaimed Lance. "When did this happen?"

"It has been some months now," said Palomides, "during this past winter."

"But how did it happen?" asked Lance.

Kahedin struggled to speak, but each time he tried to tell his tale, his throat became choked with sobs until finally his eyes implored Palomides to explain for him.

"From what I have gathered," Palomides said, "Tristram convinced Iseult to leave her husband, Lord Mark. She and Tristram left Cornwall and were on their way north to the land of the Picts. The king there had offered to make Tristram a general in his army. But Lord Mark followed them with a band of his men, quickly catching up to them. Kahedin was accompanying Tristram and Iseult, but he had gone off foraging for food one morning when Lord Mark and his men ambushed Tristram and quickly cut him down. Kahedin returned just in time to see Tristram bleeding on the ground. Iseult refused to return with Mark to be his wife, so she fell into her lover's arms and begged Tristram, with his last ounce of strength, to crush her to death, and so the two lovers died together."

"Oh!" cried out Kahedin. "If only I had been the one crushed to death in Tristram's arms so this prolonged agony of living without him might be ended."

"Do not speak such nonsense," said Morgana. "Your father and sister would not wish such a thing."

"But he was all my world," Kahedin replied. "The noblest man who ever lived."

"He was an adulterer," Palomides said, frowning. "And you know it, for I have told you so many a time while we have been in prison, and yet you remain under his spell."

"I cannot help it," said Kahedin. "I cannot help what I am. I loved him. I wish I were dead so I might share his grave."

"You shall not die," said Morgana. "You shall live, and in time, you will be wiser and stronger for what you have endured."

"Live?" said Lance. "But you just said he had but a day or two to live."

"Yes," said Morgana. "Under normal circumstances that would be true, for I cannot save him myself, but I believe there is another way to save him—and that Constantine can aid us in this matter."

Upon hearing this remark, Constantine burst forth with defiance.

"You will not do this!" he shouted at the woman he still believed to be Gwenhwyvach. "You know you will not. You told me to keep it hidden. You would not use it now for good, not to heal. You said we were to destroy it so mankind might lose hope."

"Hold your tongue!" the False Gwenhwyvach ordered. "I will do as I please. You do not give me orders, little worm. You only obey me."

"But this will destroy all our plans—it will—"

"One more word and I will have your tongue torn from your mouth," the False Gwenhwyvach warned, and the fire in her eyes caused Constantine not only to cease talking, but to crumple to the floor in tears.

"But I don't understand," said Lance. "What has been hidden away?"

"Tell me, Sir Lancelot," said Morgana. "Do you think it a coincidence that I asked you to come with me to this tournament?"

"No, I do not know why you did, but I imagine you wished me to release Palomides and the others."

"Yes," said Morgana, "but also so you might fulfill the quest you were given when you first arrived in this land."

"The quest?" asked Palomides, suddenly becoming animated. "You mean his promise to aid me in destroying the Beast Glatisant?"

"No," said the False Gwenhwyvach, rolling her eyes in such an irritated manner that the man dared not speak another word. "Think, Sir Lancelot."

"I don't understand," said Lance. "What quest? All I wanted when I arrived was to find Tristan, and now he is dead, and—"

"And..." continued Morgana, "you were given a quest you refused."

"You mean...but Viviane didn't understand. She wanted me to find the True Cross, but...." Then understanding came to Lance. "You mean that I am to find the True Cross?"

"You have already found it," Morgana replied, "or close enough, for if my guesses are correct, Constantine knows where it is, and as soon as he tells us, we will go to it."

"You know damn well where it is!" exclaimed Constantine from the corner where he was curled up like an abused child. "I will help you no longer after the way you have spurned my love in favor of this lily-livered Sir Lancelot."

"Do you think," said the False Gwenhwyvach, stepping up to him, "that I have time to concern myself with details. I can't remember everything. I give you one task—to find and keep that stick of wood until I am ready to use it while I am busy plotting to overthrow a kingdom. Do you think I have time to remember where it is?"

Constantine looked at her blankly, like a child rebuked by his teacher and fearing a whipping.

"I am lost," he cried out, his eyes turning into pools of despair. "What does it matter now? I have nothing without your love. The True Cross is in a mountain cave two miles west from here."

"Ah, yes, now I remember," said the False Gwenhwyvach, smiling.

"But I still don't understand," said Lance. "How can the True Cross help make Kahedin well?"

"Think upon what Viviane told you," Morgana replied. "How did the Empress Helena determine it was the True Cross?"

Lance thought a moment, and then his memory served him. "She had a sick woman brought forward, and when the woman touched the Cross, she was instantly healed."

"Exactly," said Morgana.

"And that means," said Palomides, "that it can heal Kahedin."

"In Christ's great love for humanity, all things are possible and all things made right," Morgana replied.

"And...and does it mean...?" Lance now had tears in his eyes, too frightened to ask his question.

"Speak," said Morgana.

"Might we...might we also bring the True Cross to Brother Baudwin's cottage and use it to restore...to bring back to life...Ileana...and...Tristan?"

"Yes," said Morgana, smiling upon him.

Lance felt his heart leap up within him. He felt as if he wanted to dance and sing as King David had done when the Ark of the Lord was brought into the Temple. He wanted to cry and shout and praise God, and for a moment, he almost believed he would fly off the ground because of how his heart joyfully rose up within him.

"But first," said Morgana, "we must find the Cross and heal Kahedin."

"We must go then quickly," said Palomides.

"No, I wish to die," said Kahedin. "I cannot live if Tristram is dead."

Morgana placed her hand on Kahedin's shoulder and gently replied, "The Goddess-God would not appreciate such a death wish, for She-He is Eternal Life, as are you if you only knew it. And it may be that you are being given this test to purge your soul so that someday you may be worthy of being reunited with Sir Tristram."

Kahedin did not know what to reply to these words, but the look of compassion on Morgana's face unnerved him. It also unnerved Constantine, who felt as if he were suddenly in the role of Judas Iscariot, not understanding how everything had gone so wrong for him.

CHAPTER 6

WITHIN HALF AN hour, Morgana bid the other knights fare-well, telling them to make themselves comfortable in Joyous Gard and to treat Constantine kindly, but not to let him escape. She would decide upon his fate when she returned. By that time, the knights would have recuperated from their imprisonment and could be on their way back to Camelot or whatever courts to which they belonged.

Palomides, Lance, and Morgana now set off with a cart that the other knights had found to bear Kahedin. The cart was pulled by Papillon, while the others walked. They headed toward the mountain, which they could see in the distance. They hoped to reach it before sundown; otherwise, finding the cave would be difficult in the dark.

"How do we even know we will find the Cross?" asked Lance.

"There is only the one mountain in this area," Morgana replied, "and while it might have more than one cave in it, we must trust our instincts that we will find it. Sometimes when we act upon faith, the Goddess-God provides the answers."

Lance did not question her further. By now, he had come to realize how headstrong and foolish he had been ever since he had arrived in Arthurian Britain. If he had only done what Viviane had asked from the start, he might have saved himself a great deal of anguish.

The three continued on in silence. Kahedin had sunk back into unconsciousness, but every few minutes, they stopped to make sure he was still breathing. They traveled slowly so as not to make him uncomfortable from too jolting a ride.

When they were halfway to the mountain, Palomides remarked, "I am not worthy to go on this quest for the True Cross. I am not a Christian."

"Neither was St. Paul at first," said Morgana, "but Christ chose him to bring many people to the Goddess-God."

Palomides shook his head. "Nonetheless, I am not worthy. I have never followed God. Uncle Pellinore mocked religion, and I have allowed him to influence me in my beliefs. Now I am beginning to feel I was wrong; still, I will try to believe if it means the Cross can save Kahedin."

"You and Pellinore both had a bad example in your religious fanatic uncle Bron," said Morgana. "If you truly wish to be worthy, the first thing you might consider is to cease questing after sin."

Palomides raised his eyebrows at this remark. "I do not understand," he said. "I have not quested after sin. The Beast is itself a creature of sin. I have sought to destroy it."

"You would do better to seek to destroy the shortcomings within yourself," said Morgana. "Both you and your uncle Pellinore have been headstrong, mistreating others, being braggarts, proving yourselves irresponsible in your behavior; then you turned your self-hatred for your behavior upon the Beast. The Beast is just a simple, gentle creature you have chosen to torment and believe to be something it is not. You have engaged in a fruitless quest. It is time you relinquish it."

"Relinquish it?" said Palomides. "I have devoted my life to it."

"And what happiness has it brought you?" Morgana asked.

Palomides realized it was a rhetorical question so he did not reply. He did not want to admit it, but he knew she spoke the truth.

"You need not quest after sin," Morgana continued. "You need not even focus upon your flaws. Nor can you hope to destroy what you fear will hurt others. We must each make straight our ways with the Goddess-God. As Christ taught us, we cannot remove the speck in another's eye until we remove the log in our own."

"I do not fully understand what you are saying," Palomides confessed, "but I will think upon your words and try to do as you say."

Morgana smiled at Palomides to give him confidence. Then they all journeyed on in silence for some time until Palomides stated, "If the True Cross saves Kahedin's life, I will become a Christian. I will be baptized, and I will make better use than I have done of the life God has given me."

Upon hearing these words, Lance remarked, "I don't believe my parents ever had Tristan and me baptized. I think perhaps because we were taken away from them at such a young age."

"It is no matter," said Morgana, "so long as you have faith now. Baptism is but a symbol of faith and a desire to act in the best way possible. It is an outer sign only; what is needed is an inner change."

"I do not need my sins washed away then?" asked Lance.

"Do not you and all Christians believe that the Christ died to wash away your sins?" asked Morgana. "If that is the case, you do not need to be baptized."

"Why do you say it that way?" asked Lance in surprise. "Don't you believe what Christians believe?"

"I believe," Morgana replied, "that the Christ is the Savior in the sense that He revealed to us that we do live after death, but I do not believe in this sin paradox. I believe He would prefer we not be so obsessed with sin; our focus on it only makes it stronger. I believe He died and rose from the dead not to rid us of sin but to remind us of life after death. Nor do I believe we only acquire that eternal life by believing He came to free us from sin. I believe we are all immortal, but we have allowed the worries and fears of this world to cause us to forget it. I believe our true purpose is to learn here; not to be saved; we have never been in danger, save the danger we create for ourselves when we let fear lead us away from good. I do not pretend to have all the answers, but neither do I believe any man or religion does. I believe we simply must seek to live the best lives possible, serving one another and trusting someday we will know what is necessary for our benefit."

Lance and Palomides listened intently to Morgana's words, but neither felt a need to respond to them.

They had been traveling for an hour now, moving slowly for Kahedin's sake. When they were just a few hundred feet from the mountain, Morgana placed her hand on Papillon's halter, causing him to stop.

"I will wait here with Kahedin," said Morgana, "while the two of you go search for the cave."

Palomides and Lance agreed to this, and knowing the sun was quickly setting, they hurriedly went in opposite directions around the mountain, realizing it would take a good hour for them to meet each other on the opposite side and that they did not have even that much time before nightfall. Nor did they want to wait until morning to search for the cave, for while the True Cross had been known to heal a sick woman, it had not yet been proven able to raise the dead, and Kahedin was unlikely to live through the night.

Lance soon lost sight of both Palomides and Morgana as he walked around the mountain's south side. He carefully scanned its walls, often feeling his way along, being careful of the treacherous rocks beneath his feet while touching every crack or dent in the rock wall in case it should open some sort of door. At first, he saw nothing that looked like a cave entrance. In fact, the mountain appeared solid enough that he became doubtful it could contain any sort of caverns. Would Constantine have lied to them about where the Cross was hidden? Would he have done so just to be spiteful? Doubtless he was bitter, but would his fear of Gwenhwyvach cause him to disobey her by lying? He must have known Gwenhwyvach would return to punish him if he dared to mislead her. Nevertheless, Lance was not finding any evidence that a cave might exist in this mountain.

After a few more minutes of searching, however, Lance heard Palomides shout, "Over here! Over here! I think I've found it!"

Lance quickly scrambled over the rough terrain, returning the way he had come. As he passed Morgana, he saw she was gently leading Papillon and the cart in the same direction.

"Where is it?" Lance shouted as soon as he saw Palomides, who knelt on the ground, digging at what appeared to be a caved-in section of the mountain's foot.

"It's an entrance," said Palomides. "It's been hidden over with rocks, but I think there must be a good-sized chamber down there."

Lance could see a decline in the earth beside the mountain, as if a slanted tunnel had been dug into it. But it was now covered over with rocks, large rocks requiring two hands to lift them; most of them weighed twenty to fifty pounds, and it took Palomides and Lance both to lift several of them because of how unwieldy they were. The two men worked quickly until, after a few minutes, they realized Morgana was standing behind them, observing.

"We'll never get all these rocks cleared away before nightfall," Lance complained to her, "and then it will be too dark for us to see to enter the cave."

"Step aside," Morgana replied.

"Milady," said Palomides, "you cannot lift these stones. Sir Lancelot and I can barely do so."

But Lance pulled Palomides away, stating, "Do as she says."

Palomides looked doubtful, but he allowed himself to be pulled away. He did not even know this woman's name—he had thought it would be indecorous to ask; it was enough for him to know she was Sir Lancelot's friend, but regardless of who she was, she could not lift those stones. Palomides was surprised when instead she raised her hands in the air, and after she chanted some words neither man understood, the rocks began to roll away from the entrance and out into the field.

"What?" exclaimed Palomides. "How is this possible?"

"She is Morgana, Lady of Avalon," Lance told him.

"Lady Morgana!" gasped Palomides. "I have often heard of you, but...forgive me, milady; I did not know."

"It matters not," said Morgana, smiling at the open entrance. "Come; we must not waste time."

The entrance was still sloped and treacherous, nearly too steep to walk down.

"Should we go in to find the Cross and bring it out?" asked Lance, "or should we try to bring Kahedin inside?"

"We will bring him inside," said Morgana. "We do not want to risk being seen; and we do not know who else might seek the True Cross."

"But the horse and cart will be seen," Lance objected.

"Go fetch Kahedin and all will be well," Morgana replied.

Palomides and Lance obeyed her, not understanding how, but yet believing she would make all things right. Once they had lifted the unconscious Kahedin from the cart, Morgana released the cart from Papillon, and then she waved about her hands until a powerful wind arose. It was all any of them could do to remain standing in the wind, and in a second, the cart was blown away in a gust.

"We will not be needing it again," Morgana said as the wind died down. "Kahedin will walk back with us."

Morgana now whispered in Papillon's ear, and then he ran off.

"He will watch from a distance so his presence does not give us away if Constantine has had us followed," said Morgana. "He will return when we are ready to leave again."

Palomides and Lance now made their way to the cave's entrance. Carefully, they started down the sloping entrance into the subterranean cave, bearing Kahedin between them. Morgana followed them, stopping once she was inside the cave to say another chant that caused the stones to roll back and cover the entrance.

Again, Palomides and Lance were amazed by her powers, but since there was now no light in the cave, Lance could not help remarking, "But we cannot see now, so how will we find the True Cross?"

Morgana replied by muttering another spell. Instantly, several torches lit up along the cave's walls.

"This place has been visited many times in the past," said Morgana. "All we need here has been provided for us."

The men were almost as amazed by the light as they were by the cave's interior. Everywhere along the walls were exquisite and colorful frescoes depicting scenes from the Bible as well as various saints, kings, and queens; they reminded Lance of cave paintings made by medieval monks that he had once seen in Cappadocia; he would have loved to stand and look at them for hours, but this desire was soon overcome by the disappointment he felt when he viewed the cave's interior. It ran about fifty feet in length and was perhaps thirty feet wide—and it was completely empty.

"Where is the True Cross?" asked Lance in dismay.

"Look about you," said Morgana.

Obeying her, Palomides and Lance gently laid Kahedin on the cave floor, and then they began to look more carefully at the paintings on the walls. After a few minutes, Lance found himself standing before one of the Crucifixion.

"Here; it must be here," he said, and he began to pat the wall, looking for a door or something that would reveal the True Cross' hiding place.

After a moment, Lance's hand passed over the image of Christ Himself, and as his hand came to rest over Christ's side, his finger slipped into a hole barely noticeable in the painting. Feeling like St. Thomas fingering Christ's wounds, Lance slid his finger into the hole and found a trigger mechanism inside. He pushed and pulled at it for a moment, and then he managed to release it. With a loud gravelly sound, the wall moved back several inches. Lance then realized it was like a pocket door, and giving it a push with his finger still in the hole, he began to slide it open.

By now, Morgana and Palomides were standing behind Lance, breathless with excitement. Once the door was open and Lance stepped back, they all saw a large piece of wood, a crossbar for a Roman cross with holes where nails had once been pounded into it. It was leaning up against the back wall. And—perhaps it was only Lance's imagination—it seemed to glow.

"The True Cross!" Lance gasped.

"Yes," said Morgana.

"Quickly; we must bring Kahedin to it," said Palomides, and he stepped toward where Kahedin lay just behind Morgana. Lance, however, remained in the doorway of the little cubbyhole where the True Cross resided; he felt too overcome with emotion to move yet.

Then just as Lance was about to turn to assist Palomides, they all heard a great rumbling sound. In another second, they realized the stones blocking the cave's entrance were again being removed.

"We are too late," moaned Morgana.

"Or perhaps I am just early," said Gwenhwyvach, the cave ringing with her cackling laughter.

CHAPTER 7

"**YOU HAVE NO** right to be here, Gwenhwyvach!" exclaimed Morgana. "This is holy ground."

"Do you not think I myself am holy?" asked Gwenhwyvach, entering the cave. "I who was among the first created by the Goddess-God?"

"Leave us," Morgana persisted, refusing to back down. "I will not allow Kahedin to die."

Gwenhwyvach stepped farther into the cave until she was just a few feet in front of Morgana. She cast a look of disdain upon Kahedin's limp body; then—her tongue dripping with venom—she said, "I do not want Kahedin to die. I want you all to die."

"You have no right to be here," Morgana repeated. "We are in the presence of the True Cross. You know the Christ will not accept it."

"Accept it? He accepts your trickery, your masquerading as me to confuse my dear Constantine. You act as if I am the deceiver here, yet you have been full of lies. I don't like it when people tell me lies."

"There was no other way," said Morgana. "You cannot imprison people against their will, nor is it allowed for you to poison people's minds with your venomous words."

"Come, Morgana," Gwenhwyvach snarled. "Do you really think you can get away with this? Did you truly think I would not catch you?"

"I knew you would follow us," Morgana admitted, "but I had hoped we'd have left with the Cross before you reached the cave."

Gwenhwyvach stepped closer, smiling upon Morgana, as if mocking her. "Come now; we are both women. Why don't you join me? I understand you have the gift of the sight, so you know that in time I will destroy Arthur and all his kingdom. You know my power is far greater than your own. But I am willing to spare you; it might be useful to me to have Arthur's sister among my servants."

"I will not be your minion," said Morgana. "I will not do that which is against the very laws of the universe that the Goddess-God has set in place."

"Very well," laughed Gwenhwyvach. "You have made your choice."

Her hand whipped up and touched Morgana's breast. And Morgana, as if she had been struck by lightning, suddenly crumpled to the ground.

"No!" screamed Palomides, pulling out his sword and charging Gwenhwyvach. But before he could reach her, Palomides' sword flew out of his hand, flashed through the air, pierced his armor, and tore into his heart. Lance watched in shock as the knight joined Morgana upon the ground. For a moment, Palomides' eyes remained open. "I was never baptized," he said, and then his eyes closed and he was still.

Lance knew not what to do. He could not defeat Gwenhwyvach. As she began to walk toward him, he backed into the cubbyhole where the True Cross rested. He backed up until his leg pressed upon the Cross. By then, Gwenhwyvach stood in the doorway of the small chamber. Desperate, Lance reached around and grabbed the Cross, wrapping his arms about it.

"Come now; let's not be a fool," said Gwenhwyvach. "You can't really believe that a five-hundred-year-old piece of wood has magical powers."

"It is the True Cross, which Christ died upon," said Lance, "and we know that He rose from the dead and also that the Empress Helena used it to heal a sick woman."

"How do you know this? Those are stories, but you do not know that they are true."

"They are stories told by people of faith."

"Or deluded, wishful thinkers, if not downright liars," scoffed Gwenhwyvach, "and even if they are true, do you really think Christ cares about you—why would he care about a spoiled little rich boy, for that is all you are. And even if he did care about you, he could not possibly care for that dying perversion lying there on the floor, or a pagan knight, or worst of all, a priestess of a pagan religion—a woman who claims, no less, to have knowledge beyond the norm like I myself. Has it not always been the case that your religion has claimed women are the root of evil in this world?"

"However you wish to twist the truth or how mankind has twisted it," Lance replied, "I believe God only loves us and we have nothing to fear."

"You have me to fear," she laughed.

"No," he said. "You can kill me, but I believe I will be reunited with my parents someday regardless. There is no death, only life, and so in the end, you have no power."

Gwenhwyvach did not reply to these words. She just stood there, staring at him, as if she had a problem and was trying to determine how best to solve it.

As he waited, Lance looked at the fallen figures of his friends. How could they have died? Especially Lady Morgana—how could she have died when he knew she would yet live for centuries and meet his parents in the future? Had the whole future in some way changed because he had been ill-fated enough to travel back in time? He was tired of it all, tired of the headache of trying to understand everything. He just wanted to go home or end it all.

Unable to stand it any longer, Lance shouted, "Why don't you just kill me the way you did Palomides and Lady Morgana?"

Gwenhwyvach only sneered, her eyes mocking him, as if wanting to savor her victory.

"Come on, you witch!" Lance shouted. "Kill me and get it over with."

After a moment, Gwenhwyvach breathed through her nostrils, sighed, and said, "I want the Cross."

Lance could barely comprehend her words. But he instinctively gripped the Cross tighter.

"I cannot kill you," Gwenhwyvach admitted, "while you are holding the Cross."

"Then I'll never let go of it!" he shouted, wondering whether he could walk past her while holding it.

"I won't let you out," she said, as if reading his mind. "I could have you buried for all eternity in this cubbyhole, and as long as you are holding that Cross, you will doubtless live forever. But is that what you want—to spend eternity in a little cave?"

Lance did not know how to answer.

"I want the Cross," Gwenhwyvach negotiated, "and in exchange, I will give you what you want."

"How can you know what I want?" Lance demanded.

"I know that since you have arrived in this time, all you have wanted is to return to the twenty-first century."

Lance knew too well her trickery to be fooled by her false promises. He did not reply or let go of his hold on the Cross.

"I'll make you a deal," Gwenhwyvach continued.

"I do not make deals with the devil," Lance spat out.

"Now you're just being insulting," said Gwenhwyvach. "I would think by now that you and your family know there's no such thing as the devil."

"I will make no bargain with you regardless," said Lance.

"Oh, I think you will. You will give me the Cross, and I will send you home to your own time and to your parents."

"How do I know you will do this?" Lance demanded. "How do I even know whether it's in your power to do so?"

"Such skepticism," scoffed Gwenhwyvach, shaking her head. "Very well. Look!"

She lifted her hands and pointed them toward the cave wall.

Slowly, the rock grew white, seeming to glow, and then Lance saw some flickering on it, as if it were a movie screen—no, a fog parting, and then there before him, as if standing on the other side of a glass partition, he saw his mother and father. For a moment, Lance nearly let go of the Cross to reach out and touch them. He longed to run to them; he nearly did, but then he felt the Cross in his arms.

"Stop!" he demanded. "Stop! What trickery is this? These are just images."

"They are not images," Gwenhwyvach replied.

"We are real, Lance," said his father, Adam Delaney.

"We are waiting for you to come home, Lance," said his mother, Anne Delaney.

"How do I know you are not spirits," Lance replied, wanting to cry because of his confusion and longing, "evil spirits doing her bidding?"

"You fool," snapped Gwenhwyvach. "It is a portal to your own time. Can you not see? Look behind them. Can you not see they are in the library of Delaney Castle? Can you not see they are waiting for you?"

Lance looked. He saw she spoke the truth. If it were a portal, then...maybe he could....

"You can step into it this very moment if you let go of the Cross," said Gwenhwyvach. "You can be with your parents in less than a second if you only agree to my terms."

"We love you, Lance," said his mother.

"Come home, son," said his father.

Lance felt tears coming into his eyes. "Mom, Dad, I love you. I want to come home, but...but...."

He looked at the Cross in his arms. Then he understood.

Looking up at Gwenhwyvach, he said, "I do not know how I will get home, but I know I cannot return home without my brother. This Cross will bring him back to life, and I will use it also to restore Palomides and Morgana and Kahedin and Ileana to life, and I will not let you stop me. I choose the lives of those I love over my own happiness."

"You are a fool," said Gwenhwyvach. "I already told you I will not let you leave this cave."

"Then I will not go home, and you will not obtain the True Cross," he said firmly.

"You would really rather stay here and save your brother and friends?" asked Gwenhwyvach, looking doubtful.

"Yes, yes, I would," said Lance, turning back to his parents. "Mom and Dad, I love you, but I hope you will understand. I can't come home without Tristan."

"Is this your final decision?" asked Gwenhwyvach, "because in a moment, I will rain down stones to hide this cave and you for all eternity."

"It is my final decision," Lance replied. "I choose to forsake my happiness for others and to trust that God will make all things right in the end."

"Then so be it," said Gwenhwyvach.

Immediately, it was as if a great explosion were taking place. Before Lance's very eyes, Gwenhwyvach dissolved into thin air, and the cave around him began to collapse. Rocks fell from the cave's ceiling, but not one rock touched him where he stood, still clinging to the True Cross. For a minute, he watched the roof fall around him, and then he was astonished to see the rocks dissolve into the earth beneath his feet.

Next, a blinding white light came charging down from the sky above him. It surrounded him, surrounded him completely until he could not see the rock walls any longer—he could not even be sure they were there. He could not be sure anything existed except for himself, the True Cross, and the white light.

And then everything became completely quiet. After a few seconds came a gentle murmuring of the wind, a cooling and comforting breeze, and then through the blinding light stepped Lance's parents.

"Mom! Dad!" he exclaimed, feeling both joy and confusion simultaneously. "But I don't understand. Gwenhwyvach said...the portal...did I go through the portal regardless? I—"

And he began to cry.

"Why do you weep?" asked Anne.

"I failed!" he confessed. "I failed, but it's not my fault. Please don't be angry. It's all been like some horrible game, and I didn't know what the rules were, and...."

"And you were having a marvelous time regardless?" said a male voice. It was a familiar voice, but Lance could not place it until he looked behind his father.

There, before him, looking stronger and healthier than ever before, was his brother Tristan.

"But...but...I don't understand," said Lance. "I thought you were dead."

And releasing his grip on the Cross, Lance ran and embraced Tristan.

"How can this be?" Lance asked. "How did you come back to life? I thought you were dead."

"I am dead," said Tristan.

"What?" Lance asked. "What are you saying?"

"I am dead; at least in terms of my life on earth," Tristan replied.

"We are all dead," said Adam, placing his hand on Lance's shoulder.

"But I don't understand," said Lance, looking from his father to his brother and then to his mother.

"We all died when the comet hit," said Anne. "All of us but you."

"But no, I—but Tristan was with me. I—I don't understand. Why—you can't be dead! You're standing before me, and—but why didn't you all time travel with me? Why—"

"You did not time travel," said Adam.

Lance stared blankly, looking at each of them in turn. How could he have not time traveled?

"You are having a near-death experience," said Anne. "You and Tristan were both knocked unconscious by the comet's debris. When the comet passed over Britain, it killed millions of people, almost the entire population of the island—in fact, it killed nearly every person on earth. There are only a handful of survivors; a few hundred perhaps—I'm not sure. For a short time, Tristan, like you, was in a coma, but he is dead now too. You, Lance, are still in a coma."

"But...a coma...a near-death experience?" Lance repeated.

"Yes," said Anne.

Lance could not seem to understand what all this meant.

"You are still alive," said Adam. "You have had a great adventure in your mind, but it is almost time for you to return to your life now."

"I don't understand. If you are dead, then, then...are we in...?"

"Your soul has been in Arthur's Bosom," said Anne. "It is one of the many forms of heaven, a transitional place really, for us to learn and prepare for the next stage of life, whether spent in heaven or on earth. When we die, we go to the most desirable place for us to transition in. As a lover of Arthurian lore, Arthur's Bosom is the heaven you have gone to."

"But I'm not dead?" asked Lance.

"No; as with most near-death experiences, you have had time here to review your life, to learn what you need to know so you can better fulfill your mission on earth."

"My mission?" said Lance.

"Yes," said Tristan. "Your mission. I wish I could be with you for it, Lance, but we will all be helping you from here."

Suddenly, Lance realized that a host of people stood behind his brother.

"All of us," Tristan added.

Lance looked more closely at who these people were. Why, he knew these faces! There was his grandfather, Cedric, and his great-grandfather, Quincey. They must have also died when the comet struck. And these other faces he did not remember seeing with his own eyes but he recognized them from family photographs. His grandmother, Mary Morgan, was holding hands with his grandfather, Bram Delaney, and his great-grandparents, Joseph and Elizabeth Morgan, were there, and looking beyond them he saw many whose faces and names were unfamiliar to him, and yet he recognized them instantly—King Arthur, Mordred and Edythe, Meleon and Rachel, Melusine and Raimond, Charlemagne, Roland, Ogier the Dane, Gloriana, Meurvin and Asalah, Vlad Tepes, and a host of others whose names he knew within a split second.

"We are all here," said another voice. Turning to his right, Lance saw Palomides holding Isolde's hand. The Saracen knight said, "All of your ancestors. We will all be helping you on your mission."

"I don't understand," Lance confessed. "What mission?"

Then the white light grew brighter, and through it, he saw another man and woman approaching him.

"The mission you have always known deep inside yourself that you were to fulfill," said the man as he drew closer.

"To be the king of your people," said the woman.

And then Lance recognized them as Merlin and Morgana.

Lance felt amazed to see them.

"Merlin and I," said Morgana, "did not survive the comet either, but that is as it should be. It was decided long ago that a new chapter in the world's history would begin now. The old world has passed away, and a new and better one is about to be born. You, Lance, will be part of that world. But before you return, understand that when the comet hit, it created a new reality—the reality in men's imaginations that was waiting to spring forth if they only believed. It was only in the moment of their destruction that they dreamt hardest of what they wanted. Most chose to end their earthly existence to do their work in a different dimension, but you and a few others have chosen to remain on earth. Deep in your subconscious, you have always longed for the Arthurian world to exist, for Camelot to return, and so because your intention and desire was so powerful, you have achieved it, you have turned your imagination into your reality, and it has allowed you to have this wonderful adventure and dig into the deepest depths of your soul. You must now return to the world and lead those who remain, teaching them the full power of imagination—that by believing in the good and working for it, you can erase fear and all the negative emotions that have crippled humanity for centuries. If you choose to believe the future will be good, then so it shall be. Couple imagination with love and the two will create the world you dream of for humanity. This is the great secret that humanity has been waiting to realize. You have always had the power to imagine and create your own destinies, to transform your dreams into realities."

When Morgana finished speaking, Lance could only nod in acceptance, for deep in his being he understood that all she spoke was true.

"Life may be hard for the first few years," Merlin stated, "but with time, the sun will return, the earth will grow warm again, and life will flourish more fully than it did before. Until that time, you, Lance Delaney, must act as a true king would, both leading and serving your people. And you know now where to find the True Cross, and with it, you will also find the Thirteen Treasures of Britain that I hid away when Arthur was king. They will serve you in this endeavor so Britain will both regain and surpass its ancient splendor. But the true question is: Are you ready for this task?"

Lance shook his head and humbly replied, "No...no one can be ready for such a task, but...but I will do the best I can and learn as I go."

"Well said," said Merlin. "It seems you have learned something since Viviane showed you your past when your ego got the better of you."

"Yes," said Lance. "I—I no longer desire to be a king, but I will accept it if it is what I must do to help the world become a better place. Will you still be able to help me?"

"Not on earth," said Merlin, "but from another dimension, yes."

Then from the host of people, King Arthur stepped forth and stood before Lance.

Lance bowed and humbly asked, "What advice do you have for me, Your Majesty?"

"It is not for me to give you advice, Your Majesty," Arthur replied. "But I do ask one boon."

"Anything," said Lance, feeling overcome to be shown such reverence by the greatest of kings.

"I ask only that you keep our memory alive—mine and Morgana's and Merlin's, and the memories of all those whose stories you have come to know, for we are all your ancestors. Keep the glory of Britain alive. Keep the glory of all the human race alive. Tell the tales of how we lived our lives. Forgive us for our flaws and remember what we tried to do that was good and right. Remember also that when we failed, we gave into fear and the faults that come with it— greed, jealousy, anger. Protect yourself from fear and teach others to do the same. And do not forget that all of us are part of you. We are your ancestors, and if we had not lived, you would not be. As long as you remember us and tell our stories now, we will not desert you. And most importantly of all, do not forget how Christ loved us and taught us to love one another."

Lance felt incredibly humbled by such a request. Suppressing the choking feeling in his throat, he said, "I will not forget. I will tell my children and tell them to tell their children. We will never forget."

And then Anne Delaney said, "It is time now. Know that we all love you."

"We love you," said Adam and Tristan together.

And then, before Lance could say another word, he felt himself being pulled through a portal. In a second, he lost sight of everyone. Instantly, everything was spinning about him. He seemed to be floating through the universe, among the constellations and planets. And then, before he could even blink his eyes, he found he was floating above his own body, his own body lying in a hospital bed, eyes closed and several tubes hooked up to him, and someone was sitting beside his bed. And then he felt himself being pulled back into his body.

EPILOGUE

LANCE OPENED HIS eyes.

"You're awake!" said Elaine, smiling.

Was it really Elaine sitting there beside him? Was it her hand holding his? Was he truly alive and lying in a hospital bed?

"Elaine," he said, joy spreading across his face. But then he remembered Tristan. "Elaine, you know my brother is dead?"

"What a thing to say for your first words?" she replied, laughing but with tears streaming down her face. "Yes, yes, I know, although I don't understand how you know since you have been in a coma all this time. But you are all right. At least you appear to be. Don't think about what we've lost just now. First, you must get better."

"Is it true?" asked Lance. "Is almost everyone dead?"

"Yes," she said. "There are only a few dozen of us in all of England. We have all gathered here—in this small village. You are in the village hospital. There is one doctor and two nurses among us. They have kept you alive."

"How did you survive? How did any of us?"

"Shh, we can talk about all that later," she said. "How are you feeling?"

"I feel fine," said Lance. "In fact, I don't think I've ever felt better in my life. I know those I love are gone, and yet they live, and I know there is a reason why I have survived."

"Oh, Lance," said Elaine, lifting his hand to kiss it. "Lance, I hope there is a reason. I...I know you think I loved Tristan, and he was a wonderful man, and my best friend, but I was always in love with you. You were just...."

"I know; I was a pompous braggart," said Lance, smiling as he looked into her eyes and wondered whether she could really be as beautiful as she now appeared. "But I believe I've changed now. If you truly love me, I know I'll be a changed man."

"I'm sure you have changed," said Elaine, squeezing his hand. "And it's all going to be all right now. We must rebuild. We must start over. Many of the survivors are in despair. The damage is unbelievable, and I know many of them are overcome by grief, but I told them this is our chance to create a new world. A better world. I'm so glad you've survived. We need someone strong like you to lead us."

"To lead?" he asked.

"Yes. You always did wish to be a king, didn't you? It's already been decided. When I told people you were the son of Adam Delaney and grandson of Bram Delaney, they wanted you to be their leader; you are the highest in rank among those of us who survived, but that matters less than the fact that I know you are the one with the most charisma. You are our greatest hope, and the others will understand that once they get to know you. It will be difficult, but I'm sure that we can—"

"Kiss me," Lance interrupted her.

Once upon a time, a terrible comet struck the earth and wiped out most of the human population. In its aftermath, the land of Britain was turned into a wasteland, as was much of the world. Because the comet had struck in the summer, all the crops and vegetation in Britain were destroyed and very little grew before winter set in, making survival very difficult for the people.

However, among the survivors was a man of ancient and noble lineage. He was acclaimed as king among the handful of British who survived. King Lancelot took the throne with all humility, and his wife, Elaine the Gracious, sat by his side. Together, the royal couple ruled justly and were well-loved by their people.

In those times, miracles were not uncommon because the survivors of the comet's devastation understood that they had been chosen to create a new world, and their faith allowed many remarkable occurrences to come about.

Foremost among these marvels was a dream that King Lancelot had. In it, the ancient hero-king, Arthur Pendragon, appeared to him. King Arthur told King Lancelot where the holy priestess Helena, Mother to the Roman Emperor Constantine, had hidden the True Cross, which she had brought back to Britain from the Holy Land three centuries after the Christ had died upon it. Following the instructions he received in his dream, King Lancelot and his people traveled into the west of Britain where they found a cave, and within it, the True Cross. There also they found the Thirteen Treasures of Britain, which Merlin had hidden away and which would aid them in countless ways in the future.

But most remarkable was the ancient and holy relic of the True Cross. Because it was the tree upon which the Christ had died, it had remarkable healing abilities, not only for people but for the land. The comet had turned Britain into little more than a wasteland, but King Arthur had told King Lancelot to take the cross to Salisbury Plain and set it up in the ground there, and then a miracle would occur. And so, King Lancelot and Queen Elaine and their people carried the True Cross to Salisbury Plain, and there beside the ancient circle of Stonehenge, they stood it upright in the earth.

What happened next no one then living would ever forget. The beam of wood, when it was struck into the earth, caused an underground spring to burst forth, and suddenly, a river flowed out across the barren and decayed plain. Almost instantly, the water provided life to the dried-up, dead earth. Flowers sprung up, burnt and dead trees blossomed and grew fruit, animals came to drink, and the water sustained every living creature so it could multiply again. In all ways, life was restored and abundance flourished to be enjoyed by all living things.

Perhaps just as amazing, the True Cross itself grew roots and branches and transformed itself into a beautiful, towering, magnificent apple tree. But perhaps that is not so remarkable, for legend has it that the True Cross had been cut from a tree that was itself a seedling of the very Tree of Knowledge that had once graced the Garden of Eden. And when the people ate of the tree's fruit, they found new life and energy coursing through their veins like they had never imagined.

"We will build a castle here," King Lancelot then told his people. "We will recreate Camelot in this sacred place. But our castle will not be a fortification—it will be a monument to the human spirit and a testament to our relationship with the Great Creator."

"We will create a veritable Garden of Eden," Queen Elaine agreed, "where all will be equal, with the king being only the first among equals. It will be a place where all will be welcomed."

And yet another marvelous thing also happened, for Stonehenge was one of the powerful energy points upon the earth, and the True Cross had struck down into the source of that energy. The True Cross' newly sprung leaves then acted like receptors, sending out waves to all the energy points across the earth. Survivors of the human race in other lands had also been drawn to the sacred energy places upon the earth, and so when the True Cross sent out vibrations, it was as if invisible messages spread to all the other sacred places, sending word to other survivors—to Macchu Picchu and the Great Pyramids of Egypt, to Merlin's Tomb in Brittany, to Mt. Fuji in Japan and Mt. Shasta in California, to Lake Titicaca in Peru and to Uluru/Ayers Rock in Australia, to Sedona, Arizona and to the Bermuda Triangle, to the volcanoes of Maui and to the Himalayan Mountains, to Mecca and to the Ganges River, to the seven holy places of Hinduism in India and to Lumbini in Nepal where the Buddha had been born, and, of course, to Mount Sinai and to the Mount of Olives. And in all these places where the last human survivors had assembled, there grew in people's hearts a great desire to search for others.

King Lancelot and Queen Elaine and the rest of the British people were very surprised when in the next year numerous streams of people began to pour into Camelot. They came sometimes in groups as small as two or three, and sometimes in groups as large as a hundred—they came from Asia, from Africa, from Australia and the Pacific Islands; they came from across Europe and the Americas. They came all to Salisbury Plain and the Summer Country—an old name for Southern England that had now become true, for with the striking of the comet, the earth's axis had slightly shifted so that now it was perpetual summer in England, always temperate, always the Garden of England, now transformed into a second Eden. They came to this new garden—144,000 people in total, the entire remains of the human race. And they all accepted Lancelot and Elaine as their rulers, for they too had seen visions and knew the destiny of the human race lived within this couple. But in truth, there was no need for rule, for all these people had endured so much pain and misery prior to the comet's strike that they had learned to love one another, to show mercy and forgiveness, gratitude and humility. And they married amongst one another until within a few generations, they were all one people in culture and language and ethnicity, not seeing color or differences, yet remembering and honoring their own ancient pasts. They were one people, one nation, one family.

And then the last and perhaps most wondrous event of all happened—for birth is always a miracle. Queen Elaine conceived and bore a child, and she and King Lancelot named him Arthur.

And in time, Arthur grew to manhood. It is said that there among the stones of Stonehenge, mankind's first friend Wisdom returned to earth to tutor Arthur so he would grow into a king both wise and just. And so it did happen, for Arthur proved himself a marvel in many, many ways until the day he reached maturity, and then King Lancelot gladly abdicated in favor of his son, and so Arthur was crowned King of Britain and Emperor of the Earth.

And so the Golden Age of Mankind began, and it has continued ever since. For endings are never anything but new beginnings.

AFTERWORD

AND SO THE Children of Arthur series comes to a close. It's been just shy of a quarter-of-a-century project. I began writing the first book, *Arthur's Legacy*, in 1993, but once I realized how much research I would need to do, I decided I would also write my master's thesis on Arthurian literature to get credit for doing the research. That thesis eventually became my book *King Arthur's Children: A Study in Fiction and Tradition* (2011). As for *Arthur's Legacy*, I thought it was finished in 1997, but when I couldn't find a publisher for it, I turned to writing The Marquette Trilogy and my other Marquette novels and let King Arthur sit on a shelf—or on my computer—for a while.

Then in 2009, I went back to revising *Arthur's Legacy*—I did some heavy revising, being able to see its faults after several years, but I also realized then that I wanted to know what happened after the story ended, so I wrote the next three books in the series. After I finished those, I realized I hadn't really satisfied the desire for King Arthur to return, and so my one book that had turned into a four-book series now turned into a five-book series. I wrote the first draft of *Arthur's Bosom* in the winter of 2013-2014, and only after I had completed it did I go ahead and begin to publish the series. I waited to publish until all five novels were drafted because I had read other series in which different books contradicted each other due to the author forgetting in a later book what he had said in an earlier one. I wanted my series to be free of such errors, and I also wanted to have the freedom to go back and change things in earlier books as I developed the themes and characters in the later ones. Hopefully, that has made the entire series more coherent.

This final book was, in many ways, the greatest challenge of the five precisely because it was the conclusion of the series. I wanted to bring the characters back to Arthur's time where the series began, but I also wanted to move the story forward. Most importantly, I had to figure out how to arrange for King Arthur to return. Several authors have tried to pull off King Arthur's return in the past, but I have always been disappointed by these books because if I were to suspend my disbelief and enter into their world, they ultimately made me feel like I had missed Arthur's return in the real world. That meant King Arthur's return had not really made a difference to me since it hadn't changed my life.

To resolve this issue, I set Arthur's return in the future—the near future, but still the future. I also did not want a fifth century warrior to show up and try to cope with twenty-first century life—which would be comical rather than dramatic—so I had Arthur return as the child of Lance and Elaine, with the hope of a Golden Age yet to come. I also wanted to return to the Blakeian imagery that ended the first novel so that the story would feel like it had come full circle. Whether this depiction of a Golden Age works is up to my readers to decide.

Beyond the concern of Arthur's return, readers may also be interested in some of the specifics to the background of the characters and storyline in *Arthur's Bosom*. I admit I'm not overly anxious to find out the truth about the historical Arthur since I think the fictional Arthur is far more important and interesting, but I do read many of the books that are published about the search for the historical King Arthur. There are so many theories to explore, and I do not pretend to be an expert on ancient Britain and its Celtic cultures, but I do find these books interesting and several of their theories have informed my writing over the course of this series.

Two of the most controversial writers of Arthurian historical research have been Baram Blackett and Alan Wilson. Their theories have been espoused in such books as *The King Arthur Conspiracy* by Grant Berkley and *The Holy Kingdom* by Adrian Gilbert. While I can't claim to know enough about the topics they discuss to determine how much truth there might be in them, and I acknowledge that many scholars dispute their theories, I did find two of their theories fascinating enough to influence me in writing this book.

One theory was the possibility that a comet struck Britain during the time attributed to King Arthur and that it caused enough destruction that it led to part of Britain being known as the Wastelands, which explains references in Malory and other Arthurian writers to the Wastelands. I think this is a plausible theory, and it appears to be backed by science that a comet did hit during this time. In the novel, I have simply connected that circa 500 A.D. comet with a twenty-first century one that wreaks even greater destruction upon the earth.

Blackett and Wilson's other theory I chose to use was that St. Helena, mother to the Emperor Constantine, was of British origin (scholars still dispute over her origins) and that she brought the True

Cross back to Britain with her and possibly hid it in a cave, most likely somewhere in Wales. The True Cross does not figure in the Arthurian legend otherwise, but it was constantly of concern to the medieval mind, especially during the Crusades.

Almost everything else in the novel has some source in Malory. Palomides is in Malory, as is his love for La Belle Iseult and his jealousy of Tristram. Tristram himself abandons La Belle Isolde of Brittany (there are various spellings for these women's names but I have chosen to use the two most common and assign one spelling to each woman to distinguish them). Isolde of Brittany's brother, Kahedin, does befriend and travel with Tristram, which I found astonishing after how Tristram treated his sister, so I finally came to the conclusion he must have been in love with Tristram. The tournament in Ireland is much as I described it in Malory. The Questing Beast is likewise in Malory and seems to be symbolic of sin since it first appears after Arthur unknowingly commits incest with his sister. The tale of Castus and Incestua is completely of my own making, designed to sound like something a religious fanatic would come up with. I prefer to think the Questing Beast had some sort of real component, and several scholars agree that he was likely a giraffe, a creature misunderstood by medieval people. No doubt he arrived in Britain on a ship, perhaps was shipwrecked off the coast, and then wandered about the island, unable to return to Africa.

In the afterword to *Arthur's Legacy*, I discussed why I made Constantine and Gwenhwyvach my primary villains in the Arthurian world. Their roles in this novel have no basis in tradition, but in Malory, Lancelot is captured and held prisoner by four queens, is freed by a young woman he promises to aid, and does battle and conquer the Copper Knight; he then frees that knight's prisoners, takes ownership of the castle, and changes its name from Dolorous Gard to Joyous Gard. It only seemed logical then that the Copper Knight could be Constantine.

Lyonesse is usually a land in Britain, which tradition says later sank into the sea. Many have theorized about Atlantis' connections to Britain in ancient times, so I simply expanded on such theories, which added nicely to an explanation for the Lady of the Lake who lives underwater. I have used Tennyson's name, Viviane, for her. Ileana's name is my own invention—another form of Helen.

Brother Baudwin is also directly from Malory—a knight who decided to become a hermit, which was not uncommon in those very religious times. In Malory, even Sir Lancelot becomes a monk after Guinevere's death. Lancelot also goes mad because of his love for Guinevere so I made Lance Delaney have his stint with madness, though for different reasons. I also had fun showing how modern-day Lance Delaney is misunderstood and becomes the embodiment of the fictional Sir Lancelot. Lancelot actually has no historical basis in Arthurian times but was created by the eleventh century French romancer Chretien de Troyes; eventually, Lancelot took the place of Sir Bedwyr, who was probably the greatest warrior in the Arthurian canon until then (which is why Bedwyr plays a prominent role in *Arthur's Legacy* while there is no Lancelot in that novel). My insertion of Lance in the Arthurian world suggests another way the tale of Sir Lancelot may have been created.

All that said, the sources I used and how I put my own spin on an old legend is far less important than the message of the series. What allows the Arthurian legend to remain so popular is its ability to renew itself continually for each generation. It is a pliable legend because we do not know the historical truth about King Arthur, and therefore, we can do whatever we like in our depictions of him. I choose to see Arthur as a symbol that inspires our imaginations to expand as we ourselves expand; as our consciousnesses grow and humanity evolves, King Arthur also expands and evolves with us. And why not? Why do we have to settle for the past? Why can we not recreate history and use it to make a glorious future for ourselves? A little quantum physics never hurts.

Overall, the goal of this series has been to challenge readers to rethink what they believe they know about history. What if we could change history through the power of our imaginations? Films have often depicted characters who can travel back to the past and thus change the future, but why do we have to travel back in time? The human mind is capable of far more than we know, and quantum physics tells us time is not linear, so why can't we change the past right now? Imagine if we could erase the Holocaust and countless other atrocities, making the past better and thus making the future even greater than we can dream. What if we could erase fear, violence, and war, and replace them with deeply meaningful, spiritual experiences and knowledge passed down from our ancestors? The Children of Arthur series has been based in such speculation, such hope. Is it not a better goal than the constantly dark and apocalyptic depictions of the future we have been bombarded with in recent science fiction books and films? Why not instead believe man can progress and bring about a Golden Age? Why not believe that the power of the imagination can bring about the betterment, indeed the salvation, of mankind? Even if we never achieve a Golden Age, believing in a better world will help us get closer to making a happier future a reality.

If my readers come away knowing one thing after reading this series, I hope it is that the imagination has the power to create a better world for us. So I challenge you now to go out and live the story of Camelot in your daily life—seek a better world, do each day what is right, and act in a way that will help humanity progress. Believe that a better world is nothing short of humanity's destiny, and inspire others to do the same.

Tyler R. Tichelaar
Marquette, Michigan
May 1, 2017

ACKNOWLEDGMENTS

FIRST AND FOREMOST, I want to thank my many readers who followed me through all five volumes of The Children of Arthur series. Several times while I was working on the later volumes and sometimes feeling frustrated, I would get an email, a letter, or a phone call from someone who really enjoyed one of the earlier books, and that motivated me to complete the series. Authors usually work largely in solitude, not knowing whether anyone will ever want to read what they are investing thousands of hours in creating. I daresay less than 1 percent of readers who enjoy a book ever make a point of telling an author how much it meant to them or post a review online so the author will know the book was appreciated, but when they do, it makes a huge difference and inspires the author to keep writing. Thank you!

Secondly, I thank my predecessors. It is impossible to write about the Arthurian legend without acknowledging the debt to the many Arthurian writers who came before me. For this book, specifically, more so than any of the others, I am indebted to Sir Thomas Malory and his wonderful *Le Morte d'Arthur,* which was the culmination of the medieval legend and has inspired the countless retellings that have come since it was published over five hundred years ago.

Next, I wish to thank Larry Alexander, who helped to see not only that these books made it into print but that they would be beautiful inside and out. He is a master book and cover designer, and I am grateful that he continues to keep me as a client for each successive book I write.

Diana Deluca and Roslyn Hurley deserve special thanks for reading my early drafts in piecemeal and giving feedback as I tried to figure out just where I was going. They often gave invaluable advice that kept my story from being too outlandish.

Jenifer Brady has been a faithful proofreader of this series and many more of my novels. Not only does she catch typos and point out awkward sentences, but she is always so enthusiastic about my books that she gives me that final boost of courage I need to see them into print.

I also wish to thank all the authors who gave me testimonials for the books. I am afraid I will forget some of their names if I try to list them all here, but you can find their names in the fronts of all the books in this series. Each one of them is a fine writer in his or her own right so I encourage you to explore their books.

I also must thank the staff at U.P. Health System in Marquette, Michigan. Just weeks before finishing this book, I had to go to the emergency room with a ruptured appendix. I could have easily been gone from this world as a result, but the staff there kept me alive and patiently helped me through my recovery.

And finally, I thank the Goddess-God, who knew it wasn't my time to go because this boy has many more books to write and, hopefully, is providing a service for the betterment of mankind in doing so. It is an honor that every day I get to spend time doing what I love.

A SPECIAL REQUEST

IF YOU ENJOYED this book, please write a book review for it at Amazon, Barnes & Noble, Goodreads, or another bookseller or booklover website. Authors rely on book reviews and word-of-mouth to sell their books, so you can make the difference in helping this book to succeed. Readers also rely on reviews to help them make their decisions on which books to purchase and read. Even just a couple of sentences will be appreciated. The author thanks you for your time.

Don't Miss Any of the Exciting Books in

THE CHILDREN OF ARTHUR
SERIES

Arthur's Legacy
The Children of Arthur:
Book One

Melusine's Gift
The Children of Arthur:
Book Two

Ogier's Prayer
The Children of Arthur:
Book Three

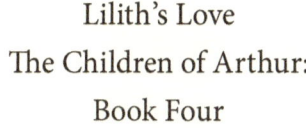

Lilith's Love
The Children of Arthur:
Book Four

Arthur's Bosom
The Children of Arthur:
Book Five

For more information and to order,
visit www.ChildrenofArthur.com

ABOUT THE AUTHOR

TYLER R. TICHELAAR holds a Ph.D. in Literature from Western Michigan University, and Bachelor and Master's Degrees in English from Northern Michigan University. He is the owner of his own publishing company, Marquette Fiction, and of Superior Book Productions, a professional book review, editing, proofreading, book design, and web design service.

Besides The Children of Arthur series, Tyler is the author of numerous historical novels, including *The Marquette Trilogy* (composed of *Iron Pioneers*, *The Queen City*, and *Superior Heritage*), *Narrow Lives*, *The Only Thing That Lasts*, *Spirit of*  the North: *a paranormal romance*, and *The Best Place*. He has also authored non-fiction titles that include *My Marquette: Explore the Queen City of the North*, *Creating a Local Historical Book*, *The Gothic Wanderer: From Transgression to Redemption*, and *King Arthur's Children:*

A Study in Fiction and Tradition. An avid genealogist, Tyler has been fascinated by the Arthurian legend and medieval history since childhood.

Visit Tyler at:

www.MarquetteFiction.com
www.GothicWanderer.com
www.ChildrenofArthur.com

www.ingramcontent.com/pod-product-compliance
Lightning Source LLC
Chambersburg PA
CBHW022204030726
47494CB00019B/253